THE ATLANTEANS

THE ATLANTEANS

A Contemporary Novel

An adventure romance, in an unusual setting, leading to a story of mystery and suspense

Dorothy Cora Moore

iUniverse, Inc.
New York Lincoln Shanghai

THE ATLANTEANS

A Contemporary Novel

www.TheAtlanteans.com

iUniverse books may be ordered through booksellers or by contacting:

iUniverse
2021 Pine Lake Road, Suite 100
Lincoln, NE 68512
www.iuniverse.com
1-800-Authors (1-800-288-4677)

ISBN-13: 978-0-595-33044-7 (pbk)
ISBN-13: 978-0-595-66735-2 (cloth)
ISBN-13: 978-0-595-77834-8 (ebk)
ISBN-10: 0-595-33044-4 (pbk)
ISBN-10: 0-595-66735-X (cloth)
ISBN-10: 0-595-77834-8 (ebk)

Printed in the United States of America

DEDICATION

This book is dedicated to those decent, humane
and enlightened Atlantean souls,
of every nation
and on every continent,
who will inherit the Earth
as we move further into the Third Millennium
to bring forth a bright and promising future,
and 1,000 years of peace.

CONTENTS

▲

ACKNOWLEDGEMENTS

The writing of this work was difficult, but getting it to the reader even more so, in that *The Atlanteans* began as an original screenplay that, together with its sequel, has become this novelization.

There have been so many individuals along the way who have read and critiqued this story, children and adults alike, to whom I will be forever grateful for their positive input. However, I am especially thankful to Jeanne Robinson, Vivien Williams and Sharon Seymour, who helped me proof my final drafts and get this story ready for publication. A special thanks also goes to the professional staff on the reference desk at the Prescott Public Library, who tirelessly found sources of information as part of my research, and answered many difficult questions for me.

I had immeasurable technical help and advice from Jim Plagenhoef of the America's Cup Team 1987, Ed Dahlberg, retired, CBS Television in Chicago, Leonard J. Cerullo, M.D., founding Director of the Chicago Institute of Neurosurgery and Neuroresearch (CINN), Thomas L. Trezise, retired, Chief of Police, Lake Forest, Illinois, and the Newton F. Korhumels, Whippoorwill Farm, Lake Forest, Illinois.

In addition, I want to thank posthumously, W. P. Phelon, M.D. and Viola Petitt Neal, Ph.D.

Dr. Phelon, through his own work completed more than a century ago, gave a true vision of Atlantis and its laws, which I have, in part, included in my opening.

Last, but not least, I want to thank Dr. Viola Petitt Neal, writer, lecturer, scientist, and the past founder and Director of the Biometric Research Foundation in Beverly Hills, California, who inspired me to begin writing this story, so many years ago.

I hope you find it entertaining.

"BRIDE OF THE SUN"

By

Viola Petitt Neal, Ph.D.

From "Fragments of Experience"

Sapphire, topaz and emerald green,

Jewelled planet

Bride of the Sun.

Move to the step of his cosmic dance

Out thru the bridal night of space.

Treasure the seed of his glorious life

Bring forth your sons of immortal joy.

The skyways await

The tread of their feet.

FOREWORD

"The Prophesy"

The Mystery Schools in China and Greece, and the Temple Schools in Egypt, have in common a teaching called the *"Ageless Wisdom,"* or *"Ancient Wisdom,"* wherein there lies a record of a revered and mystical empire called Atlantis—an island continent, ruled by magicians and destroyed by nature some 25,000 years ago at the commencement of the age of Aquarius.

It is further told that a large mass of land, equal in size to old Atlantis, would be set aside and preserved for her people—protected and waiting—until their return. Then, when the call went out by the watchers of the race, they would come together again from all over the world. Some believe that place to be America.

The legend goes on to say that the Atlanteans, having lost an earlier opportunity, have waited in time until an entire cycle of ages passed, an entire round, before they could come together once more to fulfill their destiny—a destiny of bringing in a new and prosperous age, reestablishing peace, harmony, and tranquility to a troubled planet and, once again, restoring the Kingdom of God on Earth.

CHAPTER 1

▲

MIAMI

For twelve treacherous hours, without the slightest reprieve, the skies opened up over the Miami coastline, and pounded the sea and land in a deluge of deafening fury.

It was 2:00 a.m. and Teddy Townsend found he could not sleep. He moved his tall, masculine form away from where he had been cradling his wife, Terese, and slipped out of bed without waking her.

Standing at the sliding glass doors of their room at the Dupont Plaza Hotel, Teddy could barely see beyond their balcony, where the light of the hotel below reached across to their yacht at its mooring.

He stood there watching the storm for twenty minutes or more, and wondered whether the race he had been preparing to enter for more than six months now would be postponed. They had left an unexpected mid-March snowstorm in Chicago, and it seemed the bad weather had followed them all the way to Florida.

Teddy wiped his strong, well-kept hand through his soft, blonde and wavy hair, as he thought about how frustrated his crew would be. It had taken quite a bit of planning to get everyone together. He had brought them all in from his old yacht club in New York City. They were to sail in the Miami-Nassau Regatta. Now the storm might ruin everything.

Being only in their mid-thirties, Teddy and Terese Townsend led a very privileged life. Conversely, upon first meeting either one of them, they never showed the wealth they enjoyed. Teddy and Terese always gave the impression of just being middle-class, family-oriented Midwesterners, even though Teddy's family had very old money, some of which he had inherited when he came of age. So, it was not that Teddy minded the expense of bringing everyone down to Miami, but rather the disappointment of the race being put off because of the threat of weather.

This was to be the last open-ocean race Teddy would enter before he brought the *Lady Leah*, his custom-designed 52-foot racing yacht, through the St. Lawrence Seaway. He planned to permanently bed her in Lake Michigan, immediately after the winter thaw.

Teddy needed a break from his work as a partner with a large national law firm. He had thought his transfer and move, from New York City to Chicago, would make him more content with the practice of law, but it had not—although he continued to keep his discontent to himself. He had a very happy marriage and family life, which made it all more bearable. But still, he needed this break. He needed a fun adventure.

Suddenly Teddy stepped back, as a piece of patio furniture was lifted by the wind and hurled forcefully into the sliding glass doors, cracking the glass.

Terese shot up out of bed with a start. "What happened?" she asked, looking toward the patio doors.

"It's nothing," Teddy assured her. "It's just the storm."

"It feels like a hurricane," Terese said, with a frightened tone entering her voice.

"No, it's just a bad storm," Teddy said, closing the draperies tight, and then getting back into bed. "It should be fairly well spent by morning."

Teddy did not want Terese to see the broken glass, for fear it would worry her.

"You're not sailing in this?" Terese asked.

"It'll be clear by our start time," Teddy predicted. "And it should give us a good wind."

Terese just looked at him.

"Don't worry," Teddy said laughing, as he pulled Terese back into his arms. "You'll see. Everything will be perfect."

By five-thirty the rain had subsided, almost as quickly as it had begun, and an hour later the warm Miami sun rose slowly on the horizon.

Teddy woke feeling something cold and wet near his ruggedly handsome face. When he opened his eyes, he was met with the damp cool nose of his golden retriever, Leah, as she nudged him awake. Her large brown eyes were staring at him. She had to go out.

"Do you have to?" Teddy whispered.

Leah gave him another nudge, this time with her paw, and then began climbing a little farther up on the bed.

"All right, all right," he said, in a low voice, "I'll take you."

Teddy yawned, feeling he needed a couple of hours more sleep, and reached over for his watch resting nearby on the night table. With the drapes closed tight, the room was still dark, and he could not imagine why Leah had to go out so early.

Leah was already standing by the door waiting for him. She looked unhappy about the fact that he was taking his time.

Looking at his watch, Teddy saw with shock that it was ten-thirty in the morning, and he quickly jumped out of bed.

"Terese," he called, gently waking her. "We overslept. We never got our call."

Teddy ran into the bathroom and climbed into some clothes, while Terese slipped her raincoat on over her nightgown, and grabbed a pair of deck shoes.

"Throw some things in that sea bag, will you Terese?" Teddy called.

"It's all ready to go," she answered, having packed it the night before.

Teddy ran back into the room, shoved his shaving kit into the bag, and within two minutes they were flying out the door, with Leah in close pursuit.

Two members of Teddy's twelve-man crew, Jimmy Wilder and Jerry Levendowski, had just searched the hotel and restaurants for him. Not knowing that the phone to his room was dead from the storm, they had called him twice before going back to the *Lady Leah* to report to the rest of the crew.

There was one stranger on board. Ryan Stuart. The other men had just met him at dinner the night before. Ryan was an old roommate of Teddy's from his early days at Harvard, and Teddy had invited him along for the race. He was Teddy's oldest and closest friend.

Ryan's tall, lean and athletic frame stood out where he had positioned himself on deck. His healthy, dark mahogany hair was swept back by the onshore breeze and glistened in the morning sun. Unlike the rest of the crew, who had sailed the boat down to Miami from New York, and were all well tanned, Ryan's skin showed only the slightest hint of color. But, there was something more than that that caused him to stand out from the others.

Ryan Stuart had striking good looks, and took meticulous care of his clothing. His white shorts were pressed with a distinctive crease, and his kelly green polo shirt, with its white collar, looked new.

The rest of the crewmembers were wearing navy blue shorts, with matching white polo shirts. Each of their names had been personalized over their front pockets, and the *LADY LEAH* was written across their backs, in a matching navy blue.

With his hands pitched into his slim hips, Ryan's keen blue eyes gazed up at the hotel looking for some sign of Teddy Townsend. Appearing restless and anxious, Ryan Stuart soon began pacing back and forth, muttering to himself.

Ryan led a very precise life, and the trip had already proven to be a disaster. Everything imaginable had gone wrong since he left Chicago, and by the time he reached the hotel last night, he wanted to go home. Nothing was right, not the least of which was that his accommodations at the Dupont Plaza Hotel were not to his liking.

As he thought back, he could envision the woman who was sitting next to him on the plane. Twenty minutes into the flight, she had vomited all over his perfectly tailored Italian suit. Then, when he reached the Miami Airport, it took two hours before he learned that his luggage had been sent to Los Angeles in error. To make a terrible situation even worse, when he arrived at the hotel, they had no record of the adjoining suite Teddy and Terese had arranged for him. Ryan had to take a less desirable room, with no view, on another floor of the hotel. And, now, Teddy was late for the race.

His temper rising, Ryan turned to one of the crewmembers coming up the companionway. "I can't believe he's late!" Ryan complained angrily, as he unconsciously smoothed his perfectly trimmed head of hair.

Pointing up to the hotel, Jimmy Wilder smiled and shook his head. "There they are now, coming across the plaza," he said, laughing. "That guy's really too much."

Ryan could see Teddy and Terese running to the pier and, in less than a minute, they had reached the yacht.

Leah happily took a running jump onto the boat, with her tail wagging to the fast beat of her heart. She was glad to see Ryan and the others, greeting each one of them in turn.

"Sorry we're late," Teddy offered.

"How can you be late for a race?" Ryan demanded, before Teddy could make any kind of an explanation.

"C'mon Ryan, the race doesn't even start till noon," he explained, good-naturedly.

"You're almost an hour late!" Ryan said, taking a step forward, and with a disgusted tone in his voice.

Ryan hated to be kept waiting, and Teddy knew this.

"Okay, okay, calm down," Teddy said, stepping onto the boat.

Teddy immediately began fitting Leah into her life preserver and, with a look of disbelief, Ryan saw that Teddy intended to take Leah with them.

"Wait. You can't take her." Ryan insisted. "What are you, crazy?"

"She always goes with us," Teddy explained. "She won't get in anyone's way. We have a couple of straps that connect to her life preserver."

"Maybe you take her sailing, but you're not taking her for the race." Ryan said, with conviction. "That can't be allowed. Have you ever read the rules? How can you enter a race and not read the rules?" Ryan demanded.

"Well nobody's complained so far," he said. "And she's been sailing for two years."

Teddy soon saw he was getting nowhere with Ryan and, with all that had occurred getting him down to Miami, Teddy decided not to push it.

He also knew how long it would take to get Ryan out of one of his black moods. Leah could stay and keep Terese company. Taking her along was not worth ruining the trip.

"All right, c'mon girl, you have to stay," Teddy said sympathetically, approaching Leah.

Leah looked at him, as if to question whether she heard him correctly. When he reached for her, she resisted, stretching her paws out and weighting herself to the deck.

Teddy knew she would not leave the boat without a struggle, and he somehow dislodged her dead weight, picking her up and carrying her off the boat and onto the dock.

Looking back and forth between Teddy and Ryan, with a pleading look in her eyes, and, not believing they actually intended to leave her behind, Leah attempted once more to step back onto the boat. Nevertheless, Teddy stopped her.

"Leah, you have to stay here," Teddy encouraged, with a gentle tone in his voice. "Now lie down."

Stretching down to a position on the dock, Leah obeyed him, whimpering all the while, and resting her head between her paws. Bending over to her, Teddy patted Leah's head, trying to comfort her.

"She should forgive you for this in a year, or two, Ryan," Teddy said, chuckling, not being able to resist the dig.

Ryan gave Teddy an intense cold stare, and then looked away.

Before climbing back onto the boat, Teddy offered Leah one final loving pat on her shoulder. Her eyes never lifted. She looked so sad and forlorn, that Teddy felt a tug in his heart, and winked at Terese in response to Leah's pathetic look.

"Get her a piece of prime rib or something, will you?" he asked, kissing Terese good-bye.

Terese nodded, as a warm smile crossed her face. "Good luck," she called, as Teddy grabbed a line and jumped down onto the boat.

Terese Townsend's shiny, blonde, and shoulder-length hair had been quickly pulled back in a ponytail, and her wholesome good looks needed no makeup. Nor did her soft, hazel eyes that she had in common with

Teddy, which looked more green than brown in the Florida sun. She and Teddy shared the same coloring, with natural sandy-blonde hair and even, well developed features. They looked far more youthful than a couple married almost twelve years.

Terese was totally unaware of how beautiful she looked—just out of bed, with her pale blue raincoat pulled around her, and an inch or two of her nightgown hanging below its hem. She had always carried a little too much weight, which seemed impossible for her to take off.

However, Teddy had invariably insisted that Terese looked perfect, and was healthy and fit. He was not the kind of man who was attracted to curve-less, bone-thin women, and he always thought Terese had a beautiful feminine softness about her. Moreover, she had never been overly preoccupied with herself—something Teddy loved about her.

The outfit Teddy had grabbed was the same outfit he wore at dinner the night before, a soft yellow and white cotton polo shirt and a pair of white shorts. His shirt appeared rumpled from hanging on the doorknob all night under a damp towel, but Teddy did not seem to notice.

There was a strong, everlasting bond between Teddy and Terese, which could never be mistaken. When their eyes met, it was with a full understanding of what the other was thinking and feeling.

Terese had been worried about something happening on this trip. She had even tried to convince Teddy to postpone their vacation, and cancel his entry in the regatta. Teddy had, however, laughed off her concern. He had never had the slightest fear of any impending danger—a trait that added to Terese's worry.

She had even had a series of nightmares, in which Teddy had been lost at sea. A week before the trip she had awakened crying, and Teddy had to hold her in his arms for more than an hour until she could fall back to sleep again.

"Nothing bad is going to happen, Terese. Nothing could ever harm me," he had reassured her, as he held her gently in his arms. "Please don't worry, it's just a bad dream," he had said.

All the same, Terese cried her eyes out that night, and could not be consoled. Terese believed in the warning of dreams. But Teddy trusted his own intuition, and felt nothing but excitement about this trip.

The yacht's engine started, and they soon began moving away from the dock and out of the small inlet.

"Be careful," Terese said, catching Teddy's eyes.

"I'll call you when we reach Nassau," Teddy called back. "Say hi to Jeanne and April for me, when you get together today."

Terese nodded, as she bent down to comfort Leah, who still looked upset and rejected, and who had just let out another small whimper.

"They'll be back in a few days, Leah," Terese said, as she stroked Leah's back. "You can stay and keep me company, okay girl?" Terese asked, gently petting her.

The yacht pulled out into the canal, and Teddy checked his watch. They were running late. Teddy never mentioned to Ryan that it was at least a 45-minute ride out to where the race would start, and it was now just after eleven.

When Teddy leaned over to pick up the sea bag he brought on board, he was met by Ryan's frozen stance.

"Are you sure you're ready?" Ryan asked, still annoyed.

"My God Ryan, what's with you anyway?" Teddy laughed.

"What's with me? I'll tell you what's with me," he said. "This is the stupidest thing you've ever talked me into. And, if I had known our accommodations were going to be at a Motel 6-like Resort," Ryan said, unable to even finish.

Teddy tried to keep from laughing, but his amusement came through by the look on his face.

"I know the Dupont Plaza is not fancy, but we could tie the yacht up here, and the entire crew didn't have to stay on the boat," Teddy explained. "We also needed to find a place on the water that would allow Leah to stay with us."

Ryan just looked at him.

"Just relax a little, will you," Teddy persuaded, seeing how uptight Ryan was. "You'll see, this is going to be a fun vacation."

"Fun? I don't call this fun," Ryan complained. "You're the typical lawyer. You're always manipulating people," he charged.

"I didn't manipulate you. You had the free choice to come down here."

"Did I?" Ryan asked.

"Year after year you do the same old thing, and go to the same old place. Do you call that a vacation?" Teddy asked.

Ryan turned around, and looked straight into Teddy's eyes. "I enjoy going fishing," he defended.

"But this is exciting. Something new. An adventure," Teddy said, with exhilaration. "And you need something new and fun in your life. We all do."

"I like my life. And I have all the adventure I need," Ryan justified, looking sharply to the north where the storm had hinged. "And look at that sky," Ryan said, pointing. "We have to be nuts going out in this. I thought the hotel was going to blow down last night!"

Teddy looked above him at the clear blue skies, and then to the north where the storm had hastened.

"It's going in the opposite direction, Ryan. Look, it's beautiful out, and the Bahamas are waiting for us," he rationalized, using his best comical tone.

Ryan remained silent.

"Here, I have something for you," Teddy said, reaching into his bag and handing Ryan his team shirts, with his name embroidered over the pocket, exactly like that of the rest of the crew.

Ryan took the shirts, but said nothing.

Teddy reached back into his bag and grabbed one of his own team shirts, and began changing into it. Seeing that there was no reaching Ryan, by the obstinate look on his face, Teddy soon turned his attention to the rest of the crew. Everyone else was in an especially agreeable mood, and Teddy knew they would all enjoy the race. All they had to do was get to the start on time.

It was a beautiful March morning, with a good breeze. White cumulus clouds filled the stunning blue sky. It seemed peaceful, as they moved down the channel and into the Miami Harbor. Two large cruise ships could be seen nearby, with one taking on passengers and another attempting to dock. The day was perfect for a race. The *Lady Leah* made her way out to Government Cut, and the wind began to pick up. Teddy searched the Horizon for the rest of the yachts, and soon spotted them far off in the distance.

When they finally made their way out to the open ocean, it was a few minutes past twelve, and, while their sails went up, Teddy grabbed his binoculars to see if the race had started yet. It had. His view took in the billowing sails of the large fleet of racing yachts moving effortlessly, as if a flock of birds, into an ordered position. Scanning the waters for the judges' boat, he soon saw that the "A" Class was halfway into its starting sequence.

"Do you see anything, Ted?" his tactician asked, breathing down his neck.

"It's the blue shape for 'A' Class," Teddy responded.

Turning the wheel, Teddy filled the sails and bore away to increase the yacht's speed. "A" Class was about to cross the start, but Teddy's 52-foot racing yacht was in the "B" Class. They had a few more minutes and a lot of distance to make up.

Teddy's eyes stayed peeled for the "B" Class flag, and a white shape warning, which would commence the timing of ten minutes to their start. Five minutes thereafter, a blue preparatory shape warning would follow. And then, a red shape which would signal the start.

Looking through his binoculars, Teddy saw the red shape go up for the "A" Class start, and then, immediately following, the "B" Class flag and the 10-minute warning went up.

"It's the white shape," Teddy yelled to his crew, watching his sails and simultaneously clicking the timing device he held in his hand.

The *Lady Leah* chased after the swiftly moving fleet of racing yachts, in the "A" Class, heading her bow directly to the line.

Just then one of the crew yelled from the stern, "Hey Ted, there's the *Eagle*," he said, pointing.

scape its only character. Teddy wanted to climb to the top of one of them, and began the trek. Ryan cautiously followed him.

Small, dark gray stones, that had been washed smooth by the action of the waves, skidded underneath the soles of their deck shoes, and they found it difficult at times to keep their balance. Just before they gave up the endeavor, Teddy wanted to investigate what appeared to be a piece of white stone, standing amidst the black rocks that formed one of the highest peaks. When they reached a point two-thirds of the way up the crest, they found there was only one place where the configuration of the rocks would permit their approach. They tested the secure seating of each and every stone; yet on two separate attempts, they slid almost all the way back down again. What they needed was a long rope, but neither one of them had thought to bring one.

"Come on Ted, let's go," Ryan insisted. "You'll never make it up there."

"I want to see what that is," Teddy said, pointing to the piece of white stone.

"It's a piece of rock," Ryan complained.

Teddy ignored Ryan, and planned a third attempt, only this time he decided to tackle a group of large boulders to the right, which appeared impossible to get a hold on.

Ryan shook his head. "You'll never get up that way," he criticized.

Soon Teddy found a place for one of his hands, and then his foot and his other hand, slowly making his way up the sheer, black, looming rock. Although he never once looked back, he knew Ryan would follow him, in that Ryan would never allow Teddy to surpass him at anything. And, as Teddy had predicted, Ryan soon began the climb, carefully searching for the best place to hold on to the rock.

After a long and intense struggle, they eventually made their way up to the summit. Ryan looked exhausted, as he pulled himself over the ledge at the top, and Teddy noticed he was shaking.

"How in the world are we ever going to get down from here?" Ryan demanded, trying to catch his breath.

"We'll just slide down the other side," Teddy said, starting to laugh.

"Right," Ryan muttered. "And what makes you think that's going to be so easy?" he asked.

As they looked around, they realized they were standing on the exposed tip of a huge tower-like structure, coming from deep below the rocks. To their fascination, the top had a ridge around it with a sunken floor.

Teddy crouched down near the center of the structure and picked up a pile of sand off the floor and moved it through his fingers. It felt cold and heavy in his hand.

"I don't know when," Teddy observed, fingering the sand, "but this hasn't always been above water. It's soaking wet underneath."

"Probably from the storm," Ryan said, resting back on the ledge, surveying their surroundings. His discerning blue eyes took in every crevice of the structure, as he intently watched Teddy excavate the bottom with his cupped hands.

Once Teddy had moved a portion of the sand away, he found a geometric symbol on a flat surface, just about a foot or so below where he had begun to dig.

"There's something under here, Ryan," Teddy said. "Why don't you take that side, and I'll take this, and we can see what's under here."

"I'm not digging with my hands," Ryan said, interrupting him. "I use these for surgery."

"Well you're a great help," Teddy said.

"If you wanted to conduct an excavation, you should have brought a couple of shovels," Ryan returned.

Teddy eventually cleared an area about twice the size of a sandbox, exposing a beautiful mosaic surface. The large tiles were made up of pastels of every color of the rainbow, and had a colorful design etched into them, although the surface was as hard and shiny as a solid piece of glass.

When Teddy stepped on the newly cleared floor, a large square piece of the tile moved down and backward, exposing a narrow flight of steps that led into a room below.

"I must have stepped on a spring or something," Teddy said, looking up at Ryan.

Ryan looked warily down the hole, and then back at Teddy. "What do you suppose this is?" Ryan asked.

"I haven't the slightest idea. But whatever it is," Teddy assumed, "it's buried under all this rock."

The sunlight was angled in such a way as to pour a shaft of light down the passageway, and felt warm on Teddy's back, as he bent over looking down the steps. He quickly stepped down into the passage, motioning for Ryan to follow him. Ryan didn't move.

"C'mon Ryan," Teddy motioned again.

But Ryan slowly shook his head no, and then stepped back a few paces.

"Ryan," Teddy insisted.

"I'm not going down there!" Ryan snapped. "What if that thing closes up on me?"

"It's not going to close up on you. C'mon, let's go," Teddy persisted.

But Ryan was defiant, and stayed right where he was.

Teddy, oblivious to any impending danger, descended the staircase alone. As he worked his way two-thirds of the distance down the steps he felt a recess in the stone to his right, and when he reached in to feel what was inside it, he lost his footing and fell clear to the bottom of the staircase.

Ryan could hear Teddy fall, and he listened intently at the opening. "Ted, are you all right?" he called, after finding his voice.

Teddy never answered.

Ryan looked around the surface and, as soon as he located a large enough stone to wedge into the open staircase, he carefully walked down the steps and found Teddy lying at the bottom.

Bending over Teddy's body, Ryan lit a match. "What happened?" he asked, his voice showing his concern.

"I don't know. I think I fell," Teddy responded.

"I can't see well enough to know how badly you've been injured. Do you think anything's broken?" Ryan asked, feeling one of his arms.

"No, I'm fine," Teddy said. "That was so strange, I don't think I even hit my head. It was like going down a slide."

"Why do you always have to take risks like this?" Ryan asked, moving his shoulder away from the thick chilling wall. It bothered Ryan not to be able to see how clean the passageway was, and he wondered who, or what, had used this place before him.

Teddy never noticed the ice-cold of the floor that penetrated through his clothing, nor did he pay any attention to the damp, moist walls. He thought only of discovering what was on the other side of the doorway in front of him.

Lifting himself up off the floor, he stepped forward to the arched opening and looked inside. "It's certainly dark in there," Teddy said, peering into the room.

Teddy had always had fairly good night vision, yet the room was so totally devoid of light that he could not see an inch in front of his face. "Hey, Ryan," he requested, "let me see those matches."

Ryan appeared frozen to the spot where he was standing, but managed to hand Teddy the small packet of wooden matches.

Lighting another match, Teddy entered a four-by-five-foot anteroom that appeared to open into a larger room.

Ryan's curiosity finally got the best of him, and he stepped up to the open-arched frame to look inside. His heart began pounding, and he could feel another chill run across his shoulders, and then over his entire body.

Although Teddy appeared completely composed, his heart was beating so loudly in his ears, that he thought Ryan had spoken to him. "What'd you say?" Teddy asked, as he quickly turned around.

"I didn't say anything," Ryan snapped, giving him a strange look. "We'd better get out of here, Ted. Right now. Let's go!"

"I just want to see what's in the next room," Teddy persisted.

Teddy walked with an outstretched match before him, and then suddenly the light went out. "Damn!" he murmured, as the match dropped, leaving them in total darkness. He was so focused on the room, that he had not noticed the match had burned down to the end, scorching his finger.

"That's just great," Ryan, said, having jumped almost a foot off the floor when he heard Teddy's cry. It was now pitch dark again, and Ryan felt so weak that when he tried to leave, his knees began to give out on him.

"Come," Polaris said, in an encouraging way. "Let me show you more, we're losing light. Seeing Atlantis again might help you work out the problems of your own civilization."

Once again, Teddy and Ryan found themselves moving. Their wonderment and exhilaration soon returned, all the while filling their entire beings with a sense of enchanting elation, as this astonishingly beautiful and magical city passed below them. They explored one beautiful home after another from above.

"Here on Atlantis," Polaris went on, "every family has a piece of property which is allocated to them for their use, and the children remain with the family unit until they marry. In fact, each couple, when they decide to marry, can apply for a piece of property from what is currently available. Or they can wait until land and/or property is made available, by its return to the Central Land and Property Bank—either because its previous occupant no longer has use for the property, or has become deceased."

"Man," Polaris went on to explain, "is not allowed to own or possess, for his own exclusive use, any of the four elements—earth, water, fire or air—for nature is the form of, or body of, the ensouling life of this planet."

"It is an ancient law that man can only own, or possess, that which he himself has created. And, I mean by that, things, not individuals. Man can never own that which is the body of God, or which God created—he can only be its caretaker."

Soon their attention was drawn to the enormous parcel of land before them. Three buildings, of exquisite design, were placed in the form of a squared off upside-down U, so as to share a common plaza and patio. The largest structure, the Great Sacred Cathedral, with its white walls and numerous ornate columns, faced south. The other two structures, which faced each other, formed the arms of the U. A large, intricately designed fountain filled the center of the plaza, and was not only beautiful to see, but its flowing clear water had a cooling effect on the surrounding air.

The obelisk rested nearby, and was attached to the back of the structure facing west, known as Temple School. Some of the buildings Teddy saw, including the obelisk, reminded him of those built around the Capitol in Washington. He thought it odd to see something so similar here.

"This is our Temple School," Polaris explained, pointing to the building on their right, with the obelisk attached to the back. "Education is a high honor here, and our children are encouraged to attend school for as long as they desire to learn, starting at an early age."

"We have two schools at your college level," he explained, "one is of concrete knowledge, mathematics and science, and the other is of the arts, philosophy and wisdom. In order for one of our citizens to vote in an election, he or she must have graduated from one or the other of these two schools, and in order to run for public office, he or she must have graduated from both schools."

The Temple School building looked quiet at this time of day, and the campus grounds, which were meticulously groomed by caretakers, were almost empty. It looked as if it were a sacred place, serene in its setting and consecrated long ago. It was, in fact, a Mystery School, different from the other two schools Polaris was telling Teddy about.

"Temple School," Polaris continued, "is of an even higher order than the other two college-level schools. It is reserved for our best students, those who have graduated from both colleges. However, Temple School is attended by invitation only. It is in this school that abstract knowledge, or metaphysics, is taught."

The term Temple School sounded so familiar to Teddy, yet he did not know why.

"Our leadership program at Temple School," Polaris continued, "lasts three years, and it is from this group of students that we choose our priests and priestesses. They, in turn, go on for another four years, seven in all, before taking their vows. It is from this group of priests and priestesses, that our teachers and Priestly Council are chosen—the Priestly Council being comparable in power to your United States Supreme Court," Polaris added, "and constituting the second highest office. Its forty-five members represent our eminently gifted priests and priestesses."

"Finally," Polaris, finished, "it is from this Council of priests and priestesses that our three Magi are elected, of which I am one."

"Do the Magi govern all your people?" Ryan asked.

"Yes, in a spiritual sense, upwards of 60 million persons, if you include the entire empire," Polaris replied.

The sky was continuing to change as the sun set, tempering its color from amber yellow to a burnished gold. Teddy watched, as the day's light dimmed on the western horizon, and dramatic shadows of evenings' rush enhanced Atlantis' beauty at the end of the day.

If there was ever a Kingdom for God, Teddy thought, it is here in this glorious place. When he turned to Ryan, he could see Ryan's eyes were fixed on the play of light.

"Who would ever have dreamt that we would see such a place," Teddy whispered.

Ryan remained silent.

Nevertheless, Teddy knew that this moment in time would touch their lives forevermore, and would never be forgotten.

CHAPTER 3

▲

THEOS AND TARAH

Before dusk fell, Polaris brought Teddy and Ryan to a magnificent white mansion set in the foothills above the city, and they soon found themselves in a grand and lavish garden at the back of the large estate. The main house was full of guests who had been invited to a party. Polaris watched their faces, in the way a father watches the wonder on the face of his young child.

"Does any of this look familiar to you?" Polaris asked.

Teddy stared for a moment. It did, but he did not know from where or when. "A little," he admitted, looking about him. "I must have dreamt about a place similar to this once."

They could hear the people within the house talking and laughing, and there was music playing, beautiful music, from what sounded comparable to an expertly tuned piano, only more penetrating and clear of pitch. In all their lives, Teddy and Ryan had never heard more beautiful tones from any instrument.

Listening closely for a moment, Teddy thought the piano music odd. He half expected another sound. But then, he thought, probably everything of wonder and design, and probably all scientific advancement today, has been brought through from some past Atlantean soul experiencing a more current incarnation.

He now wondered if your special abilities, coming into a new life, were truly a gift, or rather a recurring memory, from the deepest part of your soul, of something that you had learned before in another life. Could our past be our future, our final destiny, Teddy thought? He hoped so, for he had never felt such peace and tranquility before from any other place he had ever been in the world. It was as if he had finally come home.

Teddy and Ryan stood in the back garden of the residence, on the opposite side of a path that separated them from a large tranquil pond. When the music became evident again, they noticed an attractive young couple walking up a winding path to the house.

He was quite a bit taller than she, handsome, broad shouldered and athletic looking. They were both wearing white, and looked very much alike in their coloring. She was angelic in appearance, with her long, flowing, layered gown and beautiful blonde hair. A soft, wide, apricot sash was tied at her waist in the back, forming a large, soft bow, trailing down the back of her exquisitely designed dress. The young couple appeared to be especially happy, and very much in love.

The sight of her took Teddy's breath away. Teddy and Ryan stood watching from the side of the path, as the couple came closer and closer. It seemed as if, and it was as if, they were watching Teddy with his wife, Terese, in their early twenties.

Teddy turned toward Ryan with a look of amazement.

"Ryan," he whispered, "that's me, and Terese."

Ryan just shook his head.

Looking around, Teddy called out Polaris' name, however, he did not answer. Polaris was gone. He was nowhere in sight.

Ryan gave Teddy a look of despair. "Polaris, where are you?" he asked.

They then heard Polaris' voice coming from somewhere above them. "I'll be back for you in a minute," he said.

Ryan turned around the other way. "We can't see you. Where are you?" he asked, raising his voice.

"I'm right here," Polaris replied.

Ryan jumped, as Polaris materialized before him. Then Polaris' body started to sway, and became more and more transparent again.

"They cannot see or hear you," Polaris explained, referring to the young couple. "You are welcome to stay, if you wish to."

"Wait," Teddy said, still whispering. "Who are they? They look just like Terese and …," Teddy was speechless.

"They are you and Terese—a long, long, time ago," Polaris replied. "Why don't you and Ryan watch for a while, and I'll come back for you later. Their names are Theos and Tarah."

"How long can we stay?" Teddy asked.

"How long would you like to stay?" Polaris questioned.

"As long as we can," Teddy urged.

Polaris pondered a moment, reflectively. A sad, moving expression came across his face, and then he continued, gesturing to all of the land about them.

"You cannot stay too long, for all of this will be gone in a short while."

Teddy looked up at him. "Gone? What do you mean, gone?"

"All of this," Polaris went on, "everything you see," he said, his breath catching as he breathed in. "Surely you know the legend of Atlantis."

Teddy nodded, thinking back. "We'd appreciate staying a while," he said.

"As you wish," Polaris granted. "When you are ready to leave, concentrate on my image, repeating my name three times in succession, and I will come and take you back to your yacht."

"Thank you," Teddy responded, gratefully.

Polaris could see the worried look on Ryan's face and, reading his thoughts, tried to put him more at ease. "Nothing can harm you here, Ryan, so you need not be frightened."

Ryan just stared at him.

"He'll be all right," Teddy said, assuring Polaris.

"Just call my name three times," Polaris reminded them.

"Yes. Yes, we will," Teddy gratefully confirmed, and Polaris was gone.

Ryan looked furious. "Now why did you tell him he could leave?" he demanded, giving Teddy one of his cold looks of disapproval.

"He said he'd come back," Teddy replied.

"Well I'm ready to go now," Ryan insisted.

"You're afraid, aren't you? Admit it," Teddy challenged him.

Ryan was indignant. "You're the one who can't do anything alone!"

Teddy looked amused. "Right. Well, if you want to go, then go. But I'm staying right here."

Ryan just stared at him with an angry look in his eyes.

"Well?" Teddy questioned.

"All right, I'll stay," Ryan, returned. "But strictly out of curiosity. And understand this, Ted," he said, raising his voice, "I'm not staying for any hour or two. Fifteen or twenty minutes—that's it. And I mean it!"

"Fine," Teddy responded, looking back at the couple.

Now more relaxed and satisfied, Teddy leaned his arm against the tree at his side, and found his body passed right through it, throwing him slightly off balance. Teddy started laughing, and tested what seemed an illusion. He passed his hand through the trunk of the tree, and then through the bushes in front of him. What seemed to be solid matter was no denser than the air about them, just as was Polaris' etheric form.

Teddy turned to Ryan with an excited look on his face. "Did you see that Ryan?" he asked.

Ryan nodded, frozen, as if he had seen a ghost. "Ted," he asked in a very low voice, "do you think we're dead?"

"Dead? We're not dead," Teddy said sharply.

"Then where are we?" Ryan questioned.

"I don't know, I guess we're just in another dimension—kind of looking in."

"Are you sure?" Ryan asked, not at all convinced.

"Ryan, I'm solid, and you're solid. It's the world were looking at that isn't."

"Then how did Polaris know our names?" Ryan asked.

"How am I supposed to know," Teddy responded.

Once again, the young couple distracted Teddy, now walking only a few feet away from them. He leaned forward and called out Terese's name, but the beautiful young woman did not see or hear him. Nor did the young man, in his own image, standing so close to her. Teddy and Ryan watched, as the two walked slowly back to the house. Theos had his arm around Tarah's waist, and they were both intent on conversation.

They looked so young to Teddy, younger than he ever remembered being in his early twenties, but that was their age. Stopping abruptly, Tarah turned, looking deep into Theos' clear hazel eyes. She seemed very upset about something, and Teddy and Ryan strained to hear their conversation.

"Temple School?" Tarah questioned. "Theos, I don't want to wait three more years."

Theos tried to calm her. "Tarah, please."

"I thought we were getting married this year?" she asserted, questioning him.

A gentle breeze stroked her lovely form, and he watched her beautiful blonde hair as it moved down across her shoulders in soft waves. He was greatly moved by the sight of her beauty, and knew what she was feeling.

Theos brought her closer to him, and back into his arms in an attempt to comfort her. Tarah responded as he hoped she would, moving closer against his body.

Even though she could not help but respond to him, at that very moment she felt as though her life were threatened, and kept wondering why he was doing this.

"Tarah, please try to understand. I have to go," Theos said, trying to console her.

She turned her face to meet Theos' eyes. "Why Theos? Why Temple School?" Tarah managed.

"To study," he answered.

"Study what?" she asked, her voice catching.

"The mysteries, the esoteric studies," he replied. "Tarah, it would be wonderful if we could go together," he persuaded.

But not to Tarah's mind. Even though they had qualified for attendance at Temple School, neither one of them had ever talked about going. Moreover, the invitations had been extended three months ago. The only thing they had discussed was their upcoming marriage. Temple School was not in their plans.

Now, Tarah thought, he had changed his mind. She was too intelligent to deny to herself that there were only two reasons you went on to Temple

School. And, she wondered if Theos just wanted the assurance of a high office, or if he ultimately wanted to be a priest.

Tarah could feel Theos' hand reach across her back, as he affectionately pulled her toward him again, and soon his mouth was warm and wanting against hers. She found herself relaxing into him, totally consumed by his powerful, masculine presence. But she knew she had to make him understand her feelings, and she had to be certain about why he wanted this.

Pulling gently away from him, Tarah looked up into his strong, handsome face. "Theos," she managed, "why can't we just get married, as planned?"

He tenderly moved his hand down the side of her face, still breathing deeply from the passion that had so quickly risen inside of him. "Will you just try it," he whispered, "just for me?"

Tarah felt weak. She was giving in to him.

As she turned away, Theos caught her hand and gently pulled her back to him. "Please, Tarah," Theos repeated, gently persuading her.

Again Tarah felt the urge to give in to him. Theos had a compelling presence about him, which could be both charming and captivating. She could still feel his warmness from being close to him, and she knew she had to get away.

"Give me some time to think about it," she finally said, as she started to walk back up to the house.

"Wait," Theos called to her, with a concerned look on his face. "Where are you going?"

Tarah didn't answer him. She quickly glided up the path leading to Theos' house, slightly lifting her long gown an inch or two above the ground, so as not to trip. Her world was falling apart, and she did not know how to recapture it. All she wanted at that moment was to be alone, and she fought back the tears that would later stream down her face.

When Tarah reached the patio steps at the back of the house, she passed Theos' best friend.

Aryan, named for the star Orion, touched Tarah's arm as she walked up the steps. He could see something was wrong. Aryan was a very tall, slender, fashionable young man, and his dark, reddish-brown hair contrasted with his deep blue eyes.

"I was just trying to find you," Aryan said, gently.

But before he could finish, Tarah interrupted him by lifting her hand to stop him from going any further.

"I know," she said wearily. "My father's looking for me."

A look of compassion crossed his face, as he watched Tarah walk into the house. After a moment or two, he continued down the steps into the garden. He found Theos standing alone, looking out at the pond, where two large white swans stroked long, V-shaped grooves into the water. Theos turned when he heard his friend approaching.

"I take it you told her," Aryan said.

Theos nodded that he had.

"And?" Aryan asked.

"I couldn't break our engagement. I just couldn't," Theos explained. "I love her too much."

Aryan drew his hands up, and placed them defiantly on his hips. "What did you tell her?" he asked, anger coming into his voice.

"That I wanted her to go to Temple School, and…" Theos could not finish.

"And what?" Aryan queried, impetuously.

"And that I wanted her to come with me."

Aryan impatiently looked to the side, and then back again. He could not believe what he was hearing. "And is she going?" he asked.

Theos moved closer to the pond, watching the swans. "She said she'd let me know," he finally answered.

Aryan looked relieved, but that expression soon changed when Theos looked back again.

"But I'm going to talk her into it," he said seriously.

"I don't believe you!" Aryan stormed.

"Believe what?" Theos asked.

"You know you're going with the hope of being chosen for the priesthood. Why do you insist on holding on to her?"

Theos looked annoyed. "I love her and nothing is for certain yet. I haven't been asked, and I haven't accepted."

"And if you are asked after your third year?" Aryan asserted.

"Look, you don't understand," Theos, continued.

"I don't understand?" Aryan questioned sarcastically.

Theos returned Aryan's cold, angry look. "Who knows, I'll probably just go for the leadership program."

"I don't believe that for a minute," Aryan responded.

"Tell me Aryan, why shouldn't I go? You're going, aren't you?"

"You lost that opportunity when you asked Tarah to marry you," Aryan judged.

"I want to marry her, but I also want this opportunity. It's something I was born wanting. And I have to know, and I have to find out if I..." Theos stopped without finishing.

Forever it seemed he had wanted to study the mysteries and become a priest.

"Well priests are not supposed to be physically and emotionally centered," Aryan reprehended. "They're supposed to be mentally and spiritually focused, and dedicated to serving others," he said indignantly.

"Like you?" Theos questioned, staring at him.

"What's going on with you anyway?" Aryan asked, in an angry, condemning fashion. "One day you're happy, planning your wedding, and the next, all of a sudden, you have this driving ambition to become a priest again."

Theos looked at him thoughtfully for what seemed an endless moment.

"To become one of the Magi," Theos corrected.

This astounded even Aryan. It was one thing to seek the priesthood, another to be one of the Magi. With slow intent, Aryan drew in a deep breath and went on.

"Tell me Theos, how could I have known you all my life, and not have known that?"

Theos turned away, and looked back at the pond.

"Secret ambition, I guess."

"I guess," Aryan ranted. "Well priests don't marry, or do you plan to change that."

"I'm fully aware of the vows I'll have to take, Aryan. Do you think I am so self-centered, and narcissistic, as to believe that a religious order should change its tradition, or intent, because of my own unchecked desires?"

Aryan did not answer him.

Theos' anger began to fall away, as did his voice. "This is my problem, and I'll work it out in my own way," he said quietly. "No one is more aware than I of the choice I have to make."

Aryan mumbled some remark, which Theos could not clearly hear.

Theos' eyes quickly snapped back at him, as he looked keenly at his childhood friend, measuring his thought. "And why are you going?" he asked, as Aryan walked away.

Becoming a priest was something that Aryan had always wanted, but would never admit to. He would only talk about wanting to take the leadership program at Temple School. Aryan would never take the risk of letting anyone know what he actually wanted, until it had been offered to him. His ego would not allow it, and it was difficult to become an Atlantean priest. Only one in ten candidates were invited in.

Stopping short, Aryan turned to face him. "Maybe I'll just hang around until Tarah sees the light, and then *I'll* marry her," he said.

"Right," Theos answered.

"Try me," Aryan returned, challenging him.

"You wouldn't," Theos replied, testing his intent.

Aryan grinned, pleased with himself. "Oh, but I would," he said, as he headed up the path toward the house. "Don't think I won't!"

Theos followed close behind him, and they argued continuously until they fell out of sight.

Teddy and Ryan looked at each other, with amazement. It all seemed quite impossible—this conversation, this event—for it had to have taken place thousands of years ago. They had different names, but they were definitely the same individuals.

With a smile on his face, Teddy turned to Ryan, referring to Theos' and Aryan's arguing in a jesting manner.

"I guess some things never change," he said.

"I guess not," Ryan, responded, anger edging back into his voice.

"Are you ready to go?" Teddy asked, knowing Ryan, having seen himself in the form of Aryan, would not want to leave.

"I don't mind staying a little longer," Ryan admitted nonchalantly.

Teddy wondered why all this was happening. In due time he would discover that their Atlantean past, and their American future, were bound as tightly together as were the spiritual, mystical men who formed America into a united nation so many years before.

Atlantis was gone. No one could bring her, or her people, back. However, they were invited to see, through divine intervention, what this continent once was, what it represented, and how it failed.

A record had been kept, and they were privileged to view it. It was as if Polaris had made an archive available, a permanent record, which was to remain for all mankind on holographic film, in another dimension.

It was not by accident that he and Ryan discovered the obelisk—or by chance that they had met Polaris. Teddy and Ryan would stay, and watch from afar, until the very end.

CHAPTER 4

▲

LEAH

ATLANTIS

Saturday

The elegant and elaborate estate belonging to Theos' family had been handed down from generation to generation for centuries past, and was kept in flawless condition by a meticulous staff of custodians and gardeners.

Theos' light and airy apartment was located on the second tier of the house facing east, and his magnificent, expansive bedroom was filled with enormous pots, of different sizes and design, containing an assortment of tropical plants and several small varieties of trees.

Theos woke early, and watched his room change color with the warm rosy light of dawn, and listened to the sounds of birds in the garden. Theos always enjoyed this part of the day, and waking early gave him time to think through his thoughts—especially now that he had decided to go on to Temple School.

There was some unknown force driving him toward this decision, and he had not one moment's peace until he had given in to it. He was certain he had made the right decision. Certain about everything except Tarah—what would he do about Tarah?

Theos had pondered this for weeks now, and it troubled him. He had never felt about anyone the way he felt about her, and she filled a part of him he had not known was even missing, until she came into his life.

There were no words to describe the oneness he felt with her, and losing Tarah would be his greatest sacrifice, for he was overwhelmingly compelled to fulfill his ambition. Why, he did not know.

Almost an hour went by before the light tapping sound of Leah's paws interrupted his thoughts, as she trotted across the inlaid beige and white marble floor of the veranda outside his bedroom.

Leah had awakened early, too, and was investigating the house and garden. She had hoped to find something special to eat, after the big party on Friday evening, but the staff had cleaned the house and grounds before retiring.

Four large, arched, double doors stretched across the opening to the terrace from Theos' room. When Leah passed by, and saw Theos was awake, her eyes brightened, and she quickened her pace coming through one of the open doors. She was soon at Theos' side, sitting down next to his bed, nuzzling her face into the covers so he would pet her.

She had the perfect line of an Atlantean golden retriever. Her thick coat was a honey cream, with pale feathering. Leah also had a beautifully shaped head, with large expressive brown eyes, that conveyed in an instant her every emotion.

Her tail happily thumped the thick beige rug centered under Theos' bed, which expanded halfway across the beige marble flooring of his room, and she looked very excited about something.

"You sure are up early this morning," Theos said, as he reached his arm over to give her a hug.

Leah just looked at him innocently.

A shiver ran through Theos, as he eased his arm away. She was cold and damp to the touch. "How'd you get so wet?" he asked.

Leah nudged his arm, playfully.

"Have you been swimming with the swans again?" he questioned, starting to laugh.

Resting her head next to Theos on the bed, she snuggled closer, working her nose under his arm. After a moment or two, she started to jostle something around in her muzzle.

"What's in your mouth, Leah?" Theos asked, reaching for her.

Leah quickly moved her head away.

"Come on, let's see," Theos urged.

When he pried her mouth open, he found a small turtle inside. It peeked its little head out of its shell, none the worse for the warm moist ride in Leah's mouth.

"You better take that back to the pond, and let it go," he insisted. Trying to look serious when he spoke to her.

She gave him an earnest, and pleading, look, but Leah could soon see he was not going to give in.

Theos gave her a reassuring pat on her shoulder, as she dropped her head with disappointment. "Go on," he encouraged.

Leah got up, her head slung low, and she slowly sauntered out to the veranda, and down the steps to the back garden. She had been trying to catch that turtle for three weeks now, and she had no intention of letting it go. When she reached the yard, she looked back up to see if Theos was watching her. When she saw he was not, she happily turned around, picking up her gait, in search of a private place to play—her newfound friend balanced on the crest of her tongue.

Smiling to himself, with thoughts of Leah, Theos stretched out on his bed, clasping his hands above his head. Despite her young looks and rejuvenescent spirit, Leah was almost twelve years old. She had never lost that quality of wonder about her, and because of her loving, easygoing nature, she was everyone's favorite in the family.

The family consisted of Theos, his older brother, his mother and father, and his paternal grandfather. Theos' older brother had recently married, and moved to the continent southwest of their own, known as the Southern Americas. He had been assigned to a new scientific observatory there, and Theos missed having him around the house. They were close in age, and had always spent a great deal of time together.

Their parents were a source of pride to both Theos and his brother. Theos' father was quite famous in his own right, as a prophetic writer and philosopher, and his mother was an accomplished artist. Her crystal sculptures, some of which were museum pieces, were known throughout their empire, and were forever sought after by collectors.

Theos and his grandfather shared a close, enduring friendship over the years. His grandfather was a gracious and kind man, an intellectual in his late seventies, possessing an extraordinary wit, a quick gait, and electric blue eyes.

From childhood, Theos tended to emulate him in every way, and he always felt that his grandfather was the one person who truly understood him, and in whom he could confide his innermost thoughts.

Then, of course, there was Leah. Theos remembered the day she came into their lives. She was sick and hurt, and it took almost a year to nurse her back to health. But there were no signs now of the early abuse she had suffered, so many years before, when she first joined their family. Theos would never forget that day. It stuck in his mind, as a thorn into flesh.

It was Theos' tenth birthday when they first found her. He and his grandfather were testing a kite-like device they had designed together. The wind was not satisfactory at home, on their estate, so they had decided to go to a nearby park located in the lower foothills at the edge of the city. Climbing one of the highest hills for the best wind, they could see the activities of others in the park all about them. It was there that they spotted Elias, whose Atlantean name was pronounced Ee'lee-es.

Elias was a handsome, dark-haired youth in Theos' class at school, who had, at a very early age, the reputation of being something of a tyrant. From where Theos and his grandfather were standing, they could see him dragging a small puppy, against its will, across a far slope.

They watched the sight with deep aversion. It was obvious Elias showed no concern for the little dog. As they continued to watch, they saw him turn around suddenly, and with some rod-shaped tool, violently strike the small animal, knocking it to the ground.

Theos shuddered with the sound of her piercing yelp, as a hot electrical current from the device singed through her coat to the flesh.

Horrified at the sight, Theos' grandfather yelled for Elias to stop, but Elias did not hear him.

Both Theos and his grandfather ran toward the hill where Elias was standing. However, before they could reach the small puppy, Elias had already rendered another charge.

They could see Leah collapse, and retch on the ground, as she gave out one last piercing sound. Then Elias' foot cruelly penetrated hard into her ribs, as he kicked her across the grass.

Whatever air was left in her lungs had been violently expelled, and when she finally rested on her side, he kicked her once more. Looking down at her, Elias finally seemed satisfied, for she appeared to be dead.

Now only a short distance away, Theos' grandfather bolted up the hill-side, with Theos alongside of him. Elias turned sharply, when he saw their angry approach, and quickly ran off in the opposite direction, deserting the small animal where she lay unconscious.

They soon reached Leah's stricken form, and the sight of her was appalling. Theos' grandfather passed his hand over her small golden body, and took her pulse. She expelled a final, shuddering breath of death.

When Theos' grandfather touched her, the heat from his hand flowed evenly through her. Then, miraculously, her heart began beating again, as her lungs slowly shuddered open, and filled with the cool crisp air of late afternoon.

Theos knelt quietly at her side, with streams of tears running down his face. He looked up at his grandfather, trying to find his voice. "Can you heal her?" he questioned.

His grandfather looked down affectionately at him. "Let's see if she can get up on her own. It's always better that way," he said.

Lifting his hand to the small puppy's face, Theos ran the tips of his fingers tenderly across her cheek, gently smoothing away a piece of loose grass from where it had fallen close to her eye. One of his tears fell from his young round cheek, and onto her muzzle, and Theos watched the droplet as it disappeared into her soft fur coat.

His body filled with loving compassion for this tiny creature that, he thought, could not possibly understand such cruelty. He wished with all his heart she would respond to him. Theos whispered gentle reassuring

Twice Tarah had tried to tell her mother of her fears, but her mother had dismissed her without listening, and the situation was getting worse. And, Tarah's fears were valid.

Shortly after her last attempt to tell her mother of her father's abhorrent, aberrational behavior, he quite slyly had entered her room one night, and stood by her bed just staring at her. He thought she was asleep, although she had seen him enter her room, and only pretended to be—hoping he would leave without harming her. For some unexplainable reason, she feared for her life, almost as if he was contemplating how he could get rid of her.

Tarah had been so distressed by his presence that she found she could not move. It was as if she were paralyzed. Her heart had begun pounding so loudly that she thought the sound itself would give her away. She had never known such fear in her entire life, and she began to pray for divine intervention.

It was an instinctive thing to do and, unknown to Tarah, it was the most potent thing she could have done to protect herself from the evil that had entered her room that night.

Her father did not waken her, nor did he attempt to touch her. But he stood there, contemplating the act, for a very long time before he finally left her room.

It had now come to the point where she was afraid to fall asleep at night for fear he would come into her room again, even though she now locked her door. She knew, in reality, that this actually gave her little protection, because her father had access to all the household keys. However, it would at least give her some warning.

On the night of the party, she had planned to tell Theos about what had happened to her, but instead, he had told her of his plans to go on to Temple School. Now, she knew if she told him what had happened, he would feel obligated to marry her, as planned. And, she could not live with the thought that he would feel trapped in his relationship with her because of her circumstances at home—or, even worse, coerced.

Nothing was right, everything was wrong, and there was very little Tarah could do about it. The one comfort in her life was that she did have

Theos, and that meant more to Tarah than Theos would ever know. He had truly become her entire life.

Tarah cried herself to sleep that night, knowing she was no longer in control of her destiny. If she lost Theos, she lost everything. So, reluctantly, seeing no alternative, she prepared herself to go to Temple School, and accepted the delay in their marriage for three more years.

Monday

On Monday morning, at seven-thirty, the transport Theos had ordered waited outside the gates of his family's estate. Theos went through his morning routine as quickly as possible. After saying goodbye to Leah, he hurriedly made his way down the long path in front of their home, to the transport.

The heavy, ornate fence surrounding their compound was tall and strong despite its age. Theos quickly opened the gates by touching a fastening mechanism, and was soon inside the vehicle and speeding across the city.

Picking up Tarah next, and then Lucina and Aryan, it was not long before their transport approached the Temple School grounds. The air of excitement was all about them.

From their point of view, they looked across a plateau of many acres in extent, where the gradually rising ground began to break into the foothills. The whole surface of the Great Square was elevated and paved with a shiny marble-hard covering. Along the entire extent of the front and two sides of the platform extended a series of seven long steps leading up to each of the three buildings.

Their transport slowly descended at the walk bordering the grounds, and they all got out. A moment later, after the doors of the transport automatically shut, the vehicle slowly elevated and sped off to return to its main docking area.

Together they made their way up the steps, and walked across the plaza. Straight in front of them was the Great Sacred Cathedral, and, to their left, the private living quarters of the priests and priestesses. High above the third story of the living quarters rested the large, ornate domed roof of the

Priestly Council's Meeting Chambers, with its golden inlay design glistening in the morning sun.

Looking to the east and west of the Sacred Cathedral, they could see gardens with meticulously cared for groves of trees. And connected to the eastern section of the Temple School on their right, was the school's obelisk and observatory.

Theos' eyes took in the peaceful grounds, silhouetted in the morning sun, and his exhilaration grew. He had never been inside the Temple School itself, only the Sacred Cathedral, and then only on special occasions with his parents, and grandparents.

The school consisted of three stories, the first being constructed of several rows of white pillars that rose up around the entire school. The enormous pillars supported arches that in turn held up the second and third stories of the school.

Once inside, Theos led them across the first floor to a wide curving staircase that led to the second story, where the chambers for teaching and the school library were situated.

Theos knew exactly where he was going, as his grandfather had drawn the structure for him when he was quite young, and, from time to time, he would bring out the drawings and walk through the building in his mind.

Farther down the hall, on the second level, the staircase continued, leading up to the third floor, where the offices and quarters of the three ruling Magi were located. They would not be permitted on that floor, except by invitation, or for specific business.

Theos and Tarah, and Aryan and Lucina, joined the other students who were making their way up the tall staircase. The majority of students were dressed entirely in white collarless tunics, which the men wore with matching well-fitted pants, and the women with skirts of the same fine material. They, and the other first-year students, were to be fitted that afternoon for their own school attire.

The only thing that separated one group of students from another was the number of slender silver silk cords that were edged around their tunics. Each silver cord represented the number of years the student had attended the school. It was only in this way that you could tell a first-year student from those having studied two or three years.

The students who had been chosen for the priesthood wore simply tailored straight white robes with golden cords edging their garments, down the front and across the bottom, representing either their fourth, fifth, sixth or seventh year of instruction.

At the top of the stairs, an aide directed them to their assigned auditorium, and they walked swiftly down the hall to their class. When they reached the inside of the auditorium, Theos stopped for a moment, and watched some of the other students already seated at their long-angled, highly-polished wooden desks.

Each desk was attached to the next, extending into long semi-circles, with each of the four rows elevated a foot or so higher than the one before it. One side of the desk was used for the purpose of writing, and the other half, to the left, was devoted to supporting an inset, angled, monitor screen connected to a master teaching computer.

Theos and Tarah, and Aryan and Lucina, took seats high in the fourth row, which gave them an elevated view of the majority of the others below. When the last student slid into her seat, the entranceway was sealed. One could hear a locking sound, as the door shut tight, and the room became soundproof.

As Theos settled back, he looked around the room again. It was then that he saw Elias, sitting in the middle of the first row. At once Theos could feel the heat of his blood rise throughout his entire body.

How, Theos thought, could Leah's menacing enemy of so many years before, someone so lacking in any sense of morality or compassion, be accepted into Temple School? Theos started to say something to Aryan, but then stopped short, as the room fell silent and their teacher, Taro, entered from a side door.

Theos watched the priest as he moved across the floor, with his silver and white embroidered robe moving behind him. He was a large man, in his mid-forties, with deep auburn hair and a sharp striking manner. It seemed to Theos as if his energy pulled the entire room into focused attention, just by his presence.

Taro took his place at an elevated platform, and introduced himself. The students watched him intently, as he began instructing them in their first lesson dealing with the fundamentals of energy and its seven aspects. He had quickly captured their interest, and with a flick of his long-fingered hand, caused a beam of intense light to arc from the center of his palm. In his other hand he held a crystal prism.

Theos and his classmates watched with fascination as the priest demonstrated his point, passing the light extending from his hand through the prism.

"In the same way light passes through a prism, and breaks down into seven separate and distinct colors," Taro explained, "so too does energy, passing through matter, fall into seven distinct rays or types of energy."

Theos watched the angle of light extending from Taro's hand. It passed back through, moving around the object, breaking the prism into a spectrum of color—the rainbow arcing clear across the room.

He now understood the intuitive prompting he had been experiencing, for it was leading him down an enchanting path of original thought and new discoveries. Theos knew that he was doing the right thing by being there. He had definitely made the right decision. Deep within his heart he felt, without question, that he was about to embark on the greatest adventure of his life—an adventure in expanding his mind.

High above Taro's class, in the Magician's Chamber near the top of the obelisk-shaped Temple Tower, Polaris watched Theos and the other students through a large crystal.

It was in this, the second highest chamber of the obelisk, that the three Magicians kept constant ward and watch over the workings within the Temple School, and on the entire continent itself. Directly above the Magicians' Chamber, at the tip of the obelisk, rested the Great Observatory with its clear glass dome and pulsating light.

Polaris stood at one side of the Magicians' Chamber, studying a lighted crystal globe. So intense was his concentration that he jumped slightly, when a "zinging" sound interrupted the still silence of the room. Sirius, the eldest of the three Magicians, materialized at one of the three seats that curved around the circular table in the center of the room.

Sirius was a slight man, and one knew immediately upon looking at him that he could be more than one hundred years old. And yet, there still existed a vital quality about him that led you to know his influence and authority was unlimited, integral and complete.

As Sirius moved to rise out of his seat, Polaris looked up to greet him.

"You're early," Polaris said, somewhat surprised.

He had not expected Sirius for another half hour or so. They had planned to meet with regard to a problem they were having with the third, and youngest, of the three Magi.

"I wanted to talk some more about Merak before he arrives," Sirius explained. "We have to do something about him immediately," he directed.

Despite his somewhat shorter stature, Sirius stood strong and straight as he paced a slow even gait around the circular chamber. He was a complex man. His soul was principled, disciplined and strict—and yet, commensurate to Polaris, he had a profound love for humanity, and was always known to take the time to stop and talk to even the smallest child. Sirius was very much beloved by the Atlantean people, and revered above all. However, today he had a staid, pensive look on his face, and his intelligent eyes appeared restless as he glanced about the room. He was not himself.

Of late, Polaris too had been deeply disturbed by Merak's behavior, and had been experiencing visions and dreams which perplexed him. The dreams were violent and catastrophic in extent, leaving him with the deepest feeling of tragedy he had ever known. And Merak's face kept appearing in his visions.

It was because of these recurrent dreams that Polaris had conducted his own investigation of Merak's research and activities. When he was certain of his allegations, he confided all of this to Sirius, who concurred that he too had been having a series of visions of late.

What they had discovered about Merak was quite alarming. Merak was slowly and purposefully destroying the protective sheath of the planet, the end result of which would allow the threads of darkness to slip through the protective barrier of light, as the shield was loosened. There were undeniable signs that this had already begun.

Merak had to be stopped. They both knew that. Now they had conclusive evidence that they could, and would provide, if necessary, to the governing Priestly Council. The nature of conducting this investigation was unprecedented in all of Atlantean history, its records having been kept for many thousands of years.

Sirius turned and looked at Polaris, whose hands were still resting on the encasement of the crystal sphere.

"Well," Sirius asked, in a quiet tone, "are we still in agreement as to how we are to confront Merak with our findings?"

"Yes, of course," Polaris nodded. "Although I'm afraid I am no closer to reasoning his motive than I was yesterday."

Polaris had weighed the situation over for days now, and had gone through every possible theory. Yet he could not understand why Merak was doing this, or what he was up to. Nor could he imagine why Merak was bringing the master crystal up beyond its normal vibrations. Polaris wondered if he was trying to control something or someone?

Why would he foolishly try an experiment so dangerous that he was willing to disrupt the harmonious rhythm of their very existence? Over and over again, Polaris pondered about what Merak's intent was. No one on Earth had ever done anything comparable to this before.

Polaris met Sirius' thoughtful eyes. "Is it possible that Merak has become so absorbed with himself," Polaris asked, "that he thought his actions would go unnoticed?"

"Well," Sirius said calmly, "he should be here shortly, and we can confront him with it then." Sirius looked down into the crystal and was, for the moment, distracted by the holographic image set therein. "What's been holding your interest?" Sirius probed.

"I've been observing some of our new students in Taro's class," Polaris responded. "One is the son of Apollo."

Sirius examined the image, and made a nodding motion with his head, encouraging Polaris to continue.

All at once Polaris made a quick movement with his hand. Electrical charges emanated from his fingers and, with one complete sweep, he pulled the picture of Theos from the crystal, ballooning it into an image covering an area of once open space. Theos was now pictured standing by his seat in class, responding to a question Taro had posed.

When Polaris froze the framed image of Theos, he appeared little more than one-third his actual size, and a fine hair-like etheric structure of rapidly pulsating clear white light extended approximately two inches at right angles all about Theos' body.

Sirius studied Theos' etheric field.

"He has a clean, healthy instrument with plenty of vital energy," he observed. "And his emotional field?" Sirius asked.

Again with a sweeping movement, Polaris changed the picture, and a mutable aura of color moved over Theos, extending just two inches beyond where his etheric field left off.

"He's somewhat emotional," Sirius discerned, as he stood checking each of the seven vortices of energy within Theos' form, starting from the head down.

Polaris, trying to impress upon Sirius that training could bring Theos' emotional field into alignment, asked Sirius to take a look at Theos' mental field.

Again, with a sweeping movement, Polaris changed the picture, and an additional field appeared extending just beyond the emotional field. You could see a pale yellow light extending around Theos, with brighter extensions at the head, all of which extended beyond both his etheric and astral/emotional fields.

"Excellent!" Sirius said, with satisfaction in his voice. "He appears to have attained a great deal of knowledge, for someone so young."

Then, with a more serious look on his face, Sirius walked forward and viewed Theos more closely.

"And his soul?" Sirius asked, obviously encouraged.

Again with his hands, Polaris made a motion and an egg-shaped brilliantly shining clear white light, corresponding to a galaxy of billions of stars, surrounded Theos, extending well beyond the fields of his body—confirming the ancient knowledge that you can tell the age of a soul by its light.

"He is the son of Apollo," Sirius said, with acclamation.

"I would enjoy working with him," Polaris revealed. "On an individual basis."

Sirius thought for a moment, and then responded. "Perhaps if we can adjust his emotional field, but that is always a problem. We cannot have someone training in magic, when the fields of his body are not in perfect alignment," he insisted. "It is too dangerous."

What Sirius had pointed out was true. However, Polaris believed it was not often that a student of Theos' caliber came along. Despite his one flaw, Polaris favored him over the others, and felt he was well worth the effort of private instruction. For that reason, he continued his appeal.

"I still want to try working with him, and see what I can do about his emotional field," Polaris continued, deferring to Sirius. "He is only slightly out of alignment, and his father was a very gifted student."

"Yes, I know," Sirius said, with an apprehensive look coming across his face. "You tutored his father too, many years ago, but he never became a priest."

"Yes, that's true," Polaris, responded with a smile. "But now we have Theos."

Sirius thought for a moment, somewhat amused, as a sparkle came into his eyes. "As you wish," he finally said, in conclusion. "He has, without question, the potential to go far. And, if he does not become a priest, he will still validate what he has learned from you, by making a fine contribution in the world of men—just as his father, and his grandfather, have done before him."

Polaris looked very pleased.

"By the way," Sirius asked, laughing to himself, "how is Theos' grandfather?" He knew he and Polaris were friends, and thought that was why Polaris had such an interest in Theos.

"He's doing quite well," Polaris said.

"Please give him my regards, and tell him that his grandson is in capable hands."

"Yes, I will," Polaris said, laughing, having caught Sirius' thought.

Their conversation was abruptly interrupted when they heard a zinging sound fill the room. When Polaris looked away from Theos, his image dissolved into nothingness.

It was Merak. They watched him, as he materialized near the table. Merak was younger than Polaris by almost twenty years, and his thick chestnut hair remained without even the slightest hint of gray. Merak carried his strong, athletic frame with the greatest of ease, and complete self-control. Even his large, deep brown eyes sparked with the excitement of youth, although he was now in his late forties. Merak looked pleased to see them.

"I hope I'm not late," he announced, boyishly.

"No, not at all," Sirius replied, in a composed manner. "We were just viewing one of the students in Taro's class."

"You wanted to talk?" Merak asked, with a measure of charm, quickly moving toward them.

"Yes," Sirius said, motioning toward a place for him to sit down.

Merak took a seat, while Polaris and Sirius remained standing. And, once Merak was settled, Sirius continued on. "We understand you have been conducting some new experiments," he said pointedly.

Merak's expression became more serious. "That's correct," he answered.

"One of the scientific teams returned two days ago from an expedition," Sirius continued, "and reported that there is a great deal of disturbance in the northern mountains, as well as the western reef, and we …"

Shooting out of his seat, Merak interrupted Sirius mid-sentence. "I can assure you that my experiments have nothing to do with any disturbances," he said. Merak looked intensely at Sirius, and then to Polaris, who was still positioned close to the crystal.

Sirius straightened his body, as he peered deeply into Merak's eyes. "We are going to have to ask you to stop, until we can investigate the problem," Sirius mandated.

Merak's brown eyes turned black and heavy. "I have no intention of delaying my experiments, because of some interfering scientific team, who do not know what they are talking about!"

was time for them to go. Quietly, they made their way out of the building, and in a short while they were lost in the night.

Friday

Theos and Aryan arrived at the last minute for school on Friday morning, both having spent a restless night. Theos had called Tarah and Lucina and told them to go on ahead of them. They were running late. It was apparent that they were still very shaken from what had happened the night before, and were noticeably disturbed when they exited their transport.

Theos tried to block the thoughts of what they had seen going through his mind, but he could not. Everything was happening so fast, too fast, and it was getting out of control.

As they hurried across the plaza toward the school, Theos finally broke their silence. "What are we going to do about last night?" Theos asked.

A troubled look crossed Aryan's face. "I don't know," he finally answered.

"Do you want to see if we can get in to see Polaris this afternoon?" Theos suggested.

Aryan stopped at the top of the plaza stairs, and snapped a look at Theos. "And tell him what?" he demanded.

"And tell him what we saw," Theos compelled.

"What did we see?" Aryan countered.

"You know what we saw," Theos said, angrily.

"And who would believe us?" Aryan asked, looking impatient.

"Polaris!" Theos returned.

"And if he doesn't?" Aryan asked, challenging him.

"What do you mean, if he doesn't?" Theos asked.

"If he doesn't, I'm out," Aryan said, as he hurried on.

"Out of what?" Theos asked, coming up quickly behind him.

"Out of school," Aryan said, his tone of annoyance confirming his mood. "Who ever heard of reporting one of the Magi?"

"I think I have a lot more to lose here than you do," Theos challenged.

Aryan muttered something to himself, but Theos could not hear him. They were now making their way up the interior staircase within Temple School to the second floor. Theos could not believe Aryan's position. They rushed down the hallway toward class, and just as they passed through into the auditorium the doors closed tight, barring anyone else's passage.

When their eyes met, Theos gave Aryan a controlled look. "We're going up there after school," he whispered, as they made their way to their seats.

Aryan did not answer him. At the same moment, Taro entered the room and their class began.

When it was time for lunch, Theos told Tarah he had an errand to run and would meet everyone in class later. He needed more time to think about what had happened last night, and he wanted to talk it over with his grandfather.

Theos found the house empty when he reached home, with the exception of the cook. He was told his grandfather was planting some flowers out in back.

Walking quickly down the steps that led to the yard, Theos proceeded across the winding path, passing the pond where the swans made their home. He looked across the garden, and called out for his grandfather. Leah came running up to greet him, and his grandfather looked up from where he stood alongside a row of rose bushes at the back gate. He was surprised to see Theos at home mid-day.

"Are you home for lunch?" his grandfather asked, with interest. He could see that Theos was troubled about something.

Theos smiled, and nodded.

His grandfather was holding a young plant in his arms, and the sight of him comforted Theos.

"Are those your new hybrids?" Theos asked.

His grandfather looked down, admiring his plants. "Aren't they beauties?" he related. "This little one's the last to go in," he said, bending down again.

"What color will they be?" Theos inquired.

Another great puzzle to Theos was how Eunice, Tarah's mother, could tolerate this man for so long, and how she could possibly love him. She seemed totally unaware of how he controlled and manipulated her.

Theos remembered the adage—"*evil is he who imposes his will on another.*" Rama was evil. A saving grace, if any, was that Rama's type of evil was only effective in controlling those weaker, and of a lower mental level than himself. Tarah was not. She was strong, integrated and intelligent, and Theos never worried about her. But her parents were a problem. Something did not fit.

It was late in the afternoon, and the sun felt warm on Theos' face, as a soft onshore breeze blew his blonde, wavy hair away from his temples. The wind carried a clean fresh scent from the gardens below, where jasmine bloomed along a garden trellis. He lingered there, thinking about Tarah, her warmth, their love for each other, and his need for her. He was perplexed as to why she had come into his life. And why he needed her so.

Turning to go back into his bedroom he walked over to his bed, and, after propping up a couple of pillows, rested back in a comfortable position. Once again his mind began analyzing everything that had happened over the last year, beginning with the day he met Tarah, and everything that had occurred from that moment on. While lying there, after two hours of deep concentrated thought, his answer finally came.

During one single instant, everything became clear and came into focus. It was as if a door had suddenly opened, giving him clear insight and knowledge of things past, present, and future. Before it shut, Theos knew he loved Tarah too much to ever leave her.

He could never be a priest. Stay with Tarah, his inner voice kept saying. That was to be his final resolution. He had made his decision. She was at one with him, as he was at one with her. They could never be parted, no matter what their circumstances. What blinded him to this before, he did not know. However, at long last he had his answer. His driving ambition belonged to his personality, not to his soul. His heart won out, as it always should.

Calm and serene for the first time in days, Theos wished he could fall asleep for a while. He needed to sleep. A feeling of drowsiness passed over him, and he could feel his body relax into a new and complete contentment. Theos watched the sun, as it began dropping into the horizon, with its falling blaze turning the room deep amber.

As he relaxed on the bed a warm, gentle breeze swept bright pink petals off a flowering bougainvillea and into the room, lifting them in a magical, swirling spectacle of color and making an arrangement across the highly polished inlaid floor. As he watched, many of the petals stopped their skidding dance where the rug began, but a few had the strength and curiosity to jump on top, where they rolled happily across the plush carpet, before coming to a comfortable place to rest. When the golden setting sun slipped into the dark blue waters of eventide, his eyes became heavy, and he drifted off into a peaceful, quiet state of sleep.

While Theos slept, so many miles away Tarah began dressing for her parents' anniversary celebration. She had put off going downstairs as long as she could. Their house was full of guests, and she knew she would soon have to join them, or her father, in his insistence, would come up after her.

As she walked slowly out of her room, and down the hall, she wondered how she would get through the evening without Theos, especially knowing that those invited to the party would probably be at least twice, if not three times, her age. She stopped before she reached the stairs, and watched her mother and father welcoming some guests. Her parents looked so old to her, and she somehow felt totally separate and apart from them.

Rama was a tall, rawboned, stern looking man in his middle sixties, with small fading light blue eyes and thin gray hair. Her mother was lean and plain, with a pallid complexion. She looked older than a woman in her late fifties. Her lifeless blue eyes had long ago lost their inner expression, and the colors she wore were as gray and washed out as she was.

A closely guarded secret was that Tarah was not their own. She had been taken from her natural parents when she was only six weeks old, and had never been told of the tragic way they died.

There had been a terrible and fatal accident. Rama had caused the incident to happen while he and Eunice were on vacation. He had taken Tarah from her dying mother's arms just before their transport started burning. When Rama and Eunice returned home from their trip with Tarah, they had told their friends that Tarah had been adopted.

However, over the years, with Rama having changed his job and residence so often, their present friends and acquaintances thought Tarah was their own. Even Tarah thought Rama and Eunice were her natural parents. The actual story would never be told, not to anyone, not ever. Moreover, if anyone knew from whom she had been taken, they would also know that Rama had been responsible for her parents' death.

Tarah continued to watch the activity from the upstairs balcony as people arrived. She dreaded more than ever having to go down and mix with her parents' friends, for she had nothing in common with any of them.

It was then that a young man arrived with his mother and father. Tarah thought she recognized him, and then realized that he was in her class at school. She felt glad for the moment that someone her own age would be at the party. It was Elias, although Tarah knew nothing of his past. Theos had never told her of Elias' cruelty to his beloved Leah, when she was just a helpless puppy. In fact, she knew nothing of him before Temple School, although she had heard from Lucina that he was Merak's only nephew.

When Tarah reached the staircase to go downstairs, it became clear why her father had insisted that Theos not be invited to the party. Tarah could feel anger rise up inside of her, as she listened to her mother's conversation. She was telling Elias that Tarah would be his dinner partner that evening.

As she turned to go back into her room, her father spotted her, and called her down to meet Elias and his parents. Attempting to avoid a confrontation in front of their guests, Tarah reluctantly walked back to the landing.

The sight of her beauty struck Elias. Her long, wavy blonde hair fell below her shoulders in back, and was pulled up in the front with a beautiful jeweled barrette. Her delicate face, with its high color and natural blush, looked especially lovely, and her intelligent hazel eyes seemed to entrance him. Her long, pale, peach-colored gown flowed gently all about her, as the fine silk taffeta caught invisible currents of air, and shimmered in the soft light. Tarah's presence was so all-encompassing and graceful, that she appeared to be floating down the staircase toward him. The invited guests could not help but turn around and stare at her, and the room momentarily took on a more hushed tone.

Rama's eyes lit up, as he walked to the bottom of the stairs, and he brought Tarah over to Elias and his parents. "Tarah, there is someone here we want you to meet. You remember our friends from the Institute," he gestured.

Tarah extended her hand, first to Elias' mother, and then to his father. She had seen them once or twice before, at formal functions, but they had never been introduced.

All the while, Elias never stopped staring at her. She had not gone unnoticed by him at Temple School, and he had been looking forward to this evening all week. When their eyes met, Tarah gave him a welcoming smile. "I think you're in my class at school," she offered, in a friendly manner.

His large brown eyes were magnetic, and seemed to pull her into them. Elias was delighted she remembered him, as he gave a nod in agreement. His demeanor appeared warm and reassuring to her, and his dark, handsome and strong good looks were more appealing than ever. He felt pleased that he and Tarah would finally have this time together.

Looking back and forth between them, Rama was happy with his choice. He had every intention of seeing that Tarah found someone other than Theos to marry, and Elias was his first choice. Inwardly, he was laughing to himself, thinking that he could not have possibly found anyone more suitable for Tarah than the nephew of one of the Magi. To Rama, this was not to be equaled, and he would force Tarah, if necessary, to marry him. This was a night he would never forget. Nor, as it turned out, would Tarah.

Tarah did what was demanded of her that evening, although much to her surprise she enjoyed Elias' company. He was interesting to talk to, and Tarah found herself having fun at the party after all. She was relieved to have a diversion from her parents and their other guests, and, she and Elias

Theos could see at once, from the serious look on Polaris' face, that this was not the appropriate time to be disturbing him. Polaris invited them to sit down on the upholstered sofa at the end of the room, and then took a seat nearby on a chair angled to the right of them.

There was a silence for what seemed a long moment. Then, at the prompting of Polaris, Theos began retelling the story of the night they came across Merak and Elias in the Chamber of Mirrors.

Polaris listened intently until Theos had finished, then the room once again fell absolutely still. It seemed the longest time passed without another word spoken. Theos watched Polaris' face, so deep in thought, and waited for him to respond.

"What you are telling me is of a very serious nature, Theos, and I know it must have been difficult for you to come and talk to me."

Theos nodded his affirmation.

Polaris looked back and forth between Theos and Aryan, and made a mental note of Aryan's continued silence. Inwardly, Polaris admired Theos' courage, for in this single act, Polaris knew that he had not been mistaken about the contribution Theos would make as a priest.

Theos had endangered his entire future by coming forward and telling such a story about one of the Magi—not to mention admitting to breaking into a secret chamber, which no outsiders were ever permitted to enter. Yet Theos came, and Theos told all. Polaris knew his motive was pure. He knew that Theos was responding to what he thought were human cries that night.

Moving forward in his chair, Polaris continued. "Sirius and I have been monitoring Merak's activities extensively, for some time now, and we saw you enter the Chamber of Mirrors that evening."

Aryan looked over at Theos, with a shocked look on his face, and then back to Polaris again.

"We now plan to bring him before the Council, and formally charge him for what he has done. I am certain that you will understand why I must ask you both not to repeat this to anyone, nor speak again of what you saw that night."

Polaris seemed to know that they had not yet done so.

"I don't understand what went wrong," Theos, mused. "How did he become this way?"

A grave, heavy look came over Polaris' face. Theos thought for a moment that he probably should not have asked that question. However, Polaris, in the ordinary fashion that a teacher would respond to the inquiring mind of a student, began his explanation.

"It seems Merak has one great flaw," Polaris denounced. "His blind ambition. It is especially a tragedy in Merak's case, for he is exceptionally gifted. A genius gone wrong."

Theos looked down at his hand, as he picked at a piece of loose thread from his clothing and started to work it between his fingers. He wondered if he had had the same flaw.

"Be assured," Polaris added, "that Merak will pay heavily for this in the end."

"And Elias?" Theos questioned, his feelings apparent.

"He is young, and easily influenced, and he has fallen under Merak's control," Polaris explained.

Theos said nothing.

"Don't misunderstand me, Theos," Polaris added, seeming to read Theos' thoughts. "Even so, he is still responsible for his acts."

Polaris watched Theos' face, and read his expression.

"Elias is not innocent," Polaris continued. "He made his choice, and now he is under the influence of a Black Magician, and to that end, he is at Merak's mercy."

Theos remained silent.

Trying to ease his own tension, Polaris turned slightly, changing his position in his chair. "Let me show you something," Polaris, continued.

Theos and Aryan watched as Polaris made a quick movement with his hand, and in front of them, in open space, appeared the holographic form of a man.

"This is man," Polaris said.

Only the form of a man appeared.

"And this is his soul," he explained, as an egg-shaped white light surrounded the form.

Theos and Aryan leaned forward. They were transfixed by the holographic image, not wanting to miss even the slightest projection.

Polaris watched the illusion, holding it steadfast with his eyes. "At the first moment of conception," Polaris explained, "the soul attaches itself, and grows with the embryo form. The miracle of this enhancement begins when the first cell divides and multiplies, and it is the soul's energy that stimulates the embryo and gives it life. Within the soul is a permanent atom, with the memory and knowledge of all of its lifetimes."

Polaris' voice maintained a specific cadence, as he held their attention.

"As man moves through evolution, his soul gains more and more control, and more and more contact with its personality, or form. The soul is, as a way of explanation, your conscience. It is that silent voice inside of you that tells you right from wrong, or intuitively warns you of danger," Polaris instructed. "The more highly evolved the personality, the more contact he or she has with their soul, and the stronger the conscience, and the greater the intuition."

Theos and Aryan studied the projected image.

"It is your soul that connects you with God," Polaris clarified, "completing the Trinity, and gives you that quality of intuitive clear knowing that will protect you, and direct you onto the right path in life. It is only those individuals who refuse to listen to their own soul, their own conscience, that fall into the hands of darkness. They are free to make that choice, for God never imposes his will. Only the men of darkness do."

Theos and Aryan continued to listen attentively.

Polaris could see that they were following his thoughts, and he got up and walked over to the illusion he had created. "Now, what the Black Magician tries to do is to loosen this contact between the body and the soul, and if he is successful, he can enter and control the form in any way he wills. In addition to this, once he gets in, he can always get in, whether the person wants this or not—for that path, or opening, will always remain. This is true with any kind of hypnosis."

Aryan stared blankly, and looked truly frightened by what Polaris was saying, but Theos was intensely interested.

"Some very powerful magicians, such as Merak," Polaris continued, "can do this without an individual even being aware of it—if the circumstances are right."

Theos now knew he was correct. This was what Merak was doing that night in the Chamber of Mirrors. But why were they untouched by Merak's influence, he wondered. Had Polaris, watching through the crystal, protected them? Theos knew he must have, or they too would have become another of Merak's pawns, especially at close range.

Polaris watched them for a moment, as he read their thoughts.

"Don't forget this," Polaris said, standing up. "Never get into a position in which someone can hypnotize you."

Theos could tell that Polaris was getting some kind of a message, mentally, and knew he had to leave immediately.

"I think that is enough for now," he said, and, with a quick flick of his hand, the illusion disappeared. Their time with Polaris had come to an end.

Theos and Aryan immediately came to their feet, and Polaris walked them to the door, where he said goodbye.

"I'm glad you came to me," he said, extending his hand to both of them. "And Theos," he added with a meaningful look, "thank you."

"Of course," Theos responded, looking back, and meeting Polaris' eyes in understanding.

As they walked out of the Administrative Offices and down the hall, Theos felt relieved, and hoped perhaps that this was a sign things would start to turn around again. In reality though, just the opposite was true. Things would get worse.

When Theos caught the time on the clock at the end of the hall, he saw it was almost one o'clock, and they hurried back to class. Upon walking into the auditorium, Theos noticed at once that Tarah's seat was empty. He quickly went over to Lucina.

"Where is Tarah?" he asked.

Lucina's red hair reflected her quick temper, and her copper-toned eyes looked angry. Likewise, there was no hint of kindness in her round freckled face. "She wasn't feeling well," Lucina responded, in a cold, unmistakable tone. "Elias took her home."

Theos gave Lucina a strong serious look. "How does she know Elias?" he asked, trying to control his voice.

Lucina looked back to her console, and Theos repeated his question.

"How does she know Elias, Lucina?" he asked again.

"I think you had better ask her about that," she answered, beginning her work.

Theos could readily see that he would get no further information from Lucina. He turned sharply to leave the room, only to have the entranceway sealed before him. The auditorium fell still, as Taro entered from a side door. Class had now begun, and he could not leave. That afternoon became the longest afternoon Theos had ever known.

Directly after school, Theos went over to Tarah's house, and found the grounds were locked. When he rang the bell at the outer gates, a servant came out. However, he was refused admittance. Controlling the anger that was still burning deep inside of him, he stayed and argued with the servant for more than ten minutes, to no avail. Even after the servant left, Theos remained, watching Tarah's wing. However, after a couple of hours had passed, and she never appeared on her veranda, he finally walked home.

When Theos came into the house, he could hear his father's raised voice coming from the downstairs library. As he reached the main staircase leading upstairs, Theos could see his parents standing together near a set of double doors that led out to the patio. His father appeared angry about something.

Apollo was an older version of his son, still standing tall and strong, with a proud, prestigious personality. Theos' mother, although much heavier now, had remained refreshingly attractive, and had maintained her elegant nature. Pleiades wore her long blonde hair pulled back into a large braided chignon. It was from her that Theos had inherited his clear hazel eyes, with their long dark lashes, as well as his smooth, even complexion, with its natural high color.

Turning away from Pleiades, Apollo looked out to the open garden. "Theos and I are more than at odds," Apollo insisted. "He had no right asking Tarah to marry him in the first place, if he wanted to be a priest. Did he actually think he could enter into private instruction with Polaris without anyone finding out?"

Tarah's father had finally gotten in touch with him, and Apollo was outraged with what he had been told.

Still serene, Pleiades' voice remained gentle and calming. "Apollo, you're just angry right now."

"I'm not just angry, I'm disappointed in him. He's disgraced our family with his duplicity, not to mention what he did to Tarah."

"He's just confused right now," Pleiades defended. "He's truly very similar to you."

Apollo gave Pleiades a look of wonder, and then gently pulled her over to him, in a loving and knowing way. "Mothers are blind to the faults of their children," he said, smiling. "Did you know that?" The profound look of love in his eyes could not be mistaken, and you could tell they were still very close.

"He's just young and ambitious. He won't disappoint us," Pleiades coaxed, as she smiled up at him.

"Well, it's time he grew up," Apollo implored.

Pleiades waited for a moment before she responded. "I think he's trying to, Apollo. You have to give him a little more time."

Apollo slowly read her eyes. She had an uncanny way of calming him, whenever he felt upset, and he could feel his body relaxing. "You think I'm too hard on him don't you?" he questioned, still watching her.

"No, but you had the same ambition. You went all seven years at Temple School, and then changed your mind just weeks before you were to take your final vows."

"That was different," he said, as a gleam entered his eyes.

"How was it different?" she asked.

Apollo looked at her tenderly. "I met you," he said, pulling her closer to him again.

CHAPTER 11

▲

DESOLATION

Saturday

Theos welcomed the weekend when it came. He had never realized before how important his family was to him, and watched, in a new way, the close loving relationship his parents shared together. Their love was deep and enduring, based on years of trust and respect for each other. Nothing ever seemed to come between them.

His grandfather had appeared somewhat distracted the last couple of days, and had taken to spending long hours at a time in the small chapel at one end of their property. It was in this same chapel that his grandfather had spent endless days and nights, after his grandmother had passed away. During the times since, when his grandfather returned to it, Theos knew the chapel was a place where he could feel close to her again.

Theos never interrupted him there, for it was a private sacred place for prayer. He wished there were something he could do for his grandfather, some way to ease his pain. However, there was only time, and the day-to-day distractions of living, that could heal his grandfather's broken heart.

After dinner on Saturday evening, Theos showered and changed his clothes, and got ready to go to Tarah's. Tonight, without question, he would get in to see her, no matter what he had to do to accomplish it. Then, if she no longer wanted him, he would accept her decision, and once again pursue entering the priesthood. He knew he had lost her trust.

As Theos headed up the hill to Tarah's house, he tried to organize his thoughts, so that he could express exactly what he wanted to say to her. When he arrived, he was glad to see the gates to her residence were once again unlocked, and he let himself in.

It was almost eight o'clock, and he had no intention of going to the front door, for that would only mean rejection. Instead, he climbed up the back of the house to the veranda off Tarah's bedroom. When he pulled himself up over the railing, he was disappointed to find her rooms were dark, and he could see that she had gone out. Looking around for a moment, he decided to wait for her return, and sat down on one of the veranda chairs.

More than two hours passed before he heard the sound of a transport as it settled near Tarah's front gate. Tarah was with Elias.

Unable to control himself, Theos got ready to go down the side, until he saw that Elias was already leaving. He listened for Tarah's footsteps, until he finally heard her walk through her suite. When she reached the veranda, she was startled to see Theos' figure, and quickly flicked on the lights.

"Theos, what are you doing here?" she asked, after she saw who it was.

This was the first time that they had met alone, face-to-face, since Tarah had confronted him about his becoming a priest.

Theos took in a deep breath as he walked to where she was standing. He just looked at her, and his heart began aching with all the suppressed emotion that had been building up inside of him, and he found he could not speak.

"I told you I didn't want to see you," she said, with a tone of hurt in her voice. "You have no right coming here."

"I had to see you," Theos finally spoke. "You owe me at least that."

"I owe you nothing," Tarah responded, looking straight into his eyes.

"I need to talk to you, Tarah."

"About what?" she asked, with a strong tone in her voice.

"About Elias," Theos said.

"About Elias?" she questioned.

Theos showered, dressed, and then went downstairs. The mood was very quiet, and a heavy state of dysphoria hung in the air. The whole house seemed empty and spiritless without his grandfather's presence.

Shortly after everyone had arrived, the family left to go to the Great Sacred Cathedral for the Funeral Mass.

When they entered the silent, sanctified space, they found it was over-flowing with people who had come to honor this regally eminent and impressive man, and to give him their last respects. Both Sirius and Polaris stood at the altar, where Sirius was to officiate the ceremony. Once everyone had taken their seats, the services began.

The long, High Mass, with it's a cappella choir of more than a hundred voices, was an exceptional tribute, and was arranged by Polaris himself. He too would miss dearly his friend of so many years, and he was stricken by the loss.

Over the decades, Polaris and Theos' grandfather had deepened their childhood friendship, and it was with Theos' grandfather that Polaris would confer when he was writing. They shared many confidences, and saw situations in the same light. Polaris knew he could trust his old friend never to repeat to anyone what they discussed in private.

Polaris also knew how ill Theos' grandfather had been, and thought it miraculous that he had survived as long as he had. But despite his strong will, his form had simply worn out, and there was nothing that Polaris could do to help him—although he had tried.

All through the service Theos found he could not control his emotions, as tears welled up in his eyes, and down his cheeks, in rapid succession. His chest felt contorted, and his breathing was hampered. He could not bear the thought of never again being in the presence of this man, whom he loved so dearly. As the ceremony continued, Theos prayed for his grandfather's safe journey, where he believed he would be rejoined with his grandmother.

The Eternal Flame burned silently, at the center of the altar, from a raised massive structure ablaze with a heatless light. It was a time to reflect, a time to remember, and a time to say goodbye. The ritual of the Mass was a sacred rite, with its ancient origin and tradition, and went on for more than an hour.

On a high, gold, ornate table, slightly longer and wider than his own frame, rested Theos' grandfather's body. Beneath him was placed a beautiful gold and white woven cloth. He was dressed all in white, his hands crossed at the wrists, and his palms flat against his chest pointing toward his shoulders.

Theos' throat caught, as he tried to suppress the emotional wave passing over his body. He knew that in a few moments his grandfather would be gone forever. When he looked over at his father, an understanding came between them that had been missing before. His father had now lost both his parents within a year's time, and Theos could see that his father could no longer hold back the tears that formed in his eyes.

A young priest rang two high-pitched bells. Following that, a priestess came forward from the altar and walked over to Apollo. Apollo was then escorted to the place where Sirius stood next to his father's resting body.

Sirius nodded his head, and Apollo, in a long-honored tradition, walked over to where his father was lying, and started to wrap his body with the cloth that laid beneath it—first bringing the fabric up across his father's feet, then around each side of his body, as you would wrap an infant in a blanket, until his entire body was surrounded by the sacred cloth. Apollo then stepped away, and returned to his place beside Sirius.

Again, the two-high pitched bells chimed through the Sacred Cathedral. With a movement of his hand, Sirius caused Theos' grandfather's body to rise a few inches above the table, then moved his wrapped form across the space to the white eternal flame.

Theos watched intensely as his grandfather's body, once over the flame, crystallized together with the wrapping, and soon disappeared.

Sirius and Apollo knelt down before the flame, with the others following, and a cadence of prayers were spoken aloud by everyone in attendance. When the prayers had been recited, the choir began singing a beautiful, uplifting, hymn, and the ceremonious Funeral Mass and burial was ended.

When Sirius and Apollo rose to their feet, the others followed. Apollo bowed toward Sirius and Polaris, and then genuflected toward the flame with his hand over his heart.

Walking back to where Pleiades waited, Apollo took his wife's arm, and Theos and his brother followed them. Aryan, who had been seated with the family, followed thereafter.

Aryan had tried to repair the distance between himself and Theos, when he learned of Theos' grandfather's passing, and Theos had accepted the gesture with no further thought of what had been said between them. It all seemed insignificant now.

Outside, the day was bright and clear, and a soft breeze moved through the trees. Theos could still faintly hear the Cathedral's choir as he and Aryan, along with the others, walked down the seven Cathedral steps to the Great Plaza below. Theos was having difficulty composing himself, and found he could not yet leave the Cathedral's grounds. When they reached the edge of the plaza, Theos stopped and turned to Aryan.

"I need to be alone for a while," he said in a strained voice. "I'll meet all of you back at the house later."

Aryan nodded in understanding. He was not one to show his feelings, nor did he have the capacity to console others who were burdened with sorrow—yet, that very day, he wished he knew how.

Although Theos had not seen them, Tarah and Lucina were at the funeral too. After everyone had departed, Tarah looked for Theos, and caught sight of him as he walked through the gardens. A few minutes later, she found him sitting alone in a private part of the grounds.

So deep was he in thought, that he was totally unaware of her having followed him. Tarah watched Theos for a long time from a distance, not wanting to disturb him. Her heart ached in empathy of his loss, knowing how close he and his grandfather had been.

She too had been unable to control her emotion during the beautiful sacred Mass, and had never known of anyone, other than priests and priestesses, who had been honored with a Funeral Mass at the Sacred Cathedral.

Theos' grandfather had been a legend in his time, and had governed their empire from the highest elected office for more than 25 years before retiring. His tenure had been the longest anyone had held that position, and Tarah knew he would be long remembered.

After waiting a moment more, Tarah came up behind Theos. Her soft voice interrupted his thoughts as she touched his shoulder. "Are you saying goodbye?" she asked.

Theos looked up into Tarah's face, and nodded, unable to speak. He had not even noticed her until she had spoken.

"Are you going to be all right?" she asked.

Theos nodded again. "Thank you for coming, Tarah," he said, his voice cracking with emotion. "I'm sure it would have pleased him very much, to know that you were here today."

Tarah could not believe her eyes, for she had never seen Theos looking so ill. All of the compassion and love she felt for him came flowing though her again. Tarah bent down in front of him, tenderly touching his cheek with her hand. "I loved him too," she confided, tears welling up in her eyes. "He was always so kind to me."

Theos took her hand in his, and tried to comfort her. "My father went through his things yesterday, looking for any last instructions that he might have wanted carried out. He found a key to a private vault, and a gift with a note attached to it."

Tarah looked at the small, beautifully carved box, as Theos took it from his jacket pocket.

"It was for you and me," he explained. Tears now streamed down Theos' cheeks again, as he handed the box to Tarah. "The card is at home," he said.

Tarah slowly opened the box. Inside were two magnificently designed, and most exquisitely executed wedding rings.

"They were my grandmother's and grandfather's," he said, looking down at the rings. "He wanted us to have them, if we wished, and to wear them when we…"

Theos could not finish.

Picking up his grandmother's ring, Tarah looked at the inscription inside.

"*One With the Divinity in You,*" she read, "*One With the Divinity in Me.*" Tears came into her eyes again, as she placed the beautiful ring back into its proper place. She then closed the box, latching the small gold hook that kept it sealed tight.

The look on Tarah's face was expression enough for what she was feeling at that moment, and, when Theos stood up, he brought her up with him holding her close in his arms.

Tarah soon found herself relaxing into Theos' warm embrace, and it seemed as if they had never been apart.

"Tarah, I'm so sorry," he managed. "I never meant to hurt you. I was just confused."

She looked at him for a long moment, and pulled slightly away. "You did hurt me, Theos," she said. "More than you'll ever know, or understand."

"I know," he responded, looking deeply into her eyes. "I regret that more than I can ever express to you," he said, as he brought Tarah close to him once more, and held her gently.

Tarah could not help but respond to him.

A long moment passed, before he could speak again. "Can you ever forgive me?" he managed to ask.

Tarah pulled away once more, and studied his eyes. "I have forgiven you," she said.

"I thought becoming a priest was the most important thing I could do," he explained, "and that some day I could make some great contribution."

Tarah listened, attentively.

"I still don't know if I was doing it to compete with my father, or if it was because I wanted my grandfather to be proud of me."

Tarah listened, quietly, never speaking, while she watched his face.

"Or, perhaps," he admitted, "it was just my own blind ambition. I truly don't know. I just couldn't let go of a childhood dream," he reasoned. "But for whatever reason, none of it is important now, nor does it mean anything to me Tarah, without you at my side."

She looked for his intention. "Does that mean you're giving up studying for the priesthood?" she asked.

"If you'll have me," he answered, his breath catching.

Tarah studied his face, now understanding how conflicted he had been.

"Are you sure you'll have no regrets?" she asked.

"No regrets," he confirmed.

Tarah thought for a long moment, thinking through all that he had said.

"Will you marry me, Tarah?" Theos asked.

Theos watched her face, still unsure of her answer, and he could see she was not yet able to commit to him.

"I love you, Tarah, with all my heart and soul," he said, trying to convince her.

"Are you sure you won't change your mind?" she asked.

"I'll have no regrets, and I won't change my mind," he assured her.

Tarah looked deeply into his eyes, reading his true intent.

"Then I will," she finally answered.

Theos brought Tarah close to him again, and held her warmly for a long time. He was finally at peace. He wondered if his grandfather had known intuitively, that this would bring them back together again. Even in death, he was still guiding and helping Theos.

Theos looked over to the Sacred Cathedral, and then back to Tarah again. "Tarah, why did he have to die?" he asked.

"He was sick, Theos. More than he wanted us to know."

"I loved him so much," Theos said, tears flowing down his face again.

As the afternoon sun rose high in the sky, Theos and Tarah went back into the Sacred Cathedral, and said one last prayer before leaving the grounds together—although Theos found he was, as yet, unable to say goodbye.

CHAPTER 13

△

TIPHANE

The oppressive days that followed the funeral were difficult for Theos, and he and Tarah did not return to school. Theos knew that his life would slowly return to some degree of balance and normalcy, but a longer period of time was needed after his grandfather's death.

Theos had followed his father's example, and had written a heartfelt note to thank Sirius for the magnificent Funeral Mass that he had officiated, and to tell him how grateful his entire family was for the honor bestowed upon his grandfather.

After this, Theos wrote a second note to Polaris, thanking him for arranging his grandfather's services, and told Polaris how much it must have meant to his grandfather to be remembered in such a beautiful ceremony by his closest, lifelong friend.

In addition, Theos also thanked Polaris for his offer of private instruction, explaining his need to remain with Tarah, and that they were soon to start planning their wedding. Theos had also asked Polaris if it would be possible for them to complete the leadership portion of their studies at Temple School after their marriage—something that would have to be specially sanctioned. He had recently learned that his grandfather had done this very same thing after his marriage.

The entire week at home was spent helping his father with the difficult task of going through his grandfather's things. They were also packing away his personal papers, to be turned over to an historical librarian. They had come upon numerous unpublished works that his grandfather had authored. Some were along scientific lines, and others were short, entertaining stories. All of them were valuable, and were to be preserved by the librarian at the Atlantean National Library of Leaders.

One of the stories, in particular, had contained so much of his grandfather that Theos, after reading it over several times, began to feel an easing in his separation from him. The project of going through his grandfather's papers had also brought Theos and his father closer together again.

Nevertheless, the time went by very slowly, and Theos and his father finally finished the undertaking by the week's end. Additionally, at the end of the week, Theos learned that he and Tarah would be allowed to finish their studies after marrying.

Theos had planned to take an additional week off, but Tarah thought it would be better for him to get back into his usual routine, and hoped it might take his mind off his sorrow. After spending a quiet weekend together, they prepared to go back to Temple School.

Monday

When Theos woke early on Monday morning, the gardens below his rooms carried an unnerving stillness, and the air felt warmer than usual. A full week had passed since his grandfather's funeral. He slowly got out of bed, and went through his usual morning routine, and then ordered a transport and picked Tarah up on his way to school. Everyone else had gone on ahead of them, not expecting Tarah and Theos to return so soon.

As Theos and Tarah walked across the Great Plaza the unusual silence about them, and throughout the gardens on the Temple School grounds, was almost inexpressible. Not a single bird could be heard. Tarah could see that Theos was still feeling very sad, and she tried to be a comfort to him, giving him the solitude she sensed he still needed. When they reached the auditorium, they walked directly to their seats, where Lucina greeted them.

Looking around the room, Theos sensed within him that something was acutely different. But then everything seemed different, and always would be, with the passing of an illustrious life.

As Theos thought about his grandfather, he was comforted with remembering from his studies that all life is infinitely connected. And, as one life leaves, another enters, with the whole ever changing. The Ageless Wisdom Teachings imparted that a soul passes in-and-out of form, seeking experience and expression, until it takes all the required initiations, and graduates into the next kingdom.

A life, within a life, within a life, coming in-and-out of form in an attempt toward perfection, is what Taro had taught. With each life perfecting on its own plane, and under its own laws of evolution—and with each life affecting the greater life and forever moving forward into enlightenment—as light, and love, and power keep the plan on Earth, and benefit the ensouling life of this planet, the solar system of which it is a part, and the universe encompassing it.

Taro was not just teaching them new material, but expanding their minds by asking them to attempt to comprehend that which was abstract. He always gave them much to think about. He was a skillful teacher—a man of great wisdom.

Theos hoped, that as a measure of his own existence, he could accomplish half of what his grandfather had, and fathomed that that in itself would be difficult enough. One thing he did know was that whatever his accomplishments, he would make sure that when his grandfather did look back upon him, he would never be disappointed.

Tarah touched Theos' arm while they sat at their desks, and brought him out of his thoughts and back to the moment.

"Who's that?" Tarah asked, looking in the direction of a young woman that Aryan was staring at.

"I don't know," Theos said, noting the look on Aryan's face.

"She's very pretty," Tarah added.

In the year Tarah had known Aryan, he had never been so obvious in his attraction toward anyone before, and, what seemed remarkable, was that Aryan seemed totally unaware of Tarah and Theos having even arrived.

Theos nudged Aryan's arm to get his attention.

"Oh, hi," Aryan said, greeting Theos and then Tarah.

"Who's that?" Theos asked, looking in the direction of the young woman.

"Tiphane," Aryan responded. "She's a new student."

"Where from?" Theos asked.

"Elura. She just moved here."

"Who is she?" Theos asked. "She looks so familiar."

"She's from the Poseidon family. I just read of her father having made a recent breakthrough in a new use for etheric impulse. They must have moved here so he could continue his research at the Institute of Science."

Tarah looked over at Theos, and then back to Aryan. "Well, you certainly know a lot about her," she said, in a happy tone. "How did you meet her?"

"Oh, I haven't," Aryan, responded.

"Is this her first day?" Theos asked.

"No, she started class last week, while you and Tarah were out."

"She's been here since last week, and you haven't introduced yourself?" Theos questioned.

"Oh, no," Aryan said.

"Are you interested?" Theos asked.

Aryan looked very uncomfortable, and began talking about something else. "We've had a lot of assignments while you were gone," he said. "I forwarded my notes to both your computers."

Tarah looked at Lucina, who was sitting to the other side of her. "Is he trying to change the subject?" Tarah asked, smiling.

"Are you interested?" Theos repeated.

Aryan looked at him, and then gave a slight shrug, meaning maybe.

"Why don't you ask her to join us for lunch today," Theos suggested.

"I can't just walk up to her and ask her that," Aryan asserted.

"Why not?" Theos questioned, as he watched him for a moment.

"I truly couldn't," Aryan said.

"Sure you could," Tarah added. "It would be nice."

"No, I couldn't. What if she said no," Aryan countered, looking meeker than Theos had ever seen him before.

"You're not asking her to marry you—you're asking her to join all of us for lunch," Theos insisted.

Before Theos could say another word, Taro came into the room. There was no doubt about it, though. Aryan was definitely attracted to her. She was, to him, pure perfection.

Somehow at noon, when they broke for lunch, and with a shove from Theos, Aryan approached Tiphane and invited her to join them. As he spoke to her, with her long dark hair and green sparkling eyes, he knew she was everything he wanted in life. He felt as if they had been together before, as if he had spent an entire lifetime with her, and yet he could not remember where or when. He now understood Theos' strong attraction to Tarah. All through lunch, he wondered how anything so wonderful could happen to him.

While Theos and the others were having lunch, Polaris worked alone at his desk in his study, with numerous open books piled around him. He had been preoccupied with the events concerning Merak in the last week.

The quiet in his study was soon broken by a chiming sound, as Sirius' voice came into the room.

"Polaris, we have some visitors," Sirius informed him.

"I'll be there in a moment," Polaris answered.

Getting up from his desk, Polaris went through a door leading to the aid's office, making his way quickly across the room to the middle office, and going inside.

Several of the Council members were sitting around the room, talking in hushed tones. They all looked up when Polaris entered.

"They are here to talk about Merak," Sirius said, obviously pleased.

This made ten more from whom Merak's spell had worn off.

"In a couple of more days," Sirius said, with a tone of relief, "we should have the entire Council free from his control."

Polaris nodded, in agreement. "Now we can get down to the business of repairing the invisible sheath," Polaris said, looking relieved.

Since the night they tried to expose Merak to the Council of 45, Polaris and Sirius had been repeatedly unsuccessful in their attempts to repair the protective sheath around our planet. The imperiling damage appeared to be a large looming hole at the South Pole, with other smaller holes at different points around the earth.

More important, because this had never happened before, they were not quite sure of its potential effect. As each hour passed, the precarious situation became more and more critical, and, without a greater number of priests and priestesses, they did not have enough power to repair the damage. The mirrors had all been realigned, to correct the proper balance, and now Sirius hoped they had enough time.

When class was dismissed that afternoon, Theos and the others made their way out of the auditorium together. Just as they reached the staircase leading down to the main level, Theos realized he had left a book he needed on the shelf under his desk.

"I'll be right back," Theos said, turning to Tarah.

"We'll wait for you downstairs," Tarah called, as she and Lucina began going down the steps.

Theos hurried up the hallway and, just as he entered the auditorium, he ran into Elias. The two stopped, staring at each other, and you could not miss the hatred in Elias' eyes.

"You might think you've won her back," Elias said, in a biting, ugly voice. "But I'll tell you now, Theos, I'm not giving her up. Believe me when I tell you that one day she'll belong to me again!" Elias said, looking back with a glare.

"Over my dead body she will," Theos returned, in an angry tone.

"Perhaps," Elias said, viciously, "and that will be *my* good fortune."

Theos made his way over to his desk, grabbing the book he needed, and then walked back to the auditorium doorway. Elias was now blocking his path.

"Tell me Elias, what ever possesses you? Or should I say who?" Theos challenged directly.

A menacing look crossed Elias' face. "Nothing you have any protection against," he laughed, as an enraged look gleamed from his eyes.

Theos appeared to be unaffected by what Elias had threatened, and with great ease and strength, a strength that surprised Elias, Theos took strong hold of Elias' arms, and moved him aside and away from the doorway. Then, without exchanging another word, Theos left the room.

From around the corner at the top of the stairs, Elias stood watching Theos as he hurried to join the others, skipping quickly down the stairs. Theos was totally unaware that Elias had followed him, and just as Theos neared the bottom of the staircase, Elias created an illusion around Theos, whereby the last few steps appeared not to exist at all. Thinking he had reached the bottom, Theos fell down the remaining marble stairs to the hard floor below.

Tarah turned quickly, hearing his fall, and rushed over to Theos' side. "Theos, are you all right? What happened?" she asked, as she looked to see if he was hurt.

Theos slowly moved his body on the floor. "I'm fine," he managed, as he tried to focus his eyes.

Someone reached down to help Theos to his feet and, as Theos turned to thank him, he saw it was Elias.

"What a terrible accident," Elias said, while watching his tone, as to belie his actions.

"I can get up myself!" Theos complained with anger.

Tarah tried to intervene. "Theos, Elias was just trying to help you."

"Well I don't want his help!" he said pointedly. Theos picked himself up off the floor, and then guided Tarah out to the plaza and toward their waiting transport.

Aryan, Tiphane and Lucina followed them. When Aryan came alongside Theos, he related having seen what happened, knowing full well what Elias was capable of.

"He caught me by surprise," Theos said, lowering his voice so the others could not hear him.

Aryan looked directly at Theos in a knowing way. "I know," he said, in understanding. "It's time you told Tarah the truth about him, Theos. Tell her about Leah," Aryan suggested.

"I am going to tell her," Theos said. "I'm going to tell her tonight."

CHAPTER 14

▲

THE CONFRONTATION

Tuesday

When Theos awoke on Tuesday morning, he once again sensed something very strange in the air. As he walked out onto his patio, and looked across the gardens, he could see there was a definite lack of activity. Even the birds were silent. As he glanced up at the sky, not a single cloud interrupted the expansive vista, nor was there the slightest hint of a breeze. It was an alarming silence, and it was all about him.

Theos' body felt sore from the fall he had taken the day before, and his ribs hurt whenever he took a breath. After a few minutes had passed, he went back into his rooms. He took a long hot shower, hoping it would lessen the pain he was feeling. He soon became lost in thought, losing track of time, and then hurriedly dressed for school. The same strange feeling crept over him again while riding in the transport. Something was very wrong, but he had no clear impression of what was yet to come.

Later that morning, in class, Theos watched Elias from where he sat in the top row. He knew he had to pay close attention to Elias now, and tried to fight the hatred and malice he was feeling toward him—for Theos did not want that emotion to weaken him. Nor did he want Elias to win even the smallest encounter.

At noon, Theos and the others went directly to the cafeteria for lunch. Despite the cafeteria's openness to the outside patio and plaza, the space

CHAPTER 15

▲

THE ANCIENT ONE

Friday

A strong storm front moved over the city and raged on without stopping for two days. Almost hourly, violent tremors could be felt from deep under the ground, as the disturbance continued.

By Friday, events had turned worse, and classes were cancelled at Temple School. Many of the interconnecting canals throughout the continent had filled to overflowing, and much of the lowlands had completely flooded.

The Capital City itself had so far been spared because of its elevation close to the mountains, although the storm continued to build and there was no sign of it letting up.

Theos had invited Tarah, Aryan and Tiphane for dinner at his home that evening, but the mood was unmistakably sober. Everyone seemed to sense the devastation they were soon to face, although no one spoke of it.

After dinner, Theos' parents excused themselves, and Theos and the others went into the library to talk. The usual open patio areas of the house were closed off with sliding partitions of heavy glass, and the plants outside smashed against the windows, as they were whipped by the destructive winds.

Lightning and thunder persisted overhead, and it was truly a dreadful night. The rain was beating down so hard, that at times it drowned out their voices. Theos got up and looked out one of the glass sliding doors, and saw it was getting worse. He could see that the flowers his grandfather had planted near the house, only weeks before, were now pelted into the ground, and the garden pond had begun to overflow its banks.

The swans had been brought inside the night before to the enclosed atrium in the center of the house, and Leah seemed endlessly concerned about them.

Suddenly, the ground below them started to shake again, and the house vibrated violently for about ten seconds before the room became still. Leah was markedly disturbed. She shook at Theos' side as he tried to comfort her.

"Nothing's going to hurt you, Leah," Theos said, reassuring her.

Leah was terribly upset, and gave out a loud whimper.

When Theos looked up, he could see his father come down the steps at the other end of the room.

"Theos," he summoned, "I just received a call from a member of the Council. The Magi are calling together a special meeting at the Sacred Cathedral tonight."

"A meeting?" Theos questioned. "What's going on?"

"Your mother and I will be leaving shortly. There's another transport outside, large enough for all of you. I want you to go ahead of us," he added, before turning quickly and disappearing up the steps.

"I have a terrible feeling inside," Tarah said, as she grasped Theos' hand, "as if something horrible is going to happen."

"Me too," Theos said in understanding.

Tarah called Lucina to say they would pick her up on the way, but there was no answer. Leah wanted desperately to go with them, and tried going out the front door when they were ready to leave.

"You have to stay here, Leah," Theos explained, as he reached down and gently stroked her face. "You can't go to the Cathedral with us—they won't let you inside."

Leah looked very upset. Her large, watery brown eyes, pleaded with him.

"We'll be back in a little while," he said, reassuring her. Theos pushed Leah back inside before shutting the door. Then they all hurried down the walk to the transport, and quickly left for the Great Sacred Cathedral.

Leah scratched at the front door, but no one responded to her cry. Whimpering, she finally ran through the house and upstairs to Theos' room, where she managed to maneuver one of the patio doors and let herself out. Quickly she made her way down the back veranda steps, and across the side yard.

The ground felt muddy under her paws, and she had difficulty keeping her balance with the water rising so rapidly. Leah fell several times, hurting her shoulder and back leg, before making it to the front gate. When she finally got there, she saw that they had already gone, and the gate had been securely locked.

Leah tried to unfasten the lock by biting into it, and then began pulling on it, but she could not open the iron gate. Frantic in her efforts, Leah started to dig a hole. She whined in frustration, but her endeavor was futile. The surface was paved with a hard resistant material that would not give way.

Leah began to bark, but no one came to her aid. It was then that she spotted an area, at a lower part of the yard, where the iron fencing was being undermined by the flow of collecting water. There she found it easier to dig, and the running water aided her by moving the dirt away.

Again and again, she tried to fit through the small opening, to no avail. Several minutes had gone by before she was able to make another attempt. This time, the hole was large enough, and she was able to slide under the fence.

Once on the other side, she shook off the mud hanging from her soaked fur, and took off in the pouring rain in the direction of the Sacred Cathedral. She knew exactly where it was, for she had heard the family speak of it often. She and Theos had, on occasion, even gone to the park nearby. Leah somehow understood what was happening, and she quickly made her way through the night in search of Theos. The storm raged on, with its pouring rain and blinding wind, but nothing deterred her.

When Theos and the others arrived at the Sacred Cathedral, they were led into an anteroom where their wet coats were hung. Priests and priestesses, who were assisting those arriving, handed each one of them the same sacred white garments worn by initiates of the school. It was a hooded robe that fell to the floor, with an intricate design embroidered around its edges.

Theos wondered why they were wearing the robes of the initiates. One of the assistants in the anteroom lifted the hoods up to their heads, and then adjusted the garments so that they were worn properly, in the order of tradition.

Once everyone was ready, they quietly walked together through another set of doors, and into the Sacred Cathedral, where Theos' grandfather had been cremated just 11 days before. But tonight, the massive Cathedral glowed with an iridescent light coming from thousands of creamy white flickering lamps. The scene before them took their breath away.

The assemblage was organized in long, wide semicircles, extending across the width of the Cathedral. On their knees, in silent prayer, were all the priests, priestesses, graduates and students of the Temple School. The embroidery on their sacred robes glistened enchantingly in the soft light, as the late-night Mass and secret ceremony of the initiates, commenced.

This was the ceremony of the apostolate, with the donning of the holy robes, the prayers, and the sacred vows. Theos looked around for his parents. However, with the congregations' hoods raised up, everyone looked alike.

In front of the gathering, in their usual dress, the Council of 45 was assembled on an elevated platform to the back of the raised altar, forming five rows of nine members each, with their chairs curving forward, each row elevated above the last, and facing toward those gathered in the Cathedral that stormy night.

In front of the Council were three more chairs, simply carved, but of gold. Polaris and Sirius were sitting on two of the three chairs. The third seat, belonging to Merak, remained empty. In front of Sirius and Polaris was a single chair, of ornate gold, placed more to the front of the oval altar. Directly to the left of the altar was the Eternal Flame, glowing outward from its encasement.

A choir of young priests and priestesses filled the balconies above the great assemblage, and their beautiful voices, of perfect pitch, sang a soothing spiritual hymn. As the last notes of the descant rang out, the Sacred Cathedral's doors closed out the night and were latched shut.

Polaris and Sirius rose up together, and stood facing the convocation. At once, chiming bells of the same high pitch rang out. Polaris and Sirius crossed their arms, bringing their palms flat against their chests, with their fingers closed together pointing toward their shoulders. The assembly followed in order, and bowed their heads.

When their open eyes lifted, the ethereal figure of the Ancient One slowly began vaporizing out of thin air, and appeared sitting in the single chair at the front of the altar.

He was a tall, big-boned, elderly man, with a long white beard waving down his form to the waist. His hair was tapered at the shoulders, and his piercing eyes peered out as if they were beacons of light, flashing across the room. His magnificent presence seemed to sweep across the entire assemblage with his calm serenity. He was the epitome of love perfected—compassionate, devoted, and self-sacrificing.

The Ancient One's long flowing white robe sparkled, as if thousands of diamonds had been set within it. He looked out slowly across the room, seeming to take in the entire group. A far-reaching halo of yellow light extended about his head, with a white, crystal clear light, emanating and radiating beyond that, filling the entire room with its projection. It had been said of him, that you could see his light for miles. Raising his hands in a blessing, he finally spoke.

"I am afraid this is a very sad occasion for all of us," he said. "The protective sheath of our world has been severed, and all attempts to make repairs—both from this side, and the side of the invisible—have failed. An ancient law has been broken, and nature will now withdraw that which she has so freely given."

The Ancient One walked forward, closer to those assembled, and then continued on. "Our continent is slowly sinking, and will submerge beneath the sea within the next twelve hours. It has been decided that you will be allowed to leave, and take with you whatever of our heritage is left for the world to know and use."

You could not detect even the slightest movement on the faces of those gifted Atlanteans gathered there that evening, but you could imagine the despair they had to be feeling in their hearts. Everything that they had ever known, and almost everyone that they had ever loved, would soon vanish and be gone. All of this would happen because of the blind, selfish ambition of one man. Merak.

As Theos listened to the last rites being given by the Ancient One, he reached over and pulled Tarah closer to his side. Theos could feel her hand tremble in his. If times comparable to this measured the strength of a man, then Theos would disappoint no one, for he remained consistently focused and calm.

The Great Sacred Cathedral had a strange dreamlike atmosphere, with its flickering play of light, but this was not a dream. This was the beginning of their demise. Without any warning, a heavy tremor rumbled through the room for almost thirty seconds. And then a terrible moaning sound came from beneath the ground—as if rock were grinding against rock.

"We have very little time left," the Ancient One continued. "Outside the Cathedral is our entire fleet of inter-continental craft for your use. All our international outposts and observatories have been alerted, and are waiting for your arrival. The craft have been pre-programmed."

Once again, the room shook violently for about ten seconds, although the group assembled remained composed, and the room remained silent.

"It is almost midnight," he continued. "The Council of 45 will soon go into a penetrating meditation, in order to put all our populace, and creatures of nature staying behind, into a deep, peaceful state of sleep—so they suffer not in their last hours here."

The Ancient One looked to the side, as if receiving some kind of mental communication, and then wished them well. "You must go now," he said. "I know God is with you."

Again three bells chimed, and as suddenly as he appeared, the Ancient One vaporized into the air. His form swelled into a fog that crystallized into nothingness.

"Why don't you pick everyone else up, Aryan, and then come back for me," Theos said, as they made their way back to where Polaris was waiting. Aryan nodded.

"I'll go with you," Tarah said, stepping forward.

"No, stay with my parents, Tarah," Theos said.

"But I want to go with you," she persisted.

"Please. It's too dangerous," he explained. "Stay with my parents."

Aryan leaned forward so that Theos could hear him, without shouting. "How much time do you need?" he asked.

"Not much, just come back for me once you've picked everyone's family up. I'll wait for you at the top of the steps."

"Would you like me to go with you?" Apollo asked.

Theos took in the clear expression of commitment in Apollo's eyes. He had, in the last few years, almost forgotten how deeply he loved his father. "I can handle it," Theos said, not wanting to separate his parents.

Apollo nodded his agreement. "I know you can," he said, with the greatest of confidence.

Theos looked over to Aryan, catching his eyes. "Did you see where Elias went when you were up in the ship's control tower?" he asked. "He has Merak's pendant."

"He made it onto a transport," Aryan acknowledged. "Somebody gave him some trouble though—he had blood all down the front of him, and he looked as if he had cut his neck. I didn't see the pendant."

Tarah could not believe what she was hearing. "Theos, I want to go with you. I can help," she pleaded.

"No, you'll be safer here," Theos, insisted. "I'll be back," he assured her.

"But I'm afraid for you," Tarah confessed, as tears welled up in her eyes.

Apollo tried to comfort her, putting his arm around her shoulder, bringing Tarah close to his side. "Tarah," he urged, "don't make it harder on him. He's doing what he has to do, and he can do it more quickly, without you."

Tarah looked over to Theos, and then back to Apollo.

Pleiades stepped up, taking Tarah's hand, and tried to coax her back and away. "Why don't you come and sit with me," Pleiades persuaded, holding Tarah's hand. "We can wait together."

Tarah reluctantly gave in, and Apollo brought both her and Pleiades back inside, to a place where they could both sit and watch the scene together.

When Theos saw that Tarah was safe, he gave Aryan a final instruction. "If I'm not here when you return," Theos said, "then leave without me."

"I couldn't," Aryan, said, looking at him with far less composure.

"Aryan, if I'm not here, I'll meet you at my brother's observatory."

"And how are you gong to do that?" Aryan asked. "This is the last ship. I'll be back within the hour, and you be here!" Aryan added.

By now, all the other transports had lifted away, and were out of sight. Their ship was the only one left. Aryan piloted the craft near to where Polaris still sat on the ground, and Theos readied himself to jump off.

"You stay here Leah," Theos ordered, when he saw her edging forward.

Aryan soon reached what appeared to be a safe spot, and hovered the craft just above the ground.

The rain had now thankfully stopped, and giving a wave, Theos stepped onto the ground and hurried over to Polaris. Just as the ship began lifting away, Leah jumped off the ramp and ran to Theos.

Aryan looked annoyed, as he brought the ship back, and called out to her. "Leah," Aryan called. "Get back here."

"She can come with us," Polaris said, as Leah came up to greet him.

"Are you sure? You don't mind?" Theos asked.

"Not at all," Polaris returned.

"We're going to take her," Theos yelled, so Aryan could hear him.

Aryan nodded his head, and watched to see if Theos could get Polaris up without help.

Leah began jostling something around in her mouth, and wagged her tail as she nudged Polaris with her nose. "She seems to have picked something up," Polaris said. "I hope she won't swallow it."

"Leah always does that," Theos said. "She has quite a collection of things at home."

"Let's see, Leah," Theos requested, as she drew her head away. "Come on," he insisted, holding out his hand.

With some resistance, Leah finally deposited Merak's golden pendant, minus its chain, into Theos' hand.

Polaris smiled at her when he saw her treasure. "What a smart dog you are Leah," he said, stroking her face.

Theos looked at her with amazement. "Are you the somebody that Elias ran into?" he asked, smiling, as he patted her back, praising her. "I bet that felt good, didn't it girl."

Leah looked very proud of herself, although she had no idea that what she had torn loose from around Elias' neck was so valued. It had fallen to the ground when she attacked him. Leah was attracted to it because it sparkled.

Handing the pendant to Polaris, Theos picked him up again. They slowly made their way over the debris blocking their path, and up the remaining steps.

Aryan continued to watch, as Theos and Polaris made their way through the maze of pillars, with Leah close beside them. When they were about to climb the staircase inside, Theos turned and nodded—relating that they were safe, and they disappeared inside.

Aryan lifted his hand in response, but Theos did not see him. Securing the ramp, Aryan locked the control panel, and returned to the tower at the very top of the craft.

The control room, with its circular windows, gave a full view of all the grounds. Aryan could immediately see how this once sacred setting, had been changed so drastically by the desecrating storm. Tiphane was upstairs, and had already read into the computer each destination's specific numbering code, which was part of the same system the transports were run on.

As soon as Apollo and Aryan were secure in their seats at the command center, Apollo pulled back a lever, and the golden transport started its silent ascent and made haste to the outskirts of the city. They were later to find that the tremors had taken their toll, and the flooding had already destroyed many of the residential areas. Aryan and Tiphane had been fortunate to save both their families—however Tarah's parents could not be found, nor could many of the others in the far-reaching disaster.

A little more than an hour later, they returned to the plaza grounds. The great ship streaked across the city, then hovered near the Temple School steps. The grounds were now dark, all the lights having gone out from the flooding, and they met a very eerie scene.

It was raining again, but more lightly now. Using a spotlight on the craft, they searched the front of the school. Theos was nowhere to be seen. Again and again they circled slowly around the building to see if he had used a different exit, although to their total disappointment, he had not. The water was now rushing across the plaza floor, and edging up to the Temple School steps.

There was no consoling either Tarah or Pleiades, for they both realized at that instant, that there was now a very strong possibility that they would never see Theos again. Apollo was already directing their visual search from the control tower, and was determined to go in after his son. Aryan offered to go with him, but Apollo insisted on going in alone.

After calculating his best approach, Apollo instructed Aryan of his plan, explained where he wanted to be left off, and then went downstairs.

In absolute silence, everyone on board watched out the ship's windows. Aryan inched the enormous craft forward, over the swirling waters. The water had risen so fast that it now began crashing high against the steps, as if giant waves were coming onto a beach.

After putting on a special watertight suit, Apollo began to lower the ship's ramp. He could hear an ominous heavy grinding sound, with a deep rumbling underneath. Then, horrifyingly, the columns in front of them suddenly began to disintegrate into what looked like pieces of gravel. The entire front facade of the structure collapsed down to the foundation, just missing the ship.

Pleiades soon came running to the ramp, and Apollo knew by the look on her face what she was thinking. "I'll find him," he said, in a confident, reassuring tone.

"But Apollo…" she started, needing to convey her fears.

"He's alive, I know it," Apollo said, with certainty. "I know he's alive."

She looked at him for a long moment. "But I think he's hurt," she said. "Pleiades, please go back," he urged. "I have to let the ramp down again, and it's too dangerous for you to be standing here."

Still and all, she would not move. "I'm waiting here," she said, as Tarah came up along side of her.

Tarah put her arm around Pleiades' waist, steadying her. "Please find him," Tarah pleaded, tears streaming down her face.

Apollo picked up an intercom device, and instructed Aryan to maneuver the ship around to the back of the building where the columns were still standing. It took a couple of minutes before Apollo was close enough to the structure to jump off, but he did so successfully and began his search.

Pleiades and Tarah stood on the ramp and watched, as Apollo made his way from opening to opening, with the ship hovering close by. However, each and every entrance was sealed tight, and latched from the inside, and no one heard or responded to Apollo's hammering on the outside doors.

For almost half an hour he searched through the treacherous remains at the front of the school, but Apollo could not find even a foot-wide crevice through which someone could pass. Alarmingly, the water crept up higher and higher until he could go no farther.

Once again, Apollo circled the building, trying to get inside. After turning away from the last door, still strong and controlled, he looked back to where Pleiades was standing, and met her eyes. He knew what she was thinking. Theos had been such a special child to both of them, and Apollo could not envisage their lives without him.

Much of the land was now submerged, and the water rapidly crept higher and higher. Aryan edged the ship back over to Apollo, and, climbing back onto the ship's platform, Apollo began reevaluating the situation.

Aryan had caught the expression on Apollo's face from the command center windows. It was the look of a devastated man, but not that of a man who had given up. After climbing back onto the hovering craft, Apollo reluctantly sealed the docking ramp. He then took off his watertight suit, and stored it in a compartment on the craft. After all the gear had been stowed, Apollo went back to talk to Pleiades and Tarah. It became a long talk. With the front of the school destroyed, and every other exit sealed, they waited for some kind of miracle.

At the back of Temple School, and at the tip of the obelisk tower within the sealed glass dome, Sirius had successfully returned the crystal to its rightful place. After it was correctly positioned on its tripod, its light became brighter and brighter, as it pulsed on and off again.

Periodically, Aryan would bring the craft around, circling the building, but their efforts were futile, and the ship continued hovering, spending precious time. What they did not know was that Theos was just beyond their reach. He was lying unconscious in a corridor on the second floor, directly outside the door leading up to the Chamber of Mirrors.

Another hour passed, and the water had now risen so high that the columns at the back of the structure on the first level were hardly visible.

Inside the school, debris lay all about Theos. Leah was at his side, with her head resting across his stomach. She started to whimper, and nuzzled Theos under his arm, yet he remained motionless.

For a moment Leah thought she heard something. She got up and went to the end of the hallway, where the staircase led to the main hall below. Leah could see that the water had risen within a few steps of the floor where Theos laid unconscious, and was continuing to move forward. Leah ran back down the hallway to Theos, and nudged him once more, trying to wake him, but he did not respond.

Abruptly the earth began to quake again, and Leah could feel heavy pieces of plaster come down on top of her. She moved closer to Theos, and tried to protect his face.

After the tremor had stopped, Leah pulled herself away and shook off the debris and dust. Once again she tried to wake Theos, without success.

It was then that she heard the door leading to the Chamber of Mirrors slowly open with a creaking sound. Leah immediately investigated it, and squeezed through the small opening to find someone to help.

A minute or two later, Leah once again caught a scent, and lifting her head to the wind, she inhaled the air with an even deeper breath. When she looked back at the hotel balcony, to alert Terese, Terese was gone.

Leah's entire posture had changed. Teddy was coming back. Excitedly, she jogged back and forth, barking a call to him from the dock. Some of the crewmen from the other yachts came out of the restaurant to see what all the commotion was about. The Coast Guard had been conducting their own search, and had asked them to wait onshore in case they were needed.

A group gathered on the dock and started to cheer, as Teddy's weather-worn yacht motored its way down the channel to dock in front of the hotel. The story of the missing yacht had been in all the papers, with stories on each of its crewmembers.

"Hey, it's the *Lady Leah*!" one of them yelled.

Terese struggled to get through all the onlookers to Leah. As the *Lady Leah* neared the pier, tears, now of joy, streamed down Terese's face.

Leah angled herself at the very edge of the pier. As soon as they threw a line, she jumped onto the yacht and ran up to Teddy, stretching almost to his height. He warmly welcomed her and gave her a big hug.

Spotting Ryan next, Leah flew over to him, and he too gave her a big hug.

"Hi, Leah," Ryan said, smiling and looking over at Teddy. "It'll take her how many years to forgive me?" he said, with a look.

Teddy caught Terese as she attempted to reach across from the dock, pulling her into his arms. "Oh, have I missed you," he murmured.

Terese wiped her tears away, and tried to talk through sobs. "We'd almost given up hope. We thought you were lost in the storm."

"It's okay, Terese," Teddy said, trying to comfort her. "I'm back now."

"They couldn't search for you until Sunday afternoon, because of the storm," she continued, "and I've been so worried."

"I'm okay, honest," he assured her. "What day is this anyway?" Teddy asked.

"It's Tuesday," she said.

Teddy turned around, and looked for Ryan. "You're not going to believe this Ryan, but it's only Tuesday."

Terese just stared at them. "Are you guys all right? You don't even know what day this is?" she asked.

"We're fine, Terese, it just seemed longer," Teddy explained.

After his crew tied the boat securely, they were all helped off the yacht and greeted by friends and family. Many of the crewmembers' families had come to Miami when it was learned they were all missing. The atmosphere was very happy and lighthearted, and Teddy's crew looked relieved to be back.

"You guys sure are a sight for sore eyes," yelled the captain of the *Eagle*, from across the pier. "What'd you do, drop out of thin air?"

"Who won the race?" Teddy shouted over to him.

"No one did. We all had to turn back."

When the chatter died down, Teddy turned to Ryan. "That reminds me, I forgot the box."

"I have it," Ryan smiled, lifting the old carved box from his bag and passing it over to Teddy. "Did you know that the bucket of fish and all the specimen bags are empty?" Ryan asked.

"I thought they would be," Teddy said.

Terese looked back and forth between the two of them. "What in heaven's name are you two talking about?" she asked.

"I'll tell you later Terese, but you're not going to believe me," he said.

Terese looked up at him, not giving up that easily, but before she was able to say anything more, Teddy had pulled her close to his side.

"Honestly, Terese, I can't wait to tell you every detail. Come on," he said, "I need to get rooms for all of the crew, and give the front desk a credit card to cover any expenses they might have, and I want to call the children."

"They'll be so excited to hear from you," Terese said, a smile coming across her face.

"Do they know we were missing?" Teddy asked, with a worried look on his face.

"No, they're just upset because you haven't called them yet. They think the phone system went down in Nassau because of a bad storm."

"Oh good," Teddy said.

As Teddy, Terese and Ryan walked back up toward the hotel together, Leah romped on ahead of them. Every so often she would look behind her, to check and see if Teddy was still following her lead back to the hotel.

Terese turned to Ryan, and touched his arm. "I moved your things from your room, Ryan, when a two-bedroom suite opened up. So you can stay with us tonight," Terese said.

"Oh, thank you," Ryan answered, looking up at the hotel. For once, he preferred not being alone.

Teddy looked over to Ryan, with a big grin on his face. "Guess what, Ryan, I think they're rescheduling the race."

Ryan stopped dead in his tracks. "If you so much as asked me to go to the corner mailbox with you, I'd say no!" he returned.

Teddy just laughed.

After calling the children, Teddy showered and shaved. Then they all went downstairs to the hotel restaurant, and celebrated their return to Miami with everyone. It did not seem possible that so much had happened in such a small space of time. But it had.

Just as quickly as Polaris had taken them away to view a time far in the past held in an ancient archive, he had returned them to the pile of rocks where their raft was tied and waiting. And then, miraculously, within hours, the Florida coast appeared out of a mist, and the green flashing light was gone. Then the Coast Guard came up, meeting them, and escorted them all the way to the channel.

The crew thought Teddy and Ryan had been gone for only a few hours, when to Teddy and Ryan it had seemed a few weeks. Even though they were not able to explain what happened to them, they would in time learn to accept it. Who would believe them anyway?

Tuesday Afternoon

Late that same afternoon, the small Miami inlet showed very few signs of the ferment that had, for days, ravaged her banks. The turbulent storm had found its place of peace, leaving beautiful blue cloud-filled skies behind it.

In the hotel, Teddy and Terese lay close together in bed, sound asleep. The golden afternoon sun was set low in the winter sky, angling across their bed, warming their sleeping bodies from a corner window that faced south. They were both physically, emotionally, and mentally exhausted.

Leah rested nearby, content from the warm bath that Terese had given her, and her stomach full from the meal Teddy had ordered. She soon got up off the floor, to check and see if Teddy was still there, then walked through the two-bedroom suite to Ryan's room.

She watched him from the doorway for a moment, and then went around the bed to look more closely. A beautiful golden triangle charm had fallen from his hand onto the bedding. When she had checked on him earlier, she had seen he had been crying. Now he slept.

Crawling slowly up on Ryan's bed, Leah made herself comfortable beside him. She too felt exhausted, and didn't wake again until the next morning, when she heard a young hotel employee, with an arm full of newspapers, place the Miami paper in front of Ryan's bedroom door. Leah listened for a moment, as the sound of the footsteps fell away, and soon fell back into a sound sleep.

Later that day, on Wednesday afternoon, they would all see on the front page of the Miami paper, a large picture of Merak. He was with a group of other men, walking up the steps of the White House with the President.

The headline on the paper read:

"PRESIDENT TO MEET WITH INTERNATIONAL COMMITTEE OF BANKERS, BUSINESSMEN AND INDUSTRIALISTS TODAY, ON WORLDWIDE ECONOMIC CRISIS"

All this had taken place the previous afternoon, while Teddy, Terese and Ryan slept. And only time would tell if another enchanted land, America—the last great hope for a promising planet—would suffer the same fate as Atlantis, and be lost forevermore.

CHAPTER 18

▲

CHICAGO

Wednesday

A warm, gentle breeze swept through the open space of Teddy and Terese Townsend's suite of rooms at the Dupont Plaza Hotel, with a renewing healing effect—and a bright clear dawn filled the view through the open balcony doors. It was the morning after Teddy and Ryan's long-awaited return, and they were all going home.

Leah woke, and looked over at Ryan. He was still sleeping soundly. Leah was truly a beautiful dog, with her pale feathering and thick cream-colored coat, a color found on very few golden retrievers.

Not having moved all through the night, Leah's body felt stiff, despite her comfortable nest alongside Ryan on his bed. She stretched out as far as she could, then rolled over away from Ryan onto her other side without disturbing him. It seemed almost as if days had gone by since Terese had given her the warm bath in the tub off her room, and she thought once more about the two steak dinners she had eaten so ravenously. Leah had been so hungry that she had even eaten the vegetables on her plate, which started her thinking about food again.

Looking over at Ryan, Leah could see he had not moved all night, and then she heard Teddy talking on the phone in the living room. She quickly jumped down from the bed, and trotted out of the room to join him.

Teddy was making arrangements to fly everyone home. When they traveled with Leah, he always leased a private jet, so she could ride in the cabin with them. He never allowed her to ride alone in the bulkhead, as freight.

Leah immediately went over to him, sitting as close as she could, leaning her shoulder into his leg and plopping her head alongside of him on the sofa. Teddy reached down and gently petted her face and ears while he talked on the phone.

She continued to listen, as he arranged everything for their return home. The *Lady Leah* was to be taken to a local yard for repairs to her mast. The majority of the crew planned to fly back to New York that afternoon, together with their families, who had gathered in Miami. Teddy had already made out checks, with generous bonuses, for each of his crewmembers, and the envelopes were sealed and stacked together on the table. He had also made arrangements with the manager of the hotel to pick up any and all costs of the family members of his crew. The Miami newspaper sat nearby, unread.

Leah heard a knock on the door, and she and Teddy went to answer it. Soon, a waiter brought in a large tray of food for her. Teddy had ordered some toast, scrambled eggs and sausages for her to eat, before they all went down to have breakfast in the dining room with his crew. Teddy signed for the order, and then let the waiter out.

"Here you go, Leah," Teddy said, as he set the plate of food down on a large towel, at the end of the coffee table in front of him. Leah was accustomed to eating her food on raised dishes, which their vet suggested was better for her. He then poured some bottled water into a cereal bowl, and placed it beside her plate of food.

When Teddy finished his calls he woke Terese and Ryan up, and then took Leah out for a walk while they took their showers and dressed. Everything that had happened on Atlantis kept flashing back to him, moving through his mind over and over again. Teddy could not shirk the emotion that was building up inside of him, and filling his chest. He missed his Atlantean family, and wondered what had happened to his parents on that last flight to South America.

It was impossible to explain to anyone the loss he felt for his family. He still had not had time enough to get over his grandfather's passing, and now the estrangement from his parents and brother had to be dealt with. It was all very complex and confusing to him, yet he could not deny his feelings. His Atlantean past was as real to him, as the ground he was standing on at that very moment. He could never forget the people he loved on Atlantis, or his life there—even though they were now all gone, and had been for thousands of years.

When Teddy and Leah returned to the suite an hour later, his quiet mood was apparent, and Terese gave him the privacy she seemed to know he needed.

After eating breakfast downstairs with the rest of the crew, Teddy thanked everyone personally, before giving them their checks. Then Teddy, Terese, and Ryan packed their bags, and headed out to the airport in a large limousine. Their chartered plane sat on the field, and was fueled and waiting to fly them to Chicago. As soon as their car pulled up, the steward took their luggage onto the plane, and the captain introduced himself and his co-pilot.

Within minutes after boarding the plane, the sleek G-3 lifted off from a small Miami airfield, and headed out toward the ocean before making a wide turn back over the continent and proceeding northwest.

Terese sat facing Teddy and Ryan, with her legs stretched out on a long sofa, and with her back leaning against a wood closet. She reached into a large canvas bag, and pulled out the same red journal that she had been writing in earlier that morning. Finding a pen, she opened the book and began making entries into it again.

Teddy watched Terese from his seat farther back on the plane. He had known from the first moment he had met her, that he could never love anyone more. Now he knew why. They had been mated to each other for an eternity.

He never tired of looking at her. And, despite having turned thirty-six in October, Terese had never lost her wholesome, all-American good looks, with her smooth, unlined complexion, and high color on her cheeks. Her soft hazel eyes were bright and clear, and her shiny blonde hair, with its soft waves, was pulled back into a ponytail.

She was totally unaware of Teddy watching her, as she sat writing. She wore a comfortable pair of white slacks, and a pale pink cotton sweater. Teddy noticed that she had slipped her deck shoes off. A pair of clean white socks covered her feet and kept them warm, as she propped her legs up on the sofa in front of her.

Terese had a very special presence about her. One of the qualities Teddy loved most was the way she seemed to cause almost everyone to brighten, and feel happier, after they were with her for a short while. Always carefree, and energetic with others, Teddy knew her to be more than the personality that won people over upon first meeting her. Her soul was deep and complex, which caused her to have a sense of mystery about her. She could also be direct when she needed to be—something Teddy had come to appreciate and respect. And when she did speak her mind to him, she always managed to do it in a nice way.

The writer in Terese preferred to be in the position of the observer, studying people's character, motive and personality. She would do this up close, as well as at a distance. And, she always knew to whom she was talking. No one ever seemed a stranger to Terese. It was as if she could read one's soul.

Looking over at Leah next, Teddy laughed to himself. She was lying on her back, sound asleep on the sofa in front of Terese, with her head comically hanging off the side. Every once in a while Leah's feet would tap Terese, as she experienced her dream. He had never known an animal more adaptable than she, or one that could make itself at home, as she could, in strange surroundings.

Ryan sat across from Teddy at the table, toward the middle of the small craft, staring silently out the window at the flat landscape below. He was wearing the same well cut, freshly cleaned and pressed, brown tailored suit he had worn down to Miami. Ryan had not uttered a single word since they boarded the plane. In fact, he had been silent all through breakfast, as well.

Getting up from his seat, Teddy walked down the aisle to where Terese sat quietly writing in her journal. He too was dressed casually, wearing a pair of dark sea green slacks with a matching cotton sweater. Teddy was such a tall, handsome, well-built man, and they looked as if they belonged together, in the way that true soul mates often do.

Terese looked up when Teddy came along side of her, catching his eyes. The only sound on the aircraft, above the hum of the engines, was Leah's soft snore.

Teddy gazed down at Leah, and then over to Terese. "God must have given her to us," he said, laughing, and gesturing to Leah, "so we'd have some comic relief in our lives."

Terese looked affectionately at Leah, and then at Teddy again.

"I think she's exhausted," Terese said. "She stayed at that pier for two days and nights after the storm lightened, waiting for you to return. She wouldn't eat, and she wouldn't come in," Terese added, as a large wave of emotion washed over her again, and tears welled up in her eyes. "We really thought we had lost you, Ted."

Crouching down in front of her, Teddy kissed her warmly on the mouth, and then again more deeply. "I'm sorry you had to go through that Terese. I know how you must have felt, being all alone."

"Jeanne and April came over every day, and offered to have us stay at their places," Terese shared.

"Why didn't you?" Teddy asked, knowing they were both childhood friends—one living in Miami, and the other in Plantation.

"I didn't want to leave the hotel," Terese explained, "nor did Leah."

Teddy smoothed back a couple of hairs from her face and studied her expression. Then, with a great deal of sensitivity, he tried to lighten her mood.

"It really was an exciting race," he said, gently. "The start was incredible."

"I never want you to go sailing again," Terese responded, meeting his eyes.

Teddy just looked at her in a loving way. "You don't really mean that," he said.

"Yes I do. I couldn't go through this again. Never Ted. Please promise me you'll never go sailing."

"You'll feel differently," he said, cheerfully. "Do you know what the chances are of that happening again?"

"No chance," Terese confirmed, "because you're not going sailing."

Teddy kissed her once more, and then looked down at her journal. "Are you writing?" he asked, changing the subject.

Terese nodded.

"Do you have any magazines, or a paper to read?" Teddy asked.

Showing him what she had brought on board, Teddy took a couple of magazines and the morning paper out of her large canvas bag.

"Do you want to join us?" he asked, referring to where Ryan was sitting at the table.

"In a couple of minutes," she said, "let me just finish my thought."

Teddy got up, as the steward came down the aisle heading for the cockpit. "We'll be serving lunch in about forty-five minutes Mr. Townsend"

"Smells good," Teddy replied. "It must be chicken."

Terese looked up and smiled. "Leah should enjoy that," she said. "It's one of her favorites."

"Yeah, I hope you made enough," Teddy said, laughing.

"I wondered why you ordered food for five, in addition to the crew, when there are only three of you," the steward smiled, as he turned and went back down the aisle to the galley.

Looking down at Terese again, Teddy touched her cheek in an affectionate way. "Don't be too long," he said, kissing her. Then he walked back up the aisle, taking the seat across from Ryan at the table.

The steward came over again, asking Ryan if he could get anything for him, but Ryan did not seem to notice the steward standing there. Nor did he look up when Teddy sat down to join him again. Ryan just continued to stare out the window, almost in a trance.

"He'll order something later," Teddy finally answered, before the steward went back to the galley. Teddy sensed Ryan's sadness, and knew what was wrong. "Are you okay, Ryan?" he asked.

Ryan just nodded.

"What're you thinking about?" Teddy asked.

Unable to speak, Ryan motioned something to mean nothing in particular, and then, he continued to stare out the window.

"Is it Tiphane?" Teddy asked.

Without looking up, Ryan nodded again.

"Atlantis is gone Ryan, and we can't bring any of that back—not the place, and not the people we loved."

"You did," Ryan answered, meeting his eyes.

Teddy paused for a minute, as he looked down the aisle at Terese, and then to Ryan. "I know you must miss Tiphane very much," he said.

Ryan just gazed back out the window.

Overhearing the conversation, Terese looked back at them with concern, and caught Teddy's eyes with a knowing glance. She got up, with her journal under her arm, went into the galley, and spoke to the steward. After ordering wine for Teddy and Ryan, and juice for herself, she walked back to the booth-like seating, and joined them, taking the seat next to Ryan. Terese reached over, and touched Ryan's hand.

"We've all been through a lot, Ryan, and it's going to take some time before we feel normal again," Terese said, trying to comfort him.

After giving Terese her tall glass of tomato juice, the steward brought the Chablis, and served it to Teddy and Ryan. Taking a sip of the wine, Ryan relaxed back into his seat, and started drifting away from them again.

Reaching across the table, Teddy picked up Terese's log. "Is this the journal I gave you at Christmastime?" he asked.

Terese acknowledged that it was.

"You must have done a lot of writing while we were gone. It's almost filled," he said leafing through the pages.

"I started to tell you about it yesterday afternoon, after you told me what had happened to you and Ryan, but you fell asleep."

"Tell me now," Teddy said, with interest.

"Well," Terese answered, "you know how story ideas always come to me in dreams—well, all the time you and Ryan were missing, I kept having these vivid dreams, and I wrote them all down."

As Ryan's interest piqued, Teddy quickly moved through the journal, stopping now and then to read a page. When Teddy finally set the journal back down on the table, he had a shocked look on his face.

"Ryan," he said, "you're not going to believe this—it's everything that happened to us. Getting caught in the storm, going inside the tower, meeting Polaris, Theos, Tarah, Aryan and Tiphane. All of it. It's all here."

Ryan reached for the journal. "Let's see," he asked, pulling it over to him.

Teddy looked at Terese again. "No wonder you believed me when I told you the story," he said. "You must be clairvoyant."

Looking down at the table, he caught sight of the picture of Merak on the front page of the morning newspaper. "Oh my God!" he said, with alarm.

"What is it?" Ryan asked.

Teddy picked up the paper and turned it around so that Ryan and Terese could see the picture.

"It's Merak!" he exclaimed, pointing at the picture. "Right here." Teddy said.

"Are you sure?" Terese asked.

Inspecting the paper more closely, Ryan and Terese scrutinized every frame.

"It's Merak all right, or his double," Ryan considered, as he began reading the story.

Terese looked at the paper. "This is why all this happened," she said.

"Who is he?" Teddy asked, pulling the paper back over to read it.

Ryan looked at him. "It didn't say," he observed, as Teddy read the article for himself.

"That reminds me. Where's the box?" Teddy asked, as he looked about the cabin.

Ryan reached under his seat. "I stowed it away during takeoff," he said, as he set the old carved box on the table.

"When are you going to open it?" Terese asked.

"I guess this is as good a time as any," Teddy said, reaching into his pocket and taking out the gold key. "Okay with you, Ryan?"

"Sure," Ryan acknowledged.

Slipping the key into the lock, Teddy slowly opened the top, revealing a beautiful golden pendant, together with its distinctive and elaborate gold chain, appearing to be exactly like those worn by Polaris and Sirius on Atlantis.

"I don't believe it," Ryan blurted. "It's the sacred pendant. I thought Polaris was giving you the writings of the scribe."

"So did I," Teddy admitted, as he picked up the pendant and held it in the light. "This is an omen, Ryan."

"What do you mean, it's an omen?" Ryan questioned.

"Terese is correct," Teddy said. "There's a reason why we were taken back to Atlantis. Everything we saw, what happened to us. What Merak was."

Teddy picked up the paper again, and shoved it over to Ryan. "Now this newspaper with Merak's face plastered on the front page. We open the box and find the protective pendant."

"You're jumping to conclusions, Ted," Ryan interjected.

Teddy paused for a moment, and lowered his voice. "We're supposed to do something about him."

Ryan just looked at him. "Oh, no—don't even think about it," Ryan finally said, "I'm not getting involved. I want to get back to my practice, see my patients, do my work at Northwestern."

But Teddy insisted. "We have to Ryan."

"No we don't have to Ted. And I don't want to talk about it either."

Terese looked at Teddy in a way to suggest letting it go for now. Placing the pendant back in the box, Teddy locked it safely inside, and then returned the key to his pocket.

"You're just tired right now," Teddy said, looking back at Ryan again.

When the steward came up with placemats and napkins, and began setting the table, no one said another word. Ryan turned and stared out the window again, and Teddy continued reading the article.

During lunch, Terese cheerfully changed the mood, as they talked mostly about the family, and the time passed quickly. Teddy and Terese told Ryan that they were expecting another child in August, right around

Ryan's birthday, and he came back into their conversation for a short while.

An hour later, their craft began its descent, as they neared Meigs Field on Northerly Island. Meigs Field was Chicago's little-known lakefront airport, used for private planes. It consisted of a long, narrow strip of land situated across the harbor from Soldier Field, and was virtually hidden from view—although shortly it would be closed, as the city had earmarked the land for another use.

Their small jet slowed as it made its way across Lake Michigan. They could see the protected yacht harbor, and the unending stream of parks stretching uninterrupted for miles and miles on Chicago's lakefront. Dotted here and there were patches of woods, which opened to planned parks, museums and other public buildings. The museums all had a classical architectural style, with Grecian facades, and stood out along the lakefront.

The city was blanketed by a recent snowfall, when March decided to do its own thing by going *out as the lion*, and the light gray skies hinted more was on the way. Teddy watched the automobiles making their way up and down Lake Shore Drive. He remembered the first time he visited Chicago, back in the days when he and Ryan were attending Harvard together as undergraduates.

He was surprised to find that the city had so much character. Her people were warm and inviting, with a good sense of humor, and he wondered who, along the way, had so wrongfully spoiled her image. Chicago never stopped giving, and had so much to offer.

It was probably, he thought, the era of gangsters who had imposed themselves upon Chicago decades ago, and who were wrongfully glamorized on film. Then again, a few of her politicians were not above controversy. Their behavior, at times, did not reflect the essence of this heartland city, with her compassionate soul and intelligent mind.

Boston had her refined, educated people, and her age-old waterways, landmarks, and places of history, and he had loved growing up in such an historic city. And, he found New York to be stylish, impulsive, and full of life during the years he practiced law there. New York also had her intellectual side, and was somewhat well read, so to speak, as was Teddy.

But Chicago, with her 3 million residents, was different. The city seemed content with its own intuitive knowledge. Chicago had no ego to prove, and seemed to hold no pretenses. She was just a warm and reassuring city, in a friendly midwestern way. From the very beginning, Chicago held its standards high, having long ago chosen to plan parks for its people along its 35 miles of shoreline, rather than industry. Parks children endlessly played in, and adults enjoyed as well, with a season of fun concerts and food festivals.

In Chicago, Teddy soon found, people came first before material things. It was the kind of town that slipcovered an old chair, rather than throwing it away. A town where close family ties were still important, with honesty and hard work more the rule than the exception. Teddy had grown to love this city, and he wanted to raise his family here.

When their plane landed, just off the shoreline, Teddy could feel the city draw into him, similar to a mother checking her child after a prolonged absence. It felt good to be home. Their G-3 soon taxied across the field, and over to their waiting limousine. The steward brought them their winter coats, then removed their luggage from the back of the plane and put it into the trunk of their car.

In no time at all they were heading out of the airport driveway, across the small connecting bridge of land leading onto Lake Shore Drive. No one spoke in the car, and Teddy found himself listening to the drumming sound of the tires as they made their way over the cold pavement. The car soon turned west on Monroe, taking them across the Chicago River, and onto the Kennedy Expressway.

Leah chose to sit in the front, and Teddy chuckled to himself when he saw her give the driver a disgusted look when he attempted to light a cigarette. Terese soon lowered the window between them asking the driver not to smoke, and they continued on their way—more to Leah's satisfaction.

It had always amazed Teddy that Terese could completely understand two separate conversations at once, even while talking on the phone, and still be monitoring the room, her children and their pets. It was as if she were conducting an orchestra, with everything in perfect rhythm and harmony.

Terese sat between Teddy and Ryan in the back, with Teddy's arm around her, and her head resting against his shoulder. She began to fall asleep from total exhaustion. The quiet in the car carried only silent thoughts as they began their one-hour journey north.

With the carved box, petrified into a stone-hard material, on his lap, Teddy reached into his pocket and took out the gold key. The window, separating them from their driver, was once again shut tight, and he knew he could speak privately.

"Ryan," Teddy whispered, not wanting to wake Terese, "will you keep this for me?"

Ryan took the key in his hand, and examined it for a moment.

"I think it would be better," Teddy explained, "if we kept the key separate from the box, just until we can figure out what we should do with the pendant."

Ryan slipped a long gold chain from around his neck, and added the golden key to Tiphane's antique golden triangle.

"You brought that with you?" Teddy asked, referring to the charm.

"Polaris placed it in my hand when we said goodbye," Ryan responded. "I purchased the chain at the gift shop at the hotel," he added in explanation, before falling back into silence.

Teddy watched the view out the car window. He soon found himself focusing on the patterns of frost forming on the glass, then he began thinking about Atlantis again, and what an enchanting existence they all had there. He still could not believe what happened to this breathtakingly beautiful empire.

About forty-five minutes later, their car pulled off the Tri-State Tollway onto Town Line Road, and then onto Waukegan Road until they reached Deerpath—taking them once again toward the Lake Michigan shoreline. They soon entered the attractive and affluent lakefront town of Lake Forest.

Lake Forest had been established in the mid-1800s, and was now a city of more than 20,000. However, it remained as quaint as an English village with its unique clock tower, Tudor-designed train station, and old-world red brick buildings forming a market square. Despite its modern hospital, college campuses, libraries, cultural and recreational facilities, the town had kept the original architectural style that had always lent Lake Forest a certain unmistakable charm.

Teddy first heard of the town when Robert Redford filmed *Ordinary People* there, and showed the beauty of Lake Forest, its parks, and the woods that sheltered the town from the storms coming off Lake Michigan. Little did he know then that Ryan, and then he and his family, would be living there years later.

Their car moved quietly down the tree-lined street of opulent, well-appointed homes, then through the village, continuing down Ryan's street as it graciously wound its way to the lakefront.

"It's the next house on the right," Ryan instructed the driver.

Taking a turn into the driveway, the car pulled up to Ryan Stuart's two-story brick Tudor home, and parked close to the recently shoveled walk.

The yard was lined with a thick, low hedge of privet. A variety of leaf-less trees graced the yard and its perimeters, with two huge old firs on the side that were brushed with the recent snow. Christmas holly bushes, glistening under sparkling snowflakes, gave the front its only color, and bent forward to greet them. The remainder of the yard appeared to be neatly trimmed under the cover of snow.

Jen, Ryan's houseman, came running out of the house, as soon as the car pulled in the driveway, and was muttering something excitedly in Chinese. Ryan got out of the car and said hello to him, while the driver opened the trunk and removed Ryan's luggage.

"Come on over after you get settled in, Ryan," invited Terese, who had just woken up. "I'm sure the children will want to see you."

"Thanks, but I'm beat. Maybe tomorrow," he said.

As they backed out of the driveway, Ryan waved goodbye, and they were soon off in the direction from which they had come. It was getting darker now, and light snowflakes began to fall.

While pressing the intercom, Teddy spoke to the driver. "Our place is just ten minutes from here, Charles, I'll tell you where to turn."

Teddy and Terese loved Whippoorwill Farm. Their house sat on many acres of land, mostly wooded, and had an interesting history, with each owner having added their own specific touch.

The original house was built in the 1920s and was modest in size, with a couple of outbuildings. In the 1930s, the second owners turned the farm into a showy estate. They brought over a French architect who expanded the house, a center-hall colonial, to fourteen rooms, and built a master's barn and stable.

The one-story stable, facing the front of the property, was beautiful in design, having a long, narrow European look, with a high-pitched roof. The circular drive was centered on the stable, rather than the house. A cottage for a caretaker was attached to one end, and a four-car garage to the other end, near the house. A large carriage arch was designed in the center of the stable for the horses to pass through, allowing you to see from front to back.

The final owners, in the 1950s, built a more modern stable on the farm for their show horses, and, through the years that followed, lovingly raised their family there. Teddy and Terese had recently leased Whippoorwill Farm for one year, while their new estate was being built.

The area outside of Lake Forest had become built up over the years, and was no longer as rural as it once was. Because of this, Teddy and Terese had decided to move a little farther out into the countryside. In the meantime, the farm was their home. Their new place would be a copy of Whippoorwill—nothing else would do.

This was a real home, and the first time they saw it, Teddy and Terese had felt so much love and warmth coming from it, they knew instantly that this was where they wanted to bring their family when they moved back to Illinois from New York. It was ideal for them, instead of living right in Lake Forest, as they could keep their horses with them on the farm. So it was in this way that they had come to live in this lovely country home.

The limousine traveled back down Deerpath, and they soon reached the four-lane road that Lake Forest called Kennedy, but was known as Town Line or Route 60 farther out. They would soon pass beautiful acreages of land. Woods, heavy and thick with brush, had been cleared in small sections revealing new houses and patches of pastureland, where here and there large oak trees remained dotting the landscape.

As they made their way down Town Line Road, snow began falling in large soft flakes, and the trees and bushes were transformed into a fantasy of sparkling elegance with a fresh coating of snow. Only once did they pass another car. Snow piled up on the windows about them, preventing Teddy and Terese from seeing out, and the driver slowed down considerably.

Terese nestled more comfortably into the back seat, as Teddy pulled her close to him. "It's a shame about Ryan," Teddy said, "falling in love with Tiphane the way he did, and then losing her so soon."

"He didn't lose her," Terese responded.

"What do you mean?" Teddy asked.

"They were married," Terese answered.

"How do you know that?" Teddy asked.

"It was part of one of my dreams," Terese said, pausing for a moment as she thought back.

It was becoming more and more apparent to Teddy that the same archive Polaris had opened for him and Ryan, had also been opened to Terese while she was in a state of dreaming.

"Go on," Teddy said, "tell me about your dreams," he added, prompting her to come out of her thoughts.

"I was just thinking about the first day I met Ryan," Terese said, as they drove along.

As long as she had known Ryan he had never been especially close to anyone. There were plenty of girlfriends when he attended high school, where he had been a popular basketball star, but no one stuck.

"Go on," Teddy said once again, bringing Terese out of her thoughts.

"Well, I first met Ryan when his sister, Mary, asked me over to their apartment after school. Ryan was graduating that year from the eighth grade at St. Phillip's, and I remember thinking he was so cute. I had a crush on him for the longest time."

"You never told me that," Teddy said, not hiding his feelings.

"I never told anyone," she said. "But anyway, that all changed when Ryan brought you home from Harvard for Thanksgiving, several years later," she added, when she saw the hurt look on his face.

"Sounds as if you carried the torch for a long enough time," Teddy said, looking out the window.

"Ryan and I went to different high schools, and I barely ever saw him."

"Mary's your best friend, isn't she?"

"Well, of course."

"Well then you saw Ryan," Teddy finished.

"I was 11 years old when I liked Ryan, and I fell in love with at least four boys after that in high school."

"I don't want to hear about it," Teddy said.

Terese could not help but laugh.

"But you were my first true love," she said, pulling him back over to her, "and the only man who has ever touched me in my whole life," Terese finished.

"Yeah, well I thought I was," Teddy said, feeling better.

"You were," Terese assured him, almost amused by his mood. "What brought this up anyway?" she asked.

"I don't remember," Teddy said, rubbing the moisture off the window with his glove so he could see where they were. Teddy flicked the intercom again, so that he could talk to the driver.

"Our place starts when you come to the white crisscrossing fence," Teddy said. "Just go in the second driveway close to the house."

As they pulled into the wide circular driveway, they could see their large, white two-story colonial house, partially covered with snow. The dark green shuttered windows beamed out yellow light into the cold night air, and large, soft snowflakes continued to fall. The home's dark green roof was completely covered with a thick layer of snow that hung slightly over the edges.

Huge old elms, with their long-reaching arms, seemed to guard the house with their magnificence, and the setting was peaceful and serene.

"Oh look Ted, there's Katie," Terese said, as she pointed to one of the white-paned windows in front.

The face of a small child was framed where the curtains were tied back, then she was gone. Light soon poured out the front door of the house, and an older couple, the Swensens, came out, with Mrs. Swensen carrying three-year-old Katie. Her two older brothers—Matthew, six, and Michael, nine—quickly followed, as they stormed down the staircase from upstairs.

Katie had her soft, blonde hair pulled back from her fine-boned face with a pretty pink ribbon. She reached out to Terese first, for a hug and a kiss, and then was passed over to Teddy.

Leah had already flown out the driver's door of the car and greeted each one of the children, practically knocking them down. Then Leah ran to greet the Swensens.

Young Matthew, blonde and very much Katie's look-alike, and his older brother Michael, with sandy brown hair and a strong athletic build, waited their turns. Both received warm hugs and kisses from their parents. The children seemed to be very excited, and were happily talking all at once.

Pulling some money out of his pocket, Teddy thanked their driver, who had already taken the luggage out of the car, and carried it into the front hall of the house.

Teddy and Terese continued walking up the flagstone walk, talking to Mr. and Mrs. Swensen on the way. Katie was still in Teddy's arms, his coat wrapped warmly around her, and they all went into the house together.

Mrs. Swensen wiped her hands on her apron, and called out to everyone before returning to the kitchen. "Dinner's about ready," she said. "We have one of those rib roasts that you like, Mr. Townsend, and some Yorkshire pudding."

"Thank you, Mrs. Swensen."

"And two apple pies." Katie said, excitedly.

"Matthew and I got some of that cheddar cheese you like Dad, the kind from Wisconsin," Michael added, turning to his father.

"And ice cream too," Katie said, happily.

Mr. Swensen had built a roaring fire in both the living room and dining room fireplaces, and the family was still laughing and talking excitedly when the front door shut out the cold snowy night. It was truly a wonderful homecoming.

CHAPTER 19

▲

THE PERSUASION

Saturday

Being a partner of a large, national law firm had its advantages for Teddy, as other attorneys at his offices could handle all of his ongoing casework during his absence. As he had originally planned when he was arranging his vacation leave, Teddy took the remainder of the week off after returning home from his trip to Miami on Wednesday evening. Teddy was in no hurry to return to work, and the trip to Miami had not eased his discontent with his job.

During the remaining week at home, Teddy attempted to learn more about who Merak was, and more about the story that appeared in the Miami paper, without success. An editor he knew at the *Washington Post* newspaper had no information about him, and related that the photo and story Teddy had read had come over the wire service from the Associated Press.

When his attempt along that line failed, Teddy checked with the Associated Press—although they claimed they had no list of names to go with the photograph. What perplexed Teddy most of all, was that it was as if Merak did not exist at all.

Another problem was Ryan, and his adamant refusal to get involved. Ryan was excellent when it came to research, and could spend endless hours of diligent effort pursuing a line of thought or inquiry. Teddy needed that help, but Ryan was unrelenting, and refused getting involved at any level.

Teddy had invited Ryan over for lunch that afternoon, in a final attempt to arouse his interest in finding Merak. However, when Ryan had not shown up by 1:00 p.m., they finally went ahead and started eating without him. Just as the family was finishing lunch, the doorbell rang, and Teddy got up to answer it.

The sign on the truck in the driveway read "Southerland's Book Finders—Rare Books," and a deliveryman had just carried a large box to the front door.

"Are you getting more books Dad?" Matthew asked, as he followed his father to the door.

"Just a few," Teddy answered, as he signed for the delivery.

Terese came up with Katie, and looked at the large carton. "Why don't you boys put that box in the library for your father, before going out to the horses," she suggested.

Michael and Matthew took the large carton of books, one on each side, and started arguing as they moved through the entrance hall.

"I always go backwards," Matthew complained.

"Do you want to help me or not?" Michael demanded.

"That's not the point," Matthew quarreled.

"Forget it!" Michael yelled, grabbing the box away from him. Matthew soon lost his grip and the books fell near the staircase landing, and spilled out all over the floor.

"You see what you made me do!" Michael said, giving Matthew a shove.

"I offered to help," Matthew defended. "Just because you're older, you think you can have everything your own way!"

Terese came back to the front hall, and gave both boys a look that meant the mission was to be carried out without another word.

Matthew helped Michael put the books back into the box and then they carried them sideways, maneuvering themselves so that neither one of them was going backward. When they got to the door leading into the library, Michael stopped, refusing to turn his back and go through first.

Staring at each other for a long moment, Matthew managed to negotiate the turn without turning around, and soon they were both inside.

When the deliveryman left, Terese gave Teddy a hopeless look. "I'll be upstairs," she said, "I want to put Katie down for a nap."

"I'll talk to the boys," Teddy promised her, not liking their rude behavior in front of a stranger. And he did so, in no uncertain terms.

As soon as his sons left the library, Teddy began going through the box. Hours went by while he pored over the new volumes of books. It was the second delivery that week, and all the books had references to Atlantis within them, including some very abstract works on the subject.

The library was located in a small cozy, wing extending from the back of the house at the center. Teddy, from time to time, would look up from his large, antique desk, thinking he heard a car that sounded like Ryan's making its way down Town Line Road. From his desk he could see out a pair of tall library windows to the side yard. He sat quietly for a moment, and watched the bare countryside scene, as a rabbit scampered across the snow, making its way back to its warren before nightfall.

It had been a cold crisp day, with clear blue skies, and the sun was now dipping behind the woods that bordered their property to the west. Teddy could see from the thermometer attached to the window outside, that the temperature was dropping fast, and it promised to be a very cold night.

An hour later, Teddy's reading was interrupted again when he heard the engine sounds of Ryan's dark green Porsche. The frozen snow crunched under the car's tires, as Ryan pulled into the circular driveway, and up close to the front walk.

Teddy began organizing the material he had assembled for Ryan to look at, and hoped he could convince him of how important it was for them to find Merak. Something deep inside of Teddy told him that Ryan was part of the key to unlocking the mystery surrounding Merak's sudden appearance, and disappearance, and that Ryan somehow had to be a part of his efforts before Merak could be found again.

When Ryan rang the front doorbell, Katie ran down the stairs to answer it. She peeked through the beveled glass of the sidelight that framed the door, and, when she saw it was Ryan on the other side, she quickly opened it.

"Hi Uncle Ryan," she said, excitedly.

Ryan swept her up into his arms, and gave her a kiss on the cheek. "Ummmm," he said, laughing, and seeing her freshly painted bright pink nail polish. "You smell just like acetone."

"What's acetone?" Katie asked, in her small clear voice.

Ryan could hear Terese yelling down from the upstairs hall, looking for Katie.

"She's down here, Terese," Ryan answered.

"Oh, hi Ryan," Terese said, as she came part way down the curving staircase. "Teddy's waiting for you in the library, and Mrs. Swensen left some homemade soup for you, in a crock, in the warming drawer."

"Thanks," Ryan answered. "Sorry I couldn't make lunch—I had an emergency at the hospital."

Terese just smiled. "Come on Katie, and I'll finish your manicure," Terese called.

"Mommy's making me pretty," Katie, said, as Ryan set her down.

As quickly as she appeared, Katie ran back up the stairs, and was soon out of sight.

Walking through the main entrance hall of the house, Ryan went directly into the library.

"What was the emergency?" Teddy asked. "We waited lunch for you for an hour."

"I had to go forward with the surgery on the Robinson child," Ryan said, "and it took longer than we first thought."

"How's he doing?" Teddy asked.

"We won't know for a while," Ryan responded, "but I think the surgery went well."

"That gives hope," Teddy responded.

Ryan nodded. "What are you up to?" he asked, seeing all the books piled around Teddy's desk.

"I've been doing a little reading on Atlantis," he responded.

"Why?" Ryan asked. "We just got back from there."

"I've decided to hire an investigator," Teddy said.

"To do what?" Ryan asked.

"To find out who Merak is," Teddy explained.

"Ted, you can't be serious," Ryan responded.

"I want to see who he is, and what he's up to. I made a lot of calls, on Thursday and Friday, with no success. I can't even sleep at night thinking about him."

"Maybe he's changed," Ryan offered.

"A man like Merak doesn't change overnight, Ryan."

"Ted, it hasn't exactly been overnight," Ryan defended. "It's been about 25,000 years."

"I don't think it works that way—not exactly, anyway," Teddy said, as he pulled out a book. "I've been reading about what happened."

A comical look came over Ryan's face. "I thought we knew what happened," he asserted.

"That's not what I'm saying," Teddy explained.

"Well, what are you saying?" Ryan questioned.

"What I mean is, that I think we've been caught in time," Teddy continued. "At least the Atlanteans have been," Teddy added.

"My God, where do you get this stuff?" Ryan criticized.

"In here," Teddy said, as he searched through the book he held in his hand. "I read all about it."

Teddy handed Ryan the thick book, with its small print. A torn piece of paper marked the page he was talking about, and Ryan tried to find the passage.

"Where?" Ryan asked.

"Right there at the bottom of page 754."

"You've read 754 pages of this?"

"No, no," Teddy explained. "I've just been reading all the sections referencing Atlantis in the index."

"And so what does this have to do with us?" Ryan questioned.

"I read a translation of an ancient manuscript," Teddy said, as he took the book back to find the writing. "It told of a black magician who was responsible for the destruction of Atlantis."

"So what else is new?" Ryan asked cynically.

"It explained," Teddy went on, "that the people were cut off, trapped in time, as if they had committed suicide, and their souls had to wait until it was time again before they could reenter and move on in evolution."

"And you believe that?" Ryan asked, with annoyance.

"Yes, I believe that," Teddy acknowledged.

"So then you think that everyone is coming together again?" Ryan queried.

"Exactly." Teddy exclaimed. "Including the bad guys."

"I don't know about that Ted," Ryan said, shaking his head.

"The probability of Merak changing, Ryan, is rather slight. I think he's just as evil, and just as cunning, as he's always been, and we need to find out what he's up to."

"You mean *you* need to find out," Ryan returned, as he looked at some of the titles Teddy was reading. "I don't want to get involved."

"My God, Ryan," Teddy said, raising his voice. "Don't you care?"

"Yes, I care," Ryan, said. "Ted, you couldn't stop him anyway, even if you did find out what he was up to. If he really is Merak, he's too powerful to even approach."

"There's always a way to stop evil, Ryan."

"Not him. You wouldn't have a chance," Ryan asserted.

"So we let him go free to destroy another civilization?" Teddy asked.

"I think you're wrong about that," Ryan insisted. "That could never happen today."

"I think he's already tried," Teddy said, "and he'll try again."

"What do you mean, he's already tried?" Ryan asked.

"I think he already tried by manipulating and using the form of Hitler. And he almost made it too," Teddy confirmed.

"You think Merak was Hitler?" Ryan asked.

"I know he was Hitler. And he wouldn't have stopped, you know, with destroying the Jews and Christians that offended him. Eventually, he would have imposed his ugly, scheming, diabolical will on every single racial type, and religion, that did not fit his ideal. Do you really think that Hitler, that small ugly mouse of a man, had the power by himself to do what he did?"

"I don't know. I never thought about it," Ryan said.

"It was Merak, or it was the entity that uses Merak's form," Teddy revealed. "Hitler was into all sorts of sorcery and black magic, and everyone who knows about those things knew it. This was especially true with the mystics and the metaphysicians at that time."

"How do you know that?" Ryan asked.

"Because he had every last one of them that he could find and get his hands on arrested and incarcerated when he rose to a position of power. He thought they would know how to stop him. And they did stop him."

Ryan just looked at Teddy, with amazement.

"Did you know that the Pentagon," Teddy went on, "when the United States got into the war, brought three high-level clairvoyants together in London, to plot out Hitler's future moves on a map? Our military intelligence couldn't figure out where he was going to strike next, so they fought him at another level. Magic with magic. There are always things that go on behind the scenes, Ryan. And there are always ways to stop evil—even someone as evil as Merak."

Ryan did not respond.

"He is powerful, Ryan," Teddy agreed. "I grant you that. Did you ever watch, and I mean truly watch, those armies of men that Hitler had parade in front of him by the thousands. It was as if one man was moving, one mind, and that's exactly what it was. Think about it. Why were they so synchronized? They blindly worshiped him, and some of the more ignorant and weak-minded still do. My God, some of them thought him to be the Christ!"

Ryan just shook his head, as he stared down at the floor, thinking.

"The next time you see those films on the History Channel, Ryan, take a good look at Hitler's eyes, and what he does with his hand. He hypnotized them. Only it wasn't Hitler, it was Merak. He was controlling all of them, as one would a puppet. He is vicious Ryan, and he is mean-spirited, and he is still capable of destroying this planet."

"What are you trying to do, frighten me?" Ryan asked.

"I'm trying to get you to pull your head out of the sand, and take a good look," Teddy provoked.

"If Merak used Hitler's body before, then why isn't he using someone else's now?" Ryan asked.

"He probably is, when he wants to," Teddy said. "Just look at the darkness seeping into the world today, Ryan. Polaris was correct. There are examples of it everywhere.

All you have to do is to look at the insidious content and images in the music business today, not to mention the violent, menacing and demoralizing movies being made for young people. And don't get me started on basic TV, the sexual content in programming and in commercials—a lot of it is pornography."

Ryan nodded, in agreement.

"Children are being constantly barraged with images sanctioning ill-manners, immorality, the abuse of alcohol and other substances—not to mention the sick perversion invading the world today. It has never been worse than this. Young girls dressing like whores, and young boys like they're in street gangs. It's disgusting!"

"I agree," Ryan admitted.

"Every time that I see on TV, or read in the newspapers or a magazine, a shocking story—thinking it is the worst thing I have ever heard or read—the next day there is something even worse being reported."

"I agree with you," Ryan repeated.

"The world is falling under the control of evil forces, Ryan. That's why we have to find out who Merak is. He is the man of darkness that we know. And he is the one who we are supposed to stop."

Ryan just shook his head.

"We have to find out what he is up to Ryan," Teddy persuaded, "and we have to find out who his circle of friends are. Any one of them could be his pawn. Don't forget what we were taught in Temple School—darkness can move through the one, and move through the many, at will, once it has a path."

"And you want to go in there, and take him on?" Ryan asked.

"There is a reason all this happened to us Ryan," Teddy validated. "And we do have the magical pendant."

"You mean I get to wear it if we run into him?" Ryan asked.

Teddy started laughing. "Well, you know, I always figured you'd bargain for it."

Ryan smiled, and then looked down at the floor, as he began thinking about what Teddy had said.

"Will you help me?" Teddy asked.

"Why do you always have to get so involved?" Ryan asked.

"Because it's our responsibility to do so, and because he's not just some industrialist, or banker. He's Merak," Teddy persisted, "and I need your help."

"He's too much to take on, and it's much too big a risk, Ted. Besides," Ryan added, "it'll take too much of my time."

"I have that worked out," Teddy said. "Like I said earlier, I'm going to hire an investigator to do most of the legwork—at least insofar as finding him."

"Yeah, it looks like it," Ryan said, referring to the pile of books on Teddy's desk.

"That's just a little reading," Teddy defended.

"And then what?" Ryan asked, giving him a critical look. "My God, Ted, we've only been back for three days!"

"That will depend on what the investigator comes up with," Teddy continued.

"Well, keep me posted," Ryan responded, turning away, and walking out the library door.

Teddy got up, following after Ryan. "Are you leaving already?" he asked.

"Already?" Ryan answered, turning around. "I feel as if I've been here for hours."

"You've been here fewer than twenty minutes, and you know it. And I still want to talk to you about this."

"Well, I don't want to talk to you," Ryan said.

"Besides" Teddy insisted, "Mrs. Swensen left some food warming for you."

"I know, Terese told me. I ate at the hospital," Ryan said, continuing through the entrance hall.

"We're going to order some pizzas in about an hour, if you want to wait, Ryan," Teddy offered.

Ryan kept walking toward the front door.

"Mrs. Swensen baked an almond torte today, with a homemade custard sauce," Teddy said, knowing it was Ryan's favorite. "And there's still some fresh whipped cream left."

"You think you can bribe me with food?" Ryan asked, turning around.

"Well, at least have a cup of coffee, or tea," Teddy said. "I think the boys are around, and Matthew wanted to show you a spider he found in the basement."

"Are you sure you can drag yourself away from your books?" Ryan asked.

"I think I can spare a minute or two," Teddy said, laughing. "You know if you'd help me, Ryan, I'd do the majority of the work."

"Ted, I'm not going to get involved in any more of your adventures. I still count myself lucky to be alive after the last one, and this time you're on your own," Ryan finished.

"Come on, Ryan," Teddy persuaded.

"I mean it Ted, I said no. Now don't ask me again!"

Ryan walked past Teddy, through the dining room, and into the kitchen, and then paused for a moment looking around.

"I thought you said Mrs. Swensen baked an almond torte?"

Teddy pointed to the refrigerator, as he started to make some tea. "It's in there," he said, "and the custard sauce is in the pitcher on the top shelf, next to the whipped cream."

Teddy took the crock of vegetable beef soup out of the warming drawer and decided to eat it himself, while Ryan had dessert.

Knowing Ryan, Teddy was certain that he had reached an end to the discussion, and decided to drop the subject, at least for the time being.

For Teddy, tomorrow was always another day. He had not even begun to give up on Ryan.

CHAPTER 20

▲

THE INVESTIGATION

Despite Teddy's valiant effort to persuade Ryan to help him, he pursued his quest in search of Merak alone. The remaining days of March had now passed, then all of April, one day leading into the next as his private investigation continued.

With the passage of time, Teddy tried to get back into his normal routine. Nevertheless, he was beginning to feel more and more anxious, and concerned about finding Merak. Contemptuous thoughts of Merak, this menacing and demonic magician, as well as what he did to the Atlanteans, kept going through Teddy's mind. Why he could not get any information on this man, he did not know. Teddy's every attempt had failed.

It was now the first Monday in May, and the countryside around Whippoorwill Farm and Lake Forest had come alive, as the landscape turned green and the flowering trees on the property began budding into color.

Mr. Swensen's showy tulips, of assorted vivid hues, had all come into bloom in a beautiful display for spring, and Mrs. Swensen had cut large bouquets of them for the house. The horses now enjoyed their days in the pasture between the house and a large grove of trees, and wild jonquils still covered the floor of the woods.

Teddy woke early that morning, as usual, and laid in bed thinking. On one wall of their bedroom were two sets of French doors, with one set on each side of Terese's dressing table. The French doors led out to an upstairs porch, overlooking the western side yard. Teddy looked out the divided light windows of the arched doors for the changing colors of first light, when the sun rose in the east.

The soft fragrance of lilacs came into the room with the light spring breeze, and he listened to the early morning calls of birds in the yard until shortly before 6 a.m. This was his favorite time of day, and the time he did much of his thinking.

Terese was still sound asleep beside him, when he quietly slipped out of bed and took his shower. After dressing, he woke her and the boys, and then went downstairs. Mrs. Swensen had already set out his orange juice and vitamins at the table in the morning room, and she started scrambling some eggs.

Teddy had always enjoyed an early start on the day, and he also enjoyed riding into the city on the train with Ryan. Sometimes they would talk about law, and other times medicine. Teddy always found it interesting to hear about the problems Ryan faced with the illnesses of some of his patients. Over a period of time, Teddy had acquired a fair knowledge of medical procedures and terminology.

He had, at first, contemplated going into medicine, except that early on he found he did not have the stomach for it. In the end he went into law, mostly as a means of avoiding going into banking with his father—a field he found dry and boring.

His chosen field in law, civil litigation, entailed a great deal of reading, writing and research into new areas, depending on the subject matter of the case he was working on. This was the one part of his job that Teddy always enjoyed.

As the years went by, he had become increasingly disappointed with every other aspect of law though, especially with the way some attorneys practiced it. It was mostly what went on in general, behind closed doors. Teddy always felt there was a price to pay for taking advantage of another human being, and that many lawyers were going way beyond the original intention of protecting the rights of their clients.

Too many lawyers were, admittedly, seeking to set their clients free and unaccountable for the charges and suits brought against them, even those clients who they knew were guilty.

Laws on the books were increasingly protecting the rights of criminals, rather than protecting the rights of their victims. People could legally plead innocent, even though they were guilty, without any penalty for doing so when the opposite was proven. A life sentence in prison could often mean the criminal would serve as little as eight years, then be paroled, even after taking another human life. It all seemed insane to Teddy, as well as corrupt. He also disapproved of lengthy, inefficient criminal trials that went on and on, for months and months, without good cause.

It had become an acceptable practice for attorneys to win at any cost. Any measure would be used to feed their own dark egos, with justice and the rights of the innocent taking a back seat. Teddy knew there were still many honorable attorneys in the world, but the numbers were dwindling, and he wanted out of his profession.

However, as much as he had thought about getting out of law, he was still unsure about what else he could do. He knew he would enjoy teaching at the college level, and politics had come to mind of late—except he did not yet have the network of friends and acquaintances in Illinois that he had in Massachusetts and New York.

He was beginning to feel trapped, and out of place, but he kept his thoughts and feelings to himself. He knew he needed to change his work, and only he could take action on that. Nevertheless, this simply was not the right time.

"Mr. Townsend," Mrs. Swensen repeated, bringing Teddy out of his deep thoughts. "You'll miss your train," she gently reminded him, as he stared out the morning room's bay window.

Teddy quickly made a sandwich out of two pieces of toast, and the ham and scrambled eggs left on his plate, wrapping the sandwich in a paper napkin, and then headed for the kitchen door. After saying goodbye to

Mrs. Swensen, he climbed into his vintage, cream-colored Jaguar sedan, and quickly backed out of the garage.

Speeding through the countryside toward the Lake Forest Train Station, Teddy slowed down only when he passed the police station and the school on Deerpath. He and Ryan usually took the 7:23 a.m. train into the city together. Teddy crossed the tracks just before the crossing gates came down, with time to spare.

Once they had settled into their usual seats, in their set routine, Teddy began to drink the cup of coffee that Ryan had brought onto the train, while eating his ham and egg sandwich from home. He then enjoyed his chocolate-covered donut.

Teddy tried reading the paper, but soon found his thoughts were drifting, and he ended up staring out the window as they passed through one lakefront town after another, on their way to Chicago.

"So, how's *I Spy* coming along?" Ryan asked, breaking the long silence.

"Not so terrific," Teddy answered, without any defense. "It's as if Merak doesn't exist at all, and no one seems to know who he is, and how to find him."

"You could always call the President," Ryan quipped.

"Very funny."

"Believe me," Ryan remarked, "I wouldn't put it past you."

"I already tried," Teddy confessed. "I couldn't get through."

"Oh, I'm sure you'll find a way," Ryan said, humorously.

"I'm hiring another investigator," Teddy concluded.

"What does this make, number two?"

"Three. I had two working simultaneously for a while in the beginning."

"Who referred the new one?" Ryan asked.

"No one," Teddy answered.

Ryan looked over at him for a moment. "You mean you just picked him out of the phone book?"

"No, it was more an omen," Teddy confided.

"Oh wonderful, another omen," Ryan said, as he straightened the French cuff on his handmade shirt.

"It was an omen," Teddy said. "Yesterday afternoon, as I was leaving the office, a man got out of the elevator in front of me, and, when he pulled something out of his pocket, I noticed that he had dropped a card."

Teddy looked over at Ryan, and read his face.

"So, I bent down to pick it up, and when I stood up again, the man was gone. And I didn't have time to call out to him, because the elevator doors were already shutting. And, so there I was, with this card."

"So what did the card say?" Ryan asked.

"*C. T. Chang—Private Investigations*, with an address in Chinatown."

"On Wentworth?" Ryan asked.

"Yes, I think so," Teddy responded.

"This is getting expensive, isn't it?" Ryan asked.

"Not much," Teddy said.

"How much, is not much?" Ryan asked.

"Not much, is not much," Teddy defended. "Aren't you the man who, just yesterday, said how ill-mannered it is to talk about money?"

Ryan never responded.

"You know, if you'd help me," Teddy encouraged, "I wouldn't have to go through all this alone."

"Why?" Ryan asked. "Because I work cheap?"

"No, it's not that. I never mind spending the money, you know that," Teddy said, thinking for a moment. "It's just that you have a nose for it."

Ryan gave Teddy an irritated look. "I hate that expression."

Teddy started laughing. "Sorry, no pun intended," he added, making the situation worse.

He knew that Ryan had always disliked the shape of his nose. It had a small bump on it from an athletic injury, but he had always been afraid to have the necessary surgery to have it corrected. Typical, Teddy thought, of those who know what actually goes on in operating rooms.

"Ryan, I'll even make a deal with you," Teddy said.

"What kind of deal?" Ryan asked, looking annoyed.

"All your legal services for the rest of your life, free. Absolutely no charge," he smiled.

Ryan gave him a funny look. "I don't pay you now."

"I know you don't, and I'm going to start billing you for our out-of-pocket costs, too. I keep having to pay for you out of my personal account."

"It can't be that much," Ryan returned.

"I'll have Pat work up an accounting. I think you might be astonished—especially since the account has remained unpaid for more than ten years, and with accruing interest and subsequent charges, that could be a surprisingly good figure."

Ryan just looked at him.

"Mind you, I'm not charging you for my time at all, just expenses," Teddy added.

"I would never charge you for my professional services," Ryan countered.

"Yeah, well fortunately, no one in my family has needed brain surgery lately," Teddy said, starting to laugh.

Ryan remained silent.

Teddy looked over at Ryan again, and a serious tone came into his voice. "I think you should help me, Ryan. I'd do it for you."

"I do a lot of things for you," Ryan returned. "I get our donuts and coffee every morning at the train station, don't I?"

"Yes, and you always charge it all on my account."

"You have a lot more money than I do," Ryan said, in explanation. "You can afford it."

Teddy just looked at him. "Ryan, no one but the Treasury has more cash on hand than you do. You're not that poor little kid from the south side of Chicago any more."

Ryan didn't answer him.

"Come on Ryan, there must be something you want. Will you think about it?" Teddy asked.

Ryan just stared at him. "You never give up do you?" he denounced. "You push, and push, and push, and push. And then you push some more."

"I can't do it alone Ryan. I need your help."

Ryan just looked at him. "No you don't," Ryan answered him.

"Yes I do," Teddy implored.

"Honestly, am I going to have to look at your pathetic, pleading face every time I turn around?" Ryan asked.

Teddy remained silent.

"Why is it so important to you that I get involved?" Ryan questioned.

"Because I need you there, if something goes wrong," Teddy admitted.

Ryan thought for a moment longer. "If I help you, will you truly do something for me?" he asked.

"Sure. Name it."

"You asked me before if I needed anything, and there is something I could use. It's a new piece of equipment for my research project."

Teddy looked at him. "What is it?" he asked.

"It's for my laser project."

"Laser project?" Teddy asked. "I thought your research had to do with epilepsy?"

"It does. This is a little different, and it looks promising, Ted," Ryan continued, enthusiastically.

Teddy thought for a moment more. "Why is it so special?"

"It's the next step," Ryan answered.

"Why don't you get the equipment you need with your grant money?" Teddy questioned.

"This is something that became available afterward, and it was not budgeted for."

"Okay," Teddy said. "Whatever it is, it's yours," he added. "Order the piece of equipment, and send me the bill."

"Just like that?" Ryan asked, not trusting him.

"Just like that," Teddy confirmed, wondering what was going to follow.

"Now for the restrictions," Ryan added, as he brushed a piece of lint off his pants. "I'll help you, but only on weekends, and only when I'm free. I don't want to be inconvenienced with this investigation of yours every time I turn around."

So what else is new, Teddy thought, thinking Ryan should be doing this to begin with, without any reward.

"I won't leave the city," Ryan continued, "and I want you to hire a competent detective to do all the legwork."

"Okay. It's a deal," Teddy said. "I'll call Mr. Chang tomorrow. When do you want to meet him?"

"I mean highly competent, Ted. Not some stranger who shared an elevator with you."

"He'll be accomplished. I know it. When do you want to meet him?" Teddy repeated.

"On Wednesday, at lunch."

"Consider it done," Teddy said, smiling.

The train was now pulling out of the Clybourn Station, and Teddy could hear the conductor calling out in the next car.

"Northwestern Station next. Next, Northwestern Station."

Ryan neatly folded his paper and put it into his briefcase, then took out an individually wrapped moistened wipe, using it to meticulously clean the newsprint off his hands. He then handed the soiled cloth to Teddy. In an unspoken routine, Teddy used the other side of the wipe after him, then stuck it between the pages of his unread paper and shoved it all under his seat.

Without another word spoken between them, they left the train, and walked hurriedly through the terminal and out onto Madison. When they reached South Riverside Plaza, they would go their separate ways. Teddy turned off to go to his offices, and Ryan continued on to catch a bus on Wacker Drive. The bus would take Ryan to his private practice on Michigan Avenue. At night they always took different trains, and they would not see each other again until the next morning.

That evening, when Teddy and Terese had finally settled into bed to read, Teddy began thinking about Merak some more.

Teddy looked over at Terese, and watched her for a moment. She was lost in writing her novel, and never looked up.

Little Katie, who looked exactly as Terese did as a child, was sound asleep, lying between them on top of the comforter, all rolled up with her arm around a stuffed animal she favored.

He was so content for the moment, and felt lucky to have the life he led with Terese and their children. His family was his one bright spot. It would be so easy to forget it all, and let Merak go his way, and they theirs. But he knew in his heart that he could never take the path of least resistance. There was a voice, strong and powerful within him, that was leading him on his way—a voice that prompted him his every waking moment. It was the voice of his soul, and he could not help but listen to it.

Teddy pulled his covers back, and began getting out of bed.

"Where're you going?" Terese asked.

"I'm just putting Katie down," he said, as he reached over to where she was nestled next to Terese. He picked Katie up carefully, hardly disturbing her sleep.

Teddy looked in on the boys, as he carried Katie across the hall. He saw Leah on Matthew's bed, and stopped to give her a disapproving look. The wicker bed he bought for her, when they moved into the house, was on the other side of the room and had not had so much as a paw rest on it yet. Leah, without looking up again, got down from the bed to lie on the floor.

Teddy continued through to Katie's room and put her into bed, adjusting her stuffed toy and covering her. Katie moved over onto her side, and Teddy readjusted her cover, looking down at her. And who are you, he wondered to himself. She was such a sweet, happy child, and so easy to please.

Michael, who would turn ten in November, reminded Teddy of his older brother on Atlantis, as well as his American father. Michael had inherited his same good looks and large athletic build. His deep brown eyes were full of expression, and his sandy brown hair was already beginning to darken. Michael was the star athlete in the family, and Teddy was very proud of how hard he worked at perfecting his skills in sports. And, at

Teddy's prompting, Michael was now keeping his grades up to at least a B average.

As time went on, Teddy was increasingly convinced of little Matthew's likeness to his Atlantean grandfather. He was such a studious child. Teddy had noticed how Matthew would carry some of the exact same expressions on his face, and walk with that same certain gait, as his grandfather.

All of his movements were quick and swift, and Matthew had the same electric blue eyes, and very light blonde hair, as his grandfather did in his youth. Teddy knew Matthew would also grow up to have Teddy's build, and would be well over six feet tall. He had just turned six in February, and was already the tallest boy in his first grade class. He was exceptional at sports too, but preferred mental pursuits to physical ones. Teddy thought that was just as well. Michael needed to be better than Matthew at something.

But Katie was a mystery. Teddy was not sure about her. She was a beautiful child, but had much more going for her than that. Katie was full of fun and personality, and she definitely had the gift of gab. Even the boys seemed to have fun with Katie, and got along well with her. They would fight with each other, but never had either of them ever so much as raised their voice to her.

Katie's room, as well as one guest bedroom facing the front, was situated over the dining room, and Michael and Matthew's room was directly over the downstairs library at the back of the house. Teddy and Terese's bedroom and bath were placed directly above the living room, and their outside patio above the game room. The doors to all the bedrooms were in very close proximity, clustered around a small upstairs hall.

There were servants' quarters as well, in the eastern wing, with a staircase leading up just off the morning room and kitchen, but it was now used as an additional area for guests, even though it was separated from the west wing of the house. The Swensens preferred the privacy of their cottage, and Mattie, who worked under Mrs. Swensen during the week, went home to her family at night. So the space remained empty.

The new baby would now take the guest bedroom/nursery off the upstairs hallway, next to Katie and across from Terese and Teddy's room.

Terese and Katie had been working on decorating it together, and it was almost ready. Katie would be getting a little sister.

In their new home, which was currently under construction, these two rooms were to be combined so that the girls could share a bedroom. Terese felt that their children should always share rooms, as well as things, so that they would bond more quickly, and grow closer over time.

After putting Katie to bed, Teddy came out into the hall and went into Michael and Matthew's bedroom. He bent down and gave Leah a pat of approval, for she was still lying on the rug. He then walked over to Matthew's bed, and covered him with his light blanket.

When Teddy crossed over to Michael, he brushed back his hair from his face, noting that he needed to take the boys into town on Saturday for their haircuts.

"Dad...?" Michael questioned, opening his eyes.

"Are you still awake?" Teddy asked, sitting down on the edge of the bed.

"I can't sleep. They're picking the new pitcher tomorrow," Michael explained.

"You'll make it," Teddy whispered. "You're a great pitcher."

"I've been practicing a lot with Matthew," Michael said.

"I know you have, and you always pitched when you played in New York," Teddy reassured him.

Teddy watched Michael for a moment, and saw him relax.

"Do you always come in, and see us, when you work late?" Michael asked.

"I try to," Teddy said. "What's the matter, you think you're too big to be tucked in?" he teased.

"No, I like it," Michael admitted.

"What time do the tryouts start tomorrow?"

"Six o'clock at Deerpath," Michael said.

"I'll catch the 5:07 and meet you there," Teddy said, getting up from Michael's bed.

"Thanks Dad," Michael responded.

"Try to get some sleep now," Teddy urged when he reached the door.

Leah picked her head up off the carpet, as she watched Teddy go back to his room. She then got up, walking slowly to the door, and listened for a moment. When she heard Teddy climb into bed, she went back into the room and leaped up onto Matthew's bed, making a soft nest on his spread.

One single dim lamp lighted the upstairs hall. Teddy left the door open to their room that night, in the same way all the other doors were left open to the upper hall, so that he and Terese would be able to hear the children if they got up during the night and needed them. Once Teddy settled in, he closed the book he had wanted to read, and put it down on his night table.

Terese had a red pen in her hand, and was still busy working on her manuscript.

"How's it coming?" Teddy asked.

"Slow but sure," she said. "I'm almost finished with my first layer of the story."

"Can I read any of it now?" Teddy asked.

"It's not ready yet, Ted," Terese answered.

Terese always wrote things over and over again, before she would let anyone look at her work. It all came to her slowly, expanding layer-by-layer, in the same way an artist would work on a complex painting. Even Teddy, who she trusted would give her an honest critique, had to wait until she was satisfied with the inner structure. She never wanted to waste his time on earlier drafts, because the telling of the story would inevitably change.

Terese looked over at Teddy with a soft smile on her face, trying to catch his mood and thought.

Teddy soon looked up, meeting her eyes.

"What are you thinking about?" Terese asked.

"Ryan agreed to meet with Mr. Chang today," Teddy shared.

"He did?" Terese questioned, with surprise in her voice.

Teddy nodded. "We're meeting him for lunch in Chinatown on Wednesday."

"That's great," Terese said, putting down her manuscript. "I think I'd call that divine intervention. I can't believe you talked him into helping you."

Teddy laughed.

"I mean it," Terese continued. "That was no small miracle."

"Are you sleepy?" Teddy asked, covering a yawn.

"Just a little—not too," Terese answered.

Teddy leaned over to kiss her goodnight. "I'm bushed, I can't keep my eyes open," he said, as he kissed her once more.

Terese watched him for a moment, as he fixed his pillow and then rolled over, away from the light. Marking her place in her manuscript, Terese added the pages she was working on to the rest of the pile on her bedside table. And, after turning out the light, she eased down on her side moving closer to Teddy.

"You don't fit so well any more," he said tenderly, turning over on his back and putting his arm around her.

"Only 14 more weeks," she sighed.

Making Terese more comfortable, Teddy pulled her over to him so that she could rest her head on his shoulder. Lying there for a minute or two, comfortable in their closeness, Terese began drifting off.

"I know things haven't been easy for you, Terese, the last five weeks, with the baby coming, and all the research I'm doing at night."

"I don't mind picking up the slack around here," Terese said. "And I think you're doing the right thing."

"I feel so strongly about it," he explained.

"I know you do," she said. "Part of my loving you is because you do care so much. I never want you to be any other way."

"That means a lot to me, Terese," he said.

"I believe in what you're doing," she said, with a great deal of sincerity in her voice. "I will always believe in you."

CHAPTER 21

▲

MR. CHANG

Wednesday

Teddy had made a few inquiries about Mr. Chang on Tuesday morning, wanting to learn what he could about him before their meeting on Wednesday at noon. All Teddy really knew was that Mr. Chang's offices were located within the large Pagoda Building, at the corner of 22nd and Wentworth, across the street from Won Kow's. No one in Chinatown would give out any personal information about Mr. Chang. That was Chinatown, protecting the privacy of one of its own.

At eleven-thirty that morning, Ryan caught a cab outside of his Michigan Avenue offices, and picked up Teddy on the way. It took only about ten minutes before the cab they hired turned onto Cermak, then traveled the few remaining blocks to the marked entrance of Chinatown on Wentworth Avenue.

"We'll get out right here," Teddy said, as he reached into his pocket and paid the driver.

Once they were on the street, Ryan began complaining.

"Now why did you do that?" he asked. "He could have pulled in and driven us right down to Won Kow's. You're going to make us late, Ted."

"It's right here," Teddy said, looking over at the restaurant's entrance. "And that's where Mr. Chang has his offices, in the Pagoda Building right on the corner across the street."

The Pagoda Building looked as if it had been constructed in another century, and had been transformed from an ancient province somewhere deep in China. It stood out distinctly against the other shops on the street, with its red pagoda spires and curving turquoise tiled roof.

Ryan looked over at the Pagoda Building, and then over to their side of the street. "I don't see a restaurant here," Ryan responded.

"It's upstairs," Teddy pointed out. "Haven't you ever been to Won Kow's?"

"No," Ryan answered.

"You grew up on the South Side of Chicago, and your parents never took you to Chinatown?"

"No, not ever. They were always working in my father's tavern."

"Oh," Teddy responded. "Well, Won Kow's is Chinatown's oldest Chinese restaurant."

"How do you know that?" Ryan asked.

"Our firm had its Christmas party here last December, in their banquet facility. The restaurant opened in 1927, around the time this building was built."

Ryan just looked around, and they both climbed the staircase leading up to the restaurant.

"Don't you go out for Chinese, Ryan, when you're in the city?" Teddy asked.

"No, Jen cooks it for me at least once a week at home."

Teddy nodded. He thought Ryan was lucky to have such an efficient servant as Jen. He had been born in a northern province of China, but received the majority of his training in Hong Kong before coming to the United States. Teddy was sure that Jen had an interesting story to tell. He was a trained Houseman, and acted as a butler and cook. He did everything for Ryan, including his laundry and ironing.

As they were taken to their table, Teddy saw that they were ten minutes early, so they ordered tea.

"That building, the Pagoda Building across the street, has quite a history," Ryan shared.

"What do you mean?" Teddy asked.

"Well, the police shut it down about ten years ago, and sold the building and all its assets. It used to be the On Leong Building. The Chinese Merchants Association was there."

"Why were they shut down?" Teddy asked.

"Something about gambling in the basement, zero tolerance," Ryan revealed.

"That's interesting," Teddy responded.

"Jen told me that it was quite the Chinatown address at one time," Ryan continued. "It was within that building that the politicians, and powerful men of influence within Chicago's Chinatown, kept their heavily guarded offices. And it was there that the merchants of Chinatown kept court."

"Kept court?" Teddy asked.

"Chinatown took care of its own business disputes. They actually had a courtroom in that building. You should have seen the artifacts and things at the sale," Ryan finished.

"Did you go?" Teddy asked.

"No, but Jen did," Ryan responded.

"Who owns the building now?" Teddy asked.

"Well, On Leong tried to buy back the building when it was being sold off, but the police wouldn't allow it. It's called the Pui Tak Building now."

Before Ryan could say anything more, Teddy caught the eye of an elderly gentleman who was being escorted toward them. He looked to be retired, and in his seventies.

Mr. Chang greeted them, as soon as he reached their table. "You must be Mr. Townsend?" Mr. Chang said, in a friendly tone, looking directly at Teddy.

Teddy was immediately on his feet, extending his hand, with Ryan following. "Ted," he smiled, "and this is a friend of mine, Ryan Stuart."

"Ryan," Mr. Chang repeated, taking his hand.

Teddy had studied Mr. Chang's face, in an attempt to get an accurate first impression, as they shook hands. Mr. Chang's oriental skin had paled with age, yet his warm gray eyes were quick and reflective. His hair was thin, and as white as snow, and Teddy had noticed that when Mr. Chang stepped forward to greet them, he walked with a slight stoop.

His every mannerism reflected life of another era in China, yet his dress was definitely American. Mr. Chang was wearing a tan-colored spring suit, with a white tailored shirt, and a brown and beige tie. His dress was immaculate in appearance. Even his nails were meticulously manicured, and his hair was neatly trimmed. Unexpected were the pair of soft brown leather loafers that he wore on his feet. Teddy could not help but grin, when he noticed them, finding the shoes a very youthful touch.

After Mr. Chang was seated at their table, the waiter asked if they wanted a drink from the bar, however they all declined. Mr. Chang poured some tea, and they began to order.

Through the following hour, Mr. Chang learned much about Teddy and Ryan—where they had grown up, where they had gone to school, and where they now lived. In return, he had shared with them his early life in China, before he and his family moved to San Francisco in the 1930s, when he was still a young boy.

After the last course of food was served, and once the last of the dishes had been cleared away, Mr. Chang once again poured some tea and turned their conversation to business.

"You never mentioned, in your phone call, why you wanted to meet with me," Mr. Chang asked. "How can I help you?"

Teddy took a photocopy of the clipping of Merak walking up the steps of the White House from his pocket, and handed it to Mr. Chang. "We were hoping you could help us find this man," Teddy said, pointing to Merak.

Mr. Chang took a long careful look at the picture. "Who is he?" he asked.

Teddy looked at him, and then the picture. "That's what we need you to find out."

Mr. Chang stared at the picture for a long time, never looking up. "I have seen this man before, and a photograph of him, but I cannot say exactly where or when."

"You probably saw this same picture, and this article, carried in the *Tribune*," Ryan suggested. "It was an Associated Press story when it appeared in the Miami paper, and I'm sure many of the other newspapers in the country printed the same piece."

Mr. Chang looked up at Ryan, and smiled. "No," he responded politely, "it was not this picture."

"Do you think you can find him?" Teddy probed.

"May I keep this?" Mr. Chang asked.

Teddy nodded, and Mr. Chang began reading the opening paragraphs of the lead story, from the Miami paper.

"Why are you interested in finding him?" Mr. Chang asked.

"It's a very long story," Teddy related, "and very difficult to explain. Will you take the case?" Teddy asked.

"Yes. I will help you," Mr. Chang answered, slipping the copy of the article into the breast pocket of his suit. "I'm going to be out of town, on another matter, for a little more than a week, and then I will be able to start on your case, if that is acceptable."

"I'm a very patient man," Teddy smiled, meeting Mr. Chang's eyes.

"I will contact you at the appropriate time," Mr. Chang further informed, "as soon as I have located this man."

"Thank you," Teddy answered, in agreement.

"I hope you will forgive me," Mr. Chang apologized, standing up, "but I am late for another meeting."

"Of course," Teddy said, coming to his feet, with Ryan right beside him.

They both shook Mr. Chang's hand, and said goodbye, thanking him for his help.

"Please stay as long as you wish," Mr. Chang offered, quickly speaking to the waiter in Chinese, as he departed.

"He's probably late for his afternoon game of Chinese checkers," Ryan said, under his breath.

Teddy just looked at Ryan, apparently not amused.

After Mr. Chang had gone, the waiter came back to their table and brought them dessert.

"We didn't order this," Teddy said, to the waiter.

"Mr. Chang did," the waiter responded.

Teddy looked a little surprised. "Will you bring us the check, please?" Teddy asked. "And we would appreciate your calling a cab for us. We're heading back to the Loop."

"A cab will be waiting for you downstairs, Mr. Townsend. And you are Mr. Chang's guest. Everything has been taken care of."

"Thank you," Teddy returned, with a surprised look on his face.

"That was very odd," Ryan finally said.

"I thought it was exceedingly gracious of him," Teddy interjected. "And he didn't even ask for a retainer."

"You don't actually think he can find Merak, do you?" Ryan asked, with a chuckle. "He's just another senior citizen, trying to find something to do in the afternoon."

"You mean because he's old, he no longer deserves our respect—even though he has the knowledge and experience of an entire lifetime?"

"I wouldn't be surprised if he just had those business cards printed up a week ago," Ryan said, ignoring Teddy's point, and starting to laugh. "He's probably been dropping them in elevators all week, and you're his first case."

"I told you before Ryan, coming across this man was an omen. He's our connection to finding Merak."

"He's a powerless old man," Ryan commanded. "And I told you before, I don't believe in that intuitive stuff."

"Well then, you're in for a big surprise," Teddy returned, taking a fortune cookie and breaking it in half.

"Come on," Ryan said, standing up, "we'd better take our cab, or I'll be late for my conference."

But Teddy knew what they had found in this man. It would just be a matter of time before they heard from Mr. Chang. Teddy looked at his fortune, as they walked out onto the street, and then handed it to Ryan as they got in the cab.

The fortune read:

Someone from your distant past
will cross your path within two weeks.

Ryan looked at the fortune, and then shook his head in disagreement. Teddy just stared at him.

"Another omen?" Ryan asked, somewhat entertained.

"Another omen," Teddy confirmed.

"Where's mine?" Ryan grinned.

"I thought you didn't believe in these things?" Teddy asserted.

"Where's mine?" Ryan asked again, having seen Teddy swoop up the remaining cookies as he left the table.

Teddy pulled an almond cookie out of his pocket, removed the cellophane wrapper, and began eating it, as the cabdriver pulled away.

"Ted, where's mine?" Ryan asked for the third time, holding out his hand.

Teddy looked at him, and then his outstretched hand. "I left it on the table," he said.

"No you didn't."

"If it's that important to you, we can always turn around and go back," Teddy said, challenging him.

Ryan didn't answer him.

"Well, do you want to go back?" Teddy asked.

"No, I don't!" Ryan returned.

Ryan did not say another word for the rest of the ride back to the Loop, and Teddy could not wait to be dropped off so that he could read Ryan's fortune.

When they got to Teddy's building, Teddy got out of the cab, and handed the cabdriver a $20 bill through his open window.

Just before the cab began pulling away from the curb, Ryan could see Teddy take the other fortune cookie out of his pocket and crack it open.

Teddy smiled, as Ryan looked back giving Teddy an angry look.

Ryan's fortune read:

You will soon find true love.

CHAPTER 22

▲

THE REUNION

Friday

Teddy followed his usual routine on Friday, and spent the morning in court on a law and motion matter for a new case his firm had recently accepted.

The Hauser case involved litigation ensuing from an unfriendly takeover by a large conglomerate, and the men involved in the takeover were going to argue in open court that which they usually settled in private.

This was not a time that Teddy wanted to take on any heavy, complex litigation. And to complicate things further, the adversary in the takeover was a close, personal friend of his father. Teddy had assumed that his father was involved in the deal at some level, and wanted to remove himself because of an apparent conflict of interest. Although when Teddy called his father, and asked about it, his father denied any association with the case, or any business dealings with Hank Hauser.

It was a difficult call for Teddy to make. They were not close, Teddy and his father. His father was a closed-minded, strong-willed man, who had always been polite in his relationship with Teddy, but never warm or loving.

He provided for Teddy's monetary needs, saw that he was educated at the finest schools, and had association with the best families, but they had never done one single thing alone together. Teddy sensed that his father felt uncomfortable around him, but he never knew why. And, despite the love Teddy had for him as a child, that love was never returned, and there was a great distance between them now, as adults.

The only contact they had over the last 10 years was about the trust that his grandfather had arranged for him, through his estate, or during the Christmas holidays, when his parents wanted to see their grandchildren. His mother and father had openly disapproved of his marriage to Terese, first because she did not come from a wealthy, powerful family, and second because she was a Catholic, which Teddy eventually converted to.

His conversion to Catholicism was the final blow to his parents, and to their long-range plan concerning him. He had argued with his father that all other major Christian religions could trace their roots to either the Greek Orthodox Church, or the Roman Catholic Church, in that both of these churches have been in existence for over 2,000 years. But his father was adamant, and refused to listen to Teddy's reasoning.

It was not that the Catholic Church didn't have it faults. In truth, it was more the teaching at its inner core that Teddy really approved of. He also found that many Catholics agreed with this. It was the Church's ancient origin, its rituals, and its liturgy or rites, which were so sacred.

As far as Teddy was concerned, all religious institutions could be improved. And many of the churches today had people entering leadership positions within them who looked like men of light, but were actually quite dark in their nature. Many churches were paying the price for this, especially the Catholic Church.

However, there were still many good priests who were dedicated to doing good work in the world. Teddy and Terese both believed that priests should be allowed to marry, as was the case early on in the Catholic Church. They could never be compared to Atlantean priests and priestesses, who were hand-picked from the most highly educated and gifted of their population, with the aid of a special vision or sight, and had dormant lower natures that allowed them to be truly celibate.

Teddy's father had wanted him to marry a Presbyterian girl—especially the daughter of one of his banking friends. His father had been born and raised a Presbyterian, and so had his grandfather. And, that was to be the end of it.

He and Terese went on with their plans, and married in the Catholic Church, although his parents did not attend the wedding, which, to Teddy, was somewhat a relief, since they would have wanted to take control of the affair away from Terese's parents.

Terese had won both his parents over since then. Nonetheless, the early years, before their children were born, were more than a little tough on her. And Teddy and his parents had more than one argument, and ensuing separation, over that period of time about the way they treated Terese.

It was only when their grandchildren were born that Teddy's parents came around with a new attitude, for Terese was a wonderful, caring, and loving mother, and they eventually put their prejudices aside. Terese somehow forgave them their cruelty, although Teddy assumed that it was probably for the sake of their children.

Deep in his heart, Teddy had always known why he was having so much difficulty with his father. There was a wall between them, because his father wanted a wall between them. Why it surprised Teddy, when he was younger, he did not know—except that it seemed inherent in almost all of us, to seek the love and approval of our parents, even as we move into and through adulthood. Teddy sought to be accepted by them, because he had always been rejected.

Teddy's mother left him in the care of others, twenty-four hours a day, from birth. He had no siblings because she refused to get pregnant again, having already provided an heir, and not wanting to ruin her figure. Her life was filled with her friends, charities she wanted recognition for helping, and her social activities. She rarely had time for Teddy.

His father did everything for the sake of power and money. And, it was in that order that he wanted Teddy to serve him. They truly had nothing in common.

Teddy could spend the rest of his life trying, but he would never earn the love and acceptance of this man. His father had a greater need—a need to reject all that was good and decent in the world. Teddy had been born to an enemy. As it has been said before, there is always one person, in everyone's family, who sets an example of what not to be, or become. For Teddy, that was his father.

With all the ranting going on in his mind, Teddy was barely aware of the walk back to his offices from the courthouse. But he knew his father was somehow involved in the Hauser case, and he would eventually turn the stone he was hiding under.

Teddy resented having to take on this case, but he had no choice. This particular matter was centered in Chicago, and had been surrounded by a lot of publicity and newspaper articles. Not only was Teddy exceedingly competent to handle the litigation, but his firm also had expertise in the area. In addition, the income to the firm was too great to pass on, and allow one of their competitors to pick up. He had to take the Hauser case, despite his personal feelings, because of his commitment to his partners.

By the time Teddy arrived at the office, he felt better inside. It was almost as if running the thoughts that he had about his parents through his mind had cleared the air. He checked in with Reception, then went back to see Pat and get his mail and messages.

Pat Morgan was a valuable asset to Teddy, and worked for him exclusively. She was a tall, attractive, bronze-skinned woman in her late thirties. In addition to handling his legal work, she also took care of all his personal matters, including his finances and investments.

Having been with Teddy for a number of years at his law firm in New York, Pat also made the move to Chicago when Teddy accepted an offer to relocate. She too had ties in Chicago, having grown up there before going to New York in pursuit of a career in modeling.

When Pat married and began having children, her career faded. She had lost her husband six years later, and sought a secretarial position to support her family. Pat was hired as a legal trainee, and she and Teddy had been paired together ever since.

Teddy found Pat to be intelligent and hardworking, with excellent skills. Teddy was a young lawyer who needed someone equivalent to Pat at his side, and he had rewarded her loyalty consistently through the years. Teddy had made all the arrangements for Pat, and her children, to move to Chicago. He even insisted on making the down payment for her on a condo located on the north side, and the firm picked up all her moving expenses.

If Teddy had tried to find someone for Ryan, he had tried twice as hard for Pat, because of her children. Yet, he could never find anyone he thought was worthy of her, and would be a caring father to her girls. Teddy regretted that there had been no love connection between Pat and Ryan. They, in truth, had no attraction for each other. In fact, Pat thought Ryan to be a bit self-centered, and uptight.

Teddy had hoped the move to Chicago would be as pleasant for Pat, as it was for him and Terese. He knew it would put Pat in closer proximity to her family and many of her childhood friends. She did seem happier, since she had moved back to the Midwest.

When Teddy walked into his office, he joked around with Pat for a while, then got into his usual routine of going through his mail and the numerous other things that Pat had left for him that needed attention. Teddy had always found Pat comfortable to be around, and completely trustworthy.

Pat would always attach notes to everything she had handled, and was a signatory on his checking account, paying all his bills. That particular morning, she had flagged one of the bills with a note before paying it. It was for the initial down payment on the piece of lab equipment that Ryan had ordered, with the balance due in ninety days when it would be ready to be delivered. Ryan had wasted no time.

Teddy got up and walked through the door of his office to where Pat sat in her alcove. A picture of her two teenage daughters, 13 and 15, sat on her well-organized desk, and she was busy writing checks.

Teddy held Ryan's invoice in his hand. "Pat," he questioned, "Did this bill come in today?"

"Yesterday afternoon," Pat responded.

"There must be some mistake," Teddy said, examining the paperwork.

"It's for Ryan's new piece of research equipment," Pat accounted.

"Over $200,000 for a piece of equipment?" Teddy asked.

"That's what the man said. I even called the supplier—it's no mistake," she explained.

"What is it?" Teddy asked.

"It's a laser," Pat answered, "and when I called Ryan about it, he said to remind you that you promised it to him. Something about a favor you owe him?"

"I don't believe it," Teddy mused. "Get Ryan for me, will you?" he asked, as he went back into his office.

"He said something about selling a few of your petroleum shares," Pat called after him, trying not to laugh.

Soon Ryan was on the line.

"Ryan," Teddy said pointedly, "I don't think this is very funny."

"You said you would do anything, Ted. Consider it a charitable write-off."

"But it's a major piece of equipment. I didn't know you meant the laser itself!"

"You couldn't spend all the money you inherited from your grandfather in ten lifetimes, even if you wanted to," Ryan countered.

"Ryan, if I had you to support, it wouldn't last five years. I have my children to think of, you know."

"Are you backing out?" Ryan asked, challenging him.

"I'll think about it," Teddy said, pondering for a moment, and then changing the subject. "By the way, did you remember to reserve a court for tomorrow morning, at the same time the boys have their lessons?"

"8:00 a.m.," Ryan confirmed.

"Perfect," Teddy answered.

Just as they were finishing their conversation, Teddy saw Susan Woods pass by his door and look in for a moment. She was with another woman, and walked on when she saw he was talking on the phone. Teddy was virtually struck speechless. The woman with Susan was Ryan's Atlantean soul mate, Tiphane.

Teddy heard the buzz of an intercom on Ryan's end of the line, and before he could get out another word, Ryan was saying goodbye.

"I have to go Ted," Ryan said. "My other line."

"Wait," Teddy yelled, but Ryan was gone.

Susan Woods had gone, too. Teddy jumped up out of his chair and rushed to the door. He watched Tiphane walk away, wanting to make sure she was, in reality, the same individual he thought she was.

"I don't believe it," he murmured to himself, while walking back into his office. "Pat, get Ryan for me again, will you?"

However, Ryan was gone. He had just left for the hospital.

Pat came back to the door, and gave Teddy a very strange look. "You look as if you just saw a ghost or something. Are you all right?" she asked.

"Oh, yeah, I'm fine. That woman looked just like someone Ryan use to know. Who is she anyway?" Teddy asked.

"That's Anne Callahan," Pat said. "She's the attorney assigned from our New York office, to work with you on the Hauser case. I made arrangements for her to stay at the guest apartment that the firm keeps at the Hancock Center."

"Where'd she go?" Teddy asked.

"Susan's taking her around to meet everyone. She'll bring her back here a little later. Don't forget you're taking her to lunch this afternoon, I already made reservations."

"I'd almost forgotten about her arriving today," Teddy admitted.

At lunch, Teddy, Pat and two of his associates, who were also working on the Hauser case, took Anne down to a nearby restaurant, and got acquainted with her.

Teddy found he approved of Anne immediately. She was intelligent, in her late twenties, down to earth, naturally pretty, and had a good sense of humor. Teddy could not wait to tell Ryan about her.

After returning to the office, Teddy and Anne spent the remainder of the afternoon going over the research he needed for her to direct, and, when the day was gone, Teddy realized that he had not yet caught up with Ryan.

Teddy felt as if he were holding a winning lottery ticket and had not yet cashed it in. As soon as he got home that night, he told Terese the entire story. They had both tried to reach Ryan several times that evening, but he had not returned their calls.

Saturday

As soon as the boys met up with their instructor, Teddy and Ryan walked out to the tennis courts together, chatting casually.

"What are you doing tomorrow for Mother's Day?" Ryan asked.

"The children and I are shopping for presents this afternoon," Teddy answered.

"I still need to get something too," Ryan admitted.

"Do you want to come with us?" Teddy asked.

"Maybe I will," Ryan said.

"Tomorrow afternoon, the children and I are taking Terese and her parents out for lunch in the city after church, at Terese's mother's favorite restaurant. Then we're all going over to Terese's brother's place in Park Ridge for dinner."

"We're all taking my mother out too," Ryan said. "Then we're going back to my sister, Mary's place."

"I tried to reach you last night," Teddy said.

"I had a faculty thing at the end of the day that went late," Ryan explained.

"By the way," Teddy said, "the new attorney arrived to help me with the Hauser case, from our New York office."

"That should make things easier," Ryan responded.

"It's a woman," Teddy went on. "Very attractive, and very single."

"Oh, no you don't," Ryan said, catching the drift of what Teddy was up to. "No more blind dates. You and Terese have to have fixed me up with every single girl between here and Gary, Indiana."

"No we haven't," Teddy defended.

"And after the last one, at Christmastime, when you had that dinner party at your place, I'm through with being fixed up."

"Who?" Teddy asked, as he started laughing.

"Ted, she was cross-eyed and wore glasses an inch thick!"

"She wasn't cross-eyed, she had a slight astigmatism. And we weren't trying to fix you up with her. She was Matthew's teacher at school."

"Then why was she my dinner partner?" Ryan asked.

"That was Matthew's idea. He asked if you could sit next to his teacher."

"He did?" Ryan asked.

"Matthew thinks you're the scientific wonder of the world. The kid talks about you to everyone," Teddy explained.

"Oh," Ryan said, somewhat taken aback.

"In any event, I think you might enjoy meeting Anne, Ryan. This one I know you'll like," he said, assuredly.

Ryan gave him a critical look. "That's what you always say."

"We'll just do lunch," Teddy said.

"Do lunch?" Ryan asked. "Are we in Hollywood now?"

"We can take her over to The Four Seasons. That's close to you," Teddy added.

"The *Seasons Restaurant,* on the seventh floor?" Ryan asked, knowing how expensive it was.

"Yes," Teddy confirmed.

"Are you treating?" Ryan asked.

"Don't I always?" Teddy countered.

"I sometimes treat," Ryan defended.

"You mean the taffy apples you bought when we took the boys to the Lake County Fair last fall?"

"You make me sound as if I were some kind of a skinflint or something," Ryan protested.

"If the shoe fits," Teddy returned.

"Well, the shoe doesn't fit," Ryan, answered. "I give money to my parents every month, and I've put two of my sisters through medical school."

"How about if we make it a little more interesting," Teddy suggested. "Since you say you've never liked any of the women we've fixed you up with, I'll bet you your new laser that you will want to take her out again."

"Oh no you won't. We don't play with that," Ryan said.

"I thought you were sure you wouldn't like her?"

"I know I won't like her!" Ryan insisted.

"Oh, you'll like her," Teddy said, with confidence.

"You're always so sure of yourself, aren't you?" Ryan judged. "You know I hate lawyers, Ted, so she doesn't have the slightest chance."

"Then bet me," Teddy challenged.

"Okay, I will," Ryan, said. "But let me assure you of this, Ted," he said, raising his voice, "you're going to buy me my new laser. No one is worth losing that."

"It's a deal," Teddy assured him. "And you'll buy lunch, if you decide you want to see her again."

Ryan got a big smile on his face. "Yes, I'll buy lunch. You want to shake on it?" he asked, extending his hand.

"With pleasure," Teddy responded, accepting his hand and sealing the deal.

"Who is she, the playmate of the year?" Ryan asked, laughing.

"Actually, she's probably too good for you, but then you'll see what you've lost on Monday," Teddy confirmed.

"You're appallingly cocky for a man about to lose over $200,000, of unearned money," Ryan measured.

"I always go with my hunches," Teddy said. "And believe me Ryan, this is a predictive hunch."

Sunday

It was Mother's Day, and Teddy and the children fixed a special breakfast for Terese. Then, with much excitement and anticipation, the children woke her with cards and presents.

This was the one holiday that the children hosted, and Terese was always delighted with the handmade cards they gave her, and the thoughtful gifts they bought for her with their allowances. It was very endearing to her, being one of her favorite days of the year, and the only holiday when she did not have to do a thing.

Terese opened Teddy's card last. He had written a beautiful poem for her. The children helped him decorate her card, and then pasted the poem inside. It was all very touching, and brought tears to her eyes.

"There's one more thing," Teddy said, taking a small box out of his pocket and handing it to Terese.

As Terese opened Teddy's gift, she saw a beautiful ring, fashioned very much like one she had seen a very long time ago. She recognized it, immediately. When she lifted the ring out of its box and looked at the inscription on the inside, she began to choke up.

The inscription read:

One with the Divinity in You - Forever My Love

Terese looked at him, still with tears in her eyes. "Thank you, Ted."

Teddy just smiled at her.

"This is the nicest Mother's Day I could ever have imagined," she said. "I don't know what I did to deserve all of you in my life, but I will always be grateful. I must be the luckiest mother in the whole world."

Terese gave Teddy a warm kiss, and the children affectionate hugs, as they all piled up on the bed around her. It was a magnificent Mother's Day morning, and one Terese would never forget.

Mr. and Mrs. Swensen had driven up to their daughter's home in Wisconsin on Saturday afternoon, just north of Milwaukee in Whitefish Bay, and would not return until later that evening. However the children had done the same for Mrs. Swensen, as they were doing for their grandmother in Chicago. They had left their gifts and cards for her, hanging in a basket on the front door of their cottage, so that Mrs. Swensen would see them as soon as they returned home.

Directly after going to church, Teddy and the children took Terese into the city. In what would become a yearly tradition, they picked up Terese's parents, and then went out for a leisurely lunch together.

Afterward, they joined up with the rest of Terese's family at her brother's home, where her brothers and sisters were waiting with their families, to celebrate this special day.

Terese's mother was a very sweet and loving woman, and the family always made the day especially nice for her. It took quite a while for her to open all her gifts, and she loved having all her grandchildren together. The day finally wound down around eight that evening, after the entire family had dinner together. Then Terese, Teddy and the children headed back to Lake Forest.

When they pulled into the driveway, the family saw that the Swensens were back home. All the lights were on at the cottage, so Teddy, Terese and the children stopped in to wish Mrs. Swensen a happy Mother's Day. The children were also excited to know whether she liked their gifts. Teddy and Terese also gave Mrs. Swensen a card with a generous gift certificate to her favorite department store, so that she could shop for something special that she might need.

By the time everyone settled in for bed that evening, it was almost ten o'clock, but it had been a very fun-filled day.

Monday

On Monday at noon, Teddy and Anne Callahan took a cab to The Four Seasons Hotel, just off Michigan Avenue, on Delaware Place.

As they walked through the beautiful lobby of the hotel, Teddy answered some of Anne's questions about the city, but all the time he kept thinking about Ryan's reaction.

When they stepped off the elevator on the seventh floor, and walked through the restaurant's foyer, the warm and inviting dining room immediately came into view, with its perfectly appointed mahogany furnishings, and beautiful fresh floral arrangements. The Seasons Restaurant was known not only for its extraordinary cuisine, but also for its romantic atmosphere, even in the daytime.

Ryan had already arrived, and sat at their table reading a medical journal he had brought along, expecting Teddy would, for one reason or another, be late.

Anne gave Teddy a look of approval, and he knew he was in. With Anne at his side, Teddy walked through the dining room to where Ryan was seated. Ryan was so focused on what he was reading, that he was totally unaware they had arrived. He just continued to read, with his glass of orange juice clutched absentmindedly in his hand.

"Hi Ryan," Teddy said, interrupting him.

Looking up, Ryan's glass slipped from his hand, almost spilling all over the fresh tablecloth.

"Ryan, this is Anne Callahan," Teddy said, introducing them.

Trying to get up, Ryan banged his knee against the table, now spilling his orange juice across the entire table.

"Please, don't get up," Anne said, extending her hand, and seeing that they had disturbed him.

"Anne's working with me on the Hauser case," Teddy said, as if Ryan did not already know.

Ryan was now out of his seat, standing tall and straight in front of her. He found Anne breathtakingly beautiful, and, in that single instant, all of his hopes and dreams had come true.

Teddy finally caught Ryan's eye, and broke the silence. "Just say hello Ryan," he jested.

Ryan laughed, coming alive with personality. "I'm terribly sorry—you just look so similar to someone I knew a long time ago," he said, taking off his glasses.

Anne looked at Ryan's face. "You look familiar too," she said, "but I don't think we've ever met before."

"Well," Teddy said, with a huge smile on his face, "why don't you both sit down, and I'll ask the waiter to get some fresh linens for our table."

"What a beautiful hotel this is," Anne said to Ryan, trying to put him at ease, "and this restaurant, and the views," she added, "well it's just wonderful. I never pictured Chicago as quite so enchanting."

"Chicago is America's best kept secret," Ryan managed. "The people are great here."

"Yes, I've already seen that," Anne agreed.

Teddy came back with their waiter, who moved them to another table close to one of the windows, and they all settled in.

"May I get you something from the bar?" the waiter asked.

"Sure," Teddy said. "Anne?"

"I'll have a club soda with lemon," she said.

"And I'll have a ginger ale," Teddy ordered, "and another orange juice for Dr. Stuart."

"Thank you," the waiter said, leaving to get their order.

"You look as if you're a little nervous today," Teddy quipped, as the waiter left their table, "I do hope you don't have any surgery planned this afternoon?"

"No I don't, and I'm not at all nervous. I'm working in my lab this afternoon," Ryan defended.

"Oh?" Teddy responded, with a grin. "Reworking some equipment orders?"

"Something similar to that," Ryan intimated.

"The food here is delicious, Anne," Teddy said. "Please order anything that you think you might enjoy."

"Yes, please do," Ryan, added. "I'm treating today."

"Trust me," Teddy added, "money is no object. He's loaded."

Anne began laughing. "Have you two known each other for a long time?" she asked.

"Longer than you can imagine," Ryan said, as he looked over at Anne, with a smile on his face.

Everything seemed to be falling into place that afternoon. The day-to-day conditions of their lives seemed to be making a turn for the better. As it turned out, Ryan's fortune was answered first, and Teddy still believed Mr. Chang could find Merak.

CHAPTER 23

▲

ANNE

Friday

The week flew by for Ryan, and he saw Anne every single night. They were, from that very first meeting at the Four Seasons, inseparable. At the end of the week, Ryan invited Anne out to his home in Lake Forest for the weekend. No one moved faster than Ryan when he wanted something.

Anne, in turn, was virtually overwhelmed by Ryan. He was tall and handsome, intelligent and protective, and her ideal in a man. As she thought back over her entire life, she had never felt this way before. The fact that Ryan was such an intellectual was another comfort to Anne, as she knew she would never have to hide her own intelligence for fear of intimidating him. She could truly be herself.

Anne could not help but think that destiny had somehow come into play. However, Anne accepted such turns in fate, for it brought her Ryan. And, exactly as was the case with Terese, Anne believed in dreams, for she had dreamt of meeting someone like Ryan several times in the past year. He had always come out of nowhere, when she visited a city on the water. It seemed very odd when she thought back about it. In her dreams though, she could never quite make out his face.

Moreover, one needed only to watch the way Ryan looked at Anne to know how deeply he felt about her, and Anne responded to him in turn. She knew in her heart that Ryan was the man she had been looking for all of her life. Anne had been raised by very loving parents. And she thought

Ryan would be a kind and attentive partner, and father. Anne wanted a large family, and she wanted to be a traditional mother, staying at home and caring for her children. Her career could be put on hold. Anne had begun falling in love with Ryan on their second date.

On Friday afternoon, after a late lunch with Teddy and Pat, Anne left the office and went home to pack a weekend bag. She left the firm's apartment with Ryan at four, and they soon caught a cab on Michigan Avenue that took them to Northwestern Station. They planned to take the train out of the city together to Lake Forest, rather than drive, or hire a car, and fight the Friday night traffic.

As the commuter train moved north out of Chicago, Anne saw one small, charming lakefront town after another. Each community had its own personality, but all were quaint. Anne felt excited, as they pulled into Lake Forest.

Lake Forest's turn-of-the-century stationhouse, that carried the same English Tudor framing as did much of the Market Square, had a decorative low black iron gate, separating the parking area from the tracks. Even the lampposts and benches were of an old-fashioned design.

Jen was waiting for them on the train station platform, and quickly took Anne's bag to the car. When they arrived at Ryan's house, only a short distance from the station, Anne was impressed. Jen had already prepared the guest room for her, and he quickly brought Anne's bag up to her room, then put her things away.

The house was spotlessly clean, and Jen had placed a round table for two on the back screened-in porch. The table was already set with beautiful china and silver, and tall, tapering candles were set off to the side to light when they sat down to dine. Jen had also prepared a feast of Chinese food in the late afternoon, which was ready to cook.

As night fell, the large tangled oaks in the backyard conveyed an enchanting atmosphere, with indirect lighting beaming up through their rich green foliage. Up-lighting the trees was an idea Ryan had, after attending a concert at Ravinia one night, and the lighting created a very romantic setting.

Ryan had never invited anyone for the weekend before, other than family, and Jen had noted the tremendous change in his disposition throughout the week. Jen had always believed Ryan would never marry, but not now. It was quite apparent to Jen, as it was to everyone else, that this was a very serious encounter.

After eating the elaborate meal that Jen had prepared, Ryan and Anne sat and talked until two in the morning. Once again, Ryan, despite the passion he felt for Anne, took her to the door of the guest bedroom, and kissed her goodnight. He wanted much more than a physical relationship with Anne, and with Anne's natural beauty, he knew that men came at her in droves.

Anne was so touched by Ryan's genteel demeanor, she was even more convinced that he was perfect for her. As an absolute rule, Anne would never date a man twice who came on too strongly with her, or mentioned any kind of sexual inferences in their first encounters. She knew, too well, that that was how insincere men tested the water, to see how easy a woman was. Anne had never been easy, and she was always offended by such gestures.

As the early morning hours went by, Anne found it difficult to fall asleep. She reviewed, over and over again, the past week she had spent with Ryan. They had gone out to the theater, attended a concert, taken walks through the park, and eaten dinner together every night. It had been the happiest week of her entire life, and she hoped Ryan was as serious about her as she was about him. Her greatest fear was that she was falling in love too quickly with Ryan, and that she might be confusing his affection for her by making their relationship into more than it actually was.

Saturday

When they had finished a leisurely breakfast together, Anne and Ryan took a walk down to the lake. Hand-in-hand they strolled along, as the path they took wound its way through the lakefront park, with its high cliffs separating it from the shore of Lake Michigan below.

"Would you prefer to go down and walk along the water?" Ryan asked.

"Sure," Anne said. "I'd enjoy that."

Anne could not get over how beautiful Lake Michigan was. It was as if she were looking at the Atlantic Ocean, for she could not see across it, nor could she see either end in any direction.

"I never realized this was such a big lake," Anne said.

"It's about 300 miles, running north to south," Ryan remarked. "It was formed during the glacial periods, and its depth reaches over 800 feet off of northern Wisconsin."

"You must be kidding," Anne said.

"No, it's true," Ryan continued, "and it can have a dangerous undertow at times, as well," he added.

"It almost sounds mysterious," Anne said.

"I guess it is mysterious," Ryan said, thoughtfully. "Ted told me once that it's believed to have a triangle within it, comparable to the one off Bermuda. I know the lake can be treacherous to sail on, when the winds start shifting."

"A triangle?" Anne questioned.

"Of course I don't, in truth, believe that," Ryan admitted.

"It looks so beautiful and peaceful today," Anne said, as they made their way down a narrow drive.

Once they reached the lakefront, Ryan and Anne continued their walk along a curving cobblestone pathway. As they made their way down to a green grassy area, with trees that separated the sandy shoreline from a parking area, a warm soft breeze seemed to enhance the romantic setting.

A series of T-shaped jetties, built from large blocks of a light-colored quarried stone, came out from the beach, and were designed to protect the sand from erosion. The jetties created calm pools for small children to play in, with openings to the lake beyond.

Anne could see several boys and girls bobbing up and down on large truck-sized inner tubes, as they played with the gentle waves coming in to shore.

"Anne?" Ryan asked, as they walked along, "Have you ever considered marrying, and having a family?"

"Yes I have," Anne smiled, "if the right man asked me."

Ryan stopped for a moment, and turned facing her. "Am I the right man?" he asked, looking into her eyes.

Anne was so touched with how direct, and vulnerable, he was with her. "You're the right man," Anne finally answered, feeling elated.

Ryan took in a deep breath, and laughed. "I have to be the luckiest guy in the world," he said.

Anne smiled, as she looked up at him. "I guess it's to my advantage to let you continue to believe that," she joked.

In what was a very moving moment, and in lieu of a ring that he had not yet purchased, Ryan placed around Anne's neck the beautiful triangular charm she had worn so many thousands of years before. As he looked at her, with the onshore breeze sweeping through her dark, shiny hair, Ryan kissed her once, and then again more deeply. And Anne responded to him, as he hoped she would, as her body relaxed into him. Falling in love with Anne was more than Ryan had ever hoped for. His life was now complete.

Ryan and Anne went to Teddy and Terese's for dinner that same evening, so that Anne could meet Terese and the children, and they all celebrated Anne and Ryan's unexpected engagement.

Terese and Anne liked each other immediately, and were soon on their way to renewing the life-long friendship that they had shared during the years they spent in the Southern Americas, after leaving Atlantis.

Terese could not get over the change that Anne had made in Ryan, as they all spent a wonderful evening together. She had never seen him so happy, and was amazed with how totally relaxed he was with Anne. Terese could instantly feel the chemistry they had for each other—it was almost sparking

Sunday

Ryan drove Anne back into the city on Sunday afternoon, and introduced her to his family. He was totally immersed in her, and he wanted nothing more than to plan his life with Anne. She was the first person he thought of upon waking in the morning, and the last person he thought about before falling asleep at night.

Despite the fact that an entire week had gone by, Ryan remained totally unaware of the fact that they had not yet heard from Mr. Chang, and he had never once thought about Merak.

Teddy looked through his own wallet, and took out six hundreds, followed by three fifties, two twenties, a couple of fives and four ones, and he started counting.

"Let's see, that's $884."

"That's $804, not $884, and, with mine, it 's $904," Ryan corrected.

"Oh, terrific. $904," Teddy repeated.

They were now pulling up to the Continental Airlines departure curb, and Teddy jumped out.

"Ryan, call Terese and Pat for me when you get back. Tell Terese what happened, and tell Pat that something unexpected came up, and to cancel my afternoon appointments. I'll call everyone tonight," Teddy said, excitedly.

Ryan sat back shaking his head, as he watched Teddy run up to the attendant at the curb, who had just taken Merak's bags. He looked at one of the tickets hanging off the side. It read "GVA."

"Is this the bag belonging to the gentlemen who just got out of that limousine?" Teddy asked.

"Yes sir. Are you on the same flight? You better hurry. It leaves at 1:15, and you have to go through security. I have to get these bags in."

"I just need to get a message to him. What's the flight number?" Teddy asked.

"Flight 1188 to Newark, and you better hurry."

Teddy turned around and looked at Ryan, who already had his window down, and was listening to the conversation.

Ryan just shrugged his shoulders, as Teddy turned and disappeared into the terminal. It was only then that Ryan realized Teddy had left him with not even so much as a dollar to pay the cabdriver.

"Where to next mister?" the cabdriver asked.

"The nearest ATM," Ryan answered.

Teddy ran into the terminal, and up to the Continental ticket counter. He stood in line impatiently, behind several other people who were trying to get on a Continental plane after another airline had cancelled their flight.

Teddy could not imagine why Merak was going to Newark, instead of JFK or LaGuardia, unless it was just the time of day. He did not have time to check now, and he regretted not having his laptop with him.

Finally the clerk was free, and Teddy plopped his wallet down on the counter. "First Class, one way ticket, Flight 1188, please." Teddy informed, showing his identification and giving the clerk his American Express card.

"Your name, sir?"

"Theodore Townsend."

"Do you have a reservation?" the agent asked, checking his screen.

"No, I don't," Teddy, responded, impatiently.

"You have to have a reservation, sir."

"You mean I can't buy a ticket at the airport?" Teddy asked.

"Not with security as it is," the agent informed.

"Where's a phone?" Teddy asked, realizing he left his cell phone with Ryan.

"I am not sure if you have time to get on that flight, sir. You have to go through the Security Check Point."

"Where's a phone?" Teddy asked again.

The clerk pointed to the bank of phones, and Teddy went directly over to them, looked up Continental's 800 number, and then called and made the reservation. Within a few minutes, he was back in line at the ticket counter, and speaking to the clerk.

"Can I help you?" the agent asked.

"Theodore Townsend, E-Ticket, Flight 1188," Teddy said.

The clerk checked his terminal. "There's only one seat left sir, in first class."

"I know," Teddy said, feeling impatient.

"Your identification sir?"

Teddy pulled his license, and a credit card, out of his wallet, while the clerk made note.

"Any luggage sir?"

"No luggage, just my ticket."

"You're in 3F, Mr. Townsend."

"Which way do I go?" Teddy asked, putting his identification back into his wallet.

The clerk pointed down the corridor, and he gave Teddy the information as to the concourse and gate number of his flight.

"You'll have to run for it, sir."

Teddy took off, while the clerk was still speaking to him, and he luckily eased right through a short line at the security checkpoint. Moving hurriedly down the concourse, he avoided the crowds of people as best he could. When he reached his gate, everyone had just finished boarding. He was the last to go through the tunnel and board the plane.

It was a Boeing 737, and Teddy was familiar with the seating in first class, as the stewardess directed him to his seat. 3F was at the back, on the right side of the 10 First Class seats—consisting of three rows on the left, and two rows on the right—with two generous seats, on each side of the aisle, in each row.

The plane was soon closed tight, and started to taxi out to the runway. When the 737 took off from O'Hare Field, it headed east across the continent toward the Atlantic.

After they were in the air a short time, Teddy unhooked his seat belt, stretched, and looked around the first class cabin. He spotted Merak at the far left side, in the front row. Merak's two seats were isolated, with no one on his right. The galley was situated almost opposite his seating, a little farther to the front. A wall and a lavatory were located directly in front of him.

Teddy decided to walk up to the lavatory, to get a better look at Merak and the man sitting next to him. However, Teddy did not recognize the other man. Nor was he able to catch any of their conversation before slipping into the lavatory.

When Teddy returned to his seat, he realized that the man sitting next to him had also been with Merak. He was the same man who had been carrying a package as they exited the shopping center. Teddy wondered whether this man, seated a respectful distance away from Merak, might be his valet. He looked as if he could be a gentleman's servant. English, perhaps, Teddy thought. The suit he wore was well tailored, if not expensive, and appeared to be somewhat worn.

When Teddy attempted to start up a conversation with the man, the gentleman only nodded, in a non-committal sort of way, and went back to reading the English publication he had with him.

About thirty minutes into the two-and-a-half hour flight, while beverages and hors d'oeuvres were being served, Merak got up from his seat to bring his briefcase back to his valet.

As soon as Merak stood up, his valet was also on his feet, and began walking quickly down the aisle to meet Merak.

"I signed the necessary documents," Merak informed him. "See that they are couriered, as soon as we touch down."

"Yes, Mr. Martel," the valet acknowledged.

Teddy perceived no discernible accent in Merak's voice, as he spoke. But then, he thought, he is a true magician, and can sound any way he wants to sound. The valet was definitely English.

Teddy remained quietly gazing out the window, but he could feel Merak's eyes penetrating right through him. He suddenly felt his heart begin racing, in the way it will when you feel you are in danger, or you are in the presence of a dominant force of evil.

Looking up, Teddy met Merak's overly large, piercing, deep brown eyes, as he stared down the aisle to where Teddy was sitting.

Merak said nothing, but had a somewhat surprised look on his face.

Teddy suddenly realized that he had stopped breathing, and attempted to draw in a long deep breath, slowly through his nostrils. He had never known this kind of fear before, and he tried to calm himself, looking back out the window.

Teddy knew this man could be a dangerous enemy. After all, he had taken on two of the most powerful Magicians on Atlantis—and won.

At that single moment, Teddy wished he had taken to wearing his protective pendant, but, of course, he had not. He was definitely on his own with this man, and would have to protect himself by his own means.

Fortunately, a stewardess came up the aisle. She was pushing a cart, covered in a long crisp tablecloth, filled with plates of hors d'oeuvres. Teddy was glad to have the interruption. It would give his body time to settle down, and adjust to what it was sensing.

"Mr. Townsend?" the stewardess asked, "would you like a glass of wine?"

"Not for me," Teddy responded.

She then showed him her selection of hors d'oeuvres.

"It all looks good," Teddy said, asking her to make up a plate for him.

The stewardess smiled, and made a selection for him.

"Do you by any chance have today's New York Times?" Teddy asked.

"Yes, I do," the stewardess responded. "I'll get it for you on my way back."

"Thanks," Teddy said.

Merak, or Martel, seemed to recognize him, but Teddy did not know how that could be. It was in the way Martel had looked at him, studying Teddy's face.

Perhaps, in the same way Teddy had sensed an evil entity, the evil entity within Merak sensed the presence of a powerful source of light. Evil always hates, and tries to destroy, that which is good. And Teddy was a good and compassionate man. Or was it that Merak recognized Theos from Atlantis?

Teddy thought of "The Great Invocation." It was an ancient and powerful prayer. Fear no evil, Teddy thought to himself, as he tried to remember the words. The prayer was so old that the source was unknown. It contained many stanzas, each relevant to different periods in history. He had found one of its stanzas in the front of each of 18 volumes of metaphysical works, written by Alice Bailey, that were delivered to the house when he first began his research. He had made an effort to memorize it.

Slowly, the words came back to him, and, when Teddy had finished the prayer, he repeated the last lines over to himself, again and again. *Let the Plan of Love and Light work out, and may it seal the door where evil dwells. Let Light and Love and Power Restore the Plan on Earth.*

Martel and his servant were still standing in the middle of the wide aisle when the stewardess returned.

"May I get you something, Mr. Martel?" she asked.

"No, I'm going back to my seat," he said, pushing past her.

"I'm sorry," the stewardess apologized. "I didn't mean to interrupt your conversation," she said, noting that she had angered him.

Martel did not speak again.

Teddy watched Martel go back down the aisle, with his servant close behind him, the briefcase clutched tightly in his hand.

"Do you know Mr. Martel?" Teddy asked, in a low voice.

"Oh yes, he takes this flight every week," she said.

"His first name is Michael, isn't it?" Teddy asked.

"Oh, I thought it was Marshall," she returned. "Marshall Mason Martel."

"That's right," Teddy, repeated, "Marshall Mason Martel."

"He looks as if he has money," Teddy said, in an attempt to keep the conversation going. "Not too many individuals travel with an entourage."

The stewardess, laughed. "I only know that he is involved with a large European banking concern. I can't remember the name."

"Oh, yes, I think you're right," Teddy said, in a relaxed way, a warm smile coming across his face.

It was apparent that the stewardess was attracted to Teddy, even though he wore his wedding ring, and she attempted to continue the conversation.

"He's not very friendly," she added.

"Not very," Teddy agreed, with a smile.

Teddy was thankful that the loud, monotonous sound of the jet's engines drowned out their conversation. Because of this, Martel would not be able to hear them, but Teddy continued to keep his voice low, just in case.

"I read an article about him recently in the *New York Times*," the stewardess divulged enthusiastically, handing him the paper. She spoke of Martel almost as if he were a celebrity.

"You did?" Teddy acknowledged.

"They've just recently opened offices in New York, and I think Chicago," she said. "There was a picture of Mr. Martel," she added, "I think he's the Chairman of the Board."

"I guess he's a very important man," Teddy responded, hoping she would tell him more. "Could it have been a Swiss firm?" Teddy asked, knowing how liberal Swiss banking laws were.

"I don't remember," the stewardess said. "But he's been a regular on this flight once a week for the last three months. I remember him because he always refuses service. He won't even accept a cold drink," she continued, smiling. "By the way, may I offer you a cold beverage?"

"I'll have a ginger ale, if you have any," Teddy requested.

"Coming right up," the stewardess smiled, turning to go back down the aisle.

As the stewardess stepped away, Teddy took the opportunity to look over at Martel again. The man sitting next to Martel, was now looking over his shoulder in Teddy's direction, and their conversation had abruptly stopped.

Martel took back the briefcase, and the servant returned empty handed, never once meeting Teddy's eyes. The valet soon picked up his periodical, and began to read. Teddy remained silent, thinking it best not to stretch his luck by offering any unwanted conversation.

The stewardess soon came back with Teddy's beverage, and he too began to read. Or, at least, he pretended to be engrossed in his reading, until dinner was served. He could not even remember what was on his plate, he was so lost in thought. This was definitely going to be a long journey, but he finally had Marshall Mason Martel in sight.

The plane landed in Newark right on time, at 4:20 p.m. East Coast time, and Teddy quickly deplaned then stayed behind, so that he could follow Martel.

It soon became obvious, that Martel was not leaving the airport. Instead, he and his party walked down the concourse, and went into Continental's President's Club. Martel was continuing on to another destination. Now Teddy wondered where?

He could not imagine where they were going. And then, Teddy remembered the luggage tag in Chicago, marked "GVA." At the time he had assumed it to be an old tag, not yet replaced, in that the attendant at the curb had said Newark.

Teddy walked back to their gate, and up to a Continental employee, setting up for an arriving flight.

"Excuse me, may I ask you a question?" Teddy asked.

"Yes, of course," the agent responded.

"The airport call letters GVA, that's still Geneva, Switzerland, isn't it?" Teddy prompted.

"Yes, Geneva Switzerland," she confirmed.

"Does Flight 1188 connect with another flight, and then go on to Geneva?" Teddy questioned.

"1188 connects with Continental Flight 80, and continues on to Geneva in about two hours," she said, looking down, and checking her screen. "Flight 80 leaves Newark at 6:15 p.m., and arrives tomorrow morning at 7:55 a.m. in Geneva."

"Are there any First Class seats left?" Teddy asked.

"You'll have to make a reservation through Continental's reservation line. Let me get you our 800 number."

"Thank you," Teddy said, wishing he had written it down before.

"It's Flight 80, leaving at 6:15 this evening," the clerk reminded him. "You'll have to get over to Terminal C."

"What terminal is this?" Teddy asked.

"This is Terminal A," the clerk advised, "but the Air Train runs every few minutes, and will get you right over to Terminal C. Our international flights leave from there."

"Thank you," Teddy said.

"You'll see the signs," the clerk added.

Teddy remembered where he had seen a bank of phones, quickly made his way towards them, and called Continental's 800 number. He soon booked a First Class seat on Flight 80. He next called Terese, and then Ryan and Pat.

Teddy wondered whether Martel and his party had made their way over to Terminal C yet. He was now thinking that they had stopped at the President's Club just to take care of connecting with the courier to deliver the documents Martel mentioned. Teddy now had time to pick up a few things at one of the terminal shops, so that he would have shaving gear and a change of clothes once he got to Geneva.

Just after Teddy passed the President's Club, Martel and the others came out behind him. Once again, a feeling of fear came over him, and Teddy tried to be as casual as possible. He followed the signs to the Air Train, and immediately boarded. As he took his seat, he could feel Martel's eyes penetrating right through him again.

Even if he did not yet know who Teddy was, Martel knew that Teddy was pursuing him for information. Information he would never get.

It had never occurred to Teddy to guard against Martel's telepathy. He should have been watchful of this, for the ability to pick up another's thoughts is not as uncommon as people might think.

Teddy soon became aware of Martel's threatening stare. He took out his gold pen, and began working the *New York Times* Crossword Puzzle, pretending not to notice them at all. Once again, Teddy found he was not breathing, and he began repeating to himself, mentally, *The Great Invocation* for protection. Almost immediately, Martel seemed to disconnect from him.

The Air Train soon pulled into Terminal C, and Teddy followed Martel and his party off the train. The tension in the Air Train had been unmistakably heavy, and the ride unbearable. When Teddy looked down, he saw that Martel was clenching the handle on his briefcase so tightly that his knuckles were white. Teddy could see the initials "MMM" on the combination lock plate.

As they went forward, Teddy turned to go to the ticket counter to get his E-ticket and boarding pass.

"I'm Theodore Townsend, I believe you have an E-Ticket for me for Flight 80 to Geneva," Teddy said, taking out his identification.

"Oh, yes," the clerk said, continuing with his paperwork. "Your passport, Mr. Townsend?"

Suddenly it hit him. He, of course, did not have his passport.

"I'm sorry," Teddy, said, going through the motions of looking in his inside jacket pockets, "I seem to have left it at home."

"Mr. Townsend, you can't go to Switzerland, without a valid passport."

Teddy now realized that it all ended right here. Martel would go on his way, and Teddy would never find him again. As he walked away from the ticket counter, Teddy began thinking through what his next move would be.

He was almost certain that if Martel did open an office in Chicago, there would be no business listing under Martel's name. He was not the kind of man to list his residence phone either. So having just his personal name, and not the name of his company, or banking concern, had its limits.

Teddy planned to visit Chicago's large downtown library, to try to find the *New York Times* article the stewardess had mentioned, as soon as he could. Perhaps, Teddy thought, Mr. Chang now had a copy of the same article from his investigation. Mr. Chang had mentioned, at lunch, seeing Martel's picture before. He would call Mr. Chang first. Teddy was truly disappointed.

And so it was over, or so he thought. Teddy could now see that two men were following him. He had been aware that these same two men had come out of the President's Club shortly after Martel's group, but Teddy did not realize they were all together, since there had been quite a distance between them.

Teddy avoided making any eye contact with either of them, but was acutely aware of them watching his every move. He now knew that Martel must have contacted someone in flight, and made arrangements for the men to meet him at the airport. Now, Teddy had to lose them before catching his flight back home. The last thing he wanted was for them to know who he was, and where he lived.

Teddy thought for a moment, trying to decide whether to get back on the Air Train, grab a cab, or order a limousine and head to New York City. A real sense of panic suddenly came over Teddy, and his soul was warning him to fear for his life. He now realized that the Air Train was not a good idea. That would only give them the opportunity they needed to get Teddy alone.

When Teddy stepped outside of the airport's doors, he saw a line of cabs forming, and walked to the front, where a manager was handling the order of the cabs that were filling with passengers.

Teddy handed him a hundred dollars. "Two men are following me. Please make sure they have difficulty getting the next cab."

The manager looked behind Teddy, and saw two men quickly approaching. "I'll do my best, mister."

Teddy nodded, and got into the cab. "I need to get to Trump Towers, in New York City, as soon as possible," Teddy said, after he shut the door tight.

"I'm almost off shift," the driver began.

"I'll make it worth your while," Teddy, said, pulling a couple of hundred dollar bills out of his wallet, and handing them to the driver.

"Trump Towers," the cabdriver repeated, as he flicked his meter and started off.

When Teddy looked back, he could see quite a ruckus behind him. The two men had shoved past the cab manager, knocking him to the ground, and quickly got inside the next cab. But the cab never moved. When the driver saw there was trouble, he quickly took his keys and exited the car. Teddy watched, as two security officers ran over and the two men were removed and escorted away. Teddy turned back around, and settled into his seat. He was very lucky—very lucky indeed.

When Teddy reached the Trump Towers, he went to a phone, ordered a ticket back to Chicago out of JFK, and took another cab to the airport.

Friday Evening

It was late when Teddy reached home. After eating a cold plate of chicken salad and fruit that Mrs. Swensen had left for him in the refrigerator, he showered the day off of himself, then checked on the children before climbing into bed alongside Terese.

Teddy never told Terese the whole story, for fear it would worry her too much. He only conveyed to her that he had learned that Merak was now Marshall Mason Martel, and the head of a banking concern. It had been a very long day, and he was glad to be home.

CHAPTER 25

▲

THE BREAK-IN

Monday

Ryan pulled his car into the Lake Forest Train Station early on Monday morning. He could readily see that the sky was beginning to darken and cloud over again. A storm had moved through the area during the night, and it looked like more was on the way. Because of this, Ryan had decided to drive to the station that morning rather than walk.

After placing his usual order of donuts and coffee at the station stand, Ryan walked over to the north side of the stationhouse, and looked out a large window to see if Teddy had arrived yet.

Ryan had picked Teddy up at O'Hare Airport on Friday night, and had learned all about Teddy's excursion to New Jersey, and New York, on the way home. As Ryan thought back on the events of Friday afternoon, he secretly hated being left behind at the airport, but his life was far more restrictive than Teddy's. He had patients he was responsible for, and could never leave town at a minute's notice without providing for their care.

Watching the movement of trees out the train station window, Ryan could see that the breeze had begun to pick up, and that he had forgotten to grab the extra umbrella in the trunk of his car. Rain began pattering on the windowpanes and, as Ryan looked beyond the spattered marks, he could see Teddy's car cross over the tracks and come into the lot. Then, alarmingly, he also saw that two men, in a dark blue car, were following him.

Ryan kept his eyes focused on the blue car. He watched as the man on the driver's side rolled his window halfway down, and stared intensely at Teddy. Horrified, Ryan saw the driver slowly take a gun out from underneath his suit jacket. With its silencer attached, the driver pointed the barrel of the weapon directly at Teddy, steadying his shot.

Frantically, Ryan attempted to open the locked window, to call out a warning to Teddy, but the window was stuck shut. Then, abruptly, with a loud crack of thunder, the sky opened up and it began to pour. Teddy quickly sprinted the rest of the way to the stationhouse, and the gunman lost his opportunity.

As soon as Teddy came in through the door on the west side of the lot, Ryan, unseen, went out the east side to get a better look at Teddy's pursuers.

The two men had just pulled into a parking space alongside two other cars, close to the cobblestone platform. As soon as the driver saw Ryan's fast approach, he rolled up his window and appeared to begin a casual conversation.

Ryan avoided any eye contact with either of them, and instead looked beyond them to where his car was parked at the far end of the lot. The driver watched his every move, as Ryan unlocked the trunk of his car and removed his umbrella.

The men soon seemed relieved that he was no one of importance, and focused once again on the stationhouse, waiting for Teddy to come out.

With his umbrella now protecting him from the heavy rain, Ryan walked back toward the train station. Once he reached the car where the two men were sitting, he glanced down at the license plate number and made a mental note. Then, wanting to get a better look at the two men, he approached their car from the rear, and knocked on the window at the driver's side of the car.

It was apparent the two men were caught by surprise. They looked startled when they saw Ryan peering in. Slowly, and cautiously, the driver reached his right hand into his suit jacket, and rolled down his window four or five inches, giving Ryan an unfriendly look.

Bending over to get a better view of them, Ryan greeted the men in a friendly tone, and pointed to the car's rear tire.

"It looks as if your right rear's a little low," he said.

"Thanks," the man said, without much expression, letting Ryan know by the look on his face that they did not appreciate the intrusion.

"Sure thing," Ryan answered, before the window was shut tight.

Lightning streaked across the darkened sky, as thunder rumbled overhead and the rain continued to pour, coming down even more heavily now. Ryan turned away, picking up his pace, as he headed back to the stationhouse. He used the same door Teddy had entered and then looked around for him.

"Where'd you go?" Teddy asked, holding the bag of coffee and donuts that Ryan had ordered.

"You're being followed," Ryan said, privately, keeping the tone of his voice low, so that no one else could hear him. "Don't look out the window, and don't talk to me right now. They're in a Buick Park Avenue—dark blue."

"Ming Blue?" Teddy asked.

"How am I supposed to know, it's navy blue with some metallic in it. They're at the end of the lot where you always park your car." Ryan lowered his voice again. "Ted, the driver has a gun."

"Okay," Teddy said, walking away.

Hearing the train-crossing warning bells in the distance, Teddy followed everyone, who had been waiting for the train, outside. He stayed to the center of the group, as everyone moved to the cover of the station's platform. Following Ryan's instructions, Teddy avoided looking in the direction of the two men, and kept his eyes staring straight ahead toward a small shop on the other side of the tracks.

Almost out of breath, Morrie Stein, one of Ryan's neighbors, came running up under the overhang to get out of the rain. He immediately engaged Teddy in a conversation about the weather, and Teddy was thankful for the diversion.

Being almost a foot shorter than Teddy's 6'7" frame, Morrie's bald head barely came up to Teddy's shoulder.

Morrie, and three of his buddies who got on the train earlier down the line, always flipped one of their seats back and played cards together on their way into the city. Teddy and Ryan would usually take the seat directly behind them. The group could always be counted on for a laugh.

They all knew one another, casually. It was almost as if they were members of a little club, with the same people, riding the same car together every morning. It had become a comfortable place to visit, drink a cup of coffee, and read the morning paper while riding the hour it took to get into Chicago from Lake Forest.

Morrie was usually the comic of the car, with a quick wit and a good sense of humor—although that morning, while Morrie chatted away, Teddy had not heard a single word.

When Ryan first moved into the house, two doors down from Morrie and his family, Morrie mistakenly thought Ryan was Pierce Brosnan, who he enjoyed in the James Bond series. Morrie had decided to throw an enormous party in his honor, and had invited all of his friends and neighbors, only to discover at the party that Ryan was just Brosnan's look alike.

The confusion had started when Morrie stopped by Ryan's to personally welcome him to the neighborhood, and to extend an invitation to Ryan to attend a barbecue that Morrie was hosting on the 4th of July. However, only Jen was at home. The next day, Jen had gone over to Morrie's to deliver Ryan's acceptance. Somehow, with Jen's limited English, most of what Morrie had expressed to him was lost, and the confusion continued until the weekend of the party, when Morrie learned Ryan's real name. People in town still laughed about it more than two years later.

As Morrie talked, Teddy found he was able to glance over his head, and catch a glimpse of the car that had followed him. The two men were still parked at the platform's edge, and Teddy wondered who they were, and what they wanted with him. He was sure that Martel was behind their presence, and wondered how Martel had learned who Teddy was, and where he lived.

Soon the train pulled into the station and, once it stopped, everyone got on board.

"So where's Ryan?" Morrie asked, noticing how distracted Teddy was. "Did he have surgery this morning?"

"Oh, no. He'll catch up to us," Teddy said, as they began to climb up the train's steps. "He wanted to check someone out in another car."

After the train pulled away from the station, Ryan got up from the seat he took at the very front of the train's first car, and made his way back, inspecting each and every passenger on both levels. He soon reached the car where Teddy was sitting. Before opening the heavy, framed metal door, Ryan looked through the glass scanning each and every seat on the lower level. When he was satisfied the men were not there, he quickly pulled the door aside, entering their car, and began checking the upper level, as would a Doberman on the hunt.

Morrie, along with Teddy and some of the others, looked up when Ryan entered their car, and Morrie immediately noted his strange behavior.

"Ryan must be looking for that guy who borrowed a quarter from him last week," Morrie quipped, drawing everyone to laughter.

Ryan was so focused on what he was doing that he never heard Morrie's remark, and continued his search, passing into the next car.

After thoroughly scrutinizing every face on the entire train, Ryan returned to where Teddy was sitting. Looking relieved, he slid into his seat near the window, and took a deep breath.

"Were you aware you were being followed?" Ryan asked in a low voice.

Teddy shook his head no. "Are they on the train?"

"No. Do you have something to write on?" Ryan asked.

Taking a pen and legal pad out of his briefcase, Teddy handed both to Ryan.

"Don't you have any pencils?" Ryan asked.

Teddy found one of his favorite pencils, with a soft roll-up eraser at its end, and handed it to Ryan.

Ryan crossed his leg and propped the tablet up on his calf and began sketching and making notes. While Ryan drew a likeness of each of the men, Teddy watched over his shoulder and ate his chocolate donut. When a piece of the donut fell on Ryan's sketch, Ryan stopped for a moment, and gave Teddy a look.

"I'm glad this incident hasn't hurt your appetite, Ted," Ryan said.

Teddy just laughed, and brushed the crumbs off and onto the floor.

"Is that to attract any cockroaches or rodents who might have come along for the ride?" Ryan asked, as he looked down at the clean floor, and then at Teddy.

"Just draw, will you?" Teddy asked.

Ryan continued on with his detailed work. A column, on the left of a ruled margin, gave a complete description of each of the men. Ryan noted their body types, hair and eye color, approximate height, weight, and bone size, including a description of their clothing and a ring that one of the men wore. In addition to this, was the make and color of the car, including its license plate number.

Teddy took another bite of his donut, and then held it out in front of him to avoid the legal pad. However, this time he dropped some of the crumbs on Ryan's shoe.

"Ever see these men before?" Ryan asked, showing Teddy the drawings.

Teddy studied their faces. "No, not that I remember," he said.

Teddy did not know that they were the same two men that Martel had ordered to follow him in New Jersey.

"They're not the two guys at the airport in Newark?" Ryan asked.

"I never actually got a clear look at their faces. They were not that close," Teddy answered. "It could be them; one was much larger than the other."

While Teddy held the legal pad and studied the drawings, Ryan looked down at his shoe and saw the donut crumbs.

"Ted, will you look at my shoe!"

"Oh, sorry," he said, absentmindedly.

Ryan took out a clean handkerchief, brushed off the crumbs, and then continued to polish his Italian-made shoe back to its original rich luster.

"Why do you have to be such a slob?" Ryan asked, with annoyance.

"I'm not a slob," Teddy defended.

"Yes you are," Ryan said, as he straightened his sock and pant leg.

"Frankly, I'd be more concerned with working in a wet suit all day," Teddy remarked.

"I always keep some extra clothes, and a couple of suits, at my office," Ryan remarked, "in case I end up staying at the hospital all night."

It was then that Ryan noticed that his coffee and donut, still in the bag, were sitting on the floor perched between Teddy's feet.

"Why is my breakfast sitting on the floor Ted? Do you know how dirty that is?"

Teddy laughed, as he picked up the bag, and handed it to Ryan.

"This car's immaculate. They clean it every night, and you know it."

"They'd have to after you ride in it for an hour," Ryan continued, closely examining the bottom of the bag.

"It's clean, Ryan," Teddy confirmed.

"You'd be surprised what you can't see," Ryan countered, opening the bag and removing his coffee.

Ryan slowly uncapped the lid and handed the cup to Teddy. "Here, hold this a minute, and try not to spill any of it on me," Ryan said, as he carefully removed his donut from its paper wrapper, and folded his napkin down around it.

"I didn't realize you could draw so well," Teddy said, changing the subject and handing Ryan his coffee.

"I like to draw," Ryan admitted.

Teddy stared at the pad, as if he were thinking about something, and then the worst scenario came into his mind.

"Ryan," he said, with a serious note of concern coming into his voice, "if you didn't see them on the train, that means they stayed back in Lake Forest, and Terese is home alone with the children."

Ryan just looked at him, as his mind started racing.

"You don't suppose they would go out to the house, do you?" Teddy asked.

"I think they followed you from the house," Ryan returned.

Their express train was just pulling out of the Clybourn station now. It was 8:07 in the morning. Teddy opened his briefcase, grabbed his cell phone, and called the house. The phone rang and rang, then their answering machine picked up.

"Try the Swensens' quarters," Ryan suggested.

"They're on vacation up in Minnesota this week," Teddy explained, as he tried dialing Terese on her cell phone.

"Then Terese truly is alone, and the house is empty," Ryan confirmed. "Didn't you get someone to come in while they're gone?" Ryan asked.

"It's only till Saturday," Teddy said. "The boys are taking care of the horses, and Mattie is still coming in to clean and do the laundry every day."

"What time does she usually get there?" Ryan asked.

"Around nine o'clock," Teddy answered, looking at his watch.

Ryan looked troubled.

"I'll be right back," Teddy told Ryan.

"Where are you going?" Ryan asked.

Teddy pointed to the space where one car was connected to the other, and he could talk privately on the phone.

Ryan nodded.

As soon as Teddy left the car they were riding in, he dialed information and got the telephone number of the Lake Forest Police Department. When someone came on the line, he asked for the Chief of Police.

The Chief's youngest son and Michael were friends, and played on the same baseball team together. Teddy and Terese often sat with the Chief and his wife when they went to the games. He knew he could be trusted to handle the matter discreetly, without alarming Terese, and he knew that Terese would feel comfortable with the Chief checking in on her.

"Tom?" Teddy asked, as he came on the line.

"Yes?" the Chief answered.

"This is Ted Townsend."

"Oh, hi Ted."

"I need to ask a favor."

"Sure," the Chief interjected.

"When I arrived at the train station this morning, I learned from Ryan Stuart that two men had been following me, and Terese is alone with the children. Our caretaker and his wife are on vacation, and Terese is not answering the phone."

"I'll go right out there myself," the Chief assured him.

"I'm very worried," Teddy, explained, "I've tried calling the house, as well as her cell phone, but there's been no answer. Terese always goes up to her office in the attic with Katie in the morning, where she writes, as soon as the boys get off to school. And, she always answers the house phone up there."

"I can check it out," the Chief said. "It's probably just the phone lines. We had some strong lightning hits this morning with the storm. Or perhaps Terese was just in the shower when you called. But I'll get right on it Ted. I can be there in five minutes."

"I'm going to switch phones now. Give me your cell number, and I'll call you right back, so we can talk while someone drives me out to your place."

"Thanks," Teddy said, giving him the number.

The Chief called Teddy back momentarily.

"We're just pulling out onto Deerpath," the Chief informed. "By the way, Ted, who was following you?"

"I don't know," Teddy honestly answered, still holding the legal pad.

"Do you have a description of them, or their car?" the Chief asked.

"Ryan does," Teddy answered, giving him Ryan's thorough depiction.

"That's a lot of detail. We should be able to get something on that," he said, after writing everything down. "Don't worry Ted, it's probably nothing to be alarmed about."

"There's a house key above the light fixture at the kitchen door," Teddy, added.

"I'll be in touch," the Chief answered.

"Tom?" Teddy called, before the Chief was gone. "Terese is super sensitive when she's pregnant. Please don't alarm her about this, if you don't have to," Teddy prompted.

"I'll keep everything low key, Ted," the Chief promised.

"Thanks," Teddy said, before the Chief cut off their transmission.

When Teddy went back to his seat, he sat down next to Ryan, who looked concerned.

"Tom is going out there right now," Teddy informed.

"The Chief of Police?" Ryan mouthed, quietly.

"Yes," Teddy nodded.

Ryan offered no further assurances. He knew better.

Unknown to them all, while Teddy and the Chief were talking on the phone the two men had already broken into Teddy's home. David Jones was on the inside, and the lead man, Ron Andrews, was watching from the outside. Jones was in the second phase of his break-in, having gone from room-to-room checking out the house's interior layout.

When he reached the downstairs library, he went directly over to Teddy's desk, and quickly found his personal address book.

Page-by-page Jones leafed through the book, photographing each and every page with a high-tech camera. When he came to the "C's," he saw Mr. Chang's card, and slipped it into his pocket.

Aware someone hostile had entered its private domain, the house exuded an alarming eerie silence. Suddenly, the doorbell rang twice, and Jones quickly let himself out a pair of French doors at the back of the house, taking nothing with him but Mr. Chang's card, and the slender camera that he slipped into his jacket pocket.

Andrews was still on the outside, standing at the front door, dressed in a plain brown suit. He was a clean-cut man, of average height and ordinary in looks, with dark brown hair and eyes. He was the kind of man who could easily blend into a crowd. When he saw the police car pull in the driveway, he acted as if he had just arrived, and rang the front doorbell.

The rain had stopped, and the air felt muggy and heavy, as the Chief drove up the circular drive. He recognized the blue Buick as being the one described to him by Teddy, and the license plate number matched.

They had already run a check on the car from the police station, and had received word as to its registration. It was a rental car.

The Chief was a good-sized man, middle-aged, with light brown hair that was beginning to gray. Another younger officer accompanied him, and they waited a moment inside the car as they surveyed the scene.

Slowly, they opened the doors of their patrol car, being careful in their initial approach, as they walked toward the front entrance of the house.

Ron Andrews was still standing at the front door, and David Jones was coming around the corner from the back of the house.

Jones' large burly frame caused him to walk with the waddling gait of a Japanese wrestler. He was an especially homely-looking man, with mousy brown hair that was thinning on top. Deep, ugly pockmarks were pitted into his red, puffy face, and he looked out of place in the large rumpled suit he wore.

"Looks like nobody's home Andy," Jones said, in a friendly tone.

"Can we help you?" the Chief asked, as he eyed Andrews at the front entrance.

Andrews extended his hand. "Hi," he said, "I'm Ron Andrews, and this is my associate David Jones."

"What are you doing here?" the Chief asked, not shaking his hand.

"We're with the Landowners Insurance Group," Andrews lied. "I have a card right here," he said.

Andrews reached into his jacket pocket, and pulled out his wallet, removing a business card that he handed over to the Chief.

"We were just looking for the Townsends," Andrews said.

The Chief looked at the card, and stuck it into his shirt pocket. "They don't seem to be home," he responded. "Did you have an appointment?"

"Not exactly," Andrews hedged.

"Then you're trespassing."

"We're just trying to get a little business," Andrews pursued.

The Chief was no man to mess with, and he detested the idea of these men entering Lake Forest and disturbing the tranquility of his lakefront town.

"What were you doing down at the train station this morning?" he demanded, throwing them off guard.

The two men looked at each other questioningly, and then back to the Chief.

"We just got into town, and we were trying to find a hot cup of coffee," Andrews replied, sarcastically. "Is that all right, or is this town closed to visitors?"

"That depends on your business," the Chief challenged them. "And if you don't want to find yourselves down at the police station for the rest of the day, you'll be straight with your answers and watch your tone," he said, powerfully.

Just at that moment Terese drove into the driveway. Katie and Leah were with her in the back of her sports van. Terese quickly got out with two bags of groceries in her arms. Her heart staggered when she saw the Chief, and the two other men, and she immediately thought something had happened to Teddy.

The second officer went over to help her, and took the groceries out of her arms, and brought them up to the house.

"Has something happened?" Terese asked, her stomach quickening as she spoke the words. She knew it could not be the boys, because she had just dropped them off at school herself.

"No, no," the Chief assured her, "we just noticed these strangers looking around your property, and stopped to question them."

Terese took a deep breath of relief. "Oh, thank God," she said. "I thought something terrible had happened."

Stepping in front of Terese, Leah began barking at the two men, as if she had a reason to be angry with them. The men backed off when they saw the mean look in her eyes, and they sensed she could harm them, if she wanted to.

"Leah, stop that," Terese insisted. "What's the matter with you?" she asked, giving Leah a strong tug on her collar. "She's usually so friendly," Terese explained.

Despite Terese's intervention, Leah barked twice more at the two men, to let them know that she could still assert herself if she wanted to. Leah then looked up at Terese, and mumbled something to her before sitting down.

Katie came up, having removed her own seatbelt. She stood beside Leah, putting her arm around Leah's neck, leaning into her while everyone talked.

Terese's cell phone began ringing where she had left it on the front seat of her car, distracting them for a moment. Terese just let it ring.

"Why are you here?" Terese asked the two men.

"They said they're selling insurance," the Chief offered, not the least bit convinced.

"We have all the insurance we need," Terese said, stepping forward.

Leah immediately stood up and nudged Terese's leg with her shoulder, so that she would not go any farther forward. A growl came from deep within Leah's throat as she stared the two men down, warning them not to make so much as a move in Terese's direction. Then, the phone began ringing in the house.

"Mommy, the phone's ringing," Katie said, as she pulled at Terese's shirt.

"Yes Katie," Terese said, impatiently, "the machine will pick it up."

Leah once again asserted herself, growling at the two men, while the house phone began ringing again.

"Mommy the phone," Katie said, tugging once more on Terese.

"Yes Katie," Terese said, turning to the Chief. "Will you excuse me for a minute, Tom. I'll be right back. I just want to catch the house phone. It might be the Swensens."

Terese ran up to the front door, trying to find the right key.

Andrews had already backed away, never taking his eyes off Leah, who looked as if she would attack at any minute. "Well, I guess we'll be off then," he said, as both men turned to walk to their car.

"Wait a minute," the Chief ordered, as he turned to Terese. "Do you want to press charges against them for trespassing, Terese?"

"No, I don't think that will be necessary," she said. "I don't want any trouble."

"You had better look through the house, and see if everything is in order," the Chief persisted.

"Mommy, the phone," Katie insisted, as it began ringing again.

"Yes, Katie, I can hear it," Terese said, raising her voice.

The minute Terese opened the door, the phone stopped ringing again, and their machine picked up the call. Katie now started to approach the two men, and Leah quickly blocked her path, sitting down sideways on Katie's feet. Katie started to giggle, as she tried, unsuccessfully, to loosen her shoes from underneath Leah's firm heavy grip.

The Chief looked down at Katie, and saw what Leah had done. "You look as if you're stuck, Katie," he said, with a smile.

"She won't move until Mommy comes back," Katie said with a sigh, as she began to play with Leah's ears. "Daddy says she has a mind of her own," she added, making everyone laugh.

Terese stuck her head out the door, just as the phone began ringing again. "Everything's okay, Tom," she acknowledged. "Katie, I want you and Leah in the house right now," she said, as she hurried to answer the phone.

Met by Teddy's concerned voice on the line, Terese began explaining what happened, as Katie ran into the house to see who was on the phone.

Still outside the house, near the front door, Leah watched the two men from her guarding position at the front porch. The Chief walked the men to their car, and gave them a final warning. As soon as they had gone, he came back to the house and talked with Teddy on the phone.

Teddy was still concerned about everyone's welfare. The Chief offered to have someone come out and stay at the house with Terese and the children until Teddy got home—just in case the two men dared to come back. Teddy thanked him, and then talked to Terese again, further explaining that he had been followed to the stationhouse. However, Teddy intentionally left out the part about the gun. By the time he hung up, he was assured that the Chief had everything under control.

When Teddy arrived home early that evening, he thanked the officer who had been staying with Terese and the children all day. He was very grateful for the attention the police had given them. Teddy walked with the officer out the front door to the driveway, then said goodbye.

As Teddy came into the kitchen, he found Terese frying chicken for dinner. It was one of his favorite meals. She would often prepare it on the days the Swensens were off, or away, because it was also a favorite with the children.

Terese filled him in on what had been going on, and he listened to her, attentively, as she retold the story of what happened that morning.

During dinner, Teddy noticed that there was an unusual tension in the air between Michael and Matthew. He looked across the table trying to pick up on what was wrong, for neither one of them had spoken a word all through dinner. Teddy glanced over at Terese next, but her expression assured him it did not have anything to do with what had happened that morning.

Michael and Matthew were at odds with each other again, something that was occurring often of late, and it usually had to do with their chores after school. Teddy found their behavior especially annoying that evening, particularly with everything else that had happened that day. He and Terese attempted to make conversation, but still there was an uncomfortable heaviness in the air. Teddy finally stopped talking and looked around the dining room table.

"All right," he said. "I want to know what's going on between you two. I've told you both before how unpleasant, and disruptive, it is when you bring your differences with each other to the dinner table. I don't appreciate it, and neither does your mother."

No one answered. Matthew continued to pick at his food, while Michael quietly ate.

Teddy looked at Michael first, and then to Matthew. "So what is it this time?" he asked.

Still no one answered.

"Matthew?" Teddy questioned.

Trying to hold back a river of tears, Matthew just shook his head.

"Michael?" Teddy asked.

"It's nothing," Michael answered.

Katie balanced one of her peas on her small fork, and started to play with it, allowing the pea to roll back and forth.

Leah was lying under the table at Katie's feet, with a pile of peas resting next to one of her paws. Just then, another pea came falling down Katie's lap, hitting Leah on the head, and then rolling off her face and onto the floor. Leah took the pea in her mouth and set it down alongside the others. She was holding out for a piece of chicken.

"Katie?" Teddy asked, looking for the truth.

"Michael moved out of their room today," Katie revealed, in her small, young voice.

Teddy turned to Michael. "You moved out of your room?" he asked. "Where do you intend to sleep?"

"In the front guest bedroom," Michael said, in explanation.

"You mean the new baby's nursery?" Teddy asked.

"Yes," Michael replied.

"You guys can't get along?" Teddy asked, looking at both of them.

"It's not that," Michael said.

Matthew looked hurt, and continued to pick at his food, never looking up from his plate. Teddy then noticed a tear fall down Matthew's sweet, young face.

"Well, what is it then?" Teddy questioned, more compassionately now. "You guys have always shared a room."

"Have you looked at that place lately?" Michael asked, raising his voice. "There are bugs everywhere!"

"They're all dead," Matthew defended, speaking up.

"That's the point. They give me the creeps," Michael explained.

"I'm going to put them all away," Matthew said. "I'm just a little behind in cataloging them."

"I feel like I'm living in the Museum of Natural History," Michael complained, with disgust in his voice.

Teddy coughed into his napkin, suppressing his laughter. Terese brought her napkin to her mouth too, trying to hide her smile.

"I like your bugs," Katie said. "Especially the butterflies."

"Well maybe you'd prefer sharing a room with him then," Michael offered, lowering his voice.

Teddy gave Michael a look of that's enough, and Michael picked up his fork, acting unaffected, and began eating again.

"If you need some help with your collection, Matthew, I'll give you a hand after dinner," Teddy offered.

"That's okay," Matthew said, in a tone barely audible.

"I want to help," Teddy said. "I like your bugs too," he continued, giving a bewildered look to Terese.

Leah's head shot up, thinking that she heard something. It was the click, click, click of a camera shutter. She strained to listen, but it had stopped as quickly as it had begun, and she was unable to get a fix on the sound.

Always on guard for any field mice that might have snuck in without her seeing them, and with her head low to the ground, Leah scanned all the baseboards. This was a prime occupation for her, next to keeping an eye on Katie all day.

The phone began ringing, and Teddy got up to answer it. It was the Chief.

"We lifted two prints off the business card from Andrews," he told Teddy, "and I got a classification on him from the crime lab."

"That was fast," Teddy said, as he sat down on a chair situated alongside the front hall table.

"We now have an identification on him, from the state police. He's an ex-CIA agent. The computer says he's been working as an independent contractor—for hire."

"You're kidding," Teddy responded.

"No, about a year ago he disappeared after being involved in a Chicago break-in. The information we have was pulled on him then, from the FBI's computers in Washington, but the Chicago police never caught up with him. There was a notation that he might have relocated in New York City."

"Were you able to get anything on the other guy?" Teddy asked.

"Not yet," the Chief informed. "We'll keep working on this Ted. We have a competent team of investigators here at the police department, and if there's anything to come up with, they'll find it. We're also waiting for the car to be turned in at the rental agency, and then we'll go over it with a fine-toothed comb. We should be able to get Jones' prints then. One thing we do know is that Andrews' leaving the CIA was not on friendly terms."

"I can't believe he was with the CIA," Teddy said.

"Well, believe it. Why do you think they were following you, Ted?" the Chief asked. "Are you in some kind of trouble, or something?"

"No, not at all," Teddy answered. "I'm not actually sure who they are."

"Anything from your past, a case you tried, or a case you were involved in where someone might have had a reason to hold a grudge against you?"

"No, not that I know of," Teddy answered.

"Any cases where you put someone away?" the Chief asked.

"I've never practiced criminal law," Teddy said, "so it can't be that. I've only been associated with a big national firm that represents large entities more than individuals. I specialize in civil litigation. It's a different kind of law," Teddy explained.

"Well, if you think of anything, call me," the Chief said, sensing Teddy was holding something back.

"Why don't you make me a list of the cases you are currently handling," the Chief suggested.

"Yes, I will," Teddy, responded, "and I genuinely appreciate the personal attention you have given us, Tom," Teddy related.

"That's what we're here for," the Chief said, as they said goodbye. "I'm glad we could help Ted. I'll give you a call tomorrow, and, in the meantime, we'll keep a close watch on your place when we patrol."

"I'd appreciate that, Tom," Teddy responded.

"Let me know if you want an officer out there again tomorrow," the Chief offered.

"Thank you, Tom. I plan to work from home tomorrow, but thanks again."

Shortly after they hung up, Mr. Chang called. Teddy had left numerous messages for him over the weekend, but this was the first contact Teddy had had with him since they were supposed to have met on Michigan Avenue, Friday at noon.

Teddy filled him in on everything that had happened earlier in the day, and Mr. Chang offered to come and stay at the house, until the Swensens returned.

Leah walked into the hallway and listened to Teddy's conversation, as he told Mr. Chang that they would have a car pick him up early on Wednesday morning. Teddy quickly jotted down Mr. Chang's residence address on a notepad at the hall table, and then made a call to the limousine service he always used. Leah wanted to go out, but Teddy was too involved to notice her.

Going into the living room next, and then through to the game room, Leah looked out through the French doors to the darkened yard. Usually she could let herself out this way. However, all the doors had been locked and secured by the police officer that the Chief had left at the house.

Leah knew someone was out there, but she did not want to start barking until she had the intruder in sight. Then she would confront them. Leah never gave herself away, preferring to stalk her prey, as would a large cat.

Mumbling under her breath, she walked back into the hallway, and gave Teddy a strong nudge, and then looked at the front door. He was talking to Ryan now. Teddy got up, and walked over to unlock the front door for her.

Once outside, Leah breathed in deeply for any lingering scents in the air, and then brought her nose down to the ground and made a sweep around the house. Twice she had their scent, but lost it again. She knew the two men who had been at the house earlier in the day had returned. She searched the grounds thoroughly, but they were now gone.

Climbing under an enormous fir tree that she favored, growing low to the ground, Leah continued to watch the house and yard for another hour or more, before going back inside.

Just the same, she remained especially watchful all through the night never sleeping so much as a minute, but the men never returned.

CHAPTER 26

▲

THE SURVEILLANCE

Wednesday Morning

Mr. Chang arrived early at Whippoorwill Farm on Wednesday morning, shortly after the boys boarded their bus to school. Terese helped him put his things away in the old servant's quarters, at the east wing of the house. The rooms Mr. Chang occupied included a small bedroom, sitting room and bath—all of which were situated above the kitchen and morning room, from which a staircase led.

During the day, Mr. Chang stayed downstairs in the library, where he found several books of interest to read. A large overstuffed chair, with its matching ottoman, rested in the corner of the room. Mr. Chang thought this to be the best spot for him. The chair looked out to the center hall of the house, and gave him a clear view of the front door. The library also offered him a view of the grounds. Mr. Chang seemed to make himself right at home, which was a relief to Terese. She was, for the most part, unaware that he was even in the house, and the first day passed uneventfully, as she kept to her usual routine.

Also on Wednesday, Andrews and Jones began setting up camp in the woods, just behind the north pasture. They had been given orders to keep Teddy's family under surveillance, twenty-four hours a day, and had made use of an old abandoned tree house that appeared to be more of a hunting blind, where the woods began.

Martel wanted Teddy out of the picture, as soon as possible. He had ordered that Teddy be assassinated. Martel did recognize him, as Theos of Atlantis, and considered him a serious threat.

No one but Leah was aware of their presence in the woods, and when she would make a fuss about someone following her out to the back pasture, everyone thought she was tracking the raccoons again and ignored her concern. The first couple of times the boys followed her out through the back pasture on their horses, they came up with nothing. This was fortunate, under the circumstances, for the men were there—waiting and watching. Michael and Matthew had just not followed Leah far enough, to where the tree house was situated, preferring to keep to the trail.

Leah knew exactly where they were hiding. There was an invisible line that she had drawn, past which she did not want any of the animals in the woods to cross. As long as the men stayed beyond that line, Leah would not chase after them.

Andrews and Jones had contemplated shooting her with one of the high-powered rifles they kept in the blind-like tree house, but they knew that would only give them away. So they decided to wait until they had finished their assignment, before quieting her once and for all.

The day they arrived, they had left some poisoned meat in the pasture, directly in front of them, but Leah would not touch it. It had their scent on it. Leah was causing them a lot of trouble, and they had to wait until she was locked inside at night before they could approach the house.

However, so far, they had been unable to get a clear shot at Teddy. Martel also wanted photos taken of the entire family. So they were completing that task when possible during the day, at a distance, and closer to the house at night.

Wednesday Evening

At seven o'clock on Wednesday evening, everyone had dinner together, and then went in different directions. Mr. Chang retired to his room to read, and the boys got busy clearing the dinner dishes and loading the dishwasher, which was an evening chore for them, even when the Swensens were in residence.

Terese felt that the Swensens, having already worked a long day, should have their dinner at the cottage while the family had their meal at the house. After dinner, Terese would put the leftover food in the refrigerator, while the boys cleared the table and loaded the dishwasher. Despite their apparent wealth, the boys always had chores to do to earn their allowances. Teddy and Terese made an effort not to spoil them by giving them too much. The boys already knew what it was like to save for what they wanted.

After Michael and Matthew had finished bringing the dishes in from the dining room, and the kitchen was clean, they both went upstairs to start on their homework. Terese and Katie followed after them, and made their way up to the large attic room on the third floor. This is where Terese shared her office with Katie, who enjoyed part of the space as her designated playroom. It was here that Terese would work at her desk on her manuscript, and Katie would play with her dolls for an hour or so before bedtime.

Teddy had brought a file home with him, and went into the library to work on a brief that he had begun to write earlier in the day. The house soon became still and quiet.

Teddy positioned a large pillow on the high-armed leather sofa, and got comfortable, with his back propped against the sofa's arm. Drawing up his long muscular legs, he propped a smaller pillow on his lap, and began writing on a legal pad. A couple of law books, which he had pulled from the library shelf, lay nearby on the floor, and he got organized for the evening.

The library was a small, cozy room, filled with books. At one end of the comfortable space was a large fireplace that they enjoyed in the wintertime. The ceiling was covered with the same light butternut paneling, as the walls. The library had been well cared for over the years, and gave off the fresh scent of recently being polished by Mattie. The room still carried the fragrance of almond oil that had always reminded Teddy of chocolate-covered cherries. On one of the shelves sat the ancient carved box that he and Ryan had brought back from Atlantis.

In the afternoons, light flooded into the room from two exposures, but at night, the library took on another inviting mood, with incandescent lighting shadowing the silent space. This was Teddy's favorite room in the house. He always spent a great deal of time here, when he brought work home from the office, or when he was in the mood to be alone. It was also a favorite place for the boys to come to talk with him, or to sit at his partners' desk and get help with their homework. But tonight, he had the room to himself.

When Teddy finally settled down, he swung the arm of a nearby floor lamp closer in to him, so that its light would pour over his shoulder. He was soon lost in his work.

Teddy wrote solidly for almost an hour, uninterrupted, before he heard Michael enter the room. When he looked up, he saw Leah quickly slip past him. She soon jumped up on the leather sofa, making a bed for herself near Teddy's feet, before Michael took her favorite spot.

This was the one piece of furniture in the house that Leah was allowed to lie on. Terese had rationalized that it wiped clean fairly easily, and it had been Leah's favorite place to take naps when they first moved to Whippoorwill.

"What's up?" Teddy asked, as Michael moved into the room.

"Oh, nothing," Michael said, as he started looking through a pile of books on the coffee table in front of the sofa.

"Looking for something to read?" Teddy asked.

"No," Michael said. "I think I left my math book in here last night. It wasn't in my book bag when I went to school today."

"Do you still have homework to do?" Teddy asked.

"Just math," Michael responded, lifting the pile of newspapers, and looking underneath.

Leah's head suddenly shot up. She quickly got up off the sofa, and ran over to a window. Looking quietly out to the yard, she watched for any discernable movement.

Before leaving the library, Leah mumbled something to Teddy, and then trotted out the door. She quickly made her way out through the entrance hall. One light, at a hall table, lit the area. Leah then proceeded into the darkened living room, looking out at the backyard. It was nighttime now, with a few clouds in the sky, but she could still see clearly. Leah waited a minute or two, not picking up any activity, then returned to the library, where she stared once more out one of the windows. Leah took in a deep breath of evening air from the open window. She could definitely smell those two men.

When Michael, who had been sitting in her spot, got up to leave the library, Leah returned to the sofa. Once again she mumbled something to Teddy, but he had diligently returned to his writing, so she soon gave up on getting his attention. Leah listened for the longest time, for any possible sound, but she now heard only the crickets calling out from the grass.

After cleaning one of her front paws, she drifted off to sleep for almost half an hour. The silence in the room was interrupted when a couple of June bugs, attracted by the light, hit one of the screens with a force of something several times their size.

When Leah woke, she saw that Katie had wandered in, and already had her pajamas on. She had fallen asleep with her head on Teddy's shoulder. Upstairs, Leah could hear that Terese was taking her evening shower, and knew that it was almost bedtime.

Leah stretched and gave a long yawn, and then nudged Teddy's foot with one of her paws. She had to go out, and all the outside doors were still locked. Teddy was deep into his writing though, and he did not want to lose his thought.

Getting up, Leah came along side him on the floor, plopping her head down on his arm, and causing his pen to drag across the page he was writing on. The situation was urgent.

"Do you have to?" Teddy whispered, not wanting to wake Katie. "You just came in about an hour ago."

Leah looked at him earnestly.

Teddy put his legal pad down on the floor, with his pen, and eased Katie into his arms so that he could carry her. Getting up off the sofa, he went through the front hall, and then crossed the darkened living room to the family's game room. He unlocked and opened the French doors for Leah. This was where Leah usually came in and out during the day, and she quickly sauntered out and into the night.

"Leah," Teddy whispered, "don't be too long."

Teddy looked down at Katie, who was still fast asleep, then tried to see where Leah was. He opened the screen door for a better look, and saw her sniffing around near the border of bushes. When he closed the screen door, Katie began waking up.

"Daddy?" Katie asked.

"Are you ready for bed?" Teddy asked.

Katie nodded.

Teddy opened the screen door. "Leah," he called, "come on girl."

But Leah was nowhere to be seen. Teddy walked out of the room, leaving the doors open, so that Leah could get back in again, and then he took Katie up to bed.

When Teddy walked past the front nursery, he saw Michael reading in the single bed that Terese had placed in the room. All of his trophies, pennants, sports pictures, and the contents of his side of his room, were piled high near the crib on the floor.

"Did you find your book?" Teddy asked.

"It was in Matthew's book bag," Michael announced.

"Did you finish your math?" Teddy asked, seeing Michael was reading a comic book.

"Yes. We just had one page. Mom checked it for me."

"Not too late, now," Teddy reminded him, "or you'll have trouble waking in the morning"

"Okay, Dad," Michael responded.

Putting Katie down, Teddy covered her with her sheet and a light blanket.

Teddy looked in on Matthew next. He was working at his desk, using a small brush to spread glue onto a piece of heavy white paper. Several different species of insects, including butterflies, were lined up along the top of Matthew's long desk. A large architectural lamp hung low over his workspace, and created a focus of light. Teddy walked into the room, and over to where Matthew was sitting.

"Can I give you a hand now?" he asked.

"I enjoy doing this part myself," Matthew said, turning to smile.

The room looked strange to Teddy with all of Michael's things removed. He was concerned about Michael and Matthew's relationship with each other, but thought this breakdown would pass. Brothers always had disagreements, especially at their young ages, and they could not possibly know how lonely it could be to grow up, as he had, without the friendship of a brother or sister.

"How about your labels?" Teddy asked.

"Mom already printed them for me," Matthew said, looking up. "It's okay Dad, I know you've been busy."

Teddy watched Matthew work, as he delicately placed a colorful beetle on the white paper. Teddy observed how meticulous Matthew was, and knew in his heart that his son's future potential was limitless. Matthew would probably become a scientist, or go into medical research, Teddy thought, and he knew the world would be fortunate to have his kind soul so willing to take care of it.

Matthew was an exceedingly capable child, with strong adept hands, and long artistic fingers. Even as a baby, he could quickly manipulate anything he touched, and had an unending curiosity for the way things were put together and worked.

In the first year or so of his life, when other children his age were cuddling a stuffed animal with one hand, and a pacifier with the other, Matthew was building something, albeit not always identifiable, with a large set of wooden blocks. By the time he reached Katie's age, he was already collecting specimens and bringing them into the house to examine under a magnifying glass.

The school system had wanted to advance him two grades right away when he entered school last fall, but Teddy and Terese rejected the idea, and felt it was better to give him more subjects to study—including an area of science that he was interested in, and a couple of languages. They thought it was more important to keep him with other six-year-olds. Matthew was mentally advanced, and could think at a high level, although he was physically and emotionally the same age as all his peers.

"Are you still upset with Michael?" Teddy asked.

"Not really. I just never slept alone before, and I prefer having someone to talk to," Matthew confessed.

"Well, your Mom and I are just next door," Teddy, offered.

"I know," Matthew said, a little embarrassed.

"Leah's still sleeping in here, isn't she?" Teddy asked.

"Yes," Matthew answered, smiling up at his father, with a twinkle in his clear blue eyes. "The one who snores, stays."

Teddy began laughing. "Well, let me know if I can help with anything," Teddy said, still chuckling about Leah as he walked out of the room.

Once in the hallway, Teddy looked in on Terese, who was already in bed.

"What's wrong with Leah?" Terese asked. "I could hear her barking out back."

"I'll go check," Teddy responded, as he moved swiftly down the curving staircase.

When Teddy entered the game room, he could sense tenseness in the air, and could tell by the sound of Leah's barking that she was way across the pasture near the woods. Then, suddenly, the barking stopped.

Teddy slowly opened the screen door. He could now hear only the sound of crickets. Then, something pelted hard into his neck, and he moved back suddenly, bringing up his hand. It was a June bug.

He quickly removed the bug from the hollow at his throat, and absent-mindedly examined it, to see if it might be something Matthew would be interested in. However, Matthew already had one that was larger.

"Leah," Teddy called. "Come on, girl."

Teddy quietly closed the screen door behind him, and listened for a moment longer. He looked carefully, as he scanned the landscape. A quarter moon gave a little light, but not enough to really see the yard and the outbuildings. Teddy's eyes searched out across the pasture to where he thought Leah had gone. Teddy walked to the edge of the patio and placed the June bug on one of the shrubs, and then called out to Leah again. He could now hear the horses whinnying, softly, back and forth to one another, responding to Leah's barking. However, Leah was nowhere in sight.

Letting out a shrill whistle, Teddy called out to her once again from the large flagstone patio off the family's game room, but still she was nowhere to be seen. Suddenly, he jumped when he heard a loud crashing sound.

A tin lid to one of Mr. Swensen's recycling cans had crashed to the ground and hit hard on the cement sidewalk near the garage on the other side of the house. Teddy walked cautiously in that direction, across the backyard, going past the darkened living room, library, dining room and kitchen. When he reached the sidewalk outside of the kitchen door, he turned and walked back toward the garbage cans. He looked carefully around, but no one was there. He bent down and replaced the fallen lid, before heading back to the house.

Once again, he could hear Leah barking, way off across the pasture, and Teddy let out another whistle.

"Leah, come on girl," he called.

Mr. Chang came out of the back door off the kitchen, to see if everything was all right. It was then that they spotted Leah running across the open field toward the house. She looked very excited when she finally came up alongside of Teddy, and was totally out of breath.

"Are you okay?" Teddy asked, taking a thorough look at her.

Leah began telling Teddy something, which he could not understand.

"I think the raccoons were in the garbage again," Teddy explained to Mr. Chang. "We have a lot of them here, with the woods and all."

"She's a very smart dog," Mr. Chang said, as he reached down to her. "And very pleasant company. She joined me in the library this afternoon for a while, when Katie took her nap."

Leah greeted Mr. Chang warmly, wagging her tail, and Teddy could see how much she liked him. He had such a calm presence about him, and even Teddy felt himself relaxing whenever he was around Mr. Chang.

"You certainly have a perfect spot here, Ted," Mr. Chang commented. "It is so removed from the city."

"I hope you're comfortable in your rooms, Mr. Chang," Teddy responded.

"Very much so, thank you," Mr. Chang responded. "Are you ready to go in?" he asked.

"Yes," Teddy answered, as they began walking toward the kitchen door. "I hope you'll feel free to help yourself to whatever is in the kitchen, Mr. Chang," Teddy added, "and if you need anything else, there's an intercom on the phone in your room. Terese and I are in bedroom #1," Teddy added.

"Yes, Terese showed me this morning. Thank you."

"Your rooms were originally designed for a governess, and the room Michael is using right now is a nursery, so you can get over into our wing by going through that bedroom, if you need to."

"Thank you," Mr. Chang said.

"I had better go back the other way and lock up," Teddy said.

"I'll get the kitchen door," Mr. Chang offered, as they said goodnight.

Teddy reached down to Leah again, affectionately patting the side of her neck, as they walked back to the game room together.

"You're a good girl, Leah," Teddy praised. "I don't know what we'd do around here without you."

He could tell she was still concerned about something, because she kept looking back to the pasture while they were walking.

"I don't think those raccoons will be back," Teddy assured her, as he opened the screen door for her. A short-knotted rope was tied to the door's handle, to help Leah open the door, when she was alone.

Once inside, Teddy quickly shut and locked the French doors, then went back to the library. Leah had already gone upstairs, looking for Matthew and his comfortable bed.

Teddy put his file and legal pad into his briefcase, and returned the law books he was using to the library shelf. Turning around, he quickly looked to see if the stone box was still in its resting place. It was. He then locked the open windows, and turned out the lights.

When Teddy reached the staircase in the hall, he stopped, and thought a moment. He then turned around and returned to the library, turning on the light again. Proceeding over to the ancient box on the shelf, Teddy picked it up and placed it under his arm. He carried it with him out of the room, flicking off the light again as he went through the door. He decided it was time to find a safer place for his treasured pendant, and before going to bed that night, he and Terese did just that.

Thursday

Andrews and Jones reported in at Martel's offices in Chicago at nine o'clock on Thursday morning. He had just returned from a trip to Europe.

Martel's ultramodern, large, and expensive offices in downtown Chicago, on Michigan Avenue, overlooked the parks and Lake Michigan shoreline. The carpeting was a deep burgundy, and appeared putrid to a sensitive eye. The furniture was pale gray, with steel and glass tables with jarring edges.

Several pieces of abstract art hung in the cold icy room, where twin beheaded sculptures, one male and the other female, with their genitalia exaggerated, perversely filled one corner of the room.

Martel, without speaking, just stared at Andrews and Jones, when they entered his office. One could see how uncomfortable they were becoming.

"I'm disappointed that you're having so much trouble completing the Townsend assignment," Martel said, with a mean look entering his eyes.

Andrews and Jones remained silent.

"You have one more week, or I'm putting someone else on the job," Martel warned them. "Not only will you lose the promised bonuses, but you can both consider yourselves fired."

Andrews silently handed Martel three envelopes, and Martel opened the first and began going through one 8x10 glossy photograph after another. Each room of Teddy's house had been photographed, and there were several shots of Teddy, Terese and their children.

Martel slowly reviewed each photograph. When he came across the pictures taken the day of the break-in, he stopped short, as his eye caught one of the shots taken in the library. It was in this particular picture that the ancient carved stone box was shown sitting on one of the library shelves.

Martel looked at the box thoughtfully for a moment and, taking his pen in hand, circled the picture of the stone box with such force that the pen ripped through the protective coating of the photograph. He flipped the photograph across his desk in the direction of Andrews and Jones.

"Get that!" he commanded, and they immediately left the room.

CHAPTER 27

▲

THE SEIZURE

Friday

The day passed by quietly at Whippoorwill Farm, as Andrews and Jones secretly watched from the woods.

Mattie cleaned the caretaker's cottage as soon as she arrived at the house, and got it ready for the Swensens return later that day.

Teddy and Terese had invited Mr. Chang to go out to dinner at The Deer Path Inn. It would be a special last evening together before taking him back to Chinatown Saturday morning.

The Inn had traditional English detailing, in a Tudor style, and the dining room was decorated giving a distinct Elizabethan atmosphere, with English period furnishings and accessories. It was an enjoyable evening, with good food and conversation, and was also a special treat for the children who were on their best behavior.

Upon arriving home after dinner, the children were met by Mr. and Mrs. Swensen who had brought each of them a souvenir from their trip. Katie received a small Indian doll, and the boys a couple of new feathered fishing flies, for when they took their next fly-fishing trip with their father and Ryan.

Once the children had gone to bed, Teddy and Terese told the Swensens what had happened earlier in the week, and to call the police if the two men dared to return.

Saturday

The household routine seemed to get back to normal again on Saturday morning. It was the beginning of Memorial Day Weekend. After the special breakfast that Mrs. Swensen had prepared, Teddy paid the boys their allowances, and they all got ready to take Mr. Chang back into the city. They all needed to get back in time for Michael's game that afternoon. The house was bustling with activity, and the children were excited about going into Chinatown.

Terese got up shortly before they were ready to leave, and went downstairs to thank Mr. Chang for his help and to say goodbye. She was feeling especially tired that morning, and had slept in later than she had intended to.

Still in her robe, she went into the kitchen, took her vitamins with a glass of fresh orange juice, and then poured a cup of tea to take up to her office. Mrs. Swensen insisted on putting together a plate of leftover bacon, some fresh fruit, and a buttered English muffin for Terese to take upstairs with her, and was readying a tray. Terese wanted to get some work done on her manuscript while the house was quiet.

Slowly Terese climbed back up the two flights of stairs to the attic. Her back was bothering her, and she had a muscle spasm in her left shoulder.

She had tossed and turned all night, trying to find a comfortable position in bed, but it was futile. Something was bothering her, yet she could not pinpoint exactly what was wrong. Terese was beginning to feel especially cumbersome with her pregnancy, and the heat did not help the situation.

They were having an especially warm spring. Terese didn't want to put the air-conditioning on so early in the year, because she enjoyed keeping the windows open for a natural breeze. She also loved the scent of the countryside, with lilacs, roses, honeysuckle and jasmine wafting in occasionally, depending on the time of day, and direction of the wind.

Before departing, Teddy came back in and yelled up the staircase.

"Terese, we're leaving," he called.

"Have a fun time," Terese answered.

"Leah's coming with us," he added.

"Okay," Terese said, trying to project her voice.

When the front door finally shut downstairs, the house was still, and Terese could work. She turned on her computer and began organizing the material she had worked on the night before.

The attic windows were open, and Terese could hear the chatter outside as the children piled into their sport van. Everyone was talking at once, and Leah was barking excitedly.

Poor Mr. Chang, Terese thought. She had suggested to Teddy that he have a driver take Mr. Chang back into the city, but Teddy wanted to show the children Chinatown, and take them into some of the small shops that lined Wentworth Avenue. And then, they were all going to have an early lunch at the same restaurant where Ryan and Teddy had first met Mr. Chang. Teddy planned to make a fun morning of it.

Soon Terese could hear the thump of the car doors closing, and the engine starting up. When the car pulled out of the driveway, the room filled with a welcome silence, and Terese was finally able to focus on her work.

Mr. Swensen had mowed the grounds around the house an hour earlier, and was now working on the area around the stable. Terese soon picked up the aroma of the fresh cut grass, as it drifted in the open window.

Not two minutes had passed when she heard the car pull back into the driveway, and the doorbell ring downstairs. Terese knew they had forgotten something, and that Teddy had failed to take his house key. He invariably did this whenever he used their sport van, and Terese waited for Mrs. Swensen to answer the door.

However, the bell kept ringing, and Terese soon realized that Mrs. Swensen had already gone back to the cottage to unpack their things, and get organized. Reluctantly, Terese got up and walked back down the two flights of stairs. When she reached the front door, she opened it wide, with an annoyed look on her face, only to be met by Andrews and Jones.

Terese quickly tried to shut the door, but Jones shoved it open and threw Terese back against the small alcove wall.

"Where is your husband?" Andrews asked.

Terese did not answer him.

"I said where is your husband!" Andrews repeated.

When Terese tried to get away, she tripped up the one step leading into the entrance hall, then fell against a side table, causing a lamp to fall and shatter across the floor. Instinctively, trying to protect her unborn child, Terese held her stomach with one hand, and tried to break her fall to the floor with the other.

Without any warning, Jones reached down and harshly grabbed her by the arm, dragging her to a nearby closet. It was only then that Terese saw the high-powered rifle he held in his other hand.

Terese fought Jones' strong steel grip without success, as hundreds of thoughts flashed through her mind. When she tried to get up, she was cruelly met by Jones' large square hand as it smashed into her chest. So brutally had he shoved her that her head hit hard against the frame of the hall closet door.

Terese, trying to hold onto the doorframe, slowly sank down to the floor. At the same moment Andrews ran into the library. Then Jones reached down, grabbed Terese roughly by the arms, and shoved her body into the closet, kicking her with his foot where her leg was still in the way of the door.

Trying to see what they wanted, Terese fought to stay conscious. Suddenly, the closet door was slammed shut and locked. Now she could only see a thin crack of light around the door's frame. Terese could hear one of them move rapidly up the staircase to the bedrooms, and she thanked God that the children were not home.

A strange tingling sensation moved over her entire body, and Terese could feel herself slipping away. Darkness moved over her, as her body went limp, and she remembered nothing more.

In what seemed less than a minute, Jones came flying down the stairs with the stone box, just as Andrews came out of the library.

"Townsend's not here," he reported to Andrews. "And the kids are gone too."

"We must have just missed him when we were on that back road, coming out of the woods," Andrews surmised. "Let's get out of here."

Soon they were both out the front door, quickly jumping into their car, and taking off by backing out the driveway onto Town Line Road. Within half a minute, they were gone.

More than an hour later, seeing the broken lamp in the front hall, and the front door left wide open, Mrs. Swensen found Terese and called the police and paramedics.

The Chief put out an all-points bulletin, and then arranged for an officer in the Chinatown area to try to find Teddy and the children. The main business district ran only a couple of blocks, so they were easy to find.

When Teddy reached the house, two police cars were in the front drive, along with three other cars, one of which was Ryan's. Mr. Chang was still with Teddy and the children. Teddy quickly parked the car, and they all hurried into the house.

Leah began barking at the investigative team, smelling the two men from the woods.

Ryan and Anne were talking to the police in the living room. Mrs. Swensen knew to call Ryan if there was ever an emergency at the house, and, fortunately, she had been able to reach him at home. Terese had refused to go with the paramedics, and when Ryan reached the house he immediately called Terese's doctor.

As soon as Teddy entered the living room, Mrs. Swensen came over to him.

"Mrs. Swensen," Teddy asked, "will you please take the children to the kitchen?"

"Of course," Mrs. Swensen replied, picking Katie up.

"Where's Mrs. Townsend?" Teddy asked, looking around.

"Upstairs with Dr. Myers," Mrs. Swensen, said, tears forming in her eyes. "Have the children had their lunch?"

"No, not yet, and Michael is not going to go to his game this afternoon," he added.

"Dad, can we go with you?" Michael asked, as Teddy headed for the stairs in the front hall.

"Not just yet. You boys go with Mrs. Swensen, and take Leah with you. I'll let you know when you can come up."

Reluctantly, the boys followed Mrs. Swensen, with Leah in tow.

"Mr. Chang, why don't you find out from Ryan what's going on," Teddy suggested.

Mr. Chang nodded, as he went into the living room.

Teddy shot up the stairs past two investigators, who were dusting the hall closet and banister for prints. He found Terese in bed, as her doctor prepared to leave.

"What happened, Terese?" Teddy asked, unable to hide his alarm. "Are you all right?"

"I'm fine," she assured him. "They came back, as soon as you left with the children."

"Who came back?" Teddy asked.

"It was the same men who were selling insurance." Terese responded.

"Oh, my God!" Teddy said.

Terese started to tremble, and Teddy moved closer to her, sitting at her side on the edge of the bed.

"They got the box," she managed. "It's gone," she added, unable to control her emotion, as tears began running down her face.

"Don't worry about that Terese. Are you sure you're all right?" he asked.

"I'm fine, really, I just feel so badly about the box being gone. It was so important. Do you know what that means?" Terese asked, crying.

"What box?" the doctor questioned, concerned about Terese's strange behavior.

"It's an antique box that I had recently acquired," Teddy explained. "We had an attempted burglary before. It was something they apparently wanted."

That seemed to satisfy Dr. Meyers, as she turned back to Terese. "Terese, would you like me to stay with you for a while?"

"Oh, no, but thank you, Dr. Meyers. I'll be all right, now that my husband is here."

"Is the baby all right?" Teddy asked, still looking at Dr. Meyers.

"Everything looks fine," the doctor assured him, "although Terese might have a concussion. I wanted to put her in the hospital, for observation, but she doesn't want to leave the children."

Teddy looked over at Terese, trying to read her thoughts.

"Ryan's here," Terese said.

"Dr. Stuart did examine her. He said he would stay here through the day, and overnight, and will keep checking in on her. It goes without saying that he knows exactly what to watch for," Dr. Meyers continued, "neurology being his specialty."

"Is there any other reason why she should be hospitalized, other than for observation?" Teddy asked.

"As long as she doesn't have any cramping or spotting, she should be all right. We just want to keep a close watch on her for any neurological changes, and keep her quiet for a few days."

Teddy looked at Terese again.

"I'm not going to the hospital, Ted. I'm fine—truly, I am."

"Is that a final decision?" Dr. Meyers asked.

"Yes, I guess so," Teddy answered, knowing Terese.

"I'll go talk to Dr. Stuart then," Dr. Meyers responded. "My offices are right here in Lake Forest, and I am just a phone call away if Terese needs me."

"Thank you," Teddy answered.

As soon as Dr. Meyers left, Terese started crying again.

"How did they know where we hid it?" she asked, as she started to get up.

"Will you please stay in bed," Teddy insisted.

"Teddy, I'm fine, really. I just hit my head, that's all."

Terese took a couple of tissues and wiped her eyes.

"I'm just furious with them. How dare they break into our house. And what if the children had been home?"

"How did they get in?" Teddy asked.

"The front door. I opened it, thinking you had forgotten something," Terese explained.

Teddy heard someone leaving, and went over to one of the bedroom windows, looking out across the front yard. Dr. Meyers was walking to her car.

"I should never have left you alone," Teddy said, walking back over to Terese. "We're going to have to hire some guards. It's not enough to have the Swensens here. Mr. Swensen is getting too old to take anyone on, even if he is an accurate shot."

"I don't want any strangers around here, or guns in the house, Ted, and I mean it. That's no environment for our children."

"I know," Teddy answered. "I don't think we have a choice right now, Terese. They're too dangerous. Will you at least go to your parents until all this blows over? You'd be safer in the city."

"No one is going to force me out of my home, Ted. Anyway, if they actually wanted to get to me and the children, they could certainly find us at my mother's."

Teddy just looked at her.

Terese thought for a moment before continuing on, her voice dropping to her usual tone. "Besides, I couldn't tell my parents about this, they worry about everything."

"Will you at least think about it?" Teddy asked.

"Yes, I will," Terese, promised.

Teddy just looked at her.

"Where are the children right now?" Terese asked.

"Mrs. Swensen took them into the kitchen, and is fixing them some lunch. We didn't want to alarm them, so they just think someone tried to enter the house after we had left. They think you were upstairs in the attic, and called the police."

"Oh," Terese responded. "That's helpful."

As Terese got up out of bed, Teddy could see for the first time the deep red marks on her arm and chest, and a large bruise on her leg.

"My God," Teddy said. "What did they do to you?"

"They threw me into the hall closet," Terese answered, still angry.

"Are you sure you're all right?" Teddy asked, with concern.

"I'm okay," Terese said, as she went into the bathroom. "I'm going to take a shower, and then I want to go downstairs," she said. "Are the police still here?"

"You're supposed to stay in bed, Terese."

"Could you stay in bed with all this happening?" Terese asked, turning on the shower.

"No, but I'm not carrying our baby either," he said, more to himself. Teddy sat down on the bathroom window seat, not wanting to leave Terese alone, in case she got dizzy.

Terese never heard his remark, and began washing her hair. About twenty minutes later, she came back out, put on a large terrycloth robe, wrapped her hair in a towel, and went into her closet to find something comfortable to wear.

"Why don't you just put on a nightgown, and go back to bed," Teddy suggested, still sitting on the window seat.

"No, I don't want the children to think I'm ill. I'm just going to throw on some slacks, and a top," she said, looking for a matching pair of canvas slip-ons.

"Terese, please," Teddy persuaded.

"I'll come back up and lie down for a while with Katie, when she takes her afternoon nap," Terese said, reassuring him when she caught the look on his face.

Terese brushed her teeth, and quickly blew her still damp hair dry. Teddy watched her as she combed through her hair, and swiftly pulled it back with a ribbon. After putting on moisturizer, and a little lipstick, Terese headed for the hallway.

"I'll just be a minute," she said. "I left my computer on."

"I'll do it," Teddy offered.

"No, I'll do it," Terese insisted. "I don't want to lose any of the material I was working on. Computers have never been your long suit," she said, smiling.

Teddy followed Terese up the stairs to the attic, and waited for her to finish shutting down her computer. Then they went downstairs together, with Teddy carrying Terese's uneaten breakfast on its tray. When they reached the entrance hall, they could see the entire group still gathered in the living room, including the Chief and the rest of his investigative team. The Chief had taken over directing the questioning, and Mrs. Swensen was giving a thorough report to him. Teddy set the breakfast tray down on the hall table, and then joined Terese in the living room.

Ryan stood pensively nearby, listening to Mrs. Swensen recount the events.

When Teddy looked out one of the back north-facing living room windows, he could see Anne and Mr. Chang outside with the children. They had been petting the horses near the back fence, and were now returning to the house.

After coming inside, Anne had suggested to the children that they all play a game of Monopoly together at the kitchen table, and Mr. Chang had decided to return to the living room now that they were all safely inside. Leah, sensing something was terribly wrong, had remained with the children, finding a comfortable spot under the kitchen table.

The first thing Mr. Chang saw when he entered the living room was a beautiful oil painting that Terese had done of the children, hanging over the fireplace. He soon took a seat at the far end of the room, in a large wingchair, in order to stay out of everyone's way. He sat quietly alone near the fireplace, attentively listening to Mrs. Swensen's account. This was the first time Mr. Chang had sat in this room, and he soon began taking in the comfortable space, while still remaining focused on the conversations.

The walls of the living room were painted a soft, pale, buttery-yellow color, which showed off the darker-toned silk taffeta draperies, with their extravagant trim and tassels. A few Chippendale pieces, beautifully carved in a dark cherry, created a refined mood, and the large, comfortable over-stuffed sofa, with two matching club chairs, rested nearby.

The entire entrance of the room was now filled with people, as the Chief continued his investigation. Mr. Chang listened to Mrs. Swensen's husband being interviewed now. He watched as sunlight poured in through the wall of tall, colonial divided-light windows, with one exposure to the south, and the other directed to the north, looking out to the back of the property. Mr. Chang counted the points of entry there were in this room alone. The whole space seemed so bright and cheerful, which did not fit with the serious mood, and emotional conversations, now taking place in the room.

Mr. Chang continued to listen to the Chief, probing for more information, as the living room sheers, under the shimmering draperies, moved with the breeze that came across the room. The home appeared to be trying to cleanse itself of the morning's events.

This was an impossible home to secure, Mr. Chang thought to himself, with so many doors and windows. It would be easy for someone to gain entry again. He began to mentally put a plan in place. He could only imagine the terror that Terese had felt when Andrews and Jones forced their way into her home.

Mr. Chang, without disturbing anyone, got up and used the phone in the small, cozy game room situated on the other side of the living room fireplace, then returned to the same chair, not speaking a word to anyone.

The Chief questioned Terese next, and she retold the story of what had happened to her. Teddy could see she was still somewhat in a daze, and he asked her twice to go back upstairs and lie down for a while. However, Terese wanted to continue so that the Chief would have the information he needed to file his report, and to apprehend the two men.

Finally, Ryan ended the interview. Terese reluctantly went upstairs with him, while Teddy promised to find Katie for her nap. He knew Terese would lie down if Katie were with her, as they always took an afternoon nap together.

When Teddy finally came back downstairs, everyone was leaving. The Chief had assured him that they would keep an eye on the house, and that he would leave one of his investigators behind for the day. He also made arrangements by phone to have three retired officers, all personally known to him, take eight-hour shifts around-the-clock at the house. This way, someone would always be there to protect the family, and Teddy had agreed to cover all costs.

A short while after the Chief and his staff had gone, the doorbell rang, and Mr. Chang offered to get up to answer it. When he returned to the living room, he had two men with him.

Mr. Chang signaled Teddy to join him in the front hall.

"I hope you don't mind," Mr. Chang said, in a low whispering voice, "but I have asked these men to come to your home. They are specialists in electronics," he explained, "and I would appreciate having your permission to take them through the house."

"You think the house is bugged?" Teddy asked, also in a whisper.

"Yes," Mr. Chang acknowledged, nodding.

"Of course," Teddy said, thankful for Mr. Chang's initiative.

"We will also need to get into your bedroom," Mr. Chang warned.

"I'll go up with you," Teddy said.

When they had finished with Teddy and Terese's bedroom, bath, closet and patio, Mr. Chang accompanied his Chinese colleagues through the rest of the house, checking each room, closet and pantry. And indeed, as Mr. Chang had surmised, after sweeping the house, they found that almost every room had been bugged, including the telephone system.

When the debugging had been accomplished, Mr. Chang and his men returned to the living room and showed everyone their catch, before taking it all out of the house. Mr. Chang was sure that Andrews and Jones, the day of the first break-in, had placed the advanced listening devices and wiretapping mechanisms. Teddy agreed with him.

Before leaving, the two men set up a sophisticated monitoring device in the front hall. When they had completed the task, Mr. Chang showed them out and then joined the others in the living room.

Terese came back downstairs again about a half hour later, and entered the living room. Teddy looked over at her, and could see the exhausted expression on her face.

Getting up from his chair, Teddy took her hand in his. "C'mon, Terese. Everyone has gone. Why don't I walk you back upstairs, and I'll lie down with you for a while in our room."

"I haven't seen the boys. Where are they?" Terese asked.

"They're playing Monopoly with Anne in the kitchen, Terese. They're fine."

"I'm so glad Anne's here," Terese said, with emotion coming into her voice, sitting down in one of the chairs. "I'm so glad you're all here. I don't know what we would have done," Terese said.

"C'mon Terese," Teddy repeated. "Let's go up."

Mr. Chang and Ryan were already on their feet.

"You should stay in bed today," Ryan instructed. "We can all take care of ourselves. Mrs. Swensen is here, if we should need anything, and I'll come up to check on you once you're settled down again."

"Yes," Mr. Chang added, "Please do not be concerned about us."

"I do feel tired," Terese said, getting up from her chair. "Ryan, when you come up, bring the boys with you, okay?" Terese asked. "I want to make sure they don't have any questions about what happened. Katie is still sleeping, and I don't want her around when I talk to them."

"I will," Ryan promised.

Teddy helped Terese up the stairs, and Ryan went to get the boys.

More than two hours had passed when Teddy came down again, and found everyone in the kitchen. Terese showed no signs of the harm she had suffered earlier in the day, and everyone was thankful. She was simply exhausted, but Teddy and Ryan did not want to leave her alone.

Ryan was now staying with Terese while she slept. Reading a book he had pulled from the library shelf, Ryan stretched out on a comfortable chaise lounge in the corner of their bedroom, near the French doors. He soon found it difficult to concentrate on what he was reading, and finally put the book down, as thoughts moved incessantly through his mind.

Downstairs, in the kitchen, the boys and Katie were just finishing eating a snack that Mrs. Swensen had prepared. Now the boys and Mr. Swensen were about to go outside to take care of grooming the horses and cleaning their stalls. Teddy thought it was best for the boys to stick with their usual Saturday routine, although Michael was staying home from his game.

Anne began putting the Monopoly game back in order, sorting the money, and Katie was helping her put the game pieces away. "Do you want to go out to play on your swing set with me, Katie?" Anne asked, knowing Mrs. Swensen wanted to talk to Teddy.

"Yes," Katie said happily, slipping off her chair.

Anne put the game away in the morning room's window-seat storage, and soon the two were out the door, walking over to the children's play set.

When Teddy sat down at the kitchen table, Mrs. Swensen turned away from the sink. "Is Mrs. Townsend all right?" she asked, with a tone of concern.

"She's sleeping now," Teddy answered. "Ryan just checked on her a little while ago, and he's going to stay with her. She's just tired."

Turning away, Mrs. Swensen could no longer fight back the tears that were falling down her face.

"You can bring a sandwich up to Ryan, though, if there are any left," Teddy suggested.

"Yes," Mrs. Swensen answered, "there's a whole tray in the refrigerator."

"Has Mr. Chang eaten?" Teddy asked.

"He said he would wait until you came down," she answered.

"I'll go get him," Teddy offered.

"I'll look in on Mrs. Townsend then," Mrs. Swensen said, wiping her tears with a tissue. Teddy watched her, as she began putting a tray together for Ryan.

"She's doing quite well, Mrs. Swensen. You know how strong she is."

"I couldn't believe my eyes this morning." She said, her Swedish accent more pronounced. "We never even heard their car," she continued, shaking her head.

"It certainly wasn't your fault, Mrs. Swensen. We're grateful you were here to find Terese."

Wiping her eyes once again, Mrs. Swensen straightened the flowered apron that covered her crisp housedress, then selected a club sandwich for Ryan, and fixed his plate with a few sweet pickles and some potato chips.

Teddy watched Mrs. Swensen, to make sure she was okay.

Mrs. Swensen then poured a glass of ice water, and added it to the tray. She and Mr. Swensen had been with the Townsends since Michael was born, and they loved the children as if they were their own. She worried about Terese, and the baby. Mrs. Swensen knew that things can sometimes go wrong, and that Terese was not yet out of danger.

"Why don't you take that up to Ryan, and I'll get Mr. Chang," Teddy offered.

"Yes, I will," Mrs. Swensen acknowledged lifting Ryan's tray.

"And don't worry about dinner tonight, I know you've had your hands full today. We'll just order something in."

"Are you sure?" Mrs. Swensen asked. "I have to go to the store this afternoon anyway. We're out of just about everything."

"You'll have enough to do tomorrow. I think everyone will probably stay over, so get enough of whatever you might need for breakfast, and I can barbecue some chicken, or something, Sunday afternoon. Get extra salads and meat from the deli, so that you don't have to prepare anything special."

"Thank you," Mrs. Swensen said, appreciating his thoughtfulness.

"Is Mattie able to come in for the weekend?" Teddy asked.

"She's already here, doing Mr. Chang's laundry and ironing in the basement," Mrs. Swensen answered.

"I'm glad she's so reliable," Teddy answered.

"Yes, she's a very good worker," Mrs. Swensen agreed.

"I also want Michael to move his things back to his own room this afternoon, so that Mattie can clean it and get it ready for Ryan."

"Michael and Matthew moved his things back early this morning, before you went to Chinatown."

"They did?" Teddy asked.

"Mrs. Townsend told me that she had a long talk with Michael yesterday afternoon, about what he was doing to Matthew."

"I was wondering why he was being so nice this morning," Teddy said.

Mrs. Swensen just nodded.

"Anne said that she could sleep in Katie's room," Teddy added.

"I'll make sure there are clean sheets on the beds," Mrs. Swensen, responded.

"Mattie can do that," Teddy instructed. "Just let us know when you are leaving for the store."

"I will," Mrs. Swensen answered. "I have an order to pick up at the bakery, too."

"We'll get through this, Mrs. Swensen," Teddy offered, to comfort her. "If you need additional help in the kitchen, perhaps Mattie's sister will be available."

"Yes," Mrs. Swensen answered, lifting Ryan's tray.

When Mrs. Swensen took Ryan's tray upstairs, Teddy went into the library and brought Mr. Chang back with him. They both made up their plates with the food Mrs. Swensen had prepared earlier, and took their lunch outside to the back of the house, where they were closer to the children.

It was a beautiful afternoon, and felt cooler at the back of the house, where a large oak tree shaded a table and chairs, and some of the other lawn furniture. Mr. Swensen washed everything down, in his usual morning routine, and Mrs. Swensen had placed a clean tablecloth on the table afterward.

Anne played with Katie on the swings, and it seemed so peaceful sitting there, as Teddy and Mr. Chang ate their lunches and watched the boys begin washing down their horses near the greenhouse.

When they took over the farm, Mr. Swensen had hooked up a hose from the greenhouse with a warm water system, and it was apparent that the animals enjoyed the ritual. Leah sat nearby, waiting her turn, and Mr. Swensen watched the boys to make sure they did a thorough job, making suggestions now and again when he felt the horses were not being rinsed thoroughly.

Mr. Swensen was an old horseman, as well as an excellent caretaker, and Teddy felt very lucky to have him and Mrs. Swensen with his family for so many years. The Swensens were assured of having a home with them for the rest of their lives, even after they retired. They were like an extra set of grandparents to the children.

While everyone watched the activities of the boys, Mrs. Swensen brought out a tray of individual homemade strawberry shortcakes. They were exactly like those she had served to everyone else after lunch, and each contained a large dollop of vanilla ice cream. Mrs. Swensen served them to Teddy and Mr. Chang.

"These look great," Teddy acknowledged, as Mrs. Swensen cleared their empty plates.

"Quite a treat," Mr. Chang added.

"I'm leaving to run my errands now, Mr. Townsend. Is there anything special that I can pick up for any of you?" she asked.

"Mr. Chang?" Teddy asked.

"No, nothing for me," he answered. "Unless you see a copy of the *New York Times*. I've already read the *Tribune*."

"We only get the Sunday edition of the Times," Teddy offered, "but the newsstand might still have a copy of today's New York papers and the *Washington Post*."

"I'll look," Mrs. Swensen offered.

"Anne," Teddy called, "can Mrs. Swensen pick anything up for you at the store?"

"No, but thanks," Anne responded

"How about some double chocolate ice cream bars," Teddy suggested. "Those have always been Terese's favorite."

Mrs. Swensen smiled. "They're already on my list. I'll be off then," she added, as she went back to the cottage for her purse and keys.

As Mrs. Swensen left, Teddy looked over at Mr. Chang. "I can't believe this happened today," he said.

"Terese is very strong," Mr. Chang offered.

"I don't think it has hit her yet," Teddy responded. "My God, they could have killed her, and the baby."

Teddy was visibly upset, and Mr. Chang let him talk.

"Terese never outwardly shows how she feels," he said, "especially when other people are around. She tells me," Teddy added, "but she usually hides her feelings from everyone else."

"Yes," Mr. Chang commented. "That is her strength."

The two sat there for a while, quietly thinking. When Katie grew tired of the swing set, she ran down to join Leah and the boys, and Anne walked back to the table where Teddy and Mr. Chang were sitting.

"Is it all right if I join you?" Anne asked.

"Of course," Teddy responded, both men standing up, and Teddy helping her with a chair.

"How is Terese doing?" Anne asked, as she sat down.

"She's resting. Ryan is staying with her," Teddy added.

"Did she know the men who broke in?" Anne asked.

"Yes," Teddy answered honestly. "They were the same two men who were found on the grounds Monday morning."

"What did they want?" Anne questioned, wanting more of the story.

"They took an antique box," Teddy answered. "It was quite valuable, and had been handed down to me," he finished.

"Was it insured?" Anne asked, "I would imagine that your insurance will cover it."

"There's more to it than that," Teddy said, thinking for a moment.

"What was in the box?" Anne questioned.

"A pendant," Teddy explained. "Quite old, and unique. It is irreplaceable," he answered, wondering how much he could tell her. Teddy decided to stop there.

"Well," Anne said, "I hope the police will recover it."

"Yes," Teddy responded, "but I also want Mr. Chang to stay at the house, and continue to run his own investigation," Teddy added.

"Then you want me to continue to help you with this?" Mr. Chang asked.

"If you're available," Teddy questioned.

"I would be honored," Mr. Chang responded.

Saturday Evening

After everyone had eaten the Chinese food that Teddy ordered in that evening, Matthew showed Anne his trove of insects, the remainder of which had now been entirely cataloged and mounted. Anne, not wanting to hurt Matthew's feelings, had shown much interest in the collection, even though she was terrified of half the assemblage.

By ten o'clock everyone had retired to his or her rooms. Ryan's twin bed in the new nursery was comfortable, and he got up hourly to check on Terese. At midnight, a new police officer came to the door and relieved the officer who had taken over at four in the afternoon. Leah was not sure if she liked the new one or not, and was quick to note that he brought no food with him. The other officer had given her part of his chicken salad sandwich, and she could still smell its fragrance on his hands when he gave her a pat goodbye.

Leah found she could not sleep, and paced the house for almost all of the night, watching the back pasture through the darkened game room. She sensed someone was still out there, watching. And, they were.

CHAPTER 28

▲

THE DISCOVERY

Sunday

The next morning Terese woke up early, showered, dressed, and then organized the children, getting them ready for church. As children will, they all seemed to have forgotten what had happened the day before, and only wanted to know the secure world their parents had created for them.

Before going downstairs, Terese wanted to look in on Anne, to make sure that Ryan's houseman had brought over her luggage. Terese softly knocked on Katie's door, hoping that Anne was now awake.

"Come in," Anne answered. She was still in bed, and just waking.

"Hi," Terese said. "Did you sleep well?"

"Very," Anne acknowledged.

"Did Jen deliver all your things last night?" Terese asked.

"Yes," Anne said, pointing to her luggage. "Thank you."

"Would you like to go to Mass with us?" Terese asked.

"I would," Anne, replied, sitting up in bed, still half asleep.

"Teddy and Ryan have already showered and dressed. Why don't you go in and use my bathroom, Anne. And help yourself to anything you need."

"Oh, thanks, Terese," Anne replied. "How are you feeling today?"

"Quite well, thanks," Terese smiled.

"What Mass are we going to?" Anne asked.

"Probably ten o'clock. You have plenty of time, Anne. It's only about eight-thirty. We'll wait for you downstairs," Terese added.

After Anne showered and dressed, she returned her things to Katie's bedroom, and headed downstairs.

When she reached the kitchen, Anne found it was full of activity. Mr. Chang was already reading the *New York Times*, and had a plate of sausages and waffles in front of him. And, another retired officer, who had come on duty at eight o'clock, had now joined Mr. Chang for breakfast. The clock on the kitchen wall now read 9:15.

"Can I get you something, Anne?" Terese asked. "Some juice or tea?"

"Juice would be perfect," Anne answered, grabbing her vitamins out of her purse.

"Would you like some waffles before we go?" Terese asked.

"Oh, no thanks. Just the juice for me."

"We'll all go out for a big brunch together after church," Terese suggested. "Mr. Chang, when Mr. and Mrs. Swensen return from their services, would you let them know we're eating out."

"Yes, I will," Mr. Chang, answered. "And thank you for the delicious waffles."

"Yes, thank you," the officer added.

"Oh, you're both welcome. There is more batter in a pitcher on the counter. We'll probably be back around two o'clock."

Soon, the entire group had assembled in the driveway, and Teddy and Ryan adjusted the seats in the sports van to fit everyone in. Leah stood by, whimpering, when she was told she had to stay behind.

"You watch the house, Leah, we'll be back soon," Teddy instructed her.

As the van pulled around the driveway, Leah took her place under the large pine, and watched them until they fell out of site. Suddenly, she caught a faint scent. It was the two men who had been hanging around their property. Leah decided to track their scents again. Slowly she looked around, and began checking the grounds near the barn. Usually the horses would let her know if anyone they didn't like was around, but they were let out to the pasture early in the morning.

"Leah?" Mr. Chang, called, coming out the back of the house. "Come here girl," he coaxed.

Leah came trotting back to Mr. Chang, who had all of the leftover sausages from breakfast in a napkin for her.

"Come in the house, girl," he said, urging her to come with him.

Following the scent of the sausage, Leah stayed close behind Mr. Chang, all the way back into the kitchen.

"That's a good girl," he said, offering her a half a sausage at a time.

When Leah had finished, she kissed Mr. Chang's hand, and continued to follow him back into the library, where she decided to take a morning nap. She was completely exhausted from not having slept the night before.

Three hours later the group returned, with everyone piling in through the kitchen door.

"I want you all to put your play clothes on before going outside," Terese reminded the children.

Teddy and Ryan went to the library, to check in with Mr. Chang. Leah was still asleep, never waking when Teddy came into the room. The officer on duty had been out on the grounds when they returned, and had nothing to report.

"What's with Leah?" Teddy asked Mr. Chang.

"I don't think she slept a wink last night," Mr. Chang offered.

"Ryan and I are going to go horseback riding with the boys for a while," Teddy informed. "Would you like to join us?" Teddy asked.

"I'll keep an eye on things here," Mr. Chang offered.

"We'll just be gone an hour or so," Teddy explained, before going upstairs to change.

Terese looked out the large bay window in the kitchen, which had a view of the backyard and barn, and saw Mr. Swensen saddling Teddy and Ryan's horses.

"Teddy," Terese asked, as he came into the kitchen, having just changed into his riding clothes, "are you and the boys still going riding this afternoon?"

"Just for about an hour," Teddy answered. "Ryan is coming too."

"Do you think you really should?" Terese asked.

"I think it'll be all right," Teddy answered.

The same strange tension that had pervaded Terese's entire being the day before had not yet left, and she felt uneasy about their going riding.

"We're trying to return to normal, right? Isn't that what you wanted?"

"Yes, I guess so," Terese answered.

When the boys and Ryan came into the kitchen, they were all excited about going on the ride. Terese offered them some bottles of water, and then watched them as they headed out for the horses.

Anne came in next, and Mrs. Swensen put some dark green mats down on the oval cherry table, setting it up for tea.

"Don't you want to go riding?" Terese asked Anne. "You're welcome to take my horse," Terese added, with a smile. "She could use some exercise."

"Perhaps another time," Anne responded. "I'd rather stay here with you today," she said, slipping into the bay-window seat that was part of the table's seating.

Mrs. Swensen continued to set the table with matching cups, saucers and dessert plates for each of them, using Terese's favorite botanical china, by Portmeirion. Bringing over the pot of tea, which had been steeping near the large stove, Mrs. Swensen began to pour a cup for both Anne and Terese. Then she began filling a plate with some large scalloped sugar cookies that had just cooled from coming out of the oven. The cookies still had the essence of grated orange peel and butter wafting up from them.

"Oh, thank you, Mrs. Swensen," Terese acknowledged. "These are one of my favorites."

"You look so much better today," Mrs. Swensen commented, touching her cheek in a motherly way.

"I'm fine, now," Terese responded.

The large, comfortable kitchen faced east, with additional windows on both the north and the south sides of the house, and was filled with light from three exposures. As Anne looked around the kitchen, she admired the hand-painted cabinets that showed off their detailed English moldings, finished in the same deep cream color that ran through each room of the house. The counters were all in matching, contrasting granite of darker tones of tan, brown and beiges, and a large island had a well-used butcher-block top. The floor was the same beautiful dark wood tone that matched the rest of the floors in the house

"Terese," Anne asked, "did you do all this yourself?"

"The furnishings are ours, but we're just renting right now until our place farther out is finished. It's going to be an exact, but updated, replica of Whippoorwill."

"I love this room," Anne said.

"It's my favorite too," Terese admitted. "We are duplicating almost everything here in our new place. The cabinets are from a special source in England, called Smallbone. I do love decorating though, and planning spaces. It has been fun working on the architectural plans, and Mrs. Swensen has had some good ideas that we are implementing."

Mrs. Swensen looked over, smiling at Terese. Terese had asked her for her input on the kitchen design, and they had made some needed changes together."

"I enjoy all that too," Anne admitted. "I always wanted to become a designer."

"Why did you go to law school, then?" Terese asked.

"My father's a lawyer. It was more his dream than mine."

"We have a great design school here," Terese, shared. "The Art Institute, in Chicago, is one of the finest."

"Is that where you went?" Anne asked.

"Yes, although I focused more on the arts—especially painting," Terese shared.

As Teddy, Ryan and the boys rode out through the pasture, they were met by a beautiful afternoon. The horses seemed excited, as they made their way down a path that the boys always used. Long blades of emerald grass felt cool under the horses' hooves, and the countryside abounded with the sounds of birds calling to one another. When they reached the paddock gate, they all stopped for a minute.

Michael quickly got down off his horse and opened the gate for everyone to pass through, while Matthew took the reins and led his horse.

"Where do you boys want to ride today?" Teddy asked.

Matthew looked far across the large pasture to the north woods, and acted as if he had seen something.

"Dad?" he asked.

"How about riding through the woods, and then over to St. Mary's Road and back," Michael interrupted, as he got back on his horse.

Matthew was still looking far across the pasture. "Dad?" he asked again.

"Yes, Matthew?"

"I thought I saw something flickering in the trees over there."

"Don't point," Teddy said quickly, when Matthew started to raise his hand. "Do you mean in the woods?" he asked.

"Yes, near that old tree house. It's as if a mirror is reflecting in the sun. Do you think it's those men?" Matthew asked.

"Whoever it is, they're trespassing," Teddy said, "and you boys are going to have to go back to the house."

"Why?" Michael asked.

"I want you to call the police station. And then get hold of the Chief at home. I'm sure he's not working today. You have his residence telephone number on your baseball list, Michael."

"What should I say?" Michael asked.

"Ask everyone to meet us at the entrance of that old gravel road, on the back side of our property. Your Uncle Ryan and I will wait for them there. And make sure the officer at the house stays at the house."

"Okay Dad," Michael said, as he started to turn his horse.

Teddy looked over at Matthew next, who looked a little left out. "You had better help him Matthew," Teddy said, "You can tell Mr. Swensen what is going on."

"Okay, Dad," Matthew responded.

"Mr. Swensen is going to want to come with us, but tell him I need him to stay with your mother and the other women, in case the officer needs help protecting them. We actually don't know how many men are involved in all this."

"Okay, Dad." Matthew acknowledged.

"Are we suppose to meet you at the same place?" Michael asked, anxious to leave.

"No. I want you boys to stay at the house with your mother."

"But how will you know if we can't get hold of the Chief?" Michael asked.

Teddy thought for a moment. "Okay," he finally said. "Why don't you meet us at that big fallen oak, at the east side of our property. It's closer, and they won't see us there. And, Michael," Teddy added, "go all the way around and keep out of sight, okay?"

"I will," Michael said.

"Oh, and Michael," Teddy added, "grab my cell phone. I left it on the kitchen counter."

Soon the boys cantered off on their horses, and returned to the house.

"Do you think it's a smart idea to allow them to come back?" Ryan asked.

"They'll be all right," Teddy assured him. "I trust them completely. If you want your children to be responsible," Teddy added, "you have to give them responsibilities."

"Well, I hope you're right," Ryan added, as they went along. "But I can't believe Terese will allow them to come back out here."

"They want to be a part of this," Teddy said, "especially after what happened to their mother. And I'm not going to place them in any danger," Teddy added.

"Still …" Ryan answered.

Teddy tried to look past Ryan from time to time, as they rode deeper into the woods. But he did not see what his young son had seen, although he never doubted Matthew's word, for he believed his observations to be as reliable as any adult's.

In a few minutes, Teddy and Ryan had reached the fallen oak and tied up their horses. The time passed slowly.

About fifteen minutes later, they could hear Michael and Matthew's approach, as their horses' hooves pounded the soft floor of the woods. They soon came into sight, and pulled up where Teddy was standing.

"The Chief said to meet him at exactly three o'clock," Michael reported, "and not to go in without him."

"Did you see them, Dad?" Matthew asked.

"Not yet, but I'm sure they're there," Teddy responded. "By the way, is Leah in the house?" Teddy asked.

"I didn't see her," Matthew responded.

"Me either," Michael added. "Mom is really upset. She almost didn't let us come."

"Do you have my cell phone?" Teddy asked, looking at Michael.

"I knew I was forgetting something," Michael answered, with a devastated look on his face.

"That's okay," Teddy said, reassuring him. "The phone calls were what was most important."

"We wouldn't be here at all," Matthew said, "if it wasn't for Mr. Chang. He said you needed to get the Chief's message, and we were the perfect messengers."

"Who is he Dad?" Michael asked. "He's kind of strange."

"What do you mean, he's strange?" Matthew defended. "I like him."

"He's kind of strange, weird, that's all. He hardly ever talks, and there's just something different about him."

"All right, all right," Teddy said, looking at Michael. "That's enough. This isn't the time or the place. But you make sure, Michael, to show the proper respect to Mr. Chang. We are all very grateful for his help."

"I will," Michael said.

"We'd better get started," Teddy suggested, turning to Ryan. "We want you boys to go back to the house now," Teddy said.

"Can't we help you, Dad?" Michael asked.

"I don't want you guys to get hurt."

"We could distract them," Matthew suggested, "so that they don't hear you when you approach the tree house."

Teddy thought for a long moment.

"We could have a race, back to the house," Michael suggested.

"We do it every day, after school, Dad," Matthew added.

"That's actually a good idea," Teddy said, turning to the boys. "Are you wearing your watches?"

"Yes," Michael answered.

"What time do you have?" Teddy asked.

"2:45," Michael answered, looking down.

"Me too," Matthew confirmed.

"Okay," Teddy said, "but I want you to be as far away from them, as you can get."

"We will Dad," the boys agreed.

"At exactly 3:15, start your race, just as you come out of the woods, and go across the eastern field to the house."

"Okay, Dad," Michael said, with excitement coming into his voice.

"And don't try to angle across, they probably have rifles. I want you both completely out of their range, understand?"

"Yes, Dad," Michael agreed.

"Matthew, can I count on you?" Teddy asked.

"Yes, Dad," Matthew assured.

"After you get back, take the horses directly into the barn, and slowly cool them down, so they don't get sick. And then stay right there, in the barn, until we get back. Don't try to cross over to the house, okay?"

"Okay, Dad," Michael agreed.

"Promise?" Teddy asked.

"Promise," they both agreed.

"Now, I want you both to keep track of the time. 3:15, right?"

"Right," they both agreed.

Teddy and Ryan then mounted their horses, and were soon out of sight, leaving the boys hidden deep in the woods, far from the men.

Andrews was now perched on top of the old abandoned tree house, with a high-powered set of binoculars held up to his eyes. A camera with a telephoto lens, mounted on a tripod, was sitting nearby. It was this lens that Matthew had caught sight of, as it reflected the sunlight. It was now focused on Teddy's house.

All the time, from the woods, they had been monitoring every move Teddy and his family had made. There was also a tent with recording equipment, which had been used to pick up telephone and other conversations from the equipment they had placed in the house.

Andrews looked out across the pasture, and saw no one. Jones stood on the ground near a big sprawling tree, and drank coffee from a thermos. They never saw Teddy, Ryan and the boys riding out from the house. They had just returned from getting new supplies, finding that they were no long able to pick up the transmissions from the house. They thought one of the monitoring devices had broken down, and had gone out to replace a major piece of equipment in Waukegan.

It was just three o'clock when Teddy and Ryan met up with the Chief at the entrance of the old road. The Chief had three officers with him. Ryan and Teddy were anxious to get started, but the Chief would not allow them to go in—not after what had happened to Terese. They were instructed to wait by the road. Teddy had argued persuasively, but the Chief insisted, and they had to stay behind. He was already upset about what the boys planned to do, for it was now too late to stop them.

The Chief, and the three other members of his special team, who were expert marksmen, spread out undetected into the woods. All but the Chief were prepared for what was ahead, and wore camouflage gear. They now had to be on the scene to protect Michael and Matthew, if anything went wrong. Silently they watched, and waited, for the boys to chase across the eastern field before they made their move.

At exactly 3:15 p.m., Teddy and the others could hear a whooping sound, as Michael and Matthew called back and forth to each other, and galloped their horses out of the woods and across the eastern edge of a far field.

"It's the kids," Andrews called down. "They're having another race."

Jones looked out from where he was standing.

Andrews watched from the old wooden platform, and began taking pictures of the boys through his telephoto lens. Jones watched the scene through a pair of binoculars.

"Look at the little one go," Jones said, excitedly.

Suddenly, a branch cracked, and Jones could be seen warily scanning the area of the woods around them. Letting his binoculars down around his neck, he reached for his rifle. He had spotted the Chief and one of his men.

Reaching into his pocket, he pulled out two grenade-like devices. Pulling both clips, Jones threw one in the direction of the Chief and his partner, and the other towards the two other officers positioned on the other side.

"Look out," Jones warned Andrews, as he let out a shot. "They're on each side of us!"

Smoke rushed out of the devices, and billowed into the air, acting as an effective screen for both Andrews and Jones to escape.

The smoke continued to billow, blocking everyone's view, and Teddy and Ryan began moving hurriedly into the woods to help. The Chief and his officers were immediately on their feet charging through the smoke. Andrews had already jumped to the ground, and he and Jones were blindly firing shots into the smoke shield.

Teddy and Ryan knew someone had been hit, as they made their approach. They heard a loud moan, then a heavy thump, as someone came down hard on the ground. The smoke was so thick it was choking them. They could not see so much as a foot in any direction.

Crawling close to the ground, Teddy and Ryan made their way toward the sound, and soon came upon one of the smoking canisters. Teddy picked up the device, and threw it into an open clearing, where the breeze picked up the smoke and carried it off and away from them. When the air had cleared, they could see what had happened.

The Chief, and one of his men, had been wounded. Andrews and Jones were gone, as well as the two other officers. While Ryan attended the one officer, Teddy went over and knelt beside the Chief, trying to see where he had been hit.

"It's your left leg, Tom," Teddy said. "Ryan will be over to help you in a minute. I'm going to use my belt as a tourniquet on your thigh."

Teddy and Ryan could hear the boys coming up on their horses at a furious pace, and they were soon on the scene. There was no time to scold them for disobeying their father's orders. Teddy knew he needed their help.

Ryan ran over to the Chief, and saw that Teddy had everything under control, then went back to the other officer who was in critical condition, bleeding from a head wound. Calling to Michael, Ryan reached into his pants pocket for his car keys.

"Michael, go to the house and have someone call for a couple of ambulances, and then get my medical bag out of the trunk of my car, and get back here as fast as you can."

Michael caught the keys as they flew through the air, and then turned his horse and galloped back towards the house.

Matthew was already at Teddy's side, and tried to help make the Chief more comfortable. The Chief's leg was shattered where the bullet went in, and was not the clean cauterized hole that movies always depicted.

"Does that hurt?" Teddy asked the Chief, as he tightened the tourniquet.

"Not at all," the Chief responded, trying to gain control. "We didn't expect to be walking into a battlefield," he said, looking up briefly at Teddy. "How are my men doing?"

"Your partner was hurt. Ryan's attending to him now."

"And my other two men?" the Chief asked.

"They went after them," Teddy explained. "Everything's under control, and Michael's calling for an ambulance. We'll have you both out of here shortly."

"Thank you," the Chief managed.

"I'm truly sorry you got hurt, Tom," Teddy conveyed.

"I'm okay," the Chief insisted.

"Matthew, I'm going to borrow Gypsy," Teddy said, as he grabbed the Chief's rifle. "When your Uncle Ryan is free, ask him to check and see if the tourniquet needs to be loosened. I want to get out to the back road, so I can show the ambulances the way in."

Matthew had already removed his shirt, and then began making a bandage by wrapping his undershirt around the Chief's leg wound, wrapping his shirt around that.

"Will you be all right, if I leave you alone?" Teddy asked Matthew.

"Of course," Matthew answered, "I'll take care of him."

Teddy went over and untied Matthew's black Arabian mare, and swung up into her saddle.

Matthew's strong little horse ran swiftly through the woods to a far open clearing, never faltering from Teddy's heavy weight. She seemed to move effortlessly across the padded path, never tripping where fallen branches blocked her way.

Teddy could see Andrews and Jones in their car. It had been driven quite a way off the road, which explained why the Chief could not find the vehicle when he arrived. The two other officers, who had trailed them from behind, were getting into one of the police cars, and were about to go in pursuit down the road—a road which Teddy knew would soon entrap Andrews and Jones where it became a dead end.

With his legs hanging loose in the saddle, Teddy pulled Gypsy up to the fence at the end of the clearing.

Dust swelled up in a rolling mass on the gravel road, and within a few seconds, Teddy could no longer see the chase. Leaning over, Teddy unlocked the wide gate, which closed off the woods from the road, and hoped the ambulances would be there soon.

Teddy could hear sirens way off in the distance, then heard the sound of cars sliding on gravel down at the end of the road. He knew that Andrews and Jones had somehow turned around, and were making their way back in his direction.

Teddy quickly slid off Matthew's horse. "Go find Matthew, Gypsy," he commanded, slapping her rump, not wanting her injured in any crossfire. Gypsy quickly took off. His own horse, and the one Ryan was riding, were tied up in the woods and out of sight.

Teddy crouched down in the ditch at the side of the road, and was well hidden from view in the thick green brush. He positioned the Chief's rifle in the direction of the car, while it flew through a wall of dust. Aiming low at the tires, Teddy pulled the trigger just as they streaked past him. The shot blasted across the road, hitting a tire, but they just sped on past him.

Next, the police car went by, and Teddy watched as the officers fired several rounds. The car soon slid off the road and into the ditch, where it finally came to a stop. The two officers were upon them in seconds. Both Andrews and Jones were hit.

The sirens were louder now, and two more police cars were turning off the main road and coming in their direction, with the two ambulances directly behind them. One of the ambulances stopped where the car went into the ditch, and Teddy waved the other forward.

While Andrews and Jones were being checked over and taken into custody, Teddy ran back down to the gate and let the ambulance driver through to where they had entered the woods, showing them where they would have to park.

"We'll need two stretchers," Teddy informed. "There are two police officers wounded, and more help in the woods."

After a few minutes, Teddy was once again beside the Chief and the other officer. Slowly, with the help of Teddy and Ryan, the paramedics lifted the Chief, and then his partner, onto their stretchers, and they all carried them through the woods to the waiting ambulance. Within minutes, the ambulance was back out on the road and racing to Lake Forest Hospital.

Teddy, Ryan, Michael and Matthew led two of the police officers who had arrived as backups, into the woods to the surveillance site. Nothing was to be touched until the Lake Forest Police Department conducted its investigation.

When they were told they were no longer needed, Teddy, Ryan and the boys rounded up their horses, and walked back to the house. By the time they returned, everyone at the house was waiting for them at the stable. Terese was in tears, and found it difficult to talk.

"It's all right, Terese," Teddy assured her. "Andrews and Jones are both in custody now."

"How could you endanger the boys like that?" Terese asked, unable to hide how upset she was.

"They were all right," Teddy said.

"They were NOT all right," Terese returned.

Teddy looked at her, and then thought for a long moment before he answered. "They're my sons, Terese, and I needed them," he said.

Michael and Matthew looked on, with a new sense of pride in their eyes.

Terese was still terribly distraught, and continued to cry as the emotions of the last two days came pouring out of her.

"Promise me" she said, to all three of them, "that you'll never, ever do anything like this again."

No one answered her.

"Promise me," Terese insisted, looking first to Teddy, and then to Michael and Matthew.

Teddy looked at the boys and nodded his head. "Okay, we promise," Teddy assured her.

Terese looked at the boys next.

"We promise Mom," Michael said, as Matthew nodded his head in agreement.

Teddy put both his arms around Terese, and pulled her closer to him. He could feel that her body was shaking, as she broke down crying again.

"It wasn't as bad as you think, Terese," Teddy said, trying to calm her down.

"It was bad enough," Terese managed.

"But it's over now," Teddy said, "and everyone's safe again."

Mr. Swensen took the horses, and they all walked back to the house together. Teddy felt relieved that his family was once again secure, and out of harm's way. However, he knew, in the back of his mind, that he needed to quash the real evil and deadly source of all that had happened.

He had to get to Marshall Mason Martel.

CHAPTER 29

▲

THE IMPLICATION

Sunday Evening

After the incident in the woods on Sunday afternoon, Teddy and Ryan knew they had to make the next move.

Around five o'clock, a detective at the Lake Forest Police Department called and asked if Teddy and Ryan could stop by the police station, to read over the report that was written, in case anything had been left out.

Teddy and Ryan went directly over there. After making a few changes, that were quickly edited, Teddy and Ryan were able to leave the police department and go over to the hospital. They wanted to see how the Chief and his partner were doing.

Shortly after six o'clock, they arrived at the hospital. As Teddy and Ryan pulled off Deerpath and onto Westmoreland, beautiful old trees gracefully marked the manicured landscape along an inviting, curving drive that eventually led to the hospital entrance.

The hospital looked similar to a late Georgian estate turned historical site, rather than a medical institution, although it had been added on to over the years. The Williamsburg brick colonial building created a warm, cheerful atmosphere for a hospital setting. The grounds also supported several other facilities, all connected to the medical needs of the community.

Teddy and Ryan followed the signs, parked in the visitors' parking lot, and walked over to the main entrance. Ryan hoped they would be able to get in to see the Chief. It would make what he planned to do that much easier.

They checked in with the reception desk on the main floor, and learned that the Chief had already been taken to his room. Teddy asked for the room number, and they proceeded to go up to see him.

When they walked into the Chief's private room, Teddy and Ryan could see he had a visitor. One of his plain-clothed investigators, Brian Stevenson, was in the room, and the Chief introduced them to him.

"The nurse at the desk told us that your partner is still in surgery," Ryan said.

"That's Danny," the Chief acknowledged, with a worried look on his face.

"They have a very capable staff here," Ryan assured him, in an effort to be consoling.

The Chief nodded. He was feeling somewhat pessimistic at the moment, having been through such a traumatic ordeal in the last few hours. He was already thinking about what he could have done to prevent any injury to his men.

"How're you feeling Tom?" Teddy asked.

"I'm okay. We're keeping a guard on Jones, while he's here at the hospital," the Chief said. "He's just coming out of recovery now, and he'll be taken up to his room, shortly."

"Recovery?" Ryan questioned.

"He was in surgery, earlier, to remove a couple of slugs in his shoulder," Brian Stevenson, said.

"How about Andrews?" Teddy asked.

"Dead on arrival," the Chief informed them. "They've already taken him to the morgue."

"Would it be possible for us to see Jones?" Ryan asked. "Alone."

"Alone?" the Chief questioned.

"We just want to ask him a couple of questions, and find out why he's been surveilling Teddy's house. He probably wouldn't talk in front of one of your men, but he might tell us," Ryan posed.

"I've never even seen Jones or Andrews up close," Teddy said. "You, Ryan and Terese have seen them, but I have not."

The Chief thought for a moment, and then looked over at Brian Stevenson and then back to Teddy.

"We don't usually allow that," the Chief said.

"Perhaps this does have something to do with one of the cases I have handled," Teddy offered. "But I won't know unless I can talk to Jones."

"He's probably still drugged from surgery," Ryan added. "Maybe we can get some information out of him."

The Chief thought for a moment more, before making his decision.

"You can see him, but I want one of my men with you," he said. "Brian will take you in."

After visiting with the Chief, they went with Brian Stevenson to where Jones was being held in recovery, and together with two members of the hospital staff who aided in the transfer, they followed Jones' gurney back to his room. As they passed a supply closet, Ryan quickly borrowed a white jacket, without missing a step, and they were soon inside Jones' room.

Carrying a bottle of intravenous fluid, an attendant hooked the container up to a bedside stand, and then checked its connection.

The floor nurse walked into the room next and looked over at the two open windows, and sniffed the air. Both Teddy and Ryan had showered and changed their soiled clothing before they went over to the police station, but Teddy had gone into the barn to check on the horses and talk to Mr. Swensen, before leaving.

"They must be fertilizing the lawns," she said, in explanation of the pungent odor, as she made Jones more comfortable.

Ryan gave Teddy a critical look, and then stared down at his shoes. "I told you that you smelled like manure," he said, under his breath.

"I guess I've gotten used to it," Teddy finally offered, ignoring Ryan's strong look. "I don't smell a thing," he said, innocently, looking at the bottom of his soles.

As soon as Jones was settled in, and the gurney was removed from the room, the nurse asked that everyone leave. They all walked out with her to the hallway, where Stevenson explained who he was, showing her his identification.

"I am going to be watching his room," Stevenson explained. "Mr. Jones is technically under arrest."

"Oh," the nurse responded.

"Until I am relieved by another officer, I have to remain with him. I also need to ask Mr. Jones a few questions," he added. "We're still conducting our investigation."

"I'll have to check with his surgeon," the nurse countered, holding back permission.

"We'll wait here in the hall," Stevenson said.

The nurse soon came back, and told Stevenson he could enter the room.

"Too bad we don't have a tape recorder," Ryan said, just before they went inside.

"I have one in my car," Stevenson offered. "Wait here. I'll just be a few minutes. I don't think he's going anywhere," he said, having noted Jones' condition.

"We'll keep watch," Ryan offered.

As soon as Stevenson was out of sight, Teddy and Ryan quietly entered Jones' room. Jones' shoulder was heavily bandaged, and he appeared to be asleep.

Ryan swiftly slipped on the white medical jacket that he had been clutching in his hand, and a pair of surgical gloves from his pocket. Just before closing the door, Teddy looked up and down the hall, to see if anyone was coming.

"Watch out the window for Stevenson," Ryan whispered to Teddy, as Teddy shut the door. "You should be able to see the front entrance of the hospital from this exposure."

Teddy went to the window and looked outside. When he turned around, he saw Ryan filling a syringe.

"What are you doing?" Teddy asked, keeping his voice low.

"Ever hear of truth serums?"

"Where'd you get it?" Teddy asked.

"You want to be implicated?" Ryan questioned.

Teddy just laughed, and looked out the window again. He spotted Brian Stevenson coming out of the front of the hospital, just as a police car swung around the circle drive in front. Teddy watched, as he stopped to talk to the two officers.

"Mr. Jones. Mr. Jones," Ryan repeated, calling him awake.

Jones tried to open his eyes, but could not keep them open. It was apparent that he was unable to focus on Ryan's face, which was to Ryan's advantage. To Jones, he just appeared to be one of the medical staff dressed in white.

"Just rest your eyes," Ryan continued. "We have to ask you a couple of questions."

Jones began falling back to sleep.

"Mr. Jones?" Ryan asked. "How are you feeling?"

Jones stirred. "Okay," he answered.

"Are you having any pain?" Ryan asked, leading him down a path of questioning.

"No, not any more."

"Do you have any family in the area we can contact?" Ryan questioned.

"No," Jones responded. "I already told you that."

Thinking it was now safe to do so, Ryan injected a minimal dose of the truth serum directly into Jones' intravenous line. He wanted to make sure it would not interfere with any of the anesthetic still in his system.

"Are you employed, Mr. Jones?" Ryan asked.

"Yes," Jones replied.

"By whom?" Ryan asked.

"I'm self-employed," he answered, trying to focus. "Are you a doctor?" Jones asked, still groggy from the anesthesia.

"Yes," Ryan said. "I'm a doctor."

Again Ryan allowed more of the drug to flow through the syringe and into Jones' intravenous line.

"Are you currently working?" Ryan asked.

"Yes," Jones responded.

"For whom?" Ryan questioned.

"Marshall Martel," Jones explained.

Teddy looked over to Ryan, and met his eyes. They finally had a definitive answer to Martel's connection in all this.

"Who is Marshall Martel?" Ryan asked, without rushing him.

"An international banker."

"What kind of work are you doing for Mr. Martel?" Ryan asked.

"An investigation."

"And who are you investigating?" Ryan probed.

"Theodore Townsend."

Ryan looked over at Teddy, who was still watching out the window. He knew Teddy was listening to every word.

"Stevenson just reached his car," Teddy said, turning to Ryan, without raising his voice.

Trying not to lose his cadence, Ryan nodded and continued on.

"Why are you investigating Mr. Townsend?" Ryan asked.

"Don't know why," Jones said.

"Does Mr. Townsend have something that Mr. Martel wants?" Ryan urged.

"Yes."

"And what is that?" Ryan asked.

"A key."

Ryan looked surprised, as he glanced over at Teddy. Teddy slowly turned around, meeting Ryan's eyes again.

"A key?" Ryan questioned. "A key to what?"

"To the stone box," Jones revealed.

"And where is the box?" Ryan asked.

"Martel has it."

"Where?" Ryan queried, maintaining a certain calm rhythm.

"In his home."

"And where is that?" Ryan inquired.

"Geneva."

"Lake Geneva?" Ryan asked. "In Wisconsin?"

"Switzerland," Jones finished.

"Why did he take it to Switzerland?" Ryan asked.

"It's safer there," Jones explained.

"Do you remember Mr. Martel's address?" Ryan questioned, hoping he would.

"It's the big place, on the lake."

Ryan looked at Teddy again, and Teddy acknowledged Ryan's thought, before he once again turned to watch out the window.

"Here comes Stevenson," Teddy warned. "He just went through the front entrance."

"We have to get the key," Jones mumbled.

"Mr. Townsend doesn't have the key. The key is lost."

"The key is lost?" Jones asked.

"Yes. You'll have to tell Mr. Martel that the key is lost. Now try to get some sleep, Mr. Jones. Someone will be in to check on you later."

Ryan capped the syringe, slipped it into his jacket pocket, and took off the white coat and the surgical gloves. Then he pushed the gloves into one of his pant's pockets.

"Let's go," Ryan ordered, as Teddy followed him out the door.

Just as the door shut behind them, Stevenson came onto the floor. He was carrying a portable tape recorder.

"All ready?" Teddy asked, as he approached them.

Stevenson nodded. "Sorry I took so long," he apologized.

"No problem" Teddy said, as they entered the room.

Teddy walked over to the bed, and took a long look at Jones.

"Do you recognize him?" Stevenson asked.

"I'm afraid not," Teddy responded.

"Mr. Jones," Stevenson called.

Jones did not stir.

"Mr. Jones?" he said, raising his voice.

"I'm a doctor," Ryan said, quickly moving to Jones' side, and checking his pulse. His first thought was that he had injected too much of the drug.

Teddy just looked on, silently.

"He's okay," Ryan said, looking relieved, after taking his pulse, and checking his eyes. He wanted Jones alive to testify, and expose Martel.

"He's just knocked out from the procedure," Ryan added. "We'll have to come back later."

"Thanks for your help," Teddy said, shaking Stevenson's hand.

"Yes, thank you," Ryan said, as they said goodbye.

On the way home in the car, Teddy could not help but come to the realization of how potent Martel still was, and wondered how he knew about the stone box. Did he remember Atlantis, or did the box just look interesting, or valuable, when Jones and Andrews first broke into the house? He realized at that moment that they must have photographed, or videotaped, the entire break-in.

Teddy knew that the encounter with Martel was getting more and more perilous, and if Martel ever got his hands on the key, and began wearing the pendant, there would be no saving anyone.

Neither one of the men had any identification on them, and to their knowledge, Jones had not contacted an attorney, or any family members. So having made no calls, Martel did not yet know what had happened in the woods.

Mr. Chang had presumed, and Teddy had agreed, that Martel would not learn of the fate of Jones and Andrews until some time on Monday or Tuesday. Someone would have to be called to take Jones' defense before his arraignment, and Andrews would have to be buried.

That same evening, together with Mr. Chang, they began plotting out their next move. Mr. Chang had convinced Teddy and Ryan that they had an advantage over Martel. For the first time, in this deplorable ordeal, they were now in the lead.

CHAPTER 30

▲

GENEVA

Monday

Teddy and Ryan put their plan to recover the pendant into action on Monday morning, Memorial Day. Ryan had intended to take the following week off, to go back East with Anne and meet her family, so for once his schedule was not a problem. He had already rescheduled his patients, and arranged for another physician to take care of any emergency calls.

With all that had happened over the weekend, Anne was understanding about postponing their trip, and told Teddy that she would remain in Chicago and make all the necessary appearances on the Hauser case. They were now free to go to Geneva.

Terese got on the phone, and checked flight times and departures. They learned they would have to leave immediately. There was only one good flight a day leaving from Chicago for Switzerland, on Swiss Airlines. That flight left Chicago at 4:40 in the afternoon, going through Zurich, and then arriving in Geneva at 9:15 the next morning.

It was already past noon, and everyone swung into action.

Teddy ran upstairs and packed his bags, and Jen arrived at the house with Ryan's luggage about forty-five minutes later. Jen would be driving them to O'Hare Airport, and Teddy quickly loaded his bags into the back of Jen's car.

This time, Teddy made sure they both had their passports. He felt fortunate that Ryan's passport was in order from his attendance at a medical conference in Italy in the past year. Ryan was not one to travel much and, when he did, he never felt comfortable leaving the United States, because of all the difficulties and strife in other parts of the world. Ryan always felt safer at home.

After Jen dropped them off at the departure level for their international flight, they quickly checked their luggage and proceeded through security. Lost in thought, neither of them spoke a word to the other.

Teddy kept visualizing scenes from the day before in the woods, almost as if a motion picture was running on a movie screen in his mind. Usually he experienced this every night, as his mind reviewed the day, and then the relevant information would be stored in his long-term memory. Often, if he missed something that was being shown to him, the movie would repeat, showing him once again what he had missed, and he would make a mental note of it. He had had this gift since his first memory, and was surprised when he discovered that many others did not.

Both Teddy and Ryan remained quiet during the long overnight flight, content in their internal analysis of everything that had happened during the weekend. Teddy's thoughts soon went back to young Matthew.

It was truly the observant eyes of this 6-year-old child that had captured those men. And a miracle that he, the boys, and Ryan had not been shot. They had had no weapons to defend themselves, yet they were safe. Almost everyone else was hurt—the Chief, his partner, Jones and Andrews. He wondered whether it was just fate, or if their mission was of such importance that they had been deliberately spared.

An open path had presented itself. Everything had fallen into place, and they would soon learn that the importance of their mission would go far beyond finding the ancient pendant.

Tuesday

The overnight flight was long and uneventful. Just after dawn their breakfast was served. Teddy looked out the window, enjoying the magnificent view of the mountains passing below in what appeared to be slow motion.

The flight soon landed in Zurich, and they had to wait half an hour until they could board the Geneva flight. It was about eight-fifteen in the morning. As they disembarked from the plane, Teddy and Ryan adjusted the time on their watches, having gained seven hours.

"I promised Terese I'd call," Teddy said, looking for a bank of phones.

"It's one-fifteen in the morning," Ryan reminded him.

"I know, I promised," Teddy explained.

"I'll see if I can get the papers, and a couple of magazines," Ryan answered, walking on beyond him.

Teddy soon called home, waking Terese.

"Hello," Terese managed, still half asleep.

"Hi, Terese, it's Ted."

"Oh, hi. Where are you?" she questioned, still very sleepy.

"We're in Zurich."

"How was your flight?" Terese asked.

"Quiet. I slept a couple of hours on the plane," Teddy answered, hiding a yawn.

"Oh good," Terese managed.

"Everything okay there?" Teddy asked.

"Yes, very. It's as if a heavy cloud has lifted," Terese said, with a measure of relief in her voice. "That terrible energy that has been plaguing me is gone."

"Well, they won't be back," Teddy assured her.

"Yes. Thank God," Terese answered.

"Well, get back to sleep, Terese. I'll call you later, okay?"

"I love you," Terese said. "Please be careful."

"We will," Teddy responded. "I love you too."

After walking around the small airport for about half an hour, they were called to the gate for their final leg of the journey to Geneva. Teddy felt a rush of anticipation, and Ryan appeared nervous, as their plane took off.

The morning sun gained its momentum, and had risen slowly in the morning sky. Large white billowy clouds cast undulating shadows over the beautiful alpine landscape below. In a short while, their plane made its descent, and they landed at the small Geneva Airport.

Terese had made reservations for them at the Hotel President Wilson, and an English-speaking driver, provided by the hotel, was waiting to meet their flight.

After leaving the plane, they went directly through customs, and then met up with their driver.

Teddy was anxious to get started. They knew that Martel traveled back and forth between Geneva and Chicago weekly, so they reasoned that he probably spent the majority of the week in the United States, and then his weekends, or odd weekends, in Geneva. If their timing was correct, Martel would not be at home.

The Hotel President Wilson, or the President Hotel, as it was commonly referred to, was one of Geneva's most sought after destinations, and was one of the hotels that Teddy had taken Terese to on their honeymoon through Europe.

Terese had enjoyed their stay at the hotel, and loved the charming Old Town, with its historic buildings. The hotel had views of the Alps and Mont Blanc, and was situated right on the shores of Lac Leman, or Lake of Geneva, as it is known to Americans. Terese remembered fondly the strolls she and Teddy took together every evening, along the waterfront promenade. When Terese made the hotel reservations for them, she felt comforted in being able to visualize exactly where Teddy and Ryan would be staying.

Their driver, Philippe, was a very agreeable young man, and once their bags were placed into the trunk of their car, Teddy asked him to take a short drive along the lake before taking them to the hotel to register.

The ride from the small Geneva airport, into town, took only about ten minutes. It was Ryan's first visit to this internationally acclaimed city, with its immaculate streets and beautiful lake. He was impressed.

The view Ryan enjoyed looking down at the mountains during their approach to Geneva had been spectacular enough. Now his eyes were filled with beautiful vistas as they drove into town.

Terese had pulled some information about Switzerland off the Internet for Ryan, and she had given it to him before he and Teddy left for the airport. Ryan had read all that Terese had printed out for him on the plane. He now knew this independent country to be less than one-third the size of the state of Illinois, but it had a 99% literacy rate.

This, Ryan believed, was an accomplishment to be proud of, and a factor he wished other nations in the world would adopt, including the United States. And, even if Switzerland is only a small nation, Ryan thought to himself, it surely is a mighty one, with its mountaintop presence, and natural beauty.

"What are you thinking about?" Teddy asked, interrupting Ryan's thoughts.

"I can't believe how beautiful this place is," Ryan said.

"Wait till you get close to the lake," Teddy responded, as they drove along. "It separates Switzerland from France, and is about 45 miles long. And it's great for sailing," he recalled, having sailed on it many times as a boy, while attending Swiss boarding schools.

Ryan remembered reading that the Swiss spoke four or five different languages, and were surrounded by Germany, Austria and Italy, in addition to France.

As they came up over a hill, he could readily see that Geneva, with her serene mood and clear blue lake, could never disappoint. Ryan wondered who, in their right mind, would not want to live there.

"Any place special Mr. Townsend?" their driver asked, breaking the silence.

"It might be enjoyable to see some of the larger homes and estates along the west side of the lake," Teddy suggested.

"Well the largest place is that gray stone mansion," Philippe offered, pointing to a beautiful French Chateau. "It's owned by the Martels."

"Marshall Martel?" Teddy asked.

"Yes. Did you come in for their daughter's engagement party tonight?" Philippe asked.

"Why, yes, we have," Teddy, said, as casually as possible, "although I was not aware of what an impressive property the Martels have here in Geneva."

Teddy and Ryan could see that several white party tents had been erected in the back of the property, near the lake, with teams of workers scurrying around.

As they drove closer, Teddy watched several people lifting large baskets of flowers out of a parked van, carrying them around to the back.

It was apparent that the caterers were already inside, preparing a feast, for there were several food and pastry trucks parked nearby. On the lawn between the back of the house and the lake, large round tables were being covered with linen tablecloths, and then set with plates and silver. Teddy noted that there had to be as many as 25 or 30 persons working on the preparations outside alone. Teddy and Ryan just watched, taking every-thing in.

A black ten-foot high, heavy wrought-iron fence, with pointed spears at the top encased in brass, surrounded Martel's elaborate residence, the back of which faced the lake. The letter *M* stood out where it was also formed in brass, embellishing the front double-gates. A long lawn extended around the property to the back of the residence, and all the way to the lake's shore.

"People have been coming in since yesterday," Philippe offered. "The hotel is almost full to capacity."

"Yes, it will be a wonderful celebration," Teddy conveyed in an agree-able tone, wondering how Terese ever got a reservation.

"I don't know the Martels personally," Philippe continued, not wanting to overstep his grounds, "but everyone knows of the Martels in Gen'eve," he added. "There was an article announcing the event in the newspaper. Over 300 people have been invited."

"How long have they had this place on the lake?" Ryan asked, probing for more information.

"I don't know sir. I am originally from France," Philippe answered.

"Mr. Martel is from France, too, isn't he?" Teddy questioned.

"His name is French," Philippe agreed. "But, I am not sure," he admitted.

"I wonder how he ended up in Geneva?" Ryan asked, nonchalantly, not wanting to attach too much importance to the question.

"Mrs. Martel is Swiss," Philippe, revealed, "she comes from an old banking family in Zurich."

How interesting, Teddy thought, looking over at Ryan, and then back to Philippe, refraining from asking any further questions.

"The Martels give the finest parties in all of Gen'eve, sir," Philippe added, "and I am certain you will have a very agreeable time this evening."

"Yes, we're looking forward to it," Teddy said, knowing they were going to have to chance going in that night.

Philippe was unaware of how diligently Teddy and Ryan were studying the structure before them. Without speaking a single word to each other, they were both calculating every possible point of entry into Martel's mansion, as well as every possible avenue of a quick escape. This was not going to be easy, in that the home was a fortress.

"Philippe," Teddy instructed, "perhaps we had better check in at the hotel now."

"Yes, Mr. Townsend," Philippe replied, as he found a place down the road to turn around.

In one way, Teddy thought to himself, this was somewhat of a break. It would be easier to get in, with all the invited guests and outside help. On the other hand, Martel was sure to be home. After all, he would never miss his daughter's engagement party. Not with 300 persons coming. And, from the look of the flowers he saw being brought around to the back, as well as the orchestra's platform being set up in a gazebo, it was definitely a formal affair.

He wondered why the engagement party was being held during the week—unless they had a similar event in Paris, over the weekend. Perhaps, Teddy thought, with school just finishing for the year, the party in Geneva was more for the couple's friends, rather than family. It was a mystery.

The more Teddy thought about it, all of this was a blessing in disguise, and he began planning the entire evening in his mind. As they drove along in the hotel's limousine, he watched the lush landscape and lakefront residences passing by.

"Have you talked to your folks lately?" Ryan asked, disturbing the silence.

"Just my father. I had to call him on the Hauser case," Teddy responded.

Ryan just nodded.

"What made you ask that?" Teddy questioned.

"Oh, I don't know," Ryan, said, referring to Geneva and its apparent affluence. "I guess all this," he finally answered.

"What do you mean?" Teddy asked.

"When I was in grammar school, I would often fantasize about how it would be to come from a wealthy family. South Shore Drive was once an affluent neighborhood on Chicago's lakefront, with the Country Club and Rainbow Park Beach."

Teddy just looked at him, trying to read his thoughts.

"You know," Ryan continued, "never having to want for anything."

"You never wanted for anything," Teddy countered.

"Oh, yes I did," Ryan quickly returned.

"You have a great family, Ryan. I use to love to come home with you from Harvard," Teddy responded.

"Well, it certainly wasn't analogous to coming home with you," Ryan exclaimed. "Not one of these homes here," Ryan pointed out, as they drove along Geneva's lakefront, "is superior to the home you grew up in."

"It was lonely," Teddy said. "We had a big house, but no one was ever home. I would rather have been raised on the south side of Chicago, and gone to school at St. Phillips," Teddy confessed. "You had a real family, Ryan."

"There never seemed to be enough of anything," Ryan remembered.

"There was enough love," Teddy said, dropping into silence.

The car made its way into the city, and soon turned off the Rue de Lausanne, past Mon Repos Park and onto Quai Wilson. Philippe soon turned down the side street onto Gautier and stopped the car in front of their hotel.

The President Hotel was very inviting. It overlooked the lake, and its interior was decorated in a traditional style with a contemporary edge. It appeared quite European in its appointments, and prided itself as one of Switzerland's finest five-star hotels.

Ryan was especially pleased with their adjoining rooms. Teddy never spared any expense, and Ryan was thankful he was picking up the tab. Their first class airfare alone was almost $9,000 each, roundtrip. Ryan gasped when he saw what Teddy was paying. He didn't even want to ask how much the hotel was charging for their beautiful view.

While a valet attended to unpacking their bags and having their clothing pressed, Ryan and Teddy went downstairs to the hotel's pool, and they ordered something to eat.

The round table they chose, with its matching round umbrella above, afforded a pleasant shaded view of the lake on one side, and the pool on the other. They felt they could talk privately there.

"The first thing we need to do," Teddy explained, looking over to Ryan, "is to find some formalwear for tonight. The party is white tie."

"White tie?" Ryan said. "How do you know that?"

"I called down and asked the Concierge," Teddy explained.

"How are we going to do that?" Ryan asked.

"The Concierge is making some calls," Teddy explained. "I told him we were missing some pieces of luggage that had our formalwear in them."

"I'm not wearing a rented suit," Ryan said, not liking to put anything on that some stranger had worn.

"They'll be ready-made, and tailored," Teddy explained. "We will have to go in for a fitting, as soon as it is arranged."

"So, we're going in tonight?" Ryan asked.

"Of course we're going in tonight," Teddy answered. "What did you think we were going to do? Go sightseeing?"

Soon a waiter came over, interrupting their conversation, and served their lunch. Once he had left, Ryan turned his head, speaking quietly to Teddy.

"Don't you think it would be better if we waited until Martel went out of town?" Ryan asked. "I thought that's what we planned on."

"That's before we knew about the party. It's a perfect cover Ryan. We couldn't ask for more."

"I don't want to go in, if Martel's there," Ryan said. "It's too dangerous."

Suddenly, they were interrupted again. It was Philippe.

"Excuse me, Mr. Townsend, Philippe said, handing Teddy a sealed envelope. The Concierge asked that I give you this note."

"Thank you," Teddy said.

Philippe stood by while Teddy read the note.

"What is it?" Ryan asked.

"We'll be out in about ten minutes," Teddy said, excusing Philippe.

"What is it?" Ryan asked, again.

"Our fittings have been arranged with the tailors. Philippe will drive us over," Teddy explained.

"Just like that, it's all arranged?" Ryan asked.

"Just like that," Teddy agreed. "Let's finish our lunch."

"I'm finished," Ryan said, looking ill.

"Eat, you're going to need it," Teddy insisted.

Ryan took in a deep breath, and drank his beverage. He couldn't eat another mouthful.

At exactly seven o'clock that evening, Philippe called Teddy's room.

"The car is downstairs, Mr. Townsend, whenever you are ready," Philippe explained.

"We'll be down in about 15 minutes," Teddy answered, promptly setting down the receiver.

Ryan was sitting in Teddy's bedroom, waiting for him to finish dressing, and just looked at the phone, and then at Teddy. "Wouldn't it be better if we arrived later?" Ryan suggested.

Ryan took a long sip of the wine Teddy had given him, hoping it would relax him.

"We are arriving later," Teddy, explained. "The invitations were for cocktails at seven, and dinner at eight o'clock."

Ryan just looked at him.

"And you've had enough of the wine, Ryan," Teddy insisted. "I just wanted you to have a glass to relax you. It was not my intention that you drink the whole bottle."

"I'm fine," Ryan explained.

"Well, we haven't eaten since lunch," Teddy insisted. "You had better eat some of the hors d'oeuvres I ordered."

"I'm fine," Ryan insisted, putting down his glass and getting up.

"Let's go," Teddy said.

They reached Martel's shortly after seven-thirty. When they got out of the car, they walked briskly up the steps, carrying themselves in the same smooth gait they had in common, although Ryan was a little high from the wine.

Both looked very handsome, and dignified, in their tuxedos. However, Teddy was wearing Ryan's dark-rimmed glasses—a touch he had thought of just before they left the hotel. He had also slicked his hair down, resembling a 1930s movie idol.

"Don't let me bump into anything," Teddy said, adjusting Ryan's glasses, his vision now blurred.

"That's such a stupid thing to do, Ted," Ryan complained. "I can only see at a distance, and you can't see at all."

"I can see about a foot in front of me," Teddy defended.

"Yeah, that's going to do a lot of good," Ryan returned.

"I'll be the reader," Teddy said, joking.

"Yeah, right," Ryan returned, starting to laugh.

"I can see well enough," Teddy insisted. "And don't forget that I'll do all the talking," Teddy reminded him.

Ryan let out a deep sigh, releasing some of his pent-up anxiety, just as they reached the front door.

Teddy handed the butler his invitation, and then asked him in flawless French to be directed to the men's room.

The party was going on strong outside, between the house and the lake, with only a few people streaming through the main rooms of the house.

Teddy had timed everything perfectly. The Martels were no longer receiving guests, and had joined everyone outside. Teddy also noted that for the most part, it was a very young crowd. His hunch had been correct.

As they made their way down the hallway to the men's room, the orchestra could be heard a distance away. When the door to the men's room was shut tightly behind them, Teddy quickly checked to see if they were alone. They were.

Ryan was breathless. "I feel as if I just snuck in to see the Saturday afternoon matinee on 71st Street," he said, laughing, unable to contain himself.

Teddy just looked at him.

"Where'd you get the invitation?" Ryan asked.

"Do you want to be implicated?" Teddy cracked, as he adjusted his glasses.

That set Ryan off, as he began laughing again.

"I look completely different, don't you think?" Teddy asked, looking at himself in the restroom mirror.

"Yeah," Ryan agreed. "It's as if we're in *The Great Gatsby*," he suggested, trying to get control of himself.

"You think?" Teddy asked, still looking innocently into the mirror.

"Please, don't make me laugh any more," Ryan, pleaded.

It was now quite apparent that Ryan had drunk too much wine. They were both tired, with little sleep, and Teddy had begun laughing too.

"Okay," Teddy agreed. "We have to get serious."

Ryan splashed some water on his face, and then dried it with a guest towel. They both smoothed down their jackets, and took a deep breath.

Teddy looked over at Ryan. "Ready?" he asked.

"Ready," Ryan responded.

Ryan opened the door slightly, and looked down the hall. Suddenly the door slammed shut again, as Ryan burst into laughter again. That got Teddy started. The wine was a terrible mistake.

"I can't believe I'm laughing," Ryan said, still trying to get control.

"I can't either," Teddy said, removing Ryan's glasses and splashing water on his face. "You know we have to do this, punchy or not," Teddy added.

"I know, I'll be okay," Ryan assured him, as he gathered his wits.

"Just remember that Martel, is only a short distance away," Teddy reminded him.

Ryan nodded. It was a sobering thought.

They waited a moment longer, while they both calmed down, and then Teddy turned to Ryan.

"Ready?" he asked again, looking at Ryan with uncertainty.

"Ready," Ryan agreed.

"Okay, let's go," Teddy said.

Again the door opened a crack, and they both looked out. A large party of people had just arrived, distracting the butler and two maids. Teddy and Ryan quickly slipped out the door.

In a slow, easy manner they moved casually away from the men's room, and walked around and through to a hallway that divided the entire north wing of the house.

Since the south hallway could only be reached by passing the butler once again, they went down the north hallway first. It was massive in size, and decorated from floor to ceiling with dark, heavy, mahogany wood, with matching carved wainscoting, showing off a gallery of priceless paintings.

The immediate doorway on the right was open. It led into a large parlor across which they had a clear view of the lake, and they could see young couples, in their early twenties, moving around outside. It appeared to be a music room, with a large grand piano placed in front of the high-arched windows.

On the left side of the hallway were matching high-arched paneled doors, concealing other rooms behind each. Moving silently, with orchestrated ease, they started down the hallway together, with Ryan on the left, and Teddy on the right. They opened each door, slowly but efficiently, and looked inside.

The next door Teddy opened exposed a library, but the one after that was locked. Teddy reached high on the door and pressed a paneled section with his hand, and the door sprang open, revealing a steep carpeted staircase leading to a room upstairs.

Ryan was still moving hastily down the hall.

Teddy snapped his fingers, to get Ryan's attention, and pointed to the opening.

Ryan nodded, and quickly made his way back over to Teddy. At the same moment, Teddy heard the voices of two women, coming from somewhere in the vicinity of the main entrance hall. Shoving Ryan inside the opening, Teddy hurriedly closed the door behind them.

"Somebody's coming," Teddy whispered, revealing his concern.

Ryan felt a grave fear come over him. They listened together at the doorway until the two women passed. When they were gone, Teddy signaled for Ryan to follow him, and they made their way up the staircase.

At the top of the steps, they could see two concealed cameras focused down on the room next door. Teddy looked through one of the lenses, and saw a meeting room with a large round table and fifteen chairs about it.

Behind the camera equipment were racks of videotapes, all labeled and showing specific meetings. As he followed the labels, Teddy could see one tape entitled *Long-Range Planning—to 2010*, and another marked *Annual Conference*.

"Ryan," Teddy called, barely audible and motioning to the tapes, "he must have been secretly taping their meetings just in case anyone got out of line."

"Whose meetings?" Ryan asked.

"How am I supposed to know," Teddy returned, looking around. "I haven't even viewed them yet."

Ryan just gave him a look.

"My God," Teddy continued. "Look at this place. Everything's American. He must have imported every piece of equipment in this room."

"What's the voltage?" Ryan asked, "American or European?"

"It's American," Teddy said, crawling under a table.

"He must have converters," Ryan said.

"Yeah, but where?" Teddy asked, looking around. "I don't see any master switch, or anything that fits into the wall sockets."

"Well at least it will be compatible." Ryan reasoned.

"What will be compatible?" Teddy asked.

"The tapes. They'll be compatible. We can run them on our VCR's at home."

Pulling two tapes from the rack, Teddy went over to a wall where new cassettes of film were stored, and he took out two new cartridges.

"What are you doing?" Ryan asked.

"I'm going to try to figure out how to duplicate these."

"It'll take too long, we don't have time for that," Ryan complained.

"We have to do it," Teddy explained.

"Why don't we just take the originals, and put the blanks in their place?" Ryan suggested. "The jackets will still read properly, and Martel will never know."

Teddy just shook his head no. "Oh, he'll find out," Teddy assured.

"Ted, those look as if they are long tapes. We don't have time," Ryan insisted, looking around.

"Can't we duplicate them on high speed?" Teddy asked.

"We don't have time," Ryan repeated, looking around. "Just take the new tapes and stick them in the labeled jackets. And you had better wipe your fingerprints off them."

Teddy went through the process, with haste, and placed blanks into the already labeled jackets. He then carefully placed each jacket back into its proper place. He then placed the originals inside the unmarked manufacturers jackets, and handed one to Ryan.

"Why are you handing that to me?" Ryan asked, indignantly.

"Because we have a better chance of getting at least one out of here if someone stops us, or we get separated," Teddy reasoned.

Ryan just looked at him.

"Take it," Teddy insisted.

Ryan reluctantly placed the evidence into his tuxedo jacket.

"Not there," Teddy said, noticing how bulky it looked. "Slip it into the back waistband of your pants," he said, showing Ryan where he was placing his. "They won't show if we unbutton our jackets."

After they finished hiding the tapes, Teddy began feeling all the walls of the room.

"Now what are you doing?" Ryan asked.

"I'm checking to see if there are any secret passageways," Teddy said.

"That's not a bad idea," Ryan agreed. "There has to be a reason why this place is run on 120 volts. He must have his own power source separate from the city's."

"Why would he do that?" Teddy asked.

"That's what I want to know," Ryan said. "Why don't you take out your handkerchief again, and make sure you don't leave any of your prints behind," Ryan said.

"You'd better do the same," Teddy agreed.

"I will," Ryan acknowledged, taking out his own.

Ryan got busy, while Teddy continued his search, carefully scanning the wood-framed walls. When Teddy suddenly stopped, Ryan looked up. Teddy's hand began to explore one particular place on the wall, over and over again. Ryan watched, as Teddy managed to find a spring, and a doorway slowly opened.

"How did you do that?" Ryan asked.

"Come on," Teddy motioned.

They went cautiously down two flights of tight circular stairs, and into an enormous basement bunker.

The room was oval in shape, with television monitors surrounding half the circumference. In the center of the room was an oval desk with a master control panel, and Teddy and Ryan quickly made their way over to it. Again, all of the equipment was American made.

"There is no doubt about his connections in the United States," Ryan commented. "This setup is very high tech."

Ryan sat down at the desk, sitting in a single swivel chair, and studied the master panel.

"Flick that," Ryan instructed, pointing to a single lever.

Flipping the lever to an open position, Teddy activated the computers and television screens. Almost at once, they all came alive with data and pictures of the planet from outer space.

"He must be tied into our spy satellites," Ryan said.

Pictures kept changing as shots changed, and Teddy could now see how each monitor was tied to a code. He was not just tied into U.S. satellite intelligence, but to everyone else's as well.

"I hope the Pentagon has this," Teddy commented. "I guess we now know why he has his own power source. Only a factory would pull this much voltage, and it would be a sure give-away to the Swiss authorities, that Martel has more than a residence here."

"He's clever," Ryan said. "You have to hand it to him."

Teddy just nodded.

"Let's get out of here, Ted," Ryan insisted, as he shut down the system. "We have to find that box, and we're going to set off an alarm or something."

Without saying another word, Teddy and Ryan went back up the double staircase to the video room, and closed the secret door behind them, cleaning their way with their handkerchiefs as they went.

They moved at a fast pace down the short staircase to the door leading to the outer hallway, and listened to hear if anyone was coming. Ryan put up his finger, asking Teddy to wait, and pressed his ear to the door. When he heard no discernible voices coming from behind the closed door, he slowly opened it. Now they had to find the stolen carved box.

Peering out both ways, up and down the hallway, they quickly went out. Just as they reached the conference room door, they heard the voices of a group of men coming in their direction. One was Martel's.

Quickly they slipped into the conference room, shutting the door quietly behind them, trying to catch their breath. Teddy and Ryan listened, as the group of men mercifully passed by the door they were hiding behind. Martel and his party soon entered the room next to them, and shut the door.

Silently, Teddy and Ryan made their way across the large conference chamber to the door leading into Martel's office, where they attempted to listen to Martel's conversation with the other men.

"I have another copy in the next room," Martel said, getting up from behind his desk.

Teddy and Ryan could hear Martel's footsteps getting louder, as he came in their direction.

"Ted," Ryan whispered, his heart in his throat, and pointing to the door. "He's coming in here."

The door started to open and they both took synchronized steps backwards, until they met the wall, staying just behind the moving door. They dared not even breathe.

"Wait there!" Martel ordered, to the men in his office, when they got up to follow him.

Martel walked into the conference room, and over to a long antique cabinet centered on the back of the hallway wall. Removing a key from behind a painting, hanging above the piece, Martel unlocked the intricate cabinet.

All the while, Teddy peered out from behind the door, revealing only one eye to Martel's back. As Martel opened the cabinet, Teddy could readily see the ancient box inside. Turning to Ryan, he mouthed the word "box."

Martel removed a large packet containing three bound volumes, with matching black binders and covers. He took only one copy of the printed report, and returned the other two to the packet, and placed them back on the shelf. Locking the cabinet door, he returned the key to its hiding place behind the painting. Martel then walked back into his office, closing the door firmly behind him.

Teddy and Ryan were still plastered to the wall behind the heavy, paneled door, almost afraid to breathe. Motioning for Ryan to wait a minute, Teddy quietly made his way over to the cabinet, as Ryan watched.

Removing the key from behind the painting, Teddy quickly opened the cabinet, picked up the ancient box, and placed it into view. Next, he took a small envelope out of his breast pocket, removed the small intricate golden key, and unlocked the box.

Without missing a beat, Teddy removed the pendant and slipped it into his jacket pocket. He then took a raw crystal out of a small clasped envelope, and began cleaning it with his handkerchief, so as to leave no fingerprints. The crystal was similar in weight and size to the sacred pendant.

Teddy then sealed and locked the box, carefully putting the sacred pendant, together with the tiny key, back into the envelope that had held the crystal, and slipped them both into the breast pocket of his tuxedo jacket for safekeeping.

Next he cleaned and then placed the stone box back, exactly where it had been positioned on the shelf before, and again remembered to wipe everything clean with his handkerchief. Teddy locked the cabinet, and placed the key to the cabinet doors back behind the painting.

A look of conquest filled Teddy's eyes, as he motioned to Ryan to follow him out the hallway door. Soon they departed, with Teddy explaining to the butler that Ryan had eaten something very disagreeable, and that Teddy needed to see him back to the hotel. Within minutes they met up with their driver, and drove off into the night.

The mission, impossible, was a success.

When the tape ran out again, Teddy looked over at Ryan. He could see that the same thoughts he was thinking were racing through Ryan's mind at a blinding speed.

"There must have been another tape," Teddy said, angry with himself for not having looked further.

Ryan just nodded his head in agreement.

Teddy used the remote again to rewind the second tape in its entirety, and the five sat together, and talked some more about what they had witnessed and what they could possibly do about it.

By midnight, they came up with an initial plan. Above all, they had to move quickly. The world had to see those tapes, for no intelligent person would believe what they witnessed in that room that night—until, and unless, they saw it for themselves. This was the only way they could expose and stop Martel and his men.

CHAPTER 32

▲

THE MAILING

Thursday

It was now the third of June. Michael and Matthew would be getting out of school in a week, and their summer vacation would begin. On their flight back from Geneva, Teddy and Ryan talked about postponing their annual fishing trip with the boys, which they would usually go on right after school let out. It would be impossible to go away now.

Because of Martel, Teddy had lost all sense of privacy in his life, and was troubled knowing that his family had to be guarded. Their home had been surveilled from the woods without their knowledge, and his family's safety had been compromised.

They no longer had the personal freedom that they once knew, and Teddy was no longer the person he once was, who was always willing to take a risk, and plan a new adventure. He was constantly on guard, always expecting the unexpected, and worried about Terese and their children. The whole ordeal was wearing on him, but he showed this to no one, not even to Terese.

Since the confrontation in the woods, it had been planned that even when the boys rode their horses around the back pasture, unknown to them, Mr. Swensen would keep watch. If they decided to ride farther out, Mr. Swensen would now accompany them, and he would take his sharp-shooting rifle with him.

The boys were also driven to and from school everyday. They were no longer allowed to take the school bus. After the incident in the woods, the Lake Forest Police Department sent an officer to their school. The officer met with their principal, early on Monday morning, about taking extra precautions when the boys were at recess, or out on the grounds. Lake Forest was a wealthy community and the school already had strict rules, and a full-time playground guard, in place.

It was true that Mr. Chang was too old to truly guard Teddy's family, in the way that the police officers could, but Mr. Chang represented a calm presence in the home, and was constantly looking out for Teddy's family.

Mr. Chang could always be counted on for his thorough analysis of every situation, which Teddy appreciated, for Mr. Chang never stopped thinking and scrutinizing every single detail and event, whether by hypothesis or theory. He was a man of few words, always consumed in thought, and when Mr. Chang spoke, everyone listened. Teddy trusted him, without question.

Teddy and Ryan followed their usual routine on Thursday morning, and took the train into the city. And, as had been predicted, Teddy saw that he was being followed as he drove his car to the train station. Martel was regrouping. Teddy knew that he would now have the opportunity to get rid of the key.

The two men who followed Teddy that morning to the train station, looked no different from the other men getting on the train, except that Lake Forest was a small enough town, that Teddy and Ryan knew just about everyone who took the train into the city at that hour, if not by name, by sight. Taking the seats directly behind where Teddy and Ryan always sat, the two men thought themselves to be incognito.

Chatting casually as they ate their bagged breakfast, Teddy and Ryan read the morning paper, and never let on that they were aware of the two predators who were listening in. The soft morning light poured through the large train windows, and Teddy, in passing, mentioned getting rid of the key to Ryan.

"How about meeting at noon," Ryan suggested, lowering his voice just enough to attract their interest. "We can do something about it then."

"Okay," Teddy agreed, turning back to his paper. "I'll get the key out of my safe at the office, and meet you downstairs at my building," he added, wanting to avoid an earlier confrontation with the two men.

They rode for a while without talking, and then Teddy jotted a note down in the crossword column, handing the folded paper to Ryan.

"Do you know what three across is?" Teddy asked.

Three across read: *Did you get a hold of your friend at the network this morning?*

"Let's see," Ryan said, as he wrote his response.

Teddy read Ryan's answer. *I called him from a pay phone when I left your place. We're supposed to meet him right before the 10 p.m. news tonight. I'll take care of the blank tapes.*

"Great," Teddy said, enthusiastically, as Ryan handed him back the paper. "That one was key. I can get the rest done myself," he added, going back to the newspaper, and jotting down a list of things he needed to do to install their plan.

Teddy and Ryan met in the lobby of Teddy's building, exactly at noon. The two men were also waiting near the bank of elevators, when Teddy came down.

Ryan grabbed Teddy's arm, as soon as he got off the elevator, and they quickly got into the cab Ryan had waiting for them at the curb. Within a few short minutes they made their way over to Wabash Avenue, to a small rundown pawnshop.

Ryan looked around, as if to make sure that no one saw them going in, managing to avoid eye contact with the two men following them in another cab. Once inside, Teddy pulled out the gold key, and handed it to the pawnbroker, who was an old man in his late 70s.

The pawnbroker picked up the solid gold key, and eyed it carefully through his thick glasses, weighing it in his hand.

"$10.00 is all I can give you for this," he said.

"That's fine. We'll take it," Teddy said.

Ryan began opening his mouth, to protest the meager price, and Teddy gave him a look that froze his thoughts.

The old man went over to the register and took out two five-dollar bills, and then wrote a receipt. Soon they were outside of the shop, heading directly across the street. They quickly entered an inexpensive shoe store, on the corner, with large plate-glass windows facing the street. Teddy began looking around, as if interested in buying some shoes, while Ryan kept an eye on the pawnshop. The shoe store gave them a perfect view.

As one of the men watched the door to the shoe store, the other went inside the pawnshop and, within seconds, came out with the key. The man on watch quickly flagged down a passing cab, and they both got inside and took off. Within minutes, it was finished. They now had the key.

When the cab was out of sight, Teddy and Ryan went back across the street and into the pawnshop. The old man looked upset, but they could see from where they were watching that he had not been harmed.

"Are you all right?" Teddy asked the pawnbroker, when they came through the door.

"A man just came in here and took your key. It was still on the counter!"

"We know, we saw him," Teddy acknowledged. "Are you all right?" he repeated.

"What's this all about?" the old man asked.

Teddy took out his billfold, and placed a $100 bill on the counter.

"This is for your trouble," Teddy said, and without making any further explanation, they both left the shop and went to lunch.

That night, Teddy and Ryan stayed in the city and planned to meet for dinner at Bennigan's at eight o'clock. Pat had remained with Teddy in order to help him prepare all the letters and labels he needed, and he invited her to join them for dinner.

When they left the office, Teddy was carrying a large box of padded, labeled mailing envelopes, with the appropriate letter paper clipped to each.

As they walked toward Michigan Avenue, Teddy wondered to himself if it was truly possible that all Martel wanted was the key. After all, Martel had come after him even before he had known of the box. The more Teddy thought about it, he knew it was unlikely Martel would be satisfied with just the key. In fact, it suddenly occurred to him, that Martel might want to finish the job, now that he had what he wanted.

"Hold on a second Pat," Teddy said, as he stopped for a moment. "I think I have something in my shoe."

Pat took Teddy's large box of envelopes, which allowed him the moment he needed to look behind him. He did not see anyone slowing their pace, or lurking about, but he was careful to check twice while he went through the motions of taking off his shoe and emptying it onto the pavement. A short while later, when they reached Michigan Avenue, Teddy turned south.

"Aren't we going to Bennigan's?" Pat asked.

"Yes, the one across from the Art Institute," Teddy responded.

"Not the North Michigan one?" Pat questioned.

"No, I've always liked the other one, better," he said, smiling. "Terese and I would always meet there, when I was on break from Harvard, and she was finishing her schooling at the Art Institute.

As they walked along, he knew he would have to remain very watchful now, and kept checking behind himself, from time-to-time, as they made their way down Michigan Avenue.

"Is something the matter?" Pat asked.

"No, not at all," Teddy responded.

"You're acting very strange, Ted. Are you in some kind of trouble?" Pat pursued.

"No, there's nothing to worry about," he assured her.

"You know, you truly haven't been yourself at all lately. In fact, things haven't been right since you came back from Miami in March."

"No?" Teddy asked.

"No," Pat confirmed. "And you don't seem the least bit interested in your work. You keep delegating everything out to the associates in our department, and, if it wasn't for Anne," she reminded him, "very little would get done."

"Well, I'm getting more into the area of bringing clients into the firm, rather than working the long hours I did before," Teddy offered in explanation.

"It's more than just client promotion," Pat said. "Something's wrong. Those letters that I typed on my computer that you're so secretive about— we've been working on them all day."

Teddy did not respond, as he thought about involving Pat more than she already was.

"And what on earth is on those tapes?" Pat asked, "And how do you know about a bunker in a mansion in Geneva?"

"I wish I could tell you Pat, but I can't. I told you earlier today that I don't want to involve you in this, in case there are hearings."

"I'm already involved." Pat stated. "And I want to help you," she added, showing him she was truly concerned.

"I know," Teddy said. "But I can't let you."

"You don't trust me?" Pat questioned.

"I trust you completely," Teddy said. "You know that I do."

"I always thought you did, until now," Pat said, showing her disappointment.

Once they reached the restaurant, Teddy stopped to open the door for her. Ryan had already arrived, and had a glass of wine sitting in front of him when they approached their table.

Teddy looked at Ryan, and smiled. "Based on past experiences, I don't know if that's a very smart idea," Teddy noted, gesturing toward the wine.

Ryan laughed, as he stood up and pulled out Pat's chair. Teddy put his box down on the extra seat at their window table, and took a seat himself.

"It's nice to see you Pat," Ryan said. "I'm glad you could join us."

"Oh, thanks," Pat responded. "It's nice to see you, too."

"I didn't want to send her home without feeding her," Teddy said, as he sat down. "But I would have, had I known I was going to be interrogated for the last three blocks."

Ryan just laughed.

Through the large restaurant window Teddy could see across Michigan Avenue, to Grant Park and the Art Institute, and he watched some of the activity on the opposite side of the street for a moment.

Just then the waiter came over with their menus, and took their beverage orders. Teddy was thankful for the interruption. However, as soon as the waiter left, Pat started in again.

"Ryan, what's actually on those tapes you two are so secretive about?" Pat asked. "And how did you come across them?"

Ryan just looked at Teddy.

"I wouldn't have involved you in this, Pat," Teddy justified, looking directly into her large, brown, almond-shaped eyes, "except that I needed for you to run the letters off for me."

"And I did," Pat said, "including getting the names and titles for the heads of all the agencies, as well as confirming all their addresses. So now I want an explanation."

"Believe me, the less you know, the better," Ryan added.

"Why? Because I'm a woman?" Pat asked.

"You don't believe that," Teddy responded.

"So, then, who are we waiting for—or should I say whom?" Pat asked.

"We're not waiting for anyone," Teddy explained. "We all worked late, and so I thought we might all have dinner together."

"Let me rephrase that," Pat said. "I almost forgot I was talking to a lawyer. If you're not waiting for someone, then you must be meeting someone. Right?" Pat asked.

Teddy looked at Ryan, and then to Pat. "We are meeting someone, but not until 9:45," he admitted.

"You're not dumping me now," Pat said.

"She might be useful," Ryan said, thinking ahead.

"I'm not involving her in this," Teddy said. "And that's that."

"I want to be involved," Pat said. "The girls are staying over at my sister's this week. My Aunt is visiting from South Carolina, and they both wanted to spend some time with her."

"If something happened to you Pat," Teddy said, "I'd never forgive myself."

"Nothing's going to happen to me," Pat defended.

"You've been working for him too long, Pat," Ryan interjected. "You not only think the way he does, now you're willing to take the same risks that he does," Ryan added.

"I truly want to help," Pat insisted.

Teddy paused for a moment, while he thought it over. "Are you sure?" he asked.

"I'm sure," Pat responded. "So who are we meeting?" she asked.

"I don't know—he's a friend of Ryan's who is going to duplicate the tapes for us, and then we're going to mail them out."

"So who is he?" Pat asked, turning to Ryan.

"We played basketball together at Mt. Carmel," Ryan offered in explanation. "He works at one of the television stations, and has access to a video room. He's going to duplicate the tapes for us, after everyone leaves tonight."

"You told him what's going on, but not me?" Pat asked.

"No," Ryan explained. "He's doing it as a favor, no questions asked. He said he would meet us in front of the network, so we can get in as guests before the ten o'clock news."

The waiter came back at that moment, and they all ordered dinner.

By the time they left the restaurant, it was almost nine-thirty. They immediately got into a cab, and went over to the network.

Unseen by any of them, in the shadows of the Art Institute across the street, was one of the men who had followed Teddy and Ryan earlier in the day.

As soon as they got in the cab, the man signaled to his partner, who was waiting in a car down the street. They followed Teddy, Ryan and Pat from the restaurant, north on Michigan Avenue. The men remained in the shadows, and waited to see what Teddy, Ryan and Pat were up to.

At exactly 10:00 p.m., a church bell in the distance chimed out ten bells, and Ryan checked his watch. He knew that his friend had to be running late, and they quietly talked among themselves. It was a warm balmy night, and there was very little activity on the dimly lit side street where they were waiting outside the network.

One of the men following them, slowly rolled down his car window, so that they could pick up Teddy's conversation with a listening device. Then his partner opened a case holding a disassembled, high-powered rifle, and began putting it together.

Ryan looked down at his watch. He was becoming anxious. The evening news was just a half-hour program, and the telecast had already begun.

"Pat, may I see the list you prepared?" Ryan asked.

Pat took the list out of the large box of envelopes Teddy was holding, and gave it to Ryan.

Ryan took out a penlight, so that he could read the list, and began slowly scanning the page.

"Do you think he changed his mind?" Teddy asked, leaning over Ryan's shoulder.

"He'll be here," Ryan confirmed.

Just then a striking, tall black man came out of the building behind them, propping the door open so that it would not close, and walked quickly over to where they were standing. It was Ryan's friend from school.

Teddy recognized him immediately. He was the evening sportscaster at the station, and an ex-professional basketball star.

In the shadows, across the street, the man with the rifle set up his shot, waiting for a clear view of Teddy. The light pouring out the now open studio door, had given the assassin the illumination he needed to make an accurate shot.

John walked up to Ryan first, blocking the gunman's shot, and held out his hand. "Sorry, but my producer stopped me about the story I'm reporting on tonight, and I couldn't get away. She caught me just as I was walking out of the news room."

"You're John Jefferson," Teddy said.

"Right," John answered, moving closer to Teddy.

"I've always wanted to meet you," Teddy said, enthusiastically. "My son Michael has a picture of you on his bedroom wall, from when you played professionally."

"Oh, that's really nice," John, said.

Teddy looked over at Ryan. "I didn't know you knew John Jefferson," he said.

"That's because you'd be hounding me to get tickets for you to all the games," Ryan said, as everyone broke into laughter.

Ryan was now standing in front of Teddy, and the gunman paused.

"Well, at least I now know where you got the playoff tickets last year that you so generously treated me to," Teddy joked, as he turned to John. "I'm Teddy Townsend, and this is my legal assistant, Pat Morgan."

"It's a pleasure," John said, looking over at Pat. "I understand you need to use our video booths, to duplicate some tapes. Are they for a trial?" he asked.

"Oh no," Teddy said. "But they do involve a confidential legal matter, so we couldn't send them out," he explained. "We'd be very happy to reimburse you for whatever the cost," Teddy added, stepping closer to John.

The gunman tried once again to set up his shot, waiting for John to move out of his way.

"No cost," John said. "Ryan sent over the blank tapes that we need to use this afternoon, and I'll bring all three of you in as my guests to observe the newscast. We can all go back to my office afterward, and talk for about a half hour, till everyone clears out. Then I can take you in to where we'll do the duping."

"Great," Teddy said.

John, who was just as tall as Teddy, was still blocking Teddy from the marksman waiting in the car.

"We have a union shop here," John said, "but the supervisor is one of my buddies. I give him, and some of the other guys, extra tickets to the games all the time. And, when I asked Barry about doing this for you, he said just to bring you in at eleven o'clock, and that there shouldn't be any problem."

"That's terrific," Teddy said, "but I do want to pay everyone for their time."

"No, really," John added. "Ryan fixed me up a few years ago, when I had a neck injury after falling on the court, and I have yet to see a bill."

Teddy looked over at Ryan in disbelief, and then to John. "Well, thank you very much," he said. "We certainly appreciate it."

"C'mon with me," John said, smiling, putting his hand on Teddy's shoulder. "And I'll get you in."

Teddy was now completely out of the gunman's view, as they entered the building. John waited for all of them to pass through, and then he closed the door behind him, and locked it.

When they walked down an interior hall, Teddy was quick to notice that both Pat and John shared the same tall, slender-boned body, and had the same bronze-toned skin and dark brown eyes. Just by looking at them, and having seen John interviewed on numerous occasions, Teddy thought they might be quite compatible. And there seemed to be chemistry between them, even in the short moment they spoke. Teddy could sense it.

While John and Ryan moved ahead of them, Teddy looked over at Pat and nudged her, motioning toward John. "Now there's somebody nice for you," Teddy encouraged. Pat started to smile. "For once, I agree with you," Pat confirmed. "He isn't married?" Pat asked, in a low tone.

"I don't think so," Teddy said. "But I'll find out before the night's over," Teddy assured her.

"Try not to be too obvious, okay, Ted?"

"Who, me?" Teddy asked, smiling.

Pat just gave him a knowing look, and dropped the conversation as they approached the guard. After they all signed in, and were given visitor passes, they proceeded directly over to a set of double doors that John opened with a key.

Teddy looked at him, and sized him up at close range, noticing he was not wearing a wedding band.

"Do you live here in the city, John?" Teddy asked.

"Yes, I do," John, answered.

"Are you married?" Teddy asked, pointedly.

"No," John answered. "I haven't had much time to settle down."

"Pat's single too," Teddy said, as John swung the door open.

John smiled, and looked over at Pat, whose eyes were now fixed on the floor with embarrassment, and who was doing her best to escape the small space.

Once again, John and Ryan took the lead. As soon as John was out of listening range, Pat turned and looked up at Teddy.

"I'll never forgive you for that," she said, under her breath.

"Yes you will," Teddy said, chuckling to himself, as they silently entered the newsroom, and found a place to stand during the telecast.

"I'll be back for you right after my segment," John whispered.

Ryan just nodded.

The last half of the telecast seemed to pass quickly. And, after John reported the sports story he had been working on, they were all led down a short hallway off the newsroom to John's office. The small room, as would be expected, was filled with things that John had collected over the years from his career playing basketball.

At 10:55 p.m. John's phone rang.

"We'll be right over," John said, hanging up, and turning to Ryan. "That was our green light," he conveyed, as he led them out the door.

When they walked through a now empty newsroom, they could see a bank of booths all set up and ready to go. The supervisor, Barry Rodriquez, came right over to them.

"This is my man," John said, as he introduced them around.

"What do you have?" Barry asked, as Teddy handed over the tapes.

"There are two tapes, and they're both just about two hours long," Teddy explained.

"That's going to take some time," he said, while he was making a mental calculation. "We have eight booths, but it will take real time to dupe these."

"Real time?" Teddy asked.

"Yeah, we don't have any high-speed duplicating equipment here, like they do at the production houses. If it's a two hour tape, it'll take us two hours to copy it."

Teddy and Ryan just looked at each other with astonishment. This was something they had not planned on.

"Are you still using typewriters, too?" Teddy asked, joking.

"I'm sure they still have a few at corporate headquarters," Barry quipped back.

"How many copies do you need?" Barry asked.

"As many as we can get," Teddy said. "We were hoping for about twenty-five."

"Well, we can originate the tapes over there," Barry said, pointing to some equipment in a separate booth. "That will be our feed point, and then I'll throw a routing switch to bring it through to all eight booths simultaneously."

"Okay," Teddy said. "How many can we copy then?" Teddy asked.

"I think we have time to make only two sets of each," Barry added.

"Let's see," Teddy said, thinking.

"That's sixteen of each tape," Ryan quickly calculated, "so that's thirty-two tapes in all, by about seven in the morning," Ryan added.

"That's correct," Barry confirmed.

"We'll have to go with sixteen of each then," Teddy said, turning to Pat. "May I see the mailing list again?" Teddy asked.

"Sure," Pat said, handing Teddy the list.

"Will you get in trouble?" Teddy asked, turning to Barry, "if someone comes in and finds us here at seven o'clock?"

"You'll have to leave here way before then," Barry instructed. "And it might be a little later than seven."

"I'll stay and get the tapes to you," John offered. "I'm often here early in the morning when I'm writing a story."

"Should I get started?" Barry asked.

"Yes, please do," Teddy, agreed.

John followed Barry over to one of the booths, carrying the box of blank tapes.

Ryan looked over Teddy's shoulder at the list.

"We'll have to drop all the foreign mailings, and also the American periodicals," Teddy analyzed, as he marked them off his list.

"But we can still mail copies to the networks, and the Associated Press." Ryan suggested. "That will at least give all the newspapers an opportunity to run an Associated Press story."

Teddy nodded his head, counting down the list.

"Let's see," Teddy said, thinking.

"That's exactly sixteen, and we can keep the originals," Ryan suggested.

"Yes, that's sixteen sets," Teddy confirmed.

John came over, and handed Ryan a key. "Why don't you all wait at my place," John suggested. "It's close by, and I can bring all the tapes over as soon as we're finished."

"Thanks," Ryan said, taking the key.

"Help yourselves to whatever," John added.

"Thanks, John," Ryan said.

"C'mon, let me get all of you out of here," John said, walking through the door.

"Why don't you go this way," John suggested, taking them to the other side of the building from where they had entered earlier. "I live just a couple of blocks up the street," John explained to Teddy and Pat. "Ryan knows the way."

Teddy looked back, not wanting to leave the tapes with a stranger, and then he followed Pat out the door. He knew he had to trust John and Barry. He had no choice.

Friday Morning

Exactly as promised, at about seven-thirty, John arrived at his apartment with both originals, and sixteen copies of each tape in a box, each one labeled exactly as were the originals.

"Did you label these for us John?" Teddy asked.

"I didn't want you to get them mixed up," John explained.

"Thank you so much," Teddy said.

"Yes, thanks, John," Ryan repeated.

"It was nothing, I just ran them off on my computer."

Teddy and Pat worked as a team, without even speaking to each other—Teddy enclosing the tapes, and Pat enclosing the letters and sealing the envelopes. At exactly 8:15 a.m., Teddy finished packing the last envelope, with Pat sealing it securely shut.

"John," Teddy requested, "I hate to ask you for anything more, but I meant to bring a piece of carry-on luggage with me to hold these envelopes."

"Oh, there's something you can use in the hall closet," he said, getting up.

"I genuinely appreciate this," Teddy said, ignoring Ryan's critical look.

"Any time," John said.

"I don't know how to thank you," Teddy expressed, as he placed all the envelopes they were using into the piece of luggage. "We could never have gotten this done without your help, John."

"It was my pleasure," John said, looking over at Pat. "I hope some day you'll let me in on what this is all about."

"Trust me," Ryan said. "Whatever Teddy is involved in, you don't want to know."

John started laughing. "Well, I'm still curious."

"You didn't have the audio on, when you were duplicating the tapes?" Teddy asked.

John shook his head no. "There were still a few employees around, and we didn't want to attract any attention."

"We'll tell you when we can, John," Teddy said, grabbing the box containing the letters and envelopes that they were unable to use.

"It was fun meeting you," John said, still full of energy, as he opened the door. "Can I drop you someplace?"

"Thanks, but Pat called a cab. It should be waiting downstairs."

"Thanks again, John," Ryan said, shaking his hand. "I won't forget this."

"Are you kidding?" John returned, "I still owe you."

"No you don't," Ryan quickly added. "Maybe we can finally have dinner next week, when things settle down. I want you to meet Anne."

"I'm looking forward to it." John said.

Soon they all piled into the elevator, with John's piece of luggage in tow, and they were gone.

The cab was just pulling up outside, as they exited the building. Teddy quickly whisked Pat into the cab, with Ryan getting in on the other side with the carry-on piece of luggage.

Once they were settled into the cab, Pat gave Teddy a strange look.

"What's the matter?" Teddy asked.

"I didn't even get to say goodbye," she sighed.

"I know," Teddy said. "Now you play hard to get. And when he calls to ask you out, you tell him you're busy on the weekend, but you're free for lunch during the week."

Ryan just laughed.

Pat looked over at Ryan, for an explanation.

"He's right," Ryan agreed. "You have to play hard to get."

"I never chase guys," Pat said, in defense.

"He has girls falling all over him," Teddy added. "And I want him to have the proper respect for you."

Pat smiled, as she rested back in the seat. She always liked it when Teddy treated her as if she were his younger sister.

"Where to, Mister?" the cabdriver asked.

"O'Hare Airport," Teddy said.

"O'Hare?" Pat questioned.

"We can drop you off first, if you prefer," Teddy offered.

"Oh, no. Why are you going to O'Hare?" Pat questioned.

Teddy looked up at the driver. "Do you mind turning up the news," Teddy requested, so they could talk in private.

"Sure thing," the cabdriver responded, as he turned up the cab's radio.

Teddy dropped his voice, so that only Pat could hear him. "We can't mail these from Chicago, Pat. They can be traced by the postmark," Teddy explained. "I have to mail them from New York."

"Is that why you didn't leave a set with John?" Pat asked.

"John's life would be in danger, if they ever thought he was involved. This way, many people will receive the tapes simultaneously, postmarked from New York City. And no one person will be thought of as being the original source of the information disclosed on the tapes—or knowing who the original source is."

Pat looked at Teddy with serious concern. "Then you are in trouble," she said.

"There are some other things involved in this Pat, that I haven't told you about," Teddy explained. "If we released the tapes in Chicago, the finger would immediately point to me."

"Hey buddy," the cabdriver interrupted, turning down his radio. "Do you have some friends following you? I think we just lost them at the light. Ya want me ta pull over till they catch up?"

"Who?" Teddy asked, whipping around.

"The two guys in the gray car. You don't know them?" he asked, looking in the rearview mirror. "They pulled out right after we left the building, and they've made every turn right behind us."

"We don't have anyone following us," Teddy spoke up to the driver. "But I did want to hear the sports news."

The cabdriver turned the radio up again.

"We should have been more careful," Ryan said.

"I was," Teddy answered, under his breath. "I didn't see anyone."

"I'll take them," Pat said. "You two get out at the next light, there's a diner on the corner, and I'll take care of the packages."

"I couldn't ask you to do that, Pat."

"You didn't, I offered," Pat said.

"It could be dangerous," Teddy warned.

"They're following you, not me," Pat said. "And once I get to New York, I'll just be another secretary bustling around the city trying to get a mailing out."

"You'd actually do that for me?" Teddy asked.

"Of course," Pat confirmed.

The morning traffic was heavy, and had slowed them down considerably. Teddy turned around, and saw that the car, with the two men pursuing them, was fairly close behind them again.

"Use cash," Teddy instructed, "and don't send them UPS or FedEx or anything—or you'll have to give too much information."

"Okay," Pat agreed.

"They have to be mailed and weighed right at the post office," Teddy further instructed. "The return address doesn't exist."

"Okay," Pat said.

"Do you have your cell phone?" Teddy asked.

"In my purse," Pat said.

Teddy handed her an envelope, filled with one hundred dollar bills, with the flight times and airlines flying to New York that morning. "Pick an airline, and then call their 800 number for an E-ticket. Buy a first class seat, round trip. Do you have your credit cards?"

"Of course I do," Pat confirmed. "I knew you'd need me," she said.

Teddy just looked at her, and smiled. "I'm more grateful than you'll ever know, Pat."

"This is the first time I've ever been able to do anything really important for you," Pat said.

"It's because of the girls that I'm so worried," Teddy said "And everything you do is important to me, Pat."

"The girls are taken care of," Pat reminded him.

"I know, but still," Teddy, said, unable to finish.

Pat turned to Ryan. "Did you know he has my daughters come up to the office when they get their report cards," Pat said, referring to Teddy. "That's why they do so well in school. They're afraid to face Teddy with bad grades," she said, laughing.

"Well, they don't have a father," Teddy said, in explanation.

"He makes them go in one by one," Pat continued, "and he's gotten on their case more than once, too," Pat added.

"I always take them to lunch," Teddy said. "I thought they enjoyed coming over."

"They do," Pat said. "So now get out at the light, and I'll call you from New York when I'm finished."

Teddy thought for a moment. "Don't call when you get to New York, it might be traced. Just come back," Teddy instructed, not yet knowing how the men, following them were tracking him.

"Okay," Pat agreed.

"Be careful, and don't take any risks," Teddy insisted.

"I'll be fine," Pat related.

Mr. Chang had sent the same electronic specialists who went through Teddy's home, over to Teddy's office. They found nothing there, so, how they were getting their information, was still a mystery to Teddy.

Reaching into his pocket, Teddy took out two more one hundred dollar bills. "We're getting out at the light, driver," Teddy said, handing the cabdriver the money. "This will cover the fare. Please take this young lady directly to the airport, and forget that you ever saw us, okay?"

"Sure, buddy," the cabdriver, acknowledged.

"Good luck, Pat," Ryan said, as they got out of the cab.

"You two be careful," Pat returned.

"Call me on your cell phone if they follow you, and have the driver bring you right back here," Teddy said, referring to the diner on the corner. "We'll wait here for an hour, just in case. We're going to have breakfast."

"Okay," Pat said.

"I can lose those guys," the cabdriver offered, "if ya want me to."

"Only if they follow you," Teddy agreed.

"This is so exciting," Pat interjected, with a smile flashing across her face.

"Don't take any chances, Pat," Teddy warned.

"I won't," Pat said, still with an excited look on her face.

As Teddy watched the cab drive away, he knew that Pat was another missing link in the puzzle. He had just not known it till now. So were John and Barry.

Teddy carried the box with the unused letters, as if he were carrying something heavy inside. He and Ryan went directly into the diner, never looking in the direction of the two men, who had pulled over. One man got out, and the other man remained in the car.

"What's your schedule today?" Teddy asked, as Ryan grabbed a couple of papers, and they made their way over to a window booth.

"Rounds this morning, and patients this afternoon," Ryan responded, as he picked up a menu. "How about you?"

"My calendar is clear. I thought I was going to be taking the packages to New York. And I had given Pat the day off, so the receptionist is taking messages for us."

Ryan nodded.

"Do you need to get home to shower and change?" Teddy asked.

Ryan shook his head no. "I still have a change of clothes at the office, and I can shower at the Club."

"I have to get home," Teddy said, as he began reading the morning paper, and thinking through his next move.

When the waitress came up, they both ordered breakfast.

After arriving at the airport, Pat called Teddy on her cell phone.

"Hi, I just got home," Pat, said, in case someone was listening in. "I'll be taking off shortly."

"See you later," Teddy acknowledged.

Ryan looked at him. "Pat?" he asked.

"She'll be taking off shortly," Teddy relayed.

"You can always count on Pat," Ryan said. "Do you know how lucky you are?"

"Yes, I know," Teddy acknowledged, hoping Ryan was not going to go into one of his diatribes.

"What's next?" Ryan asked.

"I'm going to catch a cab," Teddy answered. "Why don't you wait here. They'll follow me, and then you can get another taxi to get over to your office."

"Okay," Ryan agreed. "I'll watch from the booth."

Teddy put some money on the table to cover their breakfasts, and walked out to the street where he waved down a cab. He was still carrying the mysterious box in both arms. And, as Teddy had hoped, the two men stayed behind him all the way back to Lake Forest.

When they were within fifteen minutes of the turnoff, onto Town Line Road, Teddy called the police department.

"This is Teddy Townsend, is the Chief there?" he asked.

"Yes, Mr. Townsend, one moment, please," the operator informed, as she connected him.

"Ted?" the Chief asked, "is everything all right?"

"I have a problem, Tom. I'm in a cab coming in from the city, about fifteen minutes from Town Line Road, and I'm being followed."

"Don't go home," the Chief instructed, "come past the police station, and we'll intercept them."

"Do you have their license plate tag?" the Chief asked.

"No, but it's a current model gray sedan, with two men in it."

"We're on it," the Chief said.

"Thanks," Teddy replied.

"I'll call you right back on my cell," the Chief informed him, hanging up.

A minute later, the Chief called Teddy back, and instructed him to have the cabdriver go well over the speed limit, so they would have a reason to stop the sedan.

"Are you a police officer?" the cabdriver asked.

"No, not really," Teddy said, as he instructed the driver which exit to take.

"Working undercover?" the cabdriver further probed.

Teddy did not answer. Exactly as planned, the minute they sped past the Lake Forest Police Station, a squad car pulled out, with its flashing lights, and pulled the two men over on the side of the road. The men were questioned, and then brought into the police department on charges of speeding, possessing unlicensed firearms, and resisting arrest.

All and all, Teddy, thought, it had been a perfect night's work, and he began thinking about what Martel's reaction would be on Monday morning, when his nefarious secret plans were revealed.

CHAPTER 33

▲

THE EXPOSURE

Monday

Sitting behind his large mahogany desk, Teddy gazed out his expansive office windows at the Chicago River, and then began watching the traffic moving up and down Wacker Drive. He had too much on his mind to work.

The Chief had called, shortly after he reached his offices, to say that the two men had been released. Their bail had been set by a judge, and then paid by a Chicago attorney. The men had given the police department an address for themselves at a downtown hotel. Because neither of them had permanent Chicago addresses, the Chief felt they would soon drop out of sight. He warned Teddy to be careful.

There was nothing more Teddy could do, except to wait for the story to break. All of the packages that Pat had mailed in New York City, on Friday afternoon, were to be delivered by that very morning. Teddy reviewed in his mind, all the steps he had taken, and hoped there were no mistakes.

As he continued to stare out his windows, he began thinking about the tapes again. The final outcome would now be in the hands of other people and news agencies. They had sent one package to the office of the President, together with separate copies to be delivered appropriately to those personages who headed up the House of Representatives, the Senate, and the Pentagon.

In addition, packages went to several governors in whose states attacks were planned, as well as *ABC, CBS, NBC, CNN,* and *C-SPAN,* the *Associated Press,* the *Washington Post,* and the current head of the *United Nations.*

The letters to the President and the Pentagon told of Martel's bunker under his Geneva estate, and the elaborate spy network he had devised. The rest of the letters just named Martel, and the other men seen in the videos, who Teddy recognized.

At lunchtime, Teddy went to a neighborhood deli to eat. He had been watchful, as he walked down the street, but saw no one following him. Sitting alone, eating a large Italian beef sandwich, he thought some more about all that had happened. Something was not right, but he could not pinpoint what he had missed.

Monday afternoon dragged by and everyone waited. The supplier for Ryan's laser called, and, in a weak moment, Teddy had Pat write the needed check and put it in the mail. It was not that Ryan deserved a reward, but rather that Teddy thought that his research was important.

Shortly after three that afternoon, he left his offices. He wanted to get home in time for the five o'clock evening news, to see if the story had broken yet. Once again, as at lunch, Teddy could see no one following him, but he also realized that didn't especially mean that they were not there.

The walk to the train station was short. Once Teddy reached the Northwestern Terminal, he stopped and picked up all the available papers, and a ginger ale, then quickly headed out for his train.

As he boarded a car, he looked around to see if he recognized anyone. In the same way he knew almost all of the people in the morning, he knew, at least casually, another group who rode the same car he did at night. But he did not recognize anyone at this time of day, and the schedule showed that the ride would take over an hour. This commuter was not an express train. It would stop at every station.

Teddy took a seat at the very rear of the car, so that no one would be sitting behind him. Within a few minutes they were on their way, and Teddy began to read all the lead stories in the newspapers.

After the train had made its way north out of the city, Teddy put down the last paper he had scanned. There were no breaking stories on Martel or the tapes. Deep in thought, he stared out the train's large-framed window at the view, as they made their way through town after town, with thick patches of woods and northern Illinois meadowlands between each station.

When the train pulled into Lake Forest, the parking lot was still full of cars. Teddy walked across the cobblestone platform, to where his car was parked at the far end of the lot.

Market Square, across the street, looked particularly quaint this time of year. Colorful baskets of planted flowers were hanging from the old-fashioned lampposts, and lush emerald green grass, within the shrub-bordered common, provided a velvet carpet around the old fountain and its grounds.

Teddy had come to know each and every little shop, and shopkeeper, along the tree-lined street, as well as in the small square, and he and his family would often go there together on Saturdays. There was a favorite place for everyone, and a delectable ice-cream store around the corner. Teddy was sure that this was the one reason why Leah always insisted on going with them, whenever she heard the words "going into town."

Teddy pulled up to the stop sign just as two of Michael's friends rode past. Teddy waved to them, as they parked their bikes in front of the corner drug store, then he turned his car west onto Deerpath and headed home.

There had been news stories and articles in the local papers, a week ago, about the Chief and one of his men being injured on Sunday afternoon, and that the Lake Forest Police Department was still able to apprehend Andrews and Jones, who were camping illegally in the woods north of Whippoorwill Farm.

The talk in town, and on the news, had finally calmed down. Teddy's family was kept out of it, saying only that someone on horseback spotted a flickering light coming from the woods, and called the police.

As Teddy made his way out of town, the fresh scent of the countryside came in through his open car windows, and the blue sky above was filled with large puffy white clouds.

Pulling into his driveway, Teddy could see Michael and Matthew with their horses, as they were setting up jumps. Mr. Swensen had started their training on jumping their horses to keep them busy in the paddock closest to the house. They were both unaware of how concerned everyone still was about their safety.

Despite all that had happened, Teddy was forever grateful that they had moved to Lake Forest, and could not have hoped for a better environment within which to raise his children. And, although Whippoorwill was just a few minutes out of town, it was far enough away to give Terese a peaceful place to write.

The house was quiet when Teddy came in, and he said hello to the day guard who was reading in the front hall. Teddy noticed that the officer had a fresh cup of coffee, and a little dish of cookies, sitting next to him on the hall table. He looked content, as he reported the activities of the day to Teddy.

The aroma of freshly baked oatmeal cookies was coming in from the kitchen and, after checking the library for Mr. Chang, Teddy went in to say hello to Mrs. Swensen.

"My, you're home early," Mrs. Swensen commented, looking up at the kitchen clock.

"I caught the 3:35," Teddy explained, as he walked over to the refrigerator and took out the milk.

"I wasn't planning dinner till seven o'clock," Mrs. Swensen explained. "Do you want to eat at six instead?"

"Seven o'clock is fine," Teddy answered. "Where are Mrs. Townsend and Katie?"

"They're both up in the attic," she said, as she checked some dinner rolls that were rising on the counter. "Mrs. Townsend is working on her manuscript, and Katie is watching her tape of *Sesame Street*."

The main purpose of having only one TV in the home hooked up to an outside service, was Terese's disapproval of most of the content on television today that the FCC, Congress and the industry allowed. Teddy agreed with her.

Terese felt that too many programs and commercials, were set on sexualizing children, including teaching them vulgar language and behavior. Teddy and Terese also did not want their children to become desensitized to cruelty by watching one violent disgusting act after another. Because of this, Katie was only allowed to watch tapes of Sesame Street, and other PBS programs for young children, which came off of the VCR in the game room. Her TV could only play tapes.

Teddy poured a glass of milk, and then put the carton back in the refrigerator.

"How did everything go today?" Teddy asked.

"It's been fairly quiet," Mrs. Swensen responded. She looked over at Teddy, and a sparkle came into her pale blue eyes. "Katie certainly likes that new headset you bought for her television, up in her play area. It's just the right size for her. And I think Mrs. Townsend enjoys it, too," Mrs. Swensen said, laughing.

"I'm sure," Teddy said, smiling.

"Okay if I take a few cookies?" Teddy asked.

"That's what they're there for," Mrs. Swensen cheerfully replied.

Mrs. Swensen always wanted everyone to eat all they could, of everything she cooked and baked. Her oatmeal cookies, which were a favorite of the children, were always oversized and chock-full of dark medjool dates, and large chunks of walnuts. The fragrance of butter and cinnamon, were irresistible when they were baking.

Leah soon came running up, and looked through the screen door, wanting to come in and see Teddy. She had heard Teddy's car pull into the driveway, and had run all the way in from the woods.

Once in the house she made a beeline over to Teddy, and started to climb up on his lap to give him a nudge near his ear. He greeted her warmly, and petted her soft coat. Leah went directly over to Mrs. Swensen next, to catch her attention, and looked over at the table of cookies. The fact that Mrs. Swensen was always a soft touch had never escaped Leah, and Leah also knew the household protocol when it came to taking food. Everyone asked Mrs. Swensen.

"Yes, you can have one," she said, in her heavy Swedish accent. Leah quickly trotted back to Teddy, who had just selected a cookie for her.

"What's for dinner tonight?" Teddy asked.

"I have some baby back ribs marinating, a fresh garden salad, and I'm going to roast some seasoned potatoes on the grill with the ribs," she added, looking over to catch Teddy's expression. She knew her back ribs were one of his favorites.

"Sounds delicious," Teddy said, as he took a few more cookies, and checked his watch. "I'm going to catch the news. Will you let Mrs. Townsend know I'm home when she comes down?"

Mrs. Swensen smiled and nodded, knowing he would only eat half the cookies he took, with Leah on his trail.

Soon Teddy was back at the kitchen door. "Is Mr. Chang around?" Teddy asked.

"He's helping Mr. Swensen fix the back gate. Do you need him?"

"No, not really," Teddy explained. "I just noticed that he wasn't in the library when I came in."

"He's a very kind man, Mr. Chang," Mrs. Swensen commented. "He always offers to help, and he's very patient with the children. He's even been teaching young Matthew a little Chinese, on the side."

"Yes, I think we have made a new friend," Teddy agreed. "If anyone needs me," Teddy called back, "I'll be back in the game room."

Mrs. Swensen smiled, as she took her last batch of cookies out of the oven.

When the telecast came on, to Teddy's total disappointment, there was no mention of Martel's international band of men.

Teddy knew that it takes only so long for journalists to do their homework, and he was concerned that that needed time had passed—especially in the fast-paced world we live in today. It was not as if they did not have all the evidence they needed. He and Ryan had seen to that.

Teddy was beginning to wonder if these men, because of their high positions of power, had put a lid on breaking the story. He knew that they all had an enormous influence on other people's lives, and were probably using that influence now when they needed it most. Reporters would be contacting all of them, confirming their association with Martel. It went without saying that they were all very powerful, intelligent, and enterprising men.

And, as it would be revealed through the evening, there would be no network news concerning the incriminating tapes. Not at five, not at six and not at ten. CNN, and also MSNBC, who should have received all the material from its parent, NBC, were silent on the subject, as well.

Ryan called Teddy three times that evening—the last time right after the evening news went off the air, wondering how they could have failed at every level.

Even Teddy was beginning to doubt whether he had chosen the correct path. The letters were not on his letterhead, nor did he sign his name. He was far from giving up though, and knew that if this effort failed, then he would just have to get to someone else. He would approach individuals this time, rather than large entities. He knew that it only took the interest of one investigative reporter to break a news story. Everyone else would pick it up later.

Teddy also knew that there were plenty of people in the communications industry, men and women alike, who could get the job done. He believed that when you have an entire nation of people whose ancestors were willing to go off and begin again in a new land, then you have a nation made up of unique individuals, who have proven themselves over and over again—individuals who have the strength, and the capacity, to rise to the occasion, and do that which has to be done.

Hardworking, dynamic and humane, America was such a nation, and this was such an occasion, and Teddy began making a mental list of whom he would contact next. It was a long list.

Tuesday

Teddy found he could not sleep that night. He tossed and turned endlessly, and then, not wanting to disturb Terese, about two o'clock on Tuesday morning he went down to the library and read until dawn. He anxiously waited for the *Chicago Tribune* to arrive, and as soon as the morning paper hit the front porch at six o'clock, he was outside picking it up and scanning the front page. The story had finally broken.

After reading the lead article, Teddy felt as if a heavy shroud had been lifted from around his shoulders. He now hoped Martel would be too busy meeting with his lawyers to bother with any petty interest he might have had in him and his family.

When Teddy came back into the house, Mr. Chang came down the back staircase, already having showered and dressed, and joined Teddy in the kitchen. Mr. Chang then began reading the section of the paper that Teddy had finished. Ryan showed up ten minutes later, with every out-of-town paper he could purchase at the newsstand, and the three men went over the newspapers together for an hour or more at the kitchen table, with Teddy still in his pajamas and robe. Anne had flown back to New York on Monday, to take care of some personal matters, and to pack more of her clothes, so on this morning it was just the men.

Teddy called Pat at home, from the kitchen, and asked her to go in early that day and clear his calendar. He wanted for her to reschedule his appointments on both Tuesday and Wednesday. He would not be going into the office.

Mrs. Swensen came in shortly thereafter and started breakfast for everyone. And, once they had all finished the cheese omelets she prepared for them, Teddy, Ryan and Mr. Chang went into the game room together and turned on CNN. The station was already covering the story with live feeds from Geneva and Washington.

"Ryan," Teddy asked, when he saw the time, "are you driving into the city today? I think you just missed our train."

"No, the surgery I had scheduled has been put off," Ryan explained. "The family was hesitating, so I suggested they get another opinion."

"So, you don't have to go in today?" Teddy asked.

"I planned to catch up in my lab, but with all the breaking news, I changed my mind."

"Oh good," Teddy said.

"I have my pager with me," Ryan continued, "if I'm needed."

Once Terese and Katie had bathed and dressed, and had taken the boys to school, they joined the men in the game room. Katie immediately began pulling out her downstairs toys, while the others watched television.

By noon, CNN was reporting that the United States was attempting to extradite Martel from Switzerland. However, the Swiss wanted him first, after they had seen the convicting tape of evidence that the United States had couriered over to them.

"I can't believe this," Teddy said. "We finally have him."

"Oh, I hope so," Terese responded, reaching over and taking Teddy's hand while they watched the telecast.

It was almost as if Teddy had spoken too soon though, for before anyone could say another word, CNN interrupted its programming, stating that it had breaking news on the story, and reported that a private plane, owned by Marshall Martel, had just gone down in route from Geneva to Bern, Switzerland's capital. Teddy immediately turned up the sound.

Mr. and Mrs. Martel were in route to Bern, to respond to charges made against Mr. Martel by the Swiss authorities, when their plane went down in the mountains. Flames soon engulfed the aircraft after it crashed. There appear to be no survivors.

Teddy looked over at Ryan, trying to read his thoughts, and then turned back to the newscast.

Investigators are currently searching through Martel's estate for evidence in the alleged international plot, CNN reported.

They could not believe what they were hearing. An hour later the newscast was interrupted once again to announce that Martel's pilot had communicated that they were having problems in flight. The reporter now had a confirmation.

There were several witnesses who saw the plane going down, shortly
after takeoff, in the mountains near Geneva. The fire, resulting
from the crash, has made it impossible to find any remains.
The Martels are survived by two children.

It was all quite shocking.

"I'm going to get my shower, and dress," Teddy said, excusing himself from the room.

During his long, hot shower, Teddy thought through all that had happened. He became totally lost in thought, and had no idea how long he remained there, but the water was beginning to get cold, and he soon turned it off. After shaving, and then dressing, he rejoined the others downstairs.

They all spent the rest of the afternoon together, in the game room, going through each of the papers, and continuing to watch for any further reports and stories—switching from CNN, to MSNBC, and then to the other stations giving the news.

Mr. Swensen made a trip back to the newsstand, and purchased later editions of all the papers, and then picked up the boys from school. The entire day had been spent in the game room.

After dinner that evening, Ryan said goodnight, and took off for home. He too was tired, and wanted to call it an early evening. Mr. Chang retired to his room to read his book, and Teddy, Terese and the children began their evening routine.

Teddy, as planned the day before, took Wednesday off, too, but Ryan had to return to the city. By Wednesday afternoon, more and more people were being questioned, and arrested, in the United States and Europe.

There were also several arrests made in Asia. The news coverage began to reveal how complex the malefic international plot was—being more than what had first been reported—and that it would take several more days to arrest everyone involved.

The networks were now showing excerpts from the tapes. CNN, MSNBC and C-SPAN were showing the tapes in their entirety that evening. Now the whole world knew what was going on, as they gave witness to the great evil threat that Marshall Mason Martel had masterminded.

Ryan had called Teddy from the hospital a couple of times, and Teddy filled him in on what was going on.

It had been a very full day and, after they all had dinner that evening, and the dishes were cleared and put in the dishwasher, Terese took the children upstairs. Everyone agreed to make it an early evening.

When Teddy went into the library to say goodnight to Mr. Chang, he found him reading *John Adams*.

"Are you enjoying McCullough's book?" Teddy asked.

"I started reading it last weekend," Mr. Chang responded. "John Adams is finally getting his due respect."

"That's what I thought too. He should be on Mt. Rushmore with the others."

"Most certainly," Mr. Chang agreed.

"It has been quite a couple of days," Teddy shared.

"Yes, and quite promising." Mr. Chang agreed.

"I think I'm going to turn in," Teddy said. "Can I get you anything?"

"I'm content right here," Mr. Chang responded, "but thank you, Ted."

"Then you won't mind if I go up?" Teddy asked.

"Not at all," Mr. Chang responded.

"I'll see you tomorrow, then," Teddy smiled.

The center hall's grandfather clock was just striking eight bells. When Teddy left the library, the new police officer on guard was coming back in, after checking the grounds.

"If you get hungry, Officer Begley, there are plenty of leftovers in the refrigerator. Help yourself," Teddy said, as he walked up the stairs.

"Oh, thank you, Mr. Townsend. Mrs. Swensen left a note, saying there was a sandwich for me in the refrigerator, and a piece of cake," he responded, smiling. "I'm going to miss coming here when my assignment is over," he added.

"Well, you men certainly have done a great job looking after my family," Teddy returned.

"It's our pleasure, Mr. Townsend," Officer Begley responded.

In his usual routine, Teddy went in and saw the children. Michael and Matthew were still awake, but Katie had already fallen asleep, and Terese had tucked her into her own bed. Michael was reading a comic book, and Matthew was mounting a new insect he had found out in the yard that day.

Teddy talked to each of them, then said goodnight. When he went into his own room, he could hear that Terese was taking her evening shower in the bathroom. He quietly slipped in to brush his teeth, without disturbing her. Soon, Teddy had changed out of his clothes and into some pajamas, then climbed into bed.

Something intuitive was still plaguing him about all that had happened, however, it was not yet clear. Teddy was so tired though, that he could not focus on anything more. The last thing he remembered was listening to the water running in the shower, and then, within a minute or two, he was fast asleep.

CHAPTER 34

▲

THE FINAL RESOLUTION

Thursday

Upon waking on Thursday morning, Teddy could not remember having slept so well in months. When he looked over to see what time it was, he saw that he had overslept.

"Terese," Teddy called, gently waking her. "Terese, I forgot to set the alarm."

"I'll get the boys up," she managed, moving in slow motion, as Teddy hurried into the bathroom to shower and shave.

He did not want to miss his train. There was still so much he wanted to talk to Ryan about. And, he knew that there were probably more news stories breaking by the hour around the world while they slept.

Ryan waited at the train station, and could hear the train-crossing warning bells, as he picked up their donuts and coffee in the stationhouse. When he walked out to the platform, he was disappointed not to see Teddy's car at the northern end of the lot.

Boarding the train, Ryan took his usual seat behind Morrie Stein and his friends, and gave Morrie Teddy's breakfast.

"Teddy miss the train again?" Morrie asked.

"Once a week, right on time," Ryan responded.

Morrie laughed, reaching into the bag, and took a huge bite out of Teddy's chocolate-covered donut.

Ryan made himself comfortable, as the train pulled away from the station. Teddy's seat, alongside of him, remained empty.

Just as Ryan was settling in with his paper, Teddy came through the back of the car, and quickly made his way over to him.

"I had to park across the street and run for it," Teddy said, catching his breath.

"Will you please tell me why you can't leave the house a few minutes earlier?" Ryan questioned. "I walk here every morning, and I never have a problem."

"Where's my breakfast?" Teddy asked, looking around.

Ryan pointed at the seat in front of them.

Teddy watched, as Morrie Stein shoved the last quarter of his donut into his mouth, and then took a swig of Teddy's coffee.

"Did you give my paper away too?" Teddy asked, looking at his empty seat.

Ryan did not answer.

A small chubby hand came up, over the seat, holding Teddy's rumpled newspaper. It was obvious that Morrie had already been sitting on it.

"In the future, Ryan, you could at least wait until the train pulls out of the station before you give my breakfast away," Teddy said, as he settled into his seat. "And you had better save me half of yours!"

Ryan handed him half of his uneaten donut, and then began reviewing the articles in the *Chicago Tribune*.

When Teddy flicked the front page of his paper, to straighten it, a piece of his donut, together with its chocolate icing, dropped down on top of Ryan's knee, chocolate side up.

"Oh, listen to this," Teddy said, with pleasure, as he began reading the headlines out loud:

MORE ARRESTS TO COME OF INTERNATIONAL GROUP PLOTTING TO OVERTHROW THE FREE WORLD

"This is wonderful," Teddy exclaimed, with a sincere tone of relief. "You know this actually proves it," Teddy went on, lowering his voice.

"You think because you're just one person, that you can't make a difference."

"One person?" Ryan asked, indignantly.

"I remember being more than a little alone, through the end of March and all of April," Teddy said, in a low voice.

Ryan looked genuinely offended.

Teddy just laughed, as he looked back at the paper. "All right," Teddy agreed. "It's true. I probably couldn't have done it without you," he admitted.

Feeling justified, and with a look of satisfaction on his face, Ryan crossed his leg and the piece of chocolate donut disappeared.

The rest of the ride was spent reading portions of the paper aloud to each other, for they alone knew that they had just pulled off the biggest, most exalted, *grand coup* of all time.

As they were pulling out of the Winnetka station, Teddy had a final concern. "Ryan," he asked, still in a low voice. "Do you remember reading anything about the bunker?"

"No, I didn't," he said, thinking back.

"Do you think they're not mentioning it because they don't want anyone to know about it—or that they never found it?"

"I'm not sure," Ryan answered.

"How about the additional tapes?" Teddy questioned. "Did you read anything about them?"

"They should have found the tapes, unless they were removed and stored elsewhere," Ryan said, "But the bunker is another story, because of the secret passageway."

"That's what I was thinking," Teddy said, "and there was no mention of San Onofre either."

"No, no mention," Ryan agreed. "Maybe they couldn't understand the tape, just as we didn't at first."

"Ryan, we have to go back in," Teddy said.

"With all the press and government officials surrounding the place? You've got to be kidding," Ryan exclaimed.

"We'll go to the funeral," Teddy said. "Can you get away?"

Ryan thought for a moment. He knew Teddy was correct.

"I'll see what I can do," Ryan said. "I'd have to reschedule some appointments, and arrange for Joe Cavanaugh to take my calls again. I don't have any surgery scheduled until next Monday morning."

"Make it first thing, because we'll have to leave this afternoon."

"I'll call you later this morning," Ryan promised, still thinking through what he would have to do before leaving.

"Okay," Teddy agreed.

"Can't we just tell someone?" Ryan asked.

"Do you think the source wouldn't slip out, with all the people involved?" Teddy asked, keeping his voice low. "Can you imagine what that would bring down on us, with all the arrests that have been made?" Teddy questioned.

"No, you're right," Ryan agreed. "We'll have to do it ourselves."

Teddy now had an idea of what his intuitive thoughts and promptings were all about. This was part of what his soul was trying to communicate to him—the bunker had not yet been discovered by the Swiss.

Further, the American government probably wanted to get in there first, then destroy it, before the Swiss got their hands on Martel's Spy Network. The CIA was probably, at that very moment, putting a plan into place. It would just be a matter of time, and Teddy knew he had to preserve any evidence that might be lost, or confiscated, and never seen again.

Ryan was not actually too concerned about going back to Geneva, with Martel dead. It made quite a difference. Teddy and Ryan rode quietly for a while, thinking about what was ahead of them. They passed through Rogers Park, and Ravenswood, before Teddy spoke again.

"The last day of school for the boys is tomorrow," Teddy, said, breaking the long silence.

"Did they mind putting off our fly-fishing trip to Wyoming?" Ryan asked.

"They were really disappointed. I told them they could each bring a friend with them, when we go in August, after the baby is here. Is that okay with you, Ryan?" Teddy asked.

"You've obviously lost your powers," Teddy said, as a further challenge. "After all Merak, I should think an Atlantean Magician would not have to fire a gun to control two mortal men."

Martel had a seething intensity in his large brown eyes, as they seemed to peer into Teddy's soul.

"Then you do know who I am," he said, as he set the gun down on the oval control panel.

Teddy nodded his response.

"Are you the one who stole the tapes that are being played on television?" Martel asked, stepping forward.

Teddy did not answer him, but he didn't need to. Martel had already picked that up by reading their thoughts.

"Are you with the FBI?" Martel asked.

Still Teddy did not answer, and this time Martel picked up nothing from Teddy telepathically.

"I know you're a partner with a large national firm, with offices in Chicago," Martel revealed. "Are you also working undercover with the CIA?" Martel further probed.

Once again, Martel was met with silence.

Then, terrifyingly, a maniacal burst of laughter came from deep within Martel's throat, and he raised his hand, as if to flick a beam of light from it, but nothing came forth.

"It never was you, you know," Teddy said, his eyes fixed into Martel's. "You have never been the one with the power."

Ryan could see that Martel was beginning to tremble with rage.

Again, and again, Martel tried to bring forth the electrical charges, wanting to strike Teddy down, but he was powerless in Teddy's presence.

"He's deserted you," Teddy said. "Did you think he would stand by you when you were no longer useful to him?"

Martel never said a word.

"He's gone, Martel," Teddy confirmed.

"Lucifer," Martel called out. "LUCIFER!"

All of a sudden a gray, streaming, snake-like essence slid from under the door of the private quarters. It flew around the ceiling of the bunker, in a weaving motion, its gray body swelling for a moment above them, before it rapidly dove down into the top of Martel's head. He burst out laughing again, and his large brown eyes began to darken.

Teddy and Ryan watched the spectacle, almost in disbelief, as Martel's features seemed to distort, and his eyes curved with a cat-like, evil slant.

"NOW YOU'LL SEE WHO'S IN CONTROL!" Martel screamed.

Electrical charges began emitting from his fingers, and Ryan drew in his breath in shock.

This time the room filled up with a dark, threatening gray-toned electrical surge, which Martel threw over Teddy. It covered his entire body with snapping electrical sparks. So heavy was this force's intensity and thrust, that Ryan could no longer see Teddy's form. Teddy had completely disappeared in a thick fog.

Turning to Ryan next, and with a single sweep of his hands, Martel threw an identical electrical force at him, and Ryan became engulfed by the same destructive, dark gray electrical surge. He could feel it poking through at him, with the sucking appendages of an octopus. Soon Ryan could no longer see outside of the field of force. It seemed as if several minutes passed before it dissipated. Martel was finally satisfied that they were dead.

When the room cleared, Teddy and Ryan stood silently facing Martel, their tall, untouched forms, all but overshadowing his small frame.

Martel looked shocked and astounded. He expected their bodies to be burned to a crisp.

The two watched, as the gray, snake-like essence oozed out of Martel's head, quickly spiraling around the room, and once again slipped under the door and out of sight.

Martel turned hurriedly to exit the room, but the door to his private quarters would not open. It was now locked. Teddy and Ryan stood watching him, as he pounded on the metal seal, losing all his composure.

"LET ME IN!" Martel screamed.

"You're coming with us," Teddy said, as Martel began moaning.

"LUCIFER, HELP ME!" Martel pleaded, still pounding on the door.

"He's gone Martel. He's forsaken you, as he will all the others."

"But he promised me," Martel said, his body crumbling to the floor.

"He lied," Teddy responded.

"LUCIFER!!" Martel screamed, one more time.

Taking Martel's arm, Teddy firmly lifted him up, and led him away from the door.

As Ryan looked on, for the first time he realized what a small, weak man Martel actually was. Ryan quickly reached over to the control panel, and took possession of Martel's gun.

"There's one thing we need to know," Teddy continued. "What are your plans at San Onofre?"

Martel slowly eased himself away from Teddy's tight hold, giving him a mean, hateful look.

In what seemed a flash, Martel turned and quickly ran to an electrical panel, and began tearing at the equipment. Teddy and Ryan were on him within seconds, and pulled his hands away.

"Oh no you don't," Teddy said, thinking Martel was trying to electrocute himself, and take the easy way out.

Ryan and Teddy forced him back, away from the panel, and then onto the floor.

"That's all we need," Teddy said, "is for you to die, and come right back in again without paying the price for all that you've done."

Teddy looked at Martel, and tried to control his anger, as Ryan held him firmly to the floor.

"I want you to spend the rest of your life, Martel, in a small cell," Teddy said, standing over him, "so that you can think about what you have done to humanity on this planet, and be despised every waking hour for the rest of your desolate life!"

Martel remained motionless.

"I'm going to ask you one more time Martel," Teddy said. "What is your plan at San Onofre in August?"

Martel remained mute.

Without another word said, Ryan took a third vial out of his jacket pocket and filled a new syringe.

"This will get us what we want," Ryan said, injecting Martel, "although he is the last person I thought I might be using this on today."

Martel soon relaxed out on the floor, and Ryan let him rest for a few moments before he began questioning him.

"Mr. Martel, do you want us to help you get out of here?" Ryan asked.

Martel did not answer.

Ryan repeated the question.

"Mr. Martel, you need to answer me. Would you like for us to help you get out of here?"

"Yes," Martel finally answered.

"All you have to do is to answer one question for us. You must agree that nothing else is important now, unless you can escape from here alive. Right?" Ryan asked.

Martel remained silent.

"What is the plan at San Onofre in August," Ryan repeated.

Still, Martel remained silent.

"I want you to know that we plan to take your daughter there," Ryan revealed.

For the first time, Martel showed some interest and, again, Ryan repeated the question in a clear, measured tone.

"Mr. Martel, what is the plan at San Onofre in August?"

"That's when the delivery takes place. We're going to blow it up," Martel revealed.

"You're planting a bomb?" Ryan asked.

"No," Martel answered.

"How are you going to do it?" Ryan questioned.

"From the ocean, Martel mumbled. The shipment arrives in August," he repeated.

"August what?" Ryan asked.

"I don't remember," Martel answered.

Teddy and Ryan just looked at each other.

"Are you talking about an underwater missile?" Ryan asked.

"Yes," Martel answered.

"Do you have any other similar plans in the works?" Ryan asked, "in addition to the San Onofre Nuclear Power Plant?"

"The test was to be at San Onofre," Merak responded.

"Put him out," Teddy said, as he walked over to the door leading to the private quarters. He felt around the door, finding a releasing mechanism, and gained entry into the locked room.

The door opened immediately for him, even though it failed to open for Martel. He soon came back with Mrs. Martel, as well as the ancient stone box and its key.

"Inject her," Teddy said.

Ryan caught the look of fear on Mrs. Martel's face.

"This will only put you to sleep for a little while," Ryan said. "Fortunately for you, I'm not the kind of man your husband is."

Mrs. Martel quickly faded away, as the drug moved through her body. Teddy was shocked to see the same gray stream, once having entered Martel, now ooze out of Mrs. Martel's head. This time it went up the bunker stairs to the video room. It was obviously searching for another host it could use, and Teddy had no doubt it would soon find Mason Martel.

Teddy looked over at Ryan. "Did you see that?" he asked, referring to the dark gray stream.

Ryan nodded.

"Is this the first time you've been able to see things that appear ethereally?" Teddy questioned.

Ryan nodded in agreement, thinking for a moment, and then looked back at Martel and his wife. They had fallen into a deep, unconscious sleep. Once again Ryan carefully capped the needles, then put them into a plastic bag containing all the other used vials and needles, and returned it to his pocket.

"Do you have an extra pair of surgical gloves?" Teddy asked.

Ryan handed him his spares, and Teddy put them on.

Teddy pointed to some cabinets on the far wall. "You take that end Ryan, and I'll take this end. Pull whatever you think might be of interest to the authorities."

"You had better wipe down what you touched going into Martel's quarters," Ryan suggested.

Teddy immediately did so, and then joined Ryan.

They soon hurried through the task of going through the cabinet, creating a pile in the middle of the floor between them.

"Do you remember your etheric impulse project on Atlantis?" Teddy asked, as he reached onto the next shelf.

Ryan shrugged his shoulders. "A little," he finally answered, reading through some booklets, and then adding them to the pile.

"You should try to bring that knowledge through again," Teddy urged. "Etheric energy is free, and clean, and tapping it could change the world."

"I don't remember how it worked," Ryan admitted.

"It had a crystal power source, didn't it?" Teddy asked.

"Yes. Yes it did," Ryan answered.

"Just think about it, Ryan, and try to bring it through again."

"Why is it that you remember what you were taught on Atlantis, but I can't?" Ryan asked.

"You just have to become more intuitive," Teddy responded. "Your soul has the knowledge of thousands of lifetimes—including your existence on Atlantis. You should start listening to it more attentively," Teddy advised. "It holds all the answers."

"Is it because of the pendant, that I can now see ethereally?" Ryan asked, touching its gold chain.

"No," Teddy answered. "It is because of you."

"I can't believe you fought him off without any protection," Ryan said, for the first time admitting how powerful Teddy was.

"We all have the power to fight off evil," Teddy explained. "*Fear no evil* is an old adage, that speaks the truth. It is the fear itself that truly weakens us, not the evil."

Ryan just looked at him.

"Do you remember that class at Temple School, when we learned that light can enter darkness, much more easily than darkness can enter light?" Teddy asked.

"Yes. Yes, I do," Ryan, answered.

"And how those who stand with and defend someone who is evil, are no better themselves?" Teddy said, in explanation.

Ryan nodded his head.

"People can fight the forces of darkness, if they want to. You didn't actually need to wear the golden pendant to protect yourself from the embodiment of Lucifer. The light of your own soul would have saved you, Ryan. The more pure the soul, the greater the light, and the more protection you have."

"You're a White Magician, and you've never even had the training, Ted," Ryan admitted. "You actually could have been one of the Atlantean Magi."

Teddy just looked at him. "My Grandfather taught me a lot of things, Ryan, during my childhood. But it's all moot now," he said smiling. "We'll never know how far either one of us could have gone."

Ryan just nodded, adding more evidence to the pile.

"Your work is far more important than mine could ever be, Ryan. You are the one who heals the sick, and does good work," Teddy conveyed.

"We wouldn't be here today, Ted, if you hadn't insisted on going after Martel. I think you do good work too, and on a much larger scale."

"Ryan, your research is going to help humanity on a very large scale when it is completed," Teddy reminded him.

Removing the pendant from around his neck, Ryan gave it back to Teddy.

"Thanks, Ryan," Teddy said.

"What are you going to do with it?" Ryan asked, referring to the pendant.

"I suppose I'll just hold onto it for safekeeping," Teddy smiled, slipping it into his coat pocket. "It means a lot to me, having once belonged to Polaris. I will probably pass it on to Matthew, one day."

Ryan nodded. "Matthew is the one who will really appreciate it."

"Well, I guess that's it," Teddy added, having gone through the last cabinet.

"The box should fit into that briefcase," Ryan said, pointing to a plain brown leather case near the tapes along the wall. "I'm glad you found it."

"Me too," Teddy said, emptying the contents of the case onto the pile. "We'll have to purchase a small box somewhere, maybe at an antique store, so we have a receipt for customs."

"Yes," Ryan agreed, checking his watch. "We'll have plenty of time this afternoon."

Teddy spotted Martel's black bound reports again and, wanting to read what was in them, took one of the two remaining copies and put it in the briefcase along with the stone box. This time around, this was all he would take of the evidence hidden in the bunker. Teddy's mission was to preserve the evidence, especially now that the Swiss were involved, not to take any more of it with him.

A printed note, in French, revealed what Martel had told them about an August shipment to destroy the San Onofre Nuclear Power Plant on the coast of California. The attack would be by sea, using an underwater missile, and to please deliver a copy of the tape, together with a copy of this note, to the President of the United States, and to the Governor of California, forthwith.

Once they reached the top of the stairs, Ryan, as a precaution, disengaged the door to the secret passageway, so that it would not close. After removing the bullets from the three guns, they wiped them clean and then placed them back on the bodies of the two men.

"Here," Ryan said, never missing a detail, as he handed his glasses back to Teddy. "You had better put these back on."

"Thanks, I almost forgot," Teddy said, taking the glasses and heading down the staircase.

After opening the hallway door, and leaving it ajar and unlocked, they wiped their prints from the doorknobs, took off their surgical gloves, and went back to the gathering at the front of the house.

Ryan waited for Teddy near the front double doors of Martel's mansion. He held the briefcase, as inconspicuously as possible, at his side. The butler was now overseeing the buffet of food that had been prepared by the kitchen staff, and the maids were assisting by bringing in platters of food.

Teddy went back into the reception, walking directly over to the one man he felt was in charge of the undercover operation, and tapped him on the shoulder.

"Excuse me," Teddy asked, speaking French. "Are you a Swiss agent?"

The agent just nodded his reply, uncertain if Teddy was a guest, or part of the household staff.

"There was a gentleman in the north hall, who asked if you would meet him in the space above the conference room," Teddy said.

The undercover agent looked puzzled. "Where the video cameras were?"

Teddy just shirked his shoulders. "Perhaps I misunderstood him," Teddy said, as he walked away.

Teddy watched, peripherally, as the man he spoke to signaled to one of the other undercover agents, and they both went out in the direction of the north hallway. Teddy followed far enough behind so that he would not be seen. When the two men entered the correct door, Teddy turned around, and joined Ryan. They immediately left the house, and found their car.

As they were driving back to the hotel, Teddy asked Philippe if there were any good antique stores in Geneva that he could take them to, saying that they wanted to do something pleasant for the rest of the afternoon. Philippe said there were several, and he drove them into town.

Ryan looked at Teddy, with relief in his eyes. They could say nothing more in the car, but they were both grateful to still be alive.

Saturday Morning

Teddy and Ryan took the same early flight back to the United States that they had taken before, and, after picking up the morning papers during their two-hour layover in Zurich, they were ecstatic with all the breaking news.

The local papers were full of stories about Martel's arrest. And, there was another story about the tall, mysterious blonde Frenchman, who had told the Swiss agents where Martel could be found, and who had also exposed a Master Spy Network housed in a bunker under the estate.

Swiss authorities now had more than enough evidence to convict every member of the Cabal of 15, as well as many of their associates. It was further reported in a press release, that the written material confiscated in the bunker involved so many nations around the world, it would take weeks to sort through it all.

Teddy and Ryan were able to find an antique box, which was similar in size to the Atlantean box, after they left Martel's mansion, and Teddy had placed the receipt for it with his passport. Then, the box they purchased was left in a locker at the Geneva airport, and the key to the locker was thrown away in Zurich.

When Teddy and Ryan boarded their flight from Zurich to Chicago, Teddy opened the briefcase with the ancient treasured box inside.

"Checking to see if it's still there?" Ryan asked, with a grin on his face.

"I wanted to read the black report on the way home," Teddy explained, as he took it out of the briefcase.

"I wanted to read it too," Ryan said, looking over Teddy's shoulder, as they reviewed the report together.

It was not long before Teddy would see what he truly did not want to know.

"Oh my God," Teddy said, as he turned the first page and saw a list of names.

Ryan looked on without saying a word.

In reading the report, Teddy and Ryan saw Teddy's father's name at the top of a chart, and knew it would only be a matter of time before he was arrested. Teddy's father was one of the 15.

Teddy had now confirmed what he feared most, after viewing the videotapes first taken from Martel's estate. It was his father who sat directly to Martel's right at the conference table. Ryan thought this as well, but said nothing to Teddy. There was no way to be certain.

It was heartbreaking to Teddy to think that his father had caused so much evil in the world. And he now understood better why he had been born to an enemy. God had apparently placed him there for a reason.

The hardest thing of all for Teddy, was to have to tell Terese about his father when they returned home. However, he did just that at the end of the day when they were alone in bed. Terese began to cry, as Teddy divulged what he had read, and then she tried to comfort him as best she could. They talked about it all for a very long time, and it was quite late before they finally fell asleep.

Sunday

When the family returned from church late Sunday morning, the Swensens took the children out for lunch, and then to see *Snow White and the Seven Dwarfs*. Mr. Chang was invited to accompany them.

Ryan planned to spend the day with Anne, in the city, so Teddy and Terese had time to work on getting the mailing of Martel's black-bound report ready.

With this in mind, and not wanting to waste any more valuable time, Teddy and Terese went up to Terese's attic office, while the guard remained in the downstairs hall. It was time to take action.

After talking to Pat on the phone, Terese was able to pull up the full list of names and addresses that she needed from Teddy's laptop. This time the mailing would go out to everyone on the address list, and the entire world would benefit from reading this report. While Terese worked at her computer on the needed labels, Teddy handwrote a cover letter to go with the report that Terese later typed for him.

The information in the report also listed all of Martel's holdings, including a list of companies that would benefit from the havoc he, and his Cabal of 15, had been creating. It was very condemning evidence.

A copy of the report, as well as the cover letter telling of the plan to attack the San Onofre Nuclear Power Plant in August, would go out to everyone, including the Governor of California—just in case the Swiss had become bogged down, sorting through Martel's bunker. Every detail had been seen to.

It was also planned that Pat would meet Teddy at the office, at seven o'clock on Monday morning, so she could photocopy and bind the needed copies of Martel's report, before everyone got in. This way they would have the privacy they needed. Then the envelopes could be sealed, and Pat would make another trip to New York, to mail the packages.

After everyone returned from the movies, the children excitedly told Terese and Teddy about the film that they had seen. Then the boys helped Mr. Swensen with the horses, while Mr. Chang went to the library to read.

Terese and Teddy spent the rest of the afternoon out in the backyard with Katie, while they watched the boys jump their horses.

When it was time for dinner, Teddy ordered in Chinese food again for everyone, then they all made an early evening of it.

After Teddy and Terese finally went to bed that evening, Terese read Martel's report, in its entirety, for the first time. It was all still quite shocking, and they had another long talk.

Terese asked Teddy what he was going to do once his father was arrested. She knew her father-in-law would call Teddy, asking for his help, as would his mother.

Teddy thought for a long time before answering her. "I'm going to refuse their calls."

Terese said nothing more. She disliked both of Teddy's parents, but had never said so. However, she was greatly relieved for his decision. It was a long time in coming.

Teddy had also decided to disclose to Terese that evening, how unhappy he was with practicing law. It had not been as much of a surprise to her as Teddy thought it would be. Terese encouraged him to think it all through very carefully, after he had some needed rest, and then make the necessary decision. She told him that he had her support, no matter what he wanted to do.

Everything had fallen neatly into place. Most important, their part in disclosing what Teddy had come to believe was a master plan was now complete. Marshall Mason Martel had been captured and exposed, and soon the rest of his men would meet the same fate—including Teddy's father.

CHAPTER 35

▲

A NEW BEGINNING

Monday

Teddy and Pat met, as planned, early on Monday morning. In about an hour, all the reports had been copied and bound, and Teddy helped Pat package everything up into a piece of carry-on luggage. He then drove her out to O'Hare, and saw her onto her plane.

When Teddy returned to the office, he began handwriting his letter of resignation. Teddy was the partner who headed up the litigation department at the firm's Chicago office. It was not an easy letter to write, in that he liked many of the people he worked with.

Also, without disclosing his plan, he had extended an invitation to Anne, and the other associates in his department, including the secretaries and paralegals, to join him for a special luncheon on Tuesday. Teddy wanted to wait until Pat had returned, before he made his announcement.

Pat's trip to New York City on Monday had, once again, been successful, and she returned to Chicago Monday evening. She called Teddy as soon as she reached home. Everything had gone exactly as planned.

Tuesday

Shortly after Pat arrived at the office, and had settled into her alcove, Teddy asked her to bring her coffee into his office so they could talk. He then shut the door, so that they could have their conversation in private.

As Teddy began to explain his plan, Pat could not believe what he was telling her. She knew he was no longer interested in his work, but she never thought he would leave the firm.

"When did you decide this?" Pat asked.

"Terese and I talked it over Sunday night." Teddy said.

Pat just nodded her head, as she thought through what he had just told her.

"Pat," Teddy asked, "would you consider coming with me?"

"Of course, I'll come with you," Pat said, then thinking for a moment. "Where are we going?"

"I'm not sure yet what the future will hold, but it won't be working in law any longer."

"What will I do for you?" Pat asked.

"You'll continue to act as my private secretary, and handle all my personal matters, just as you always have."

"Oh, okay," Pat, said, "when are we leaving?"

"The beginning of August," Teddy explained.

"I thought, at first, you were going to leave me behind," Pat said, as a smile came across her face.

"I'd never leave you behind, Pat," Teddy said, reassuring her.

"Oh good, because I don't want to stay here without you," she said.

"By the way," Teddy asked, "how did your date go with John Jefferson last weekend?" Teddy knew that they had had lunch, the previous week, and that Ryan's friend had invited Pat, and her daughters, to go to a game with him on the weekend.

"It was so much fun, Ted. And both my girls like him," Pat shared.

"That's wonderful," Teddy said.

Pat was glowing.

"We'll have to have lunch at Won Kow's sometime this week, and see what your fortune says," Teddy jested.

Pat just laughed.

Teddy had shown her Ryan's fortune, the day they had lunch with Mr. Chang, and they had both had a good laugh about how furious Ryan was with him, when Teddy had withheld it.

Terese also felt that this would be a better environment for the children, and she wanted to continue with the chores they were responsible for. It was important to both Teddy and Terese that the children be raised to learn to work for any extras that they wanted, and to budget their allowances.

Even little Katie, who would turn four in October, had begun to receive an allowance of one quarter each day, which she would plunk into her piggybank after completing her chores. She would receive this only if she made her bed, and put her toys away.

Before the new baby arrived early in August, Terese planned to finish the interior design work. She had hired a decorator to act as her assistant, and to oversee the installation of what she had selected for their new home. Terese had also allowed one extra month for any unforeseen delays in scheduling and deliveries, and hoped to be at their new estate by the beginning of October, at the very latest.

For Thanksgiving, over 50 guests, friends and family alike, were going to be invited for a feast of turkey, and fun-planned events, including an old-fashioned hayride.

Terese had a large family, as did Ryan, and they were all invited, which was enjoyable for the children. Terese and Ryan's families were close, having all grown up together in the same neighborhood in Chicago. Michael, Matthew and Katie always had fun playing with Ryan's nieces and nephews, as well as their cousins from Terese's side of the family. Terese was glad that they could all be invited more often now.

A combined Christmas and Housewarming Party in December, was also in the works for the weekend before Christmas. Terese had already lined up her caterers, and had the invitations printed for an even larger crowd. Everyone in the house was excited about all the forthcoming holiday plans. It gave everyone something good to look forward to.

Terese had always made their home a fun and comfortable place to be, and Teddy loved her for this. It was not by accident that their children were so happy and well adjusted, with good characters. Terese worked on that every day, making each one of them feel special to her, as she guided them in their decision-making, and helped them work through anything that was troubling them. Good manners were also important to Terese, and their children were never a disappointment to them when they were out in public, or at someone's home.

Thoughts of the family kept moving through Teddy's mind, as he walked down the wooded path, with Leah romping on ahead of him. Leah soon stopped, to search through the floor of the woods for a stick she favored, and then happily brought it over to Teddy so that he could throw it for her.

Leah loved taking walks with Teddy, and was especially playful that morning. She too felt all the pressure of the past few weeks dissipating. Teddy played with her for about half an hour, and then they made their way back to the house.

The house held a pleasant, early morning hush when Teddy and Leah came back through the front door. Everyone was still asleep. The guards were now gone, but at Teddy and Terese's invitation, Mr. Chang had remained on at the house. When Teddy reached the top of the stairs, he cut through the nursery, and across to the door that led into Mr. Chang's suite.

"Mr. Chang?" Teddy called, gently knocking on the door.

It had been arranged, the evening before, for Teddy to drive Mr. Chang back into the city before he went to work. Teddy and Terese had asked him if he would enjoy staying with them for a while longer, and have a needed rest out in the countryside, but Mr. Chang declined, saying it was necessary that he get back to the city, as there was another matter he now needed to attend to. He had stayed as long as he could. The family was now safe, and he felt it was time to say goodbye.

"Mr. Chang?" Teddy called, a little louder this time, knocking twice more on his door.

When there was no answer, Teddy looked into the room. Mr. Chang was nowhere in sight. Teddy assumed that he might be in the shower, yet he did not hear any water running.

they could prepare individuals whose depositions were to be taken the following week in the Hauser case. Every hour was filled.

Pat had arranged to have lunch brought in at noon. And, at four in the afternoon, Hank Hauser was to arrive. They spent the rest of the day and evening questioning him, and, as it turned out, Teddy did not leave the city until after eleven.

It was almost midnight, when he finally arrived home and unlocked the kitchen door of the house. The downstairs was dark, except for the soft amber light that came from the new hall lamp that Terese had recently purchased, and the occasional nightlight that came on automatically. Teddy was glad to see the hall chair sitting empty. It meant their lives were more normal again.

Feeling exhausted, Teddy walked slowly up the curving staircase to the second floor of the house. He was glad it was the end of the week. He planned to sleep in on Saturday morning, until it was time to go to Michael's game.

When Teddy reached the upstairs hall, he saw that the light in their room was on, and Terese was sitting up in bed working on her manuscript. Teddy walked over to her, and kissed her hello.

"I was wondering what time you'd get home," Terese said. "Did you finally get hold of Ryan, to tell him about what happened when you went to see Mr. Chang?"

"He thought I was crazy, and went over there himself."

Terese encouraged Teddy to go on, wanting to hear more of the story.

"What did he find?" Terese asked.

"He soon learned that Mr. Chang never had an office in the Pagoda Building."

Terese just looked at him.

"And, then he went over to Mr. Chang's residence, the address that the driver first picked him up at, and Ryan found it was just an empty lot."

"No kidding," Terese responded, thinking for a moment.

Teddy got up from the bed, and went in to brush his teeth.

"Are you hungry?" Terese asked. "Mrs. Swensen left a couple of roast beef sandwiches in the fridge for you."

"I grabbed a bite with Pat and Anne when we left the office," Teddy explained.

"What time was that?" Terese asked.

"About ten o'clock," Teddy answered, starting to laugh.

Terese looked at her watch, and then back at her manuscript.

"Are you checking up on me?" Teddy asked, coming back to the door.

"Don't flatter yourself," Terese said, with a grin.

"So, how was your day?" Teddy asked.

"Very uneventful, for a welcome change," Terese said, looking through to the bathroom. "I really feel so much more comfortable, now that they have Martel in custody," she added, her voice soft and mellow.

"Me too," Teddy admitted. "By the way, I called the Chief today during lunch."

"How's he doing?" Terese asked.

"Quite well. The physical therapy is helping," Teddy conveyed.

"That's great," Terese said.

"And the other officer, Danny, is expected to be released from the rehabilitation center in another week or so," Teddy added.

"I'm so relieved," Terese, said, with emotion entering her voice. "Katie and I have been lighting candles for him at church, whenever we go into town," Terese added.

"I still feel responsible for what happened to him," Teddy said, as he stepped into the shower. He felt hot and sticky, and wanted to shower off his perspiration, as well as the entire day, before getting into bed with Terese.

Teddy truly felt terrible about what had happened in the woods, and there were no words to comfort him. When he called the Chief, he had asked if there was anything he could do to make it up to him and Danny. The Chief had tried to make him realize that what had happened was all in the line of duty for them, and they were just doing their job.

Nevertheless, the whole incident was still nagging at Teddy. He had decided to make a contribution to the police department, so they could purchase whatever they might need, or add the gift of money to one of the police funds.

The shower was both refreshing and relaxing for Teddy. Ten minutes later, he was drying off with a large towel, and then put on a clean pair of pajamas Mattie had recently ironed. He was feeling much better.

Terese just looked at him for a moment, when he came out of the bathroom, reading his mood.

"I'll be right back Terese, I'm going to check on the children," Teddy managed.

A soft smile crossed Terese's face, as she met his eyes, and then she looked back at her manuscript.

Walking across the hall, Teddy checked in on little Katie first, who was sound asleep. He covered her with her sheet, then placed one of her favorite stuffed animals, that had fallen on the floor, back into bed with her.

When he first came up the stairs, he had seen that Terese had finished the upstairs nursery, and that Katie had placed one of her very worn, but favorite, animals on the rocking chair in there—a very sweet and final touch.

Teddy went in to check on the boys next, who were both fast asleep. He saw that Leah, as usual, had her head hanging off the side of Matthew's bed, and was snoring softly. Teddy left her there, and went back to his room, and climbed into bed with Terese.

"Everyone tucked in?" she asked.

"Snug as a bug in a rug," Teddy answered.

"I haven't heard that expression for ages," Terese said, laughing.

"I came across it when I was reading to Katie last weekend," he said, with a smile. "I think I'm enjoying that new series as much as she is."

"It should make you happy to know then, that I finally found the two missing volumes to the *Child Craft* set," Terese responded.

Teddy started laughing. "I guess everything is back to normal."

"I guess," Terese answered, as she covered a yawn. She reached over, and put her manuscript on her bedside table.

"Sleepy?" Teddy asked.

"I can't keep my eyes open," Terese answered, "but I wanted to wait up for you."

"I'm tired too," Teddy said, kissing her goodnight.

Terese turned off her light, and then rolled over on her side, and Teddy moved alongside her back, putting his arm around her stomach. The only light entering the room came from a tiny nightlight in the bathroom, and the small lamp on the table in the upstairs hall.

Teddy felt so at ease, lying there, with Terese beside him, and he started thinking once again about what happened that morning, as he watched Polaris' body undulating before he disappeared.

"Terese," Teddy asked, "has Matthew ever mentioned to you that he sees fields of light around people?" Teddy asked.

"Yes he has," Terese answered. "He sees more than that."

"What did he tell you about it?" Teddy asked.

"Just what he saw, although not everyone looks the same to him," Terese explained. "I bought a journal for him, and told him to keep a record of each person. He filled it in no time. He draws pictures now, and keeps notes in an old 3-ring notebook I had."

"You don't see the same thing, do you?" Teddy questioned.

"No, I don't," Terese, admitted, "but I read about it once, a long time ago."

Terese thought for a long moment about what Teddy was asking, and she remembered the first time Matthew had commented about this. At Terese's prompting, he drew what he saw for her—including the spirals of energy, and vortexes of energy within each of three fields of the body.

When Terese was quite young, she found a book at the library entitled *Breakthrough to Creativity, Your Higher Sense Perception*, and had read about some sensitives who were used in medical research, for the purpose of better understanding disease. In the studies cited, disease first appeared in the outer fields of the body, before there was a pathological existence within the human form, and that six of the seven major vortexes, were all connected to the ductless glandular system of the body.

Terese found the book again at a used bookstore, and had brought it home for Matthew to read. He felt much better about his gift of sight, after reading the book.

It had not surprised her that Matthew had this gift, for he was always talking about the way people *looked* to him, when he was very young. Matthew had begun his record-keeping journal a year earlier, with the help of Terese. It was something they shared together, privately. He kept the 3-ring binder, and all of his records in one of Terese's file drawers in her attic office. At an early age, Matthew learned that his other friends did not see this.

Terese had read that for some individuals, the fields of their body were in perfect alignment, and for other individuals the fields were out of alignment.

There were also other differences. For instance, for some people, the etheric field was made of thick lines extending at right angles out from the body, and for others the etheric field was made up of fine lines extending at right angles. When someone was not well, the lines sagged where the disease had taken hold. This was also true after an injury.

In addition, for some individuals, the etheric field was a dirty gray color, and for others it was bright and clean. Some people had a slow movement to the etheric field, while others had a more rapid movement, or vibration. And then there existed everything in between. The etheric field reflected what people put into their bodies, and how healthy an instrument they were maintaining. This was all part of what Matthew was documenting.

It was very complex, especially for a child. Matthew also saw the astral/emotional field, in colorful auras, as well as the mental field, and the human soul.

Terese had actually developed a chart on her computer for Matthew to use, with the outline of four human forms on it, representing the four different categories that Matthew was charting—the etheric, astral and mental fields, as well as the human soul. Neither Matthew nor Terese yet knew exactly what everything meant. For the time being, Matthew was just collecting the data.

"You also see what Matthew does, don't you Ted?" Terese asked, thinking that he had this gift too.

"Yes, I do," Teddy shared.

"You should ask Matthew to show you his notebook some time, when Michael isn't around. Michael has already made fun of him, probably because he sees nothing at all."

"I'll do that," Teddy assured her.

There was a short pause in their conversation, and then Terese asked Teddy another question.

"Ted," Terese asked, thinking back. "What does Merak, or Martel, look like?"

Teddy thought for a moment, before answering her.

"He is almost completely devoid of light. He truly is a devil."

"He certainly is that," Terese agreed.

"I recently read that the inverted pentagram is the symbol of the devil, and Black Magic," Teddy shared. "It symbolizes darkness, and inverted power. The inverted pentagram is also the sign of the devil in Tarot Symbolism, representing Key 15."

"When you say the inverted pentagram, do you mean the five-pointed star?" Terese asked.

"The five-pointed star, with the point down," Teddy further explained. "All of that was in *Numerology and the Divine Triangle*. It was one of the books I received when we returned from Miami, and I began researching metaphysical writings, and Atlantis. Within that book, even a tarot card was shown with an inverted pentagram on the devil's forehead."

"We have the five-pointed star on the American flag," Terese reminded him.

"When the five-pointed star is shown with the point up, it is a good omen, and gives protection," Teddy explained. "It means just the opposite with the point down."

"I have seen a lot of people using the five-pointed star incorrectly," Terese added.

"So have I," Teddy agreed. "And I have always had a bad feeling when I saw the star used that way, even before I came across the metaphysical explanation for it."

"Me too," Terese agreed.

"I'm not sure if it is by accident, when people use an upside-down star," Teddy went on to explain. "I think that many people do this intentionally," Teddy surmised, "so that others, like them, know who they are, and what they represent."

"You're probably right," Terese agreed, "it truly looks unnatural, whenever I see a star shown that way."

"A lot of men are also visually giving the image of the devil when they wear goatees, or devil-looking beards," Teddy added. "It is disappointing, as well as discouraging, to see so much of that today."

For a long while, they laid quietly together, both thinking through their conversation, when Teddy posed another question.

"Terese?" he asked, "did I ever get out? It has been on my mind lately."

"Out?" Terese asked, now half asleep.

"Out of Atlantis?" he asked.

Terese turned over facing him, and lovingly touched his cheek with her hand. What he had said was so unexpected.

"Yes, you got out, Teddy. Apollo and Aryan went back for you. They rescued you by breaking into the protective dome, at the tip of the Temple Tower."

"They did?" Teddy questioned.

"Yes, they did. Polaris and Sirius arranged it, after we arrived at your brother's observatory."

"So, they got out too?" Teddy asked.

"No. They stayed behind in a sealed chamber. You and Leah were the only ones to leave."

"That explains the two piles of dust then, when Ryan and I entered the obelisk's chamber. Why didn't they come with us?" Teddy asked.

"Polaris and Sirius, and the Council of 45, thought it their duty to stay with those left behind, who died," Terese revealed. "They all felt responsible for what happened to the Atlanteans, and not being able to stop Merak in time."

"My God," Teddy said, "what a terrible death they must have suffered, after being entombed."

"Yes," Terese agreed. "Some people think of Atlantis as if it were an under-the-sea city, rather than what it really is—an under-the-sea grave, like the Titanic. It was all so very tragic."

"Yes, very tragic indeed," Teddy agreed.

"It's all in the past, now," Terese added.

"I cannot stop thinking about it," Teddy said. "My Atlantean family, our friends. Thoughts of them keep coming back, when I am quiet and alone."

"I've tried my best to recall it all," Terese said. "But it is such a complex story to tell. And, it has be to told as fiction."

"I wish I could have gone back, and somehow saved them all," Teddy admitted.

Terese thought for a moment, before answering him.

"Teddy, you cannot go back and change that which has already happened," Terese said. "We can learn from history, but we cannot change even a moment of it," Terese added, trying to comfort him. "What you viewed, and experienced, was recorded in an ancient archive. It was not happening in current time."

"Why do you think all of the Atlantean technology was lost over the ages?" Teddy asked.

"I don't know," Terese honestly answered. "The Atlanteans didn't mix with the primitive races that were also living on the planet at that time. And I have a sense that they left the buildings behind—the observatories and the outposts—that were later discovered and used by other civilizations, but not the technology."

"The buildings?" Teddy asked

"The Atlanteans did have observatories," Terese further explained, "and many outposts."

"You mean like the pyramids, and Machu Picchu?" Teddy asked.

"Yes, among others," Terese answered. "I've always thought they were all built by the Atlanteans, but that other civilizations later discovered and used them as their own."

"That's an interesting thought," Teddy said.

"I seem to remember something about a latitudinal band, around the earth, where the Atlantean observatories were built. And the outposts were spread throughout the world for trade. But that's all I can recall about it."

"You could be right," Teddy said. "Perhaps the last of the Atlanteans died off from some plague, or virus, for which they had no immunity. Or, perhaps they did blend in with other civilizations, and led a more primitive life."

"Perhaps," Terese agreed. "I know all science would be lost, if the world depended on my understanding of how to recreate it. I couldn't even come up with how electricity really works, and I use it every day," Terese said.

Teddy began to laugh. "Let me know when I can read your story, okay?" he asked.

"I will," Terese assured him.

Teddy thought about Terese's gift of clairvoyance. She was definitely a high-level, or high-functioning clairvoyant, to be able to tap into the same archive Polaris had shown to them—even if it was, as she would say, in a dream state, or when she meditated.

He remembered reading that psychic gifts come from the astral/emotional dimension, or field, and what is psychic is not always accurate, in that there is a lot of illusion, or delusion, in the astral realm. However, true clairvoyants have a higher gift, in that they are able to tap into the causal or soul level, and this information is always accurate.

Terese didn't think her abilities were all that special though, since she had had them all her life. Teddy felt pretty much the same about his own gift. It was not something that either of them had ever talked about before—and probably would not in the future, except to each other.

"Teddy," Terese shared, interrupting his thoughts, "there is one thing that I have been worried about."

"What's that?" Teddy asked.

"Well, once the novel is published, if it is published, and I tell the whole story right to the end, the whole world will know that you were the source of the tapes."

Teddy thought for a moment, before he answered her.

"Many writers are going to borrow the theme of Martel, and his men. Writers always pull from the events of the day for story ideas. Don't worry about it."

"No?" Terese questioned.

"Not at all," Teddy answered. "All you have to do is to change all the names, and put a legal disclaimer in the front of the book."

"Martel would still find out," Terese said. "I don't want any more trouble."

Teddy thought for a long moment, before answering her. He had not told her about how Martel confronted him, for fear it would worry her.

"Terese?" Teddy said, still hesitating.

"Yes," Terese answered.

"Martel already knows I took the tapes," Teddy finally disclosed.

"He does?" Terese asked.

"He confronted me in the bunker, about stealing the tapes," Teddy said.

Terese remained silent, while what Teddy had just told her began to sink in.

"I want you to publish your book, Terese," Teddy insisted. "The Atlanteans deserve to have their true story told."

"Ted, I really couldn't take any more, if there is any kind of a backlash," Terese shared.

"There won't be any backlash," Teddy assured her.

"Maybe once all our children are grown, and I'm old and gray," Terese finished.

Teddy just laughed.

"Terese," Teddy further disclosed, "Martel also thinks I'm either with the FBI, or the CIA. And if I am not mistaken, he still hasn't figured out who my father is. He's not going to do anything more, it would only dig him in deeper."

"I'll have to think about it," Terese finally answered.

Teddy held her tenderly, for a long moment, thinking how lucky he was to have her to share his life.

"I know I don't tell you often enough, Terese, but I truly do love you more than anyone else in the world."

"I know you do," Terese responded, affectionately, "but I think I love you even more. I'd really be lost without you, Ted."

They kissed once more to say goodnight, and, as Terese turned back over on her side, she silently expelled a sigh of emotion. She was grateful that they were all safe and secure, and could begin to do fun things together again, as a family. Their world truly was back to normal again.

Terese's head sank slowly into her down-filled pillow, and, as Teddy cradled close to her, all their bedtime thoughts seemed to slip away. Soon, they both fell off into a deep and restful state of sleep.

A NOTE TO MY READERS:

If you are a student of art at the high school, art school, college or university level, and have an interest in illustrating a chapter or more of this story for a future fully illustrated version of *The Atlanteans*, please visit www.TheAtlanteans.com for further information.

The Author

978-0-595-66735-2
0-595-66735-X